# BELLE GREENE

Alexandra Lapierre

# BELLE GREENE

*Translated from the French*
*by Tina Kover*

Europa
*editions*

Europa Editions
27 Union Square West, Suite 302
New York NY 10003
www.europaeditions.com
info@europaeditons.com

Copyright © Flammarion, Paris, 2021
First publication 2022 by Europa Editions

Translation by Tina Kover
Original title: *Belle Greene*
Translation copyright © 2022 by Europa Editions

Library of Congress Cataloguing in Publication Data is available
ISBN 978-1-60945-758-7

Lapierre, Alexandra
Belle Greene

Art direction by Emanuele Ragnisco
instagram.com/emanueleragnisco

Cover design: Keenan

Cover photo: Shutterstock

Prepress by Grafica Punto Print – Rome

Printed in the USA

# CONTENTS

For Frank
And for Garance, Leo, and Lavinia

"May your secret stay safe."
—Yoruba greeting, Gulf of Guinea

"Let me tell you a secret, my love. If you continue to like me, you will find that it is *in spite of* the things I do, and say, and think."

—*Letter from Belle da Costa Greene to her lover Bernard Berenson, renowned art historian and appraiser, April 1909*


"The whole trouble with me is my insatiable curiosity—a perfectly mad, irresistible desire to know everything, everybody, every emotion, every divine and hellish relation."

—*Letter from Belle da Costa Greene to Bernard Berenson, July 1910*


"I write in my diary all the things I don't dare say—awful things, impossible things, hateful, spiteful things—generally all amusing to me, for *au fond* in everything I do, everything I think, there is always *un petit sourire*."

—*Letter from Belle da Costa Greene to Bernard Berenson, July 1910*


"I have been hit by a wandering sun. [ . . . ] I don't know what color it was, whether it was dark, or purple or, as it seemed to me, a radiant gold. In any case, after such an encounter, it is a miracle that I am still alive."

—*Letter from Bernard Berenson to his friend Neith Hapgood, summer 1911*

# TO THE READER

The reader will of course be aware that, over the two and a half centuries during which slavery was practiced in the United States, masters frequently subjected their slaves to sexual abuse. Many of these women subsequently gave birth to mixed-race children who remained slaves.

This interbreeding, which lasted over more than eight generations, gave rise to a whole population of slaves with "Caucasian" features, smooth hair, and light skin. When slavery was abolished in 1865, there was nothing—or virtually nothing—in their physical appearance to distinguish them from their white owners.

At the end of the Civil War, still in 1865, federal laws were enacted granting former slaves both civil equality and the right to vote.

However, twelve years later these laws were repealed, a state of affairs that would last until the 1964 enactment of the Civil Rights Act, dividing the population into two groups on the census: *white* and *colored*. Mixed-race individuals were required to identify themselves as Black according to the "one-drop rule," which stipulated that a single African ancestor was sufficient to establish a "colored" bloodline.

In these years of the twentieth century, during which the segregation and persecution of Black people raged more violently than ever, those individuals of mixed race who appeared white found themselves facing the temptation to break the law, to hide their true identities, to cross the color barrier at the risk of their own lives.

The act of masquerading as white when one was legally Black was given a nickname that needed no translation beyond American shores: *passing.*

Readers wishing to know more about the history of passing, the origins of Belle da Costa Greene's family, and the glittering worlds of the many millionaires, scholars, and collectors who surrounded her will find, at the end of this book, a photo section, a glossary of bibliophilic terminology, and a brief bibliography.

Is there any need for me to remind the reader that the terms used to designate Black and African Americans are not my own, but taken from historical documents? Or that it would be out of the question to sugar-coat this language or strip it of its violence, given that it bears witness to an abhorrent reality?

Everything that happens in this book is based on real facts. Every character actually existed.

While the tone and technique of the novel seemed to me the only possible means of relating Belle's many adventures, I have adhered scrupulously to historical dates and to the facts as I understand them. The reader may rest securely in the knowledge that even the most novelistic scenes, the most trivial incidents, are the fruit of thorough archival research in Italy, England, and America, and that even the smallest details are based on documented evidence.

A.L.

## THE SEALED ENVELOPE

### London, 1943. Research laboratory, Courtauld Institute of Art

In late August 1943, Professor Dan Thompson, director of research on ancient painting techniques and fresco restoration, is standing at his desk, head down. He has just learned some sad news. One of his protégés in London, a young American Air Force aviator based in England, has been killed. Not on a bombing raid, but by firing a bullet through his own head. It happened on the third of August. His name was Robert Mackenzie Leveridge, and people called him Bobbie. He was twenty-four years old. He was one of the most charming young men Dan had ever met. And he was the nephew, the adopted son, the beloved child of Dan's colleague, the director of the Morgan Library in New York, the renowned Belle da Costa Greene. A dear, dear friend.

During his last furlough, in June, Bobbie had stayed with Dan and visited him at the Courtauld Institute, as he always did. Just before he'd left to return to his base, Bobbie had turned suddenly on the front steps, taken an envelope from his pocket, and held it out to Dan: "I want you to keep this letter." Dan had taken it, out of surprise as much as anything. Thinking it must be a list of Bobbie's last wishes in the event of his plane being shot down, he'd responded: "I'll put it in the safe." "No," Bobbie had replied, "I want you to read it right away." Then he'd hurried down the stairs and walked quickly away.

Dan, though no sentimentalist, had stood for a long time watching the young man's tall figure vanish behind the trees of

Portman Square. The blond head beneath the uniform helmet and the pale, long-fingered hands gave him the look of a poet, or a hero. Youth, courage, and beauty, incarnate.

Vaguely unsettled at the thought of the combat in store for the boy, Dan had turned the envelope over in his hands. It bore no stamp, merely the label *Examiner 908*. This meant that it had been opened by the Censorship Bureau, which screened all incoming mail from the United States. There was no address, but the recipient's name was written in a rounded, highly feminine hand: "Lieutenant Robert M. Leveridge, care of Mrs. Stevens."

Fearful of committing an indiscretion by reading a lady's letter not intended for him, Dan had not dared to open the envelope but had stowed it in his safe as he'd originally intended.

Now Bobbie was dead.

"Killed by a bullet wound self-inflicted in a moment of madness" was how the War Office put it.

What could have driven this young man, so far from being mad—a model of reason and health, in fact—to blow his brains out?

An incomprehensible suicide.

And to think that Dan had seen him just two months ago, and seen nothing, sensed nothing of his anguish.

Though there had been the incident of the letter that Bobbie had given him and asked him to read *right away*.

If Dan had done so, could he have prevented this tragedy?

Moving heavily, Dan Thompson goes to his laboratory safe. He takes out the envelope, sits down at his desk, puts on his glasses, and unfolds the four sheets it contains. Eight pages, front and back. It is undated, but the letterhead reads *995 Madison Avenue*.

"Darling, it's nearly impossible for me to write to you without saying all sorts of ridiculous things that mean *I love you . . .*"

So it is a letter from a woman. And a love letter, too. Probably the last letter from Bobbie's fiancée, a girl called Nina, with whom he was deeply smitten.

The more of this letter Dan reads, the more he feels a sort of vague irritation. The young lady's sweet words seem vacant, her thoughts muddled. But her simpering is nothing compared to what follows. Dan has to reread several passages in order to understand them fully.

What Bobbie's fiancée, who refers to herself in the letter as a *clean white girl*, has written to him—a soldier at the front—is beyond comprehension.

She tells him that, since last year, when she learned "the thing" her father had discovered upon conducting a private investigation, "the thing" that has made a life together impossible for them, she has no longer seen a future for their relationship.

But, she says, she's loyal by nature and will marry him anyway, on one condition: he must agree to have himself castrated.

Then she says, with numerous protestations of love, that he will have to have himself castrated no matter what happens, even if they don't marry. *You do realize that, don't you, my darling?*

Dan feels as though he might vomit.

She also says that she wouldn't be able to bear not having children because of him, that she could never resign herself to not becoming a mother. And that, in consequence, he will have to consent for her to use an anonymous donor.

She's afraid, she goes on, that Bobbie might mistreat the offspring, who won't be his. He must pledge to love them as if they were his own.

Next, she writes that the idea of living off *the money of John Pierpont Morgan's nigger whore*—this is Dan's friend and the adoptive mother Bobbie worships, Belle da Costa Greene—disgusts her, so much so that all the gifts Bobbie has given her seem dirty, tainted. The idea of spending time with this person, she continues, is so deeply appalling to her that she doesn't dare imagine the promiscuity she might be exposed to, if Bobbie continues to see her.

Despite his own disgust, his anger, Dan forces himself to keep reading.

She is aware, the young woman writes, of how attached Bobbie is to his aunt. But she asks him to consider severing the connection, so that the children will never be subjected to the same sorts of comments she herself will have to endure daily in polite society. People already say that while the famous lady director of the Morgan Library may well appear white to those who know no better, having added the noble patronym of da Costa to her name and claiming to belong to that aristocratic Portuguese family—which would explain her dark hair and skin—really, she is nothing but vermin. An authentic Negress.

This rumor has come from several sources, she says, all of them entirely objective.

Finally, she begs Bobbie to reply quickly by her dear papa's messenger; his silence, she says, will be interpreted by "Daddy" as proof of arrogance and a total lack of moral responsibility— two traits that are typical, according to Daddy, of the Black race to which Bobbie belongs.

Dan has taken off his glasses.

So, this was "the thing" Bobbie was unaware of until just last year, "the thing" that little shrew had told him during his last furlough in New York.

Despite his blond hair, his blue eyes and pale skin, Robert M. Leveridge was Black.

And in the United States, that's no laughing matter.

According to law, a single African ancestor—whether recent or going back many generations—is all it takes to give rise to a line of colored people who are required to declare themselves as such. One drop of Black blood, a single drop of Black blood in your veins, marks you out forever as a "Negro." This is the implacable one-drop rule, with its attendant segregations, discriminations, and racial persecutions.

Dan Thompson tries to imagine the shock Bobbie must have felt, this young man raised among the well-heeled denizens of Park Avenue and educated at Harvard, steeped in the customs and prejudices of his class, at learning of his African American origins. The depth of the identity crisis the discovery of his ancestry must have caused.

And Dan thinks, too, of the consequences of such a revelation for Bobbie's life as a soldier. If the American military authorities had learned that Lieutenant Leveridge was a colored officer, they would have separated him from his comrades, expelled him from his regiment, and sent him to fight with a Black unit.

In asking Dan to read this vile letter *right away*, Bobbie had been trying to share with him the crisis that was destroying his life.

Proof of the trust Bobbie had had in him, which Dan had failed to grasp.

And now? What should he do?

Dan Thompson spends several days deep in thought. Should he burn the letter? Could he bring himself to do it? This document, given to him by Bobbie less than two months before he ended his life, gives the reasons for his death. It's a kind of testament. To destroy it would be impossible.

Should he give the letter to Belle, Bobbie's adoptive mother, Dan's friend, who is tormenting herself now with questions about why her beloved nephew would commit suicide? The poor woman already suffered a heart attack when she learned the news. Rather than consoling her, reading the filth contained in this letter might deal her a final blow.

And then, why add insult to injury . . . After all, dear Belle has always carefully maintained her silence, drawn a veil of secrecy over her past. Dan could never inflict such humiliation on her as that contained in this letter, which refers to her as "Morgan's nigger whore."

She must never find out that he knows the secret truth of her origins. Their friendship couldn't withstand it. How could she bear knowing that he knows what she's never revealed to any-one—not even her own nephew?

Or that she had borne such an immense responsibility for so long, only for Bobbie to learn the truth anyway, and from the mouth of a stupid, racist little hyena?

After endless prevarications, Dan decides to do nothing. Or, rather, he contacts his attorney and sets his wishes down in writing:

"This envelope contains a document that I want no one but my dear friend Belle da Costa Greene to be aware exists.

"Because it is my express wish that this document shall be seen by no eyes but hers, I request the executors of my will and testament to take every possible measure to ensure that this envelope, with the wax seals I have affixed intact, will be hand-delivered to Miss Greene personally.

"Should Miss Greene be deceased or incapable for any other reason of taking receipt of this envelope, I ask that it not be given to her executors, nor any trustee or representative. Rather, it should be destroyed.

"I solemnly declare that the contents of this envelope belong wholly to me, and that it has no financial value as part of my estate.

"London, January 9, 1944."

Next, Dan Thompson slides the envelope Bobbie gave him into a larger one, marked with the letterhead of the Courtauld Institute of Art. He secures this larger envelope with two wax seals and, for even more security, writes on the back:

"This letter to be opened only *after my death* and *only* by the hand of

Miss Belle da Costa Greene
33 East 36th Street
New York, NY
USA."

Before applying the hot wax, and adding the seal of the Courtauld Institute to the whole, he slips a handwritten note into the large envelope:

*Dear Belle,*
*The contents of this envelope drove a noble young man to his death. Calling it a suicide is unjust. It was this letter that killed him.*

And he locks the sealed envelope in his safe. To keep the secret, so he thinks, forever.

# Book I

Too Black for the Whites
Too White for the Blacks
1898–1908

# CHAPTER 1

## BLACK
## 1898–1900

### Georgetown, Washington's Black quarter, June 1898

For weeks now, the aged and formidable Hermione Fleet, doyenne of Washington's Black quarter, had enjoyed neither rest nor peace. She shifted uncomfortably in her bed without managing to change position, so painful was the ache in her bones. And the humidity of the air in this strange June was overpowering. She had stood firm until now, always refusing to allow the infirmities of age to best her. She had shrunken and withered, certainly, but she had remained indefatigable, continuing to organize weddings and picnics and charity balls in the parish. Didn't the pastor call her "our Little Iron Lady"?

Even those times seemed far in the past now.

Her blue eyes, clouded by cataracts, scanned the flowered wallpaper for the portrait of her deceased husband. A large, full-body photo in its oval frame, along with Dr. James Fleet's diploma under glass. She couldn't make out a thing. Lying on her side, she could only imagine on the wall the figure of the man who had stood by her for so many years. With everything in her, she begged her husband to come to her aid. She needed his help.

Tonight she couldn't even manage to formulate the problem clearly; the subject alone caused uncontrollable fear to rise in her. And yet she was no stranger to anguish when it came to the behavior of her children!

Up in Heaven, the doctor must know what their daughter

Genevieve was thinking. He must have heard the rumors that were swirling.

People were saying that, in New York, Genevieve had rented an apartment from landlords who were not Black.

That she'd settled in an area where her neighbors—shopgirls, seamstresses, laundresses—were not Black, either.

That she was enjoying herself so much among these new acquaintances that she spent all of her time with them now.

*White* women.

Furthermore, they said, Genevieve had carefully avoided telling anyone where she came from. On which streets, in which part of Washington, she had grown up. But how could these neighbors of hers not be aware? Genevieve was married to one of the most famous Black activists in the country. Yes, he had left her. Certainly, she no longer needed to invoke his memory, or even mention his existence.

But to go from that to the opposite extreme! To betray her own race!

There it was. The old lady had put her finger on exactly what was bothering her so much.

Yes, Genevieve *looked* white. So what? It was a phony façade, an illusion that would fool no one but the whites. They weren't familiar with the Black community; they didn't understand it, didn't know how to see it. No Black person who met Genevieve would ever have any doubt about her origins.

Truth be told, the interbreeding of the Fleet clan went back so many generations that many of its members had pale skin and "Caucasian" features. One of Hermione's four sons may have "come out Black," it was true, but both of her daughters—petite and dainty, with golden-brown hair, green eyes, and aquiline noses—corresponded perfectly to white standards of beauty. Just like their mother.

Old Hermione had been born Hermione Peters, to a large family of mixed-race musicians that had resided in Washington since the eighteenth century. Her grandfather, a slave freed in 1797, had himself purchased the freedom of his wife and their five children from his former owner.

Dr. Fleet, who was also of mixed race, had been able to undertake the study of medicine thanks to the American Colonization Society, a white organization whose efforts were aimed at sending all Black residents back to Africa, believing they could never adapt to a civilized society. Their purpose in training Black doctors was to install these men in the American colony of Liberia, in West Africa, and they had financed the education of three physicians—all of whom had refused to leave the United States in the end. Hermione's husband was one of them.

Dr. Fleet had ministered to the Black community for nearly thirty years. Not only a doctor but a musician as well, he had led the hymns at church services and accompanied his wife on the violin at charity balls. Hermione, for her part, was a pianist, and their mutual passion for classical music was so strong that they had named their three sons Mozart, Bellini, and Mendelssohn.

Mozart had grown up to be a printer, Bellini, a teacher—though Mendelssohn, who died in childhood, never had the chance to make a place for himself in the world. Their sisters, Genevieve and Medora, had followed in their mother's footsteps by becoming piano teachers in the area's primary schools. Genevieve, in particular, was a true virtuoso at the keyboard, as well as an ardent lover of literature.

In short, then, the Fleets were among the most upper-class and cultured members of the Black community. In the eyes of their friends, they personified Washington's "Black elite." And the great paradox of all this was that they could have been taken for white.

Now, in the twilight of a long life during which she had kept her tribe—her six brothers and their wives, her five children and their spouses, her thirty nephews, and her twenty grandchildren—

tightly knit, united in the same habits, the same traditions, the same beliefs, Hermione watched as a great chasm opened at the feet of those she loved.

This disaster whose approach she felt so keenly was due to the desertion of that monster of egotism and thoughtlessness, her son-in-law. The famous professor Richard Theodore Greener, Genevieve's husband. The bane of her existence since the first day she'd met him.

Rick Greener could well pass for the most intelligent Black lawyer of his generation, the most brilliant of Black orators, the most dynamic and probably most effective of Black activists— but, in the end, he had blighted the happiness of everyone close to him. A scourge.

Of course, Hermione understood why her daughter had loved him with such constancy and passion, why she had supported him through thick and thin for so long. All that Greener said to champion the cause of his people, all he did to educate his brethren and guide them toward freedom, could only arouse enthusiasm. She herself had been seduced by his beautiful speeches and his energy. Rick had such a talent for *convincing*! And a charm that opened doors for him, that enabled him to climb the most insurmountable peaks.

His claims to fame? Unprecedented! He had been the first Black student to graduate from Harvard. The first Black man to occupy a professorship at a Southern university. The first, and so far only, Black man to have his law degree ratified and be approved to practice law by the Supreme Court of the state of South Carolina.

God knew, he *had* come a long way! The grandson of an African-born slave and an escaped mulatto woman—two fugitives who'd managed to reach the North and settle in Baltimore—he had been born with nothing, absolutely no means of raising himself up in the world. He'd had to work to support his mother from the age of eleven. Not a single weapon in his arsenal, except for his street urchin's pride and his fists. Nothing but his incredible thirst for knowledge, his curiosity about the world, his tireless work ethic, his tenacity, his eloquence, his magnetism. Hadn't he managed himself in such a way as to meet white protectors who had financed his studies? And then other white benefactors to support his applications elsewhere?

Old Hermione had to give credit where credit was due. Through the sheer force of his determination, Rick Greener had broken all the laws of destiny and risen to the extraordinary position he would soon occupy: the first African American ever appointed to serve as consul to Russia. Yes, yes; Hermione was perfectly willing to acknowledge her son-in-law's intellectual merits.

Still, she refused to recognize how unfairly she had treated him for so many years. With all due respect to the Fleet clan, Richard Theodore Greener belonged to that class of important figures who fight for the honor of humanity. His faith in the future of his Black brothers, his ardor in defending them and transmitting his knowledge to them lifted him, morally, far above the common man. He had sacrificed everything to his battle for justice and equality.

All the same, Hermione raged, on a personal level, he was worthless. The proof of that lay in his abandonment of her daughter and their five children, after thirty-five years of marriage. Truth be told, Genevieve's conjugal woes were hardly a recent development; indeed, they went back to the very start of her marriage. September 24, 1874—Hermione remembered the date perfectly. It had been one year to the day after she herself had been widowed.

The late Dr. James Fleet, who had come to know Rick when he was courting their daughter, had been under no illusions about what sort of young man they were dealing with. He might possess a degree from Harvard, might display every promise of a bright future, but for all that, the doctor did not like him. Who were his parents? To which parish, which community, did he belong? Troubled, Fleet had refused to grant his daughter's hand in marriage.

The old man was too conservative. After his death, Hermione had given in to her lovelorn daughter's pleas. A mistake. But who could have known?

Despite her sweetness and her docility, her particularly pliable nature, Genevieve was tenacious. She knew what she wanted. A woman of strength beneath her apparent submissiveness. For more than a year, she had bided her time, working subtly to convince her mother to give her consent. And she had succeeded.

Hermione saw her own stubbornness in her daughter, as well as that positivity, that zest for life that enabled them to stay the course no matter the circumstances. She knew Genevieve was capable of surviving the darkest adversities. Oh yes, she could certainly flatter herself that she'd raised the girl well! She had taught her politeness, graceful manners, the importance of dress and deportment. And resilience.

And the girl had seemed so much in love . . .

At the time, Hermione had to admit, Rick Greener had had everything going for him. Tall, slim, and elegant, with the aristocratic bearing acquired at Harvard and looks that could easily be taken for white, he was a man that would stand out in any crowd. To say nothing of his education, of which very few Black men in the United States could boast.

Those times seemed so long ago now!

So far away, those twelve years after the end of the Civil War, when the whites had "experimented" with integration and granted Black men civil equality and the right to vote. Twelve years between that period, so full of hope, that had been christened the "Reconstruction," and the abominable Jim Crow laws of 1877, with their attendant atrocities. The forbidding of Black people to ride the same trains as white passengers, to drink from the same fountains, to use the same bathrooms, to frequent the same public places, the same theaters, and, of course, the same universities.

When conservatives regained control of the Southern states, this hellish situation was firmly solidified. And the North hadn't moved to intervene, claiming that national unity and reconciliation were worth the price. The 1870 Constitutional amendment guaranteeing all male citizens the right to vote regardless of race was simply rescinded by the Supreme Court several years later. At the same time, in Washington, Congress refused to pass laws against lynching—and with reason. The 1877 elections, which had been held amid a storm of violence and corruption, had put power in the hands of Southern reactionaries.

And so Rick Greener's string of successes, his victories over ignorance and poverty, had come to a sudden end. Indeed, so quickly had the dream turned to a nightmare that he'd been obliged to resign his university posts one after the other. He'd stopped being paid. His students were taken away. He was humiliated. He was threatened. And the Black students who remained loyal to him were assaulted and harassed. No surprise, then, that he had thrown himself with such ardor into the political struggle to retain the few concessions gained during the liberals' hour of triumph! Even in the eyes of Hermione Fleet, who had built a peaceful life for herself in her parish and felt no need to venture beyond Washington's Black community, the laws being passed here were shameful . . . How could she not stand with her son-in-law against the segregation, discrimination, and racial persecution that the Northern states—ostensibly so supportive of Black emancipation—had accepted without batting an eye! *Separate but equal*, they claimed. What hypocrisy!

But from that to running all over the country speaking about education for Black folk the way Professor Greener did, leaving his wife and five children without protection, without food on the table or the means to put it there—well, that was something else altogether. Oh yes, Rick knew how to stir up a crowd from a podium, how to produce endless articles on civil rights, how to rant magnificently about equality. But when it came to the education of his own son, or bringing up his daughters properly, he was useless, in Hermione's opinion. How many consecutive weeks had he spent at home? Three? He never stayed. A few Christmases, certainly. A Thanksgiving or two, perhaps. If Genevieve hadn't had the whole Fleet clan to support her; if she hadn't been able to spend long stretches living in her mother's townhouse on the 1400 block of T street; if she hadn't been willing to shed blood, sweat, and tears to feed her five little ones through needlework and piano lessons, how would they have survived? And how would they survive now, in New York, with the head of the family, recently appointed consul to Vladivostok on a comfortable salary, preparing to sail away toward new adventures without them, and announcing that he wouldn't support any of his offspring beyond their eighteenth birthday? These were meaningless words, of course. Four of his children had already reached that age. Only the youngest was still his responsibility, and anyway it was clear that he had no intention of sending a penny to anyone. Why change the habits of a lifetime now? For nearly a quarter of a century, the lion's share of his income had been spent in the company of his mistresses, or his comrades in arms.

There was no other way to put it: his mother-in-law hated him. He had disappointed her, too.

And now, owing to her husband's imminent departure for the far side of the world, Genevieve had announced that she was arriving in Washington tomorrow. In different circumstances, the old lady would have rejoiced at her daughter's visit. But not tonight. How could she not be suspicious of Genevieve's motives in coming here?

Hermione was preparing herself for their encounter as if for a battle. At ninety years old, with Death hovering nearby, would she have the strength to overcome her daughter's willfulness and prevent her betrayal?

\*

Everything had happened just as Hermione had anticipated. Genevieve had arrived by train, without the children. This was surely not a question of money; Mozart would have paid for his nephew's and nieces' tickets, for in the Fleet clan, the wealthier family members took on the expenses of the poorer ones. They lived together; they travelled together. Never alone, unless the matter was urgent, too serious for anyone else to be involved.

The moment she'd stepped over the threshold, Genevieve had hurried upstairs to kiss her mother. Hermione, who could no longer see faces clearly, had found her daughter less pretty than she remembered, and had told her so. A reflex. She could be tender with her grandchildren, but remained critical of her daughters. "Suck in your belly and stand up straight, Genevieve, or you'll turn out as ugly as Aunt Lily!" This refrain had long ago turned into a joke within the family.

In truth, if Hermione had looked objectively at her visitor, she would have noticed how youthful Genevieve remained. Her face was a perfect oval and her hair, worn in a low chignon, smooth and golden. Her dark-colored ensemble made her look even slimmer than she was. Thanks to her skill as a seamstress, which had gotten her through many a rough patch, she wore a corset beneath her stylish peplum jacket, a long, straight skirt, and a hat she'd made herself. Despite adversity and multiple pregnancies, she retained the elegance that was her signature. Her brother Mozart, who had gone to fetch her at the station, had been struck by her allure. Genevieve—Geenie to her friends—was nearly fifty, but she looked fifteen years younger, easily.

True to form, Genevieve had been careful not to directly address the doubts and worries that had brought her here. It took several days for the two women to manage a real conversation. Hermione attacked first; the pussyfooting had gone on long enough. Each of them knew what she wanted from the other. Genevieve had come seeking the approval she needed, psychologically speaking, to do what she'd decided to do: pass herself off as a white woman. Hermione, though, had no intention of giving it. Rather, she was determined to convince her daughter to abandon this dangerous, if tempting, game.

The outcome of this mother–daughter battle would determine the future of all their posterity.

"Take care, child. Take care not to do something you can't take back," the old lady said severely, as Genevieve bent to help her out of her chair and up to bed.

"Take back, Mother?"

"If you do this, you'll have to lie and hide for the rest of your life." Hermione had batted her daughter away, clinging with both hands to the armrests of her chair. "Move to a different city, change your behavior, change the way you speak, the way you think."

Her steely tone sharpened further, her words becoming staccato as she grew short of breath. She paused for an instant to recover herself.

". . . and I—if I were to meet you in the street, I would have to pretend not to recognize you. I wouldn't even be able to look at you or speak to you, much less touch you or get near any of my grandchildren . . ."

Genevieve couldn't stop herself from interrupting. "Why not?"

Her mother continued more slowly, affecting calmness:

"Because no one can *ever* find out your secret, and no one can ever reveal it. Not the whites. Not us. No one. Ever. If you do this, you'll have to break completely with your past. Break with everyone you love—your brothers, your uncles. The whole neighborhood. If you do this, none of us will ever be able to visit you, anywhere. If you do this, we won't see each other again."

"But why not?" Genevieve cried out again.

"Because if one of us were to betray your origins by the tiniest slip, an overfamiliar word, a joke from among our people, a song from home, even the texture of their skin . . ."

The old lady exhaled, searching for the right words, determined to explain herself dispassionately.

"Your sister married a Black man. Mozart and Bellini married Black women. Their children, your nephews, are mulattos with dark skin and curly hair. Receive them in your home, in a white neighborhood, in a white building, and you will immediately be unmasked, arrested, and condemned. Twenty years in prison. And I am an optimist! Prepare yourself, Genevieve. You will have to play this role to the very end."

"How else am I to survive?" Genevieve's voice was faint. "Rick . . ."

"Damn him to hell!" spat Hermione.

"He's not coming back. If only you'd seen how quick he was to accept that post on the other side of the world!"

"Forget your husband. You can just come back to Georgetown."

"What chance will my children have in Georgetown? There's no more work. There are no more businesses, no more schools. Nothing but misery for Blacks. Here. Elsewhere. Everywhere. Look at our street; it used to be so lovely, with its new two-story houses. See what our whole block has become, how shabby it looks now. Even you aren't living the way we used to live. The neighborhood is falling into ruin, and you know it. The state of this room alone . . ."

Despite her encroaching blindness, Hermione sensed her daughter's gaze sweeping the room. She knew the wallpaper was torn, the oil lamps cracked, the carpets threadbare. But what could she do about it? Despite the efforts of her daughters-in-law, poverty was winning.

"So what?" she barked. "Life has never been easy for us, honey. Our forebears were slaves who fought to win their freedom. It falls to you to preserve what their courage and suffering bequeathed to you."

"That's *all* we did for twenty-five years, Rick and I—we battled for our people's right to dignity. Rick has fought hard; he's pugnacious, we have to give him that. And I supported him. But every year has been a step backward. And now, here we are."

"This house—this neighborhood—they're our history! *Your* history! *That's* what counts! The heritage our ancestors have passed down to us."

"What counts is our children's future. What counts is finding a way for my children to move forward in life, to progress. To live without fear."

The old lady exploded:

"If you have white skin, the world is your oyster—is that it?"

"Mother, the discrimination keeps us from finding jobs! We can only work as housemaids or drivers! *Servants!* And there's no hope that that will change! Even Rick stopped believing a better future was possible. Do you want my son to spend the rest of his days shining shoes, my daughters scrubbing bathrooms? I could only give them the education they've gotten by illegally enrolling them in white schools! The diplomas they dream of— teaching for Louise, engineering for Russell, and for Belle, a library degree—they can only earn them if they pass as white."

"Honey, their true fight is to raise themselves up as Blacks!"

"You sound like Rick used to, Mother! And you see where *that* got us!"

Night had fallen, cloaking both of them in darkness. One of them remained firmly planted in her armchair, the other standing. For a moment, neither spoke.

"So," the old lady concluded bitterly, "you would be willing to cut ties with your own family to improve your existence? To separate yourself from us for the sake of *ambition*? That, Genevieve . . . there's no word for it in any language but *betrayal*."

"It's a hopeless battle, Mother. Totally hopeless. And for those of us with mixed blood, there's more: we don't exist. For anyone. Even the word 'mulatto'—'mestizo,' 'quadroon,' call it what you will—isn't in the civil registries. In the eyes of the law, a person is either fully Black or fully white. But we're neither! We belong *nowhere!* Even in the eyes of the Black community, we don't fit in. Haven't you seen the articles that Rick's old friends have published? They've disowned him! Now they accuse him of appearing too white to protect their interests."

"That's not your problem anymore."

Unable to restrain herself any longer, Genevieve burst out: "At this point, the only thing that will save us is crossing the line that separates us from the whites!"

"It's a terrible sin to sail under false colors, to disguise your soul. A terrible sin for a colored man to pass himself off as white."

"What about passing for Black when you're white?" asked Genevieve, her tone ironic.

"What are you talking about?"

"The fact that I don't feel—have never felt—Black!"

"What do you mean, 'never felt Black'?"

"As a colored woman, I'm forced to consider myself Black, to accept not being treated like a human being . . . and yet, physically, I'm white. I don't see why I should live and die like a dog."

"If you abandon your people, you'll lose your sense of self!"

"I am the only person—the one and only—who can determine my place in this world. I demand to be accepted on that basis. And I refuse to let anyone tell me who I am, or who I should be."

"My child, being Black is about so much more than skin color.

It's about sharing the same experiences, the same memories, the same jokes, stories, songs. I've known young people who wanted to cross the line, as you say. And once they finally had, all they wanted was to go back. To go home. But it was impossible. Like them, you'll suffer from homesickness, and loneliness, and regret."

"Homesickness, for being constantly humiliated? For being rejected? Persecuted? For being burned alive or lynched? You have no idea what goes on outside the neighborhood! If Russell enrolled in an engineering school as a Black man, his classmates would treat him the same way they did that student of Rick's. Remember him? A brilliant boy. Rick helped him get accepted to West Point. His fellow recruits tied him to his bed, slashed his face, and slit his ears. And what did his professors say? They accused him of having mutilated *himself*, so he wouldn't have to take his exams and risk failing them. And then they court-martialed him, stripped him of his rank, and expelled him. *That's* the fate that awaits my children."

Hermione waved the argument away. "Our roots are stronger than any persecution. And stronger than all the so-called success of Black people who try to switch sides."

"What roots? We have as many white ancestors as we do Black ones! Why should a single drop of Black blood override all the rest?"

"It's the law."

"When a law's unjust, it should be broken."

"You don't understand," retorted Hermione, her voice quivering. "What overrides all the rest is loyalty to your ancestors' memory! What overrides the rest is respect for your history. Only our past pride can guarantee our future honor. It would be different, maybe, if you were only getting yourself into this mess. But your children!"

"My children want to become white."

"That hotheaded Russell and Belle, perhaps. But the others . . ."

"The others, too. Louise, Ethel, Teddy. They wish it whole-heartedly."

"If you push them down this path, Genevieve, if you allow them to commit this crime, you'll be condemning them to eternal exile. All five of them. Because from that, from their origins, there will be no escape."

Hermione's words shook them both deeply. Genevieve fell to her knees.

"Don't say that," she begged, the tears flowing now.

Exhausted, the old lady let her hand rest gently on her daughter's head. Genevieve didn't pull away.

Frozen in this tableau, they both wept.

Their interlaced silhouettes blurred together in the half-light, forming a dark island in the depths of the night, a tragic and powerful whole, inseparable, like a marble *Pietà*.

But when Genevieve lifted her tear-streaked face toward her mother and pleaded, "Don't curse us, Mother. Forgive my children!" Hermione couldn't bring herself to do it.

She simply took Genevieve's chin in her hand and bent close to her. Her faded eyes locking with Genevieve's, she murmured, her tone urgent:

"May your secret stay safe . . . If you do renounce your true selves, may your secret stay safe!"


### New York, 29 West 99th Street, June 1898

Genevieve had gathered her children around the table in the Greener family's tiny apartment north of Central Park. Her mother's reaction had shaken her so deeply that she'd returned from her trip to Georgetown full of doubts and misgivings.

Hermione Fleet was still the head of the family. Her wishes could not be disregarded. Should they change their minds and give up the plan? There was still time. The decision hadn't been made. No harm had been done. She could still convince her children to turn back.

The discussion that evening would affect the future of every one of them, and so she had made sure that even the youngest, Theodora—little Teddy, aged just twelve—was present, too.

"Before we discuss anything else," she began slowly, "I must warn you that I've spoken to your grandmother about our . . . about what we . . ." She searched for the right words.

Candlelight flickered from the ceiling lamp above their heads, illuminating their faces weakly. Since the departure of the *pater familias*, they'd had to be sparing with gaslight. And in this candlelight, the faces of Russell, Genevieve's oldest son, and Belle, his younger sister, looked dangerously dark. Their Mediterranean looks set them apart, and the difference worried her. Yet it was nothing new. Belle had always had to brush her hair more vigorously than Louise and Ethel, to discipline the dark mass before twisting it up into the high chignon dictated by current fashion. As for Russell, he tamed his rebellious curls by slicking them back with pomade. Nothing out of the ordinary, if they'd lived in Italy or Spain. But in America, for Black people attempting to cross the racial divide, their exotic beauty might draw attention, and put them in danger as a result.

Even more than the others, the two of them would be at great risk of being found out.

Here in New York, though segregation could not be legally imposed, it existed everywhere. And if anyone—in a café, for example—decided to ask Russell or Belle for their identification papers, which bore the stamp *colored*, they would not be served, or if they were, it would be with such ill grace that they would feel obliged to leave.

Neither Genevieve nor any of her children had ever officially declared themselves white, yet. Since their arrival in New York ten years earlier, they had simply kept quiet. *Keep your damned mouth shut*, Belle often said, in the slangy way of speaking she favored. Say nothing at all. Lie by omission.

But everyone here knew that, if they wanted to keep walking on the sidewalks with the white people rather than trudging through the gutters with the Black, to try on shoes in department stores instead of back rooms, to avoid being elbowed aside and spit on while in line for the tram, keeping silent on the subject of their ancestry wouldn't fool the people around them forever. And they were all eager to take the plunge, to falsify their birth certificates and create new identities for themselves.

"Your grandmother reacted very badly," Genevieve said now. "She predicted the worst for us, if we go ahead with this."

"What else did you expect?" exclaimed Belle. "Did you really think she'd approve?"

In the dim light, Genevieve could only see Belle's hands, resting palms-down on a portfolio. But while her face was indistinct, her husky voice was immediately recognizable. She was utterly determined, Genevieve knew, to cross the color barrier, and she suspected that her daughter was prodding the others more firmly in that direction, too.

"What about Father? Have you told him?" asked Louise, the oldest of the girls.

"Father's opinion is meaningless." Belle cut her sister off. "Father doesn't exist anymore."

Belle had loved him so much once. As a child, she'd awaited Rick's return with an impatience that far outweighed her sisters'. At night, she fell asleep dreaming of her courageous father, who stood up to the police and to judges at the risk of his own life. She'd saved up kisses to give him, questions to ask him. She'd waited for him at the corner of their street for hours whenever he came home to Georgetown for public events and holidays, refusing to leave his side, quizzing him endlessly about his travels, the people he had met, the debates he'd engaged in. But he always grew tired of her questions before he could answer them all. In truth, he preferred the less clever company of Russell, the only boy. Genevieve saw how much Belle admired her father, how she clipped and kept the articles he wrote, watched her growing up with the same passion for books and ideas—and knew that he was annoyed by his daughter. In truth, she was *too* much like him, and their temperaments, through their very magnetism, couldn't coexist harmoniously. And Belle suffered from her father's indifference.

Still, she hadn't wavered in her passionate adoration for him until she'd become aware, at around age twelve, of her mother's isolation, and the difficult situations in which he tended to leave his family. She'd been the first to realize that whenever Rick came home, another new baby followed. Genevieve was endlessly pregnant, seven times in ten years. She'd lost two little boys, and now her children were her whole life. They'd watched her work her fingers to the bone to ensure that they would have "an education." Without knowledge, she said, there could be no salvation. And she and her husband were of one mind about the necessity of studying. It might have been the only point they agreed on.

Although Genevieve almost never complained, her older children had witnessed the discord in their parents' relationship. And they knew that, in the hierarchy of their father's many concerns, they ranked last.

When Rick Greener had finally put an end to his comings and goings and summoned them to New York, they had believed that things might improve. But even living under the same roof, they were forced to recognize that Rick was as absent as ever, and even more impatient. With the passage of time, all the respect they had once felt for him had been transferred to their mother.

Their time in New York had begun with such promise. Rick Greener had been recruited by the Grant Monument Association.

To honor the great man—victor of the Civil War, President of the United States during the Reconstruction Era—shortly after his death, the liberal mayor of New York had decided to build a mausoleum in his city worthy of such an august personage. As founding members of his association, he had selected some of the wealthiest and most powerful men in Manhattan, including the tycoons John Pierpont Morgan, Cornelius Vanderbilt, and John Jacob Astor, all of whom had, like the mayor himself, belonged to Grant's abolitionist party. Grant remained an object of veneration for the people he had liberated, and so the association's board of directors had thought it appropriate to appoint a prominent figure from the Black community as their secretary. Who better than Professor Greener, the first Black man to graduate from Harvard, to represent former slaves? Greener had been personally congratulated by General Grant when the latter had visited the university in 1875, and had even been received in Washington by Grant with other delegates working on behalf of Black civil rights. What was more, he almost looked white himself—which, in the eyes of Mr. Astor and Mr. Morgan, made him acceptable.

And so Rick Greener had been charged with acquiring the funds for a gigantic mausoleum, one worthy of the general. He was also responsible for putting out calls for bids among American architects, selecting the best proposals, and submitting these to the board.

Richard Greener had flourished in the role, sinking all of his prodigious energy into the accomplishment of his mission.

Yet this titanic project, on which he labored so brilliantly for seven years, had brought him no recognition. At the splendid inaugural ceremony, his name—among the hundreds of people cited and thanked—was not even mentioned. And with reason. His protector, the mayor of New York, had just been defeated at the polls by his conservative opponent. Discredited by his rival and successor, the former mayor had been forced to resign from the Grant Monument Association. Rick, now without support, politically isolated, and newly vulnerable to the vindictiveness of the board's most racist members, quickly found himself under siege on all fronts. He'd ceased to be respected. Stopped being paid. And, in the end, been compelled to resign.

Such a rapid reversal of his fortunes did nothing to benefit either his bank account or his domestic situation.

He turned on his wife, accusing her of being responsible for all his failures, including the rumors now swirling that he had given up his political struggles and abandoned his Black brothers in favor of his own personal ambition. To hear him talk, it was because of Genevieve—who had moved them into a white neighborhood, enrolled his children in white schools, and received only white visitors in their home—that other Black activists now regarded him as a traitor and chastised him for missing their meetings. It was she who had pushed him to accept the job in service of their oppressors. How could he have found time to prepare his speeches, to write his articles and organize his debates, when he'd had to spend so many hours, minutes, seconds working for the Grant Committee? He'd worked like a maniac to feed his family! Yes, it was *Genevieve's* fault that the president of the American Negro Academy, one of his former colleagues, had refused him membership. *Her* fault that, in the Black newspapers to which he'd always contributed articles, that same president had dared to explain this veto by saying: "Mr. Greener has tried to have a finger in every pie. He's lived as a white man in New York, where he turned his back on his brethren of color. And now that his friends the whites have ousted him, he's affecting to be one of us again. I have no personal quarrel with Mr. Greener's passing himself off as a white man. But I do oppose his return to our ranks, and his intent to use his Blackness to obtain a political post if, one day, one of us is elected to office."

Rick had never recovered from this rejection.

His arguments with Genevieve about the injustices to which he'd fallen victim, the complaints now targeting him, became so violent that he finally abandoned the marital home and moved in with one of his mistresses. The thought of Rick cheating on her publicly, and spending what meager funds he did manage to earn on his own pleasure, pushed his wife to the breaking point. And when she learned that he was seeking a diplomatic post on the other side of the globe, Genevieve exploded in turn, unleashing an unrestrained flood of bitterness and reproach.

The couple eventually reached a point of such mutual fury that Uncle Mozart was dispatched from Georgetown to mediate between them. He proved unable to broker a financial agreement for a possible separation, though, and Rick announced that he would pay for neither the schooling nor the upkeep of anyone except his youngest girl, Teddy. He ended by announcing his permanent departure for Vladivostok.

"And let's hope he stays there!" concluded Belle.

This remark, uttered so firmly into the dimness, provoked a vague, uneasy stirring among her brothers and sisters.

"Goodbye, and good riddance," she insisted. "There's no use hiding from the truth; this is reality. We won't see him again. So much for the 'activist' Greener. Actually, we might as well take advantage of it," she continued, teasingly. "Since he's ruined our good name anyway, let's toss it in the trash along with him, and change it."

She'd always been extremely forthright in her speech, and her language, in its directness, often bordered on being crude. God only knew where she'd picked up all the slang that habitually crept in when she spoke of her father! At nineteen, she expressed herself however she liked.

This time, Genevieve decided not to remonstrate with her. She'd played devil's advocate too often in recent years, trying to soften Belle's intractable fury toward everything that had to do with Rick and his undertakings. Too many dashed hopes. Too many injustices. Too much violence; too many lost causes. And above all, too much shame, inflicted in the end by their own brethren. *Too white for the Blacks. Too black for the Whites.* A no-win situation that had convinced her at last of the pointlessness of the struggle for which Rick had sacrificed everything.

In Belle's eyes, her father embodied the exclusion, the marginalization, she wanted no further part of.

So. Greener's few remaining friends on the committee had gotten him this consulate post on the far side of Asia, had they? He was welcome to it!

He hadn't deigned to give his family any explanation for this prestigious appointment, or seemed to imagine, even for an instant, that they could follow him. When Genevieve had made it clear that she was opposed to his departure, and the children had sided with her, he'd stopped coming to see them. They could go straight to hell—Louise, Russell, Belle, the whole bunch of them! He had put himself on the line too often to have to justify himself to them now. For thirty years, the Fleets of Georgetown had been endlessly critical of him. His harpy of a mother-in-law had never stopped disparaging him. And if his own children were old enough to disapprove of him now, they were damned well old enough to fend for themselves without him.

Even at the moment of separation, he hadn't had a single word of farewell for his wife, nor a token gesture for anyone. Not even a few dollars to soothe his conscience. Not even a hollow promise of returning. He'd left without saying goodbye. Yesterday.

For Belle, that was the final word on the matter. He'd failed to fulfill his most basic responsibilities. The time had come for their lives to change.

"But not by changing our *name!*" protested Ethel.

"Oh, *darling*, if it were only a matter of names, passing for white would be easy as pie."

"But people know us everywhere as the Greener family!"

"We can find something similar. Something that will still be *us*, but set us apart from *him*," Louise suggested. "We could take out a letter or two, for example . . . 'Gene'? Louise Gene?"

"Hideous," said Belle scathingly. "What about 'Greene'?"

"*Mundane*," retorted Ethel.

"Exactly. There's probably only one Greener family in New York, but there are Greenes all over the United States. If we become respectable little Greenes, we can lose ourselves in the masses and disappear."

"Still mundane. And too much like Greener to erase our connection to Pa."

"Not if we add a few frills. 'Miss Belle Greene de Windsor.' That has a nifty ring to it, don't you think?"

Genevieve frowned. "Enough clowning, Belle. If you keep up in that tone, and with that vocabulary, you're leaving the table."

The girl wasn't cowed. For all that she might appear at first to be the flightiest of the children, certainly the most fanciful, she took the lead in most of their family meetings. And no one could deny that she possessed the solid common sense her older siblings, Russell and Louise, lacked. Genevieve was only too aware of the predominant trait in Belle's personality: the ability to endure life's ups and downs with the appearance of ease. Especially the downs. She saw her father's departure as a betrayal and an abandonment, but, far from ruminating on the trauma, she was making fun of it. A deliberate, systematic refusal to acknowledge any sentimentality in herself, or anyone else. She never allowed herself to yield, at least when the world was watching, to the slightest emotion. Except, perhaps, to intellectual exhilaration. When it came to talking about a book, Belle didn't hold back. Her voice would even quiver with excitement. But the rest was masked by a froth of wisecracks, sarcasm, irony. Perpetual banter. Sometimes it was funny, sometimes infuriating.

"This isn't a game, Belle," her mother insisted now.

"I know it isn't a game, Mommy. The situation's even fairly tragic. All the more reason to act decisively, and on a grand scale. All joking aside . . ."

Belle opened her portfolio, which contained a family tree covering three generations. None of them could make out the details, but her words were enough:

"Russell and I have done a bit of investigating, and here is what we propose: *Maman*—in the French way from now on; it's more chic—was born in Virginia, into a family of Southern planters that was totally ruined by the Civil War. Maman doesn't have a single drop of Black blood, you see; it's all completely blue. In for a penny, in for a damned pound . . ."

"Belle, one more rude word and you are leaving the table!"

"So, Maman becomes an aristocrat from Alexandria, descended on one side from a Dutch family with a long lineage: the van Fleets, as you see here. It could also be 'van Vliet,' if you think that makes it seem more European. On the other side, her forebears are Portuguese, which would explain Russell's dark skin, and mine. Portugal is better than Italy, I think; less known, less visited. That side of the family is the da Costa branch. There are hundreds of da Costas in Lisbon, so it shouldn't be a problem to fit in a few more. Our father, the late Captain John Greene, was English—here again, there are countless John Greenes all over the British Empire. He was an officer serving in India, the youngest son in his family. He died in Bombay, leaving his worthy widow in difficult financial straits. So, she left Virginia and moved to New York, where she earns her living giving piano lessons. Her husband's trunk, with their marriage certificate inside, was stolen in India, but she will swear on the Bible to the authenticity of their union. Maman looks so refined that no one will doubt her. As for the rest—our birth certificates, if they were even filed in Washington—did not come with us to New York. All Maman will have to do is swear that we were born in Virginia.

Oh, and good news: to muddy the waters even further, Maman subtracts ten years from her age. She's around forty now."

"Does that make me *three?*" interrupted Teddy.

"This is where things get tricky," laughed Belle. "I'd be fifteen!"

Genevieve couldn't contain her exasperation any longer.

"That's quite enough, Belle. Listening to this makes me realize just how immature you all are! *Children!* The subject is closed. And the answer is no. No one here will dishonor themselves with false testimony."

"I haven't gotten to the important part yet. The thing that will count in the future, exactly that—children. If we're white, we'll be able to marry white people and have white children. But—"

"*But,*" her mother cut her off, "You might also have Black children. You know that. It can skip a generation, and it can even happen within the same set of siblings. Look at Uncle Mozart and Uncle Bellini. One looks white; the other looks Black. What will happen if one of you gives birth to a colored baby?"

"It'll give the rest of us away."

"That's why we've taken a vow never to have children," Ethel chimed in.

"You *what?* You don't know what you're saying!" Genevieve exclaimed, appalled.

"We've all made a pact," replied Belle firmly. "Ethel, Louise, Russell, and me. We've sworn to one another that we'll remain childless, so our secret will stay safe."

Her words shocked Genevieve to the core. It was the exact phrase her mother had used.

"Even me," put in young Teddy. "I swore it on the Bible."

Genevieve, who never blew up, finally lost her *sang-froid* at this.

"I don't know whose idea it was to make such a monstrous vow, but I order you to give it up immediately. None of you can

commit yourselves to something so abominable! Your grandmother's absolutely right. I've changed my mind, and you have
to follow my lead. Crossing the color barrier is a crazy idea and
will end in disaster. It's impossible!"

"Impossible during Grandma's lifetime," agreed Belle. "But
what about afterward?"

### Freedmen's Cemetery, Alexandria, Virginia, January 1899

Hermione Fleet's coffin looked as small as a child's. Despite
the freezing rain, Georgetown's entire Black community had
gathered at her graveside.

The Fleet clan alone would have been large enough to fill the
cemetery, but many in the crowd that had come to pay its
respects had come from much further afield. Even the former
comrades-in-arms of her son-in-law, the famous Professor
Richard Greener, had made the journey, as had some of Rick's
students, men he had once championed, trained, and sometimes
defended before the courts. Every generation, every background,
every class, every caste, every shade of color was represented.
Merchants, laborers, domestic servants, the unemployed. Some
of them appeared white; Pastor Philipps spotted those individuals from far away, among the tombstones that studded the green
lawn. Next to draw his attention were those most miserable of
Blacks—The Desperate Ones, as he thought of them, because
they constantly dreamed of killing white people. Then, nearer the
grave, his usual parishioners, the Domesticated Ones, who knew
nothing of revolt and worked as servants to the whites. Finally,
there were the Educated Ones, who lived somewhere in
between, moving in polite society without any link to the whites.
It was to this third category that the family of Hermione Fleet
belonged, that Little Iron Lady of Georgetown whom the pastor
had known and loved so well.

Her descendants formed a compact group at the graveside, almost as varied in their appearance as the crowd gathered behind them. Among her flock of grandchildren, the offspring of her eldest daughter were immediately discernible. Everyone here knew Genevieve Fleet-Greener. She might not have lived in the neighborhood for a decade now, but her relationship to the parish and the affection that bound her to her childhood friends were undiminished. In the eyes of the community, the Greeners belonged inextricably to Pastor Philipps's church.

And all those, too, whom Dr. Fleet, the deceased's husband, had treated; all those who had once practiced their scales with Hermione and played piano with her daughters; those who had played in the house on T Street with Genevieve's children, with Louise, Russell, Belle, and Ethel, had come to support them, to show their loyalty. An immense group of young people surrounded the oldest grandchildren. Russell, the boy, would soon reach adulthood, and his former playmates were present and accounted for. The three girls, aged twenty-one, nineteen, and eighteen, respectively, drew every eye. Standards of female beauty in Georgetown were no different than among the whites; the paler a woman's skin, the more attractive she was. And in this respect, the Greener girls embodied the ideal. With their translucent complexions and burnished gold hair, Louise and Ethel had grown into truly radiant women. Belle, the middle sister, was noticeable as well, a pretty brunette with gray eyes. They remembered her as the liveliest girl in class, a ringleader whose sauciness had made her schoolmates laugh until she moved away in the eighth grade. Even as a child, she'd had a collection of sweethearts; more than one boy had declared his love for her, signing his missive in letters of blood. Next to Belle, the youngest sister, Teddy, on the brink of adolescence now, was in floods of tears.

None of the girls paid any attention to the many glances they received. In deep mourning, they kept their eyes cast down beneath their dripping hat-brims. They had all worshipped their grandmother, and the sight of her casket descending slowly into the earth was intensely emotional.

The ceremony at the cemetery had plunged Genevieve into bottomless grief, and the enormous gathering held after the burial unsettled her even further. Everyone she loved was there, some of them gathered around the piano, others surrounding the pastor. Despite the pervading sense of grief, children hurtled all over the place, doing their best to keep their cries low and their steps soft, but playing energetically all the same. The warmth of this family circle, the kindness, the bonds she shared with each person here, the memories . . . and their cheerfulness, even in these circumstances; the incredible zest for life of this community—how could she renounce them? She looked around the room for her children. She saw Louise and Ethel, chatting with their female cousins in a corner. Russell, comfortable and at ease among his friends. They belonged completely to the 1400 block of T Street, all five of them. What madness to have considered cutting ties; what shame to have entertained the thought for even a moment! It would have meant the heartbreak that Hermione had predicted, the regret, the longing, the loneliness.

*This* was life. Real life.

Genevieve hadn't seen her mother again after that last conversation, and she looked back on the scene now with a deep feeling of guilt, which Hermione's passing made difficult to bear. Remorse at having worried her mother with such a cruel plan in her final days gnawed at her.

Her gaze settled on Belle, who didn't look back at her. Belle, normally so lively, so boisterous, a girl whose every move was intended to capture the light, to attract interest, was standing apart from the crowd, alone, unmoving. Though her face betrayed nothing, Genevieve sensed that her daughter, too, was overwhelmed. She leaned against the wall in a corner of the room, hands behind her back, chin raised as if the heavy mass of her dark hair was pulling her head backward. Her restless body, its slimness accentuated by the black mourning attire, was almost invisible against the wallpaper. Genevieve knew what Belle was feeling, what she was trying to do.

She was listening. She was observing. She was trying to imprint on her memory these voices, these faces she had loved. The smells of this room, the colors, the noises. She was fixing all these impressions deep within herself. The air she was breathing, the objects she saw, every detail. The white porcelain globes of the oil-lamps; the brightly hued squares of the patchwork piano-cover. She was engraving on her soul this moment that she was living for the last time.

In that instant, Genevieve knew that Belle had chosen. That she had made her decision a long time ago. And that her brother and sisters would follow her. This time, the die was cast. And if she didn't want to lose her children, she would not only have to accompany them but probably also guide them in their lies, in the staging of their new lives. Six irrevocably intertwined fates, and if any one of them were to fall short, it would bring the others down with it.

And so the aristocratic family of *van Vliet da Costa Greene* was born.

# CHAPTER 2

## WHITE
## 1903–1904

**Princeton University, winter 1903**

On the Monday morning train from New York to Princeton, Belle was jubilant. The piece of paper, folded twice, that she had tucked into her reticule conferred on her, at long last, the legitimacy she'd been seeking since her father's abandonment. She knew every word on the paper by heart, yet she couldn't keep herself from taking it out of her purse again and reading it for the hundredth time.

*IDENTIFICATION OF REQUESTING PARTY*
*FOR A PASSPORT APPLICATION:*

*Name: Miss Belle da Costa Greene*
*Address: 507 West 112th Street, New York City*

*Affidavit: Genevieve van Vliet Greene swears on oath and solemnly declares that she is a citizen of the United States of America and that she is the mother of Belle da Costa Greene, the above applicant for a passport to Europe.*

*Declares that the said Belle da Costa Greene was born in Alexandria, Virginia on the 26th of November, 1885, and that she has resided in the United States since that date.*

*Declares that the said Belle da Costa Greene resides with her at 507 West 112th Street in the borough of Manhattan, city of New York.*

*Sworn before me on this third day of December, 1903.*

*Jocelyn H. Magrath, notary public, 31 Nassau Street, New York City*

. . . *For a passport application.* Admittedly, she was far from having the means to travel at all, and farther still from traveling from America to Europe. But this paper was an *open sesame* to freedom, protection from any intrusion into her family background.

Just in case.

Crossing the color barrier suddenly seemed so simple. Anyone could do it! Her mother had followed her instructions, of course, and done everything very well. And yet Belle hadn't imagined that they would be able to make the great leap with so much ease. Why weren't colored people brave enough attempt it more often, when their skin was pale enough to try? But, God knew, perhaps there were more of them than it seemed. The practice was well known; it could be summed up in a single word, with no need for further clarification: Passing. This offense, this crime of passing, could lead to the end of a noose, a threat that was enough to deter many. Belle had heard stories of these unspeakable lynchings; in one case a Black woman had been doused with gasoline and burned alive, accused of having passed herself off as white and married a white man. And as for the treatment in store for her brother Russell if he were to be found out after having slept with a white woman . . .

She looked around at the crowd of elegantly dressed travelers sharing this dawn train to New Jersey and chuckled inwardly. Who was to say that they weren't *all* Black? That old lady in the plumed hat? The slim young man in the tight frock coat? Princeton was said to be the most racist of the small towns between New York and Philadelphia, to say nothing of its university, many of whose students hailed from Southern states. The idea of this community, so prosperous and conservative, being "infiltrated" filled her with glee.

But enough kidding around.
*Never think of yourself as a colored woman again. Ever.*

She thought back over just how tumultuous the past four years had been. Their share of the inheritance left by their grandmother had enabled the new "van Vliet da Costa Greene" family to move away from 99th Street, leaving the last name of Greener behind them. They had settled down ten blocks away on 112th Street, closer to Columbia University, where Russell had just begun his scholarship-funded studies in engineering.

Louise and Ethel had earned their teaching certificates and found places in two schools north of Central Park, while Genevieve, playing the role of virtuous widow to the hilt, taught piano to the children of her new neighbors between Broadway and Amsterdam Avenue. Everyone put their income toward running the household, perpetuating in this way, without even realizing it, the tradition of the Fleets of Georgetown, a clan that pooled its resources. In this respect, Belle had to admit, she didn't contribute much to the family coffers.

But it didn't matter. She knew exactly what she wanted to do. She wanted to work with books.

Since the age of twelve, she had loved to look at books, to touch them, to breathe them in. She sensed their souls. She was deeply sensitive to the magic they emanated, the dreams, the emotion, the beauty.

There was no point in her taking classes in dressmaking or secretarial work, like so many other young women biding their time before marriage. Unlike her friends, she had absolutely no intention of marrying, ever. Books were worth more than all the husbands in the world.

This passion, though she refused to admit it, had been inherited from her father. No one had ever yearned to dedicate his life to art and literature more than Professor Greener. Before earning his law degree and embarking on a political career, he had wanted to become a writer. Lack of means, and the urgency of his struggle, had put an end to those ambitions, something he bitterly regretted.

His respect for books had been so great that he had single-handedly undertaken, during his first professorship in South Carolina, the reorganization of the university's library. It was a herculean task; the Civil War had left the library in a deplorable condition. Volumes damaged or lost, volumes borrowed and never returned, volumes ordered and never received. With his customary energy, Greener had set about restoring order. It would remain one of his fondest memories of his career. As a result of his efforts, the library had become the pride of the university. It remained so today.

In July 1900, Belle had enrolled in the summer cataloguing course at Amherst College in Massachusetts. Fortuitously, she hadn't been required to produce any family references other than her mother's approval, proof that she had graduated from high school, and fifteen dollars in academic fees. Her five weeks on a university campus had only confirmed her ambitions. By the end of the summer, she had mastered the art of bibliography.

Certificate in hand, she had quickly found an internship as a receptionist at the Lenox Library, one of New York's two public libraries, on the corner of 70th Street and 5th Avenue. Entrance to the library was by ticket only, and the reading room was frequented only by a few dedicated scholars. It was there, in the dimly lit depths of the stacks, that Belle leafed through an illuminated manuscript for the first time. She didn't know the document's history, couldn't even decipher the title, but at the sight of those splendid images painted in the Middle Ages, the richness of the colors and the delicacy of the calligraphy, she felt the kind of emotion that changes the course of a life. She consulted one of the old bibliophiles about the manuscript's provenance, firing questions at him with such ardor that he was touched.

Never would he have imagined that a young female intern would be so interested in the mysteries of a work by Cluniac monks. Belle's clear delight was enough for him to recommend her for a position as librarian at Princeton University in New Jersey.

She'd felt herself to be in paradise ever since.

With great good fortune, she had found a room in the home of the redoubtable Miss Charlotte Martins, who had been director of acquisitions for more than twenty years. She was an institution unto herself at Princeton, an unmarried woman of fifty who lived in a two-story Victorian house not far from campus with her invalid father, her widowed sister, and her two nieces. To make ends meet, she provided lodging to the young female librarians under her tutelage. Miss Martins, whom they called "Aunt Charlotte" or "Aunt Lottie," had entered into her career as a librarian like one taking up holy orders. She knew how to recognize other, similarly fervent souls who lavished books with the adoration she considered their due. She could be severe, even cruel to dilettantes. But if one of her flock displayed sufficient proof of devotion, Aunt Lottie would take that girl under her wing and train her. And out of all of them, her heart's choice over the past year had been one Miss da Costa Greene. This young woman seemed to Miss Martins, if not a revelation, then certainly a recruit full of promise at the very least. It was true that her background lacked any sort of study worthy of the name; she had only a certificate to prove that she was capable of cataloguing or drawing up an inventory. But she grasped the intricacies of the profession with lightning speed. Belle was aware of Miss Martins's partiality toward her, and returned her fondness a hundredfold, treating her with respect that bordered on reverence—a most agreeable situation for the older woman, and one that inspired her to treat her protégée with unbounded generosity.

As always, Belle refused to see that this was another trait she had inherited from her father: that vitality, that seductive power, and that devotion to a cause that attracted the benevolence of powerful protectors.

In truth, Belle lived every moment of her time at Princeton as if it were a miracle, with the constant feeling that it could all end tomorrow. Far from depressing her, though, the threat of losing what was dearest to her drove her to take advantage of every single opportunity that came her way. The result of this was that she left campus less and less often, arriving at dawn before anyone else—the library opened at eight o'clock—and combing the shelves tirelessly in search of volumes requested by the director, typing up the index cards for the cataloguing service, running endlessly between floors and from one department to another, shutting the place down in the evening. It was a murderous pace she kept up all week, often late into the night. On the weekends there were student balls and football, baseball, and hockey matches, all social events to which her admirers—the library's readers—invited her. She never turned anything down. Too many opportunities to learn. Too many opportunities to enjoy herself.

Now, however, with Christmas approaching, she thought it was time to go home and help her family get ready for the holiday festivities. Christmas remained a difficult time, awakening in all of them a longing for their uncles, aunts, and cousins in Georgetown, a nostalgia they were obliged to fight.

Their mother never said a word to indicate regret or doubt, never even alluded to their previous life, but Teddy, the youngest sister, now eighteen, often spoke wistfully of the warmth of the Fleet clan's gatherings. Though she had been born just as her parents' arguments began to get truly ferocious, and had been only two years old when they moved to New York, she tended to brood at this time of year, and to break their pact of silence regarding the past. She had only ever spoken of her feelings to her family, but these confidences would become a danger if ever they overspilled the bounds of their apartment. And so Belle intended to tighten the sibling circle again by imbuing it with fresh gaiety; she had instructed everyone in the family to invite a colleague to spend Christmas with them, someone who was alone for the holidays, whose loved ones lived far from New York. There was no shortage of these young women at the library, girls hailing from other states who, like Belle, worked day and night. There were some fifteen of them, working across six departments: referencing, loans, binding, acquisitions, inventory, and cataloguing. Their salary did not exceed five dollars a week where a factory worker earned ten; this was in accordance with a principle held by Mr. Richardson, the head curator, who claimed to hire as workers only young women from respectable families, possessing neither skills nor the need to earn a living. A hypocritical policy aimed at saving money at the expense of the staff. For the rest, Mr. Richardson devoted himself body and soul to his mission: to endow Princeton with the richest and best organized collection of all university libraries.

In fact, under Richardson's leadership, Princeton had come to possess two libraries. The older of them, the octagonal Chancellor Green library, had been built in 1875. The roof of its rotunda and its tall windows were made of stained glass to let the light in, a design that eliminated the risk of fire posed by candles and oil lamps. During the tenure of the first head curator, Miss Martins had reigned over the research room alongside him, keeping an eagle eye on the reference-seekers from atop her rostrum. No one knew better than she the contents of the volumes inventoried in the catalogues.

Yet in less than twenty years, the shelves of the Chancellor Green's circular research room had reached capacity, unable to house the forty thousand volumes Miss Martins had ordered and purchased. The university was obliged to demolish East College and the Old Chapel to build a second library, this one designed on a rectangular plan and connected to the first by a passage that

Miss Martins triumphantly dubbed the Hyphen. Belle was fully conscious of the dignity—and the privileges—conferred upon her as a priestess in this temple. She knew all too well that the sort of libraries she should have been frequenting, those reserved for Black readers, often consisted of some fifty books piled in the basement of a school, or in the corner of a shabby classroom.

But as a white woman, she could work—study—amid the collections bequeathed to the university generation after generation by former students who had forged careers as archaeologists or researchers. And, down through the centuries since 1746, the gifts had multiplied: donations of manuscripts, rare books, and periodicals in which European and American history, as well as literature in every language, were splendidly depicted.

As a white woman, Belle was able to attend any lecture that struck her fancy, on subjects as diverse as classical philosophy, archaeology, and paleography.

As a white woman, she belonged to the elite, and participated fully in the social life on campus.

And now this piece of paper.

Age: 18 years                    Mouth: wide
Height: 5 feet 2 inches          Chin: pointed
Forehead: average                Hair: dark chestnut
Eyes: gray                       Complexion: dark
Nose: average                    Face: oval

The coolness and objectivity of this description conferred upon her a legal existence in accordance with every law. And, cherry on the cake, it made her younger by six whole years.

\*

The earliest train, at five-thirty in the morning, well known to those fun-loving students who spent their nights in Manhattan's hotspots, had Belle at the library before dawn. She got off at Princeton Junction and boarded the tram, which whisked her to the very heart of town in twenty minutes. On these cold mornings in December 1903, her second winter with Miss Martins, the journey was a familiar one.

Belle loved nothing so much as spotting the ghostly silhouettes of Blair Hall's towers through the darkness, rising castlelike beyond the little tram station. She had only to cross one street and go up a flight of stairs to reach one of the arched campus entrances. There was no reason to stop at Miss Martin's to change clothes; she possessed doubles of each of her meager possessions. Two dark hats handed down from Genevieve. Two long skirts, cut slim and straight. Two white blouses buttoned to the chin. Two silk scarves that she wore tied in a bow or knotted like a necktie. Two trim jackets, fitted at the waist. The rest of her wardrobe was determined by her whim on any given day. The only constant was the woollen coat, edged with rabbit-fur, which traveled with her between New York and Princeton.

Her heeled boots slipped on the icy cobbles as she passed beneath the archway. The wind whistled through the empty courtyards and passages, making her shiver. But the orange and black banners fluttering from the flagpole atop Nassau Hall in the moonlight matched so well the colors of her own soul— orange for the joy of belonging to Princeton, black for the everpresent threat of losing everything—that she hardly felt the sting of the cold.

The campus was still deserted at this hour. How could her whole being not thrill at an exalted moment like this, when she felt as if this world of gray stone and delicate snowflakes were hers alone? She looked at the snow clinging to the bare vines and settling in stripes on the Gothic façades, festooning the mullioned windows and the crenellations of the towers, crowning statues and gargoyles, blanketing the immense lawns in white.

Her pleasure at the sight of it all was physical, almost sensual; it was a universe suspended in space and time, medieval England and modern America all at once.

She felt the same exhilaration now as she always did in the wood-paneled rooms of the library when she carried, pressed to her chest, first editions of Virgil's writings—among the *incunabla*, the early modern texts that featured in the extraordinary collection of Junius Spencer Morgan. She knew every detail of every book. The publication date of the oldest piece in the collection: 1469. Its place of publication: Rome. The names of its printers: Sweynheim and Pannartz, two Germans who had produced the very first books printed in Italy.

How could she possibly express the emotion of holding in her hands the *editio princeps* of each of Virgil's works? The pride of working alongside the benefactor who had discovered, hunted down, and brought back these European marvels?

Mr. Junius Morgan. That great scholar, a Princeton graduate, had donated the entire corpus of his *Virgiliana* to the university at a splendid ceremony seven years early. The coherence and equilibrium of this collection had, in one fell swoop, transformed Miss Martins and her handmaidens into the keepers of a priceless treasure. Since then, Mr. Junius Morgan had occupied the office adjacent to the director's; while his position might appear to be a largely honorary one, it took up all of his time, and indeed he spared no effort. When Junius was not attending sales of books or engravings, he spent his days and nights studying the illuminations that illustrated his manuscripts, comparing their calligraphy, their pigments, and the different layers of their colorization. In this way he succeeded, from time to time, in identifying the provenance and the artistic hand behind a particular work. While in matter of fact his profession lay in Wall Street finance, the truth was that he had no passion for banking and put in only the minimum effort required at Cuyler, Morgan & Co., one branch of the family empire. For all that, however, he

was a trusted advisor to his uncle, the tycoon John Pierpont Morgan, in matters of the older man's eclectic tastes in all forms of art, and acted as his agent in the acquisition of his most beautiful objects.

In short, Junius Morgan incarnated both knowledge and imagination. He was a man with both an eye and a brain, his friends said, to which were added the ineffable virtues of whimsy and imagination—and all this on top of both a sense of humor and a deep aesthetic sensibility, both unequaled. He was thirty-six years old, of average height, with a twinkle in his eye behind the pince-nez spectacles he wore. His sensual mouth often seemed almost to pout. He was, along with all his other charms, a handsome young man.

*Junius.* The man with whom Belle was madly in love, the man she was impatient to rejoin at Chancellor Green.

*The love of my life*, she thought to herself during sleepless nights at Miss Martin's. An ill-fated love. Because Junius was married, and had no intention—for now, at least—of being unfaithful to his wife. But who knew what might happen in the future?

She was shrewd enough to sense, if not that he admired her, at least that he'd noticed her. She had done what was necessary to be sure of that.

But from that to imagining that something more might be possible . . . She was well aware that her dreams could never be anything but fantasy. All the more reason to allow them free rein! And so she didn't hesitate to indulge herself, whenever she desired, in thoughts of what it might feel like to be embraced, kissed, by Junius.

\*

Heads bent over a sheaf of large-format drawings, the library's four departmental directors didn't even look up when

Belle set on the table the boxes that Junius Morgan had asked her to fetch. They contained the plans for Princeton's two libraries, which Junius wanted to compare with those of the architectural firm employed by his uncle, J.P. Morgan, who wished to construct, right next door to his New York mansion on the corner of Madison Avenue and 36th Street, a building to house his book collections. The project posed the same problems as those that the head curator of special collections, Mr. Richardson, had tried to resolve when he had envisioned the buildings of the new Pyne Library eight years earlier. How to maximize natural light and minimize the risk of fire? How to design conservation, storage, and filing spaces that were simultaneously protected, functional, and modern? Mr. Richardson had thought long and carefully about all these points, and viewed the solutions he'd found with undiminished pride. He was a man of some forty years, who looked a decade older—yet he had no need of the outward signs of age, of his receding hairline and gray mustache, to make an impression. A peerless educator, he trained the university's top classes of students in the humanities, encouraging them to travel in Europe, where he spent six months of each year himself in quest of the newest gems in the collections of the Bibliothèque Nationale in Paris, the British Museum in London, the Staatsbibliothek in Berlin. Everywhere. Being able to say you were a student of Professor Richardson's opened all sorts of doors to a career in a variety of American institutions—and, conversely, criticizing his initiatives could cost you dearly. Highly authoritarian, he had a reputation for brooking no opposition, and his colleagues were obliged to tread with extreme care when pointing out to him, in front of Junius Morgan, the few defects in the system he had designed.

"The glass floors, so cleverly proposed by Professor Richardson to allow light to pass between levels of the building, were a stroke of genius," began Mr. Bishop, head of the cataloguing department, delicately. "The problem at the Pyne Library is that . . ."

He hesitated, catching Belle's eye. She stood very still a few steps away, listening raptly to the conversation. Mr. William Bishop, the youngest of the department heads, seemed to be the only one who had noticed her presence. He had started at the library the previous year, at the same time as Belle; they had cut their teeth at Princeton together. Though he moved in social and professional circles far more exalted than hers—and was engaged to a young woman from Kentucky—Bishop was not impervious to her charms. He'd made this clear to Belle, and she had not discouraged him, questioning him with great interest when he described to her his plans for a future public library.

"The problem at the Pyne," he continued now, "is that the sound of Miss Greene's charming little boot-heels, clicking against the glass over readers' heads, is distracting to even the most serious among us."

Junius's eyes twinkled. He might be of a generally impassive nature, careful to maintain his gravity in every circumstance, but his eyes often betrayed the amusement he tried to hide. Now, looking up at the transparent ceiling, he forbore from pointing out that visitors to the library might be distracted by the view of more than just Miss Greene's boots through the glass.

Even the softest footsteps, Bishop persisted, made an extraordinary racket on the glass as people moved among the shelves. And as for the light, while the multicolored rays that fell from the stained-glass windows of the Chancellor Green Library were certainly very pretty, their red gleam tended to flicker on the page, making it extremely difficult to read.

". . . which, I'm sure you will agree, constitutes a problem in a library."

The smoke from their English cigarettes clung to the oak paneling of this corner room, designated as Seminar Room 4. The oil lamps suspended from the ceiling, with their spherical green porcelain shades, hung low above the long table covered with plans. The leather armchairs in the corners gave the room the feeling of a London gentleman's club, rather than a workspace.

Belle couldn't bring herself to leave. She knew she ought to, though, and began to reach back reluctantly for the door-knob.

"No need for you to go, Miss Greene," murmured Junius. "You're here day in and day out; what do you think of the way the premises are laid out?"

Anyone other than Belle would have lost their nerve at being addressed publicly this way. Especially because every word that came out of Junius's mouth made her heart flutter. And because every word that came out of her own could cost her her job.

Concealing every trace of emotion, she stepped closer to the table and said, measuring her words carefully:

"The fact that none of the shelves is higher than seven and a half feet, as Professor Richardson wished, is quite practical. None of us needs a stepladder or a footstool to reach the books. But . . ."

She stopped. Junius had removed his spectacles and was look-ing at her with the sharp, serious expression he habitually wore.

"But, Miss Greene?"

"I've been uneasy about the books," she answered frankly. "Especially when they are in folio. When they're carried down five flights of concrete stairs and held too tightly, the binding can be damaged. And perhaps the steps are a bit too high, and too narrow? For the rest, the loan department and display cases are perfect, as is the lighting in the attic and the basement— Professor Richardson thought of everything! And his system of cataloguing by number—a single line per index card with the author's name, title, and a description of the work—is truly unparalleled in its effectiveness. Both for the readers and for us."

Junius motioned toward the architectural firm's sketches, which he had already modified.

"And what do you think of these plans?"

She bent over them and examined them carefully, then asked, in her slightly husky voice:

"Where is the curator's office? If it's this room here, I think it should be located much closer to the stacks. Next to them, if possible." She looked up, and, making eye contact with her listeners, expounded with some heat: "Books suffer from being transported. I believe it's important for those who handle them to be aware of it. Important, too, that manuscripts and early texts never be carried through a maze of stairways and corridors."

"I shall have to seek your counsel for the organization of my own library," said Junius ironically, without elaborating further. "Thank you, Miss Greene. We'll speak about this again. Please ask Miss Martins to join us."

Belle departed. The four men looked at one another.

"Quite an intelligent girl," remarked Richardson, approvingly.

When Aunt Lottie emerged from Seminar Room 4, she was the bearer of incredible news. Mr. Junius Morgan had invited them both to take tea with him and his wife that Sunday at Constitution Hill, the grand house he'd had built in the heights above Princeton.

*

If Miss Martins was aware of Belle's feelings for Junius, she did not let on, affecting to believe that the girl's joy at the news was due simply to the exhilaration of being invited to such a palace. Accordingly, she allowed herself to be thanked over and over again, and kissed, and fawned over as if she'd secured this bounty after a great struggle. In truth, she was impressed, herself, to have been invited. Working alongside Mr. Junius Spencer

Morgan was one thing; being received in his home was another. And the idea of entering his world and meeting his wife intimidated her not a little.

Miss Martins, like everyone, knew Mrs. Junius Morgan by sight. How could she not? Mrs. Morgan presided over every charity event in Princeton, sat on several committees at the hospital, even attended football games when the president of the university—Mr. Woodrow Wilson—was there. She was the epitome of a society doyenne, who prided herself on founding the town's most exclusive women's clubs, membership in which remained far beyond the reach of a Miss Martins. Invariably to be seen wearing immense hats covered in feathers, flowers, and fruit, Mrs. Morgan traveled with her husband on his jaunts to Europe but had no interest in the Benedictine psalters and Dürer engravings he bought there unless they had belonged to a British aristocrat or a crowned head. And yet she was not frivolous. Merely conventional, and remote. Her wealth meant that she inhabited a world very far removed from that of a librarian, even a highly respected one like Miss Martins.

The older woman took every bit as long as Belle herself to dress on Sunday afternoon, and anyone watching the two of them step together into the hansom cab that would take them to the Morgan manor would have taken them for a mother and daughter paying a visit to the dowager princess of Prussia.

Aunt Lottie had never been much for frills, except perhaps when it came to her home, which displayed her marked fondness for lace doilies, beaded lampshades, and French knick-knacks. Her taste in clothes was usually understated and elegant. Today, though, she was dripping with every piece of jewelry she and her sister possessed—jet earrings, coral necklace, rings, bracelets, and an old-fashioned cameo pin—she didn't look like herself anymore. It wasn't that the result was disastrous; it was merely incongruous. She was a small, plump woman with blue eyes and a pointed nose, whose only habitual aspiration was to outdo herself in demonstrating fairness, integrity, and tireless devotion to her profession. She demanded that her trainees adhere to the same neat dress code and care for their reputations, though in spite of her strict work ethic she could be flexible, even merry, under the right circumstances. A visit to Constitution Hill, however, was not one of these situations.

She knew exactly what she was exposing herself to by venturing into these exalted circles.

First there was the name, Constitution Hill, which rang with the dignity and solemnity of History: it was there that the first constitution of New Jersey had been conceived, drafted, and signed in 1776. Then there were the grounds, spreading over more than forty hectares and boasting woods, a lake, and a park full of deer, swans, and peacocks. And the house, the first Gothic manor to be built in the area, its style copied from the great English castles of Sussex. Finally, there was the company. In addition to Mr. and Mrs. Junius Morgan, the rest of Princeton's high society would undoubtedly be there today. And while Aunt Lottie may have been a queen in her library, she found the idea of facing so many sophisticates absolutely terrifying.

Belle, for her part, was untouched by any of the anxieties plaguing Aunt Lottie. She knew the Morgan family sat at the very top of the social register; Uncle J.P. Morgan's fortune regularly made headlines in the newspapers alongside those of the Astors and the Rockefellers. But, having never moved in such circles, she had no real idea of the difficulties she might be about to run up against.

Well aware that she couldn't hope to compete with these wealthy people in terms of her jewelry or her education, she would simply rely on the strength of her own charms.

Well, not completely.

She had traveled to New York and back the previous night to

borrow her sisters' finest clothes for the occasion, including Louise's pearl-gray dress with its leg-of-mutton sleeves, which their mother had made for the holiday ball, and Ethel's little flounced wrapper, gloves, and stylish flat hat. Nothing spectacular, but still more chic than what she usually wore. She had put a great deal of effort into taming her unruly hair, twisting it into an elegant chignon. She knew she looked very pretty. This relative self-confidence, however, did nothing to relieve her nervousness. She knew that Junius must live in an unthinkably grand residence. And the whole of her excitement lay in the idea of penetrating his private space, of *seeing* where he lived. She knew, too, that he had two young children; she even knew their first names, Sarah and Alexander. Would she meet them?

The carriage struggled up the hill, the two women's tension rising along with it. Belle, who had fired questions at her companion throughout the journey—*Where did Mr. Junius meet his wife? When did they marry? How old are Sarah and Alexander?*—had fallen silent. Gazing straight ahead, she nervously adjusted the same hairpin again and again, though it hadn't even come loose. She thrust it deep into the twist of her hair now in a determined movement. Aunt Lottie had pulled her smart little veil over her face.

They turned into the long driveway, past the spruce trees bordering the immense snow-covered lawn. The cab deposited them between the balustrades at the front entrance. The red brick house with its tall Tudor-style chimneys and bow windows rose up before them, imposing and sinister.

The valet who took their coats could not suppress a dubious expression as he opened the doors to the salon for them. Belle saw nothing at first but several women standing in a group, holding cups of tea in which they were swirling delicate, tiny spoons. All of them wore large wide-brimmed hats, which obliged them to keep some distance apart so their plumes wouldn't become entangled. In spite of this, though, they formed a compact, uniform mass. All of them seemed to share the same S-shaped silhouette in their afternoon tea-gowns, their skirts pooling gracefully on the carpet. The only variations lay in the fabric of their dresses and the color of the belts tightly cinching their waists: pale pink, lemon yellow, and azure blue for the young ladies; plum and seal-gray for the matrons; black for the widows. The oldest women wore wide velvet ribbons around their necks, the wives, multiple strands of pearls. Close-fitting bracelets with delicate chains reinforcing the clasps adorned the wrists of the young fiancées.

Their first glimpse of this corseted, taffeta-ruffled world, clinking with precious metals and glinting with gems, froze Belle and Aunt Lottie in their tracks.

Paralyzed by uncertainty, unsure whether to move farther into the room or wait for someone to come and escort them, they stood still, pressed together, backs to the closed door. The assembly had turned toward them, but no one made a move to welcome them.

"Those are Junius's employees from the library," murmured one of the female guests.

"He always invites such odd people."

"That's what makes him so marvelous; he always has a surprise in store for us!"

Junius chose that moment to make his entrance through the door at the back of the room opening into the library. He was accompanied by his wife, along with a whole group of gentlemen, fresh from a tour of his collections. He quickly spotted Belle and Aunt Lottie, hovering at the edge of the room. Taking his wife by the elbow, he left his friends and joined them.

"Josie dear, allow me to introduce Miss Charlotte Martins, our exceptional librarian. And her young disciple, Miss Belle Greene."

Tall, handsome, and statuesque as a Greek caryatid, Josephine Perry Morgan was an intimidating woman, her round cheeks and large, sad eyes doing little to soften the impression she made. She was hatless and wore neither pearls nor diamonds, just a large winter rose in the belt at her waist. So great was her wealth that it would have been both impossible and inappropriate for her to exhibit her jewels at this hour of the day, when she was merely receiving guests for tea. Moreover, she was in her own home, which called for a simpler style.

Though still attractive, this was a mature woman, whose pregnancies had thickened her figure. Her husband, two years her senior, looked like an adolescent next to her. Belle was struck by Junius's youthfulness, which set him apart from Josie Dear. And from everyone else.

"My husband always speaks of you with great admiration," Mrs. Morgan said composedly, speaking only to Miss Martins. "He assures me that the library—and Professor Richardson—owe everything to your skill. You will have a cup of tea, won't you? I see that you haven't yet been served."

Aunt Lottie stammered an unintelligible reply, yes, no, it's all right.

"With pleasure, Mrs. Morgan," put in Belle quickly. "Thank you very much indeed."

She knew she was of so little consequence that, unless she made herself noticed quickly, she would forever be a non-entity in the eyes of their hostess.

"Are you any relation to our close friends, the Greens of Princeton, Miss Greene? I'm speaking of John C. Green, the patron of the Chancellor Green Library."

Belle hesitated.

"My family belongs to the English branch . . . quite a distant one. My father was an officer in the Indian army. Greene, with an *e*."

Junius, shanghaied by a portly gentleman with Victorian

sideburns, had vanished again, leaving Josie Dear to usher her two guests over to the immense silver teapot enthroned on a sideboard. Tradition dictated that Mrs. Morgan, as hostess, pour the first cup, with it then falling to her army of footmen to offer, on plates featuring the family crest, the miniscule jug with which to add the tiniest splash of milk, the lemon slice, sugar tongs, scones and marmalade, and dainty cucumber sand-wiches. Everything was done according to the rules of British etiquette. Junius had spent his boyhood in London, where his father was director of the family bank, and he and his wife had honeymooned in Sussex. The Morgans remained enthusiastic Anglophiles, and many of their guests were to be heard speak-ing with a cut-glass Oxford accent.

When Josie Dear was satisfied that her husband's guests were well-supplied with cakes, she steered Aunt Lottie toward the wife of Professor Richardson. The two women knew each other slightly, and she left them to make awkward small talk.

Belle drifted away.

Lifting the fine porcelain cup to her lips, she tried to appear relaxed and nonchalant. Observe. Observe. Observe. The objects. The paintings. She didn't dare get too close to anything. She walked with small, slow steps, being careful not to spill tea into her saucer or drop her spoon, yet she didn't miss a single detail. The logs burning in the fireplace, whole trunks, like in the Middle Ages. The coffered ceiling. The lush carpets. And the people. Her sentimental considerations evaporated at the sight of this elegant crowd, to be replaced by cool, hard curiosity. It wasn't simply about finding out where Junius lived anymore; it was about . . . seeing. And being seen, perhaps, by the dazzlingly lovely women in this room. How did girls her age dress? How did they conduct themselves? How did they speak to one another? She noted, with a pang of anxiety, that most of them were blonde, with skin so pale that hers must look black in com-parison. *Like a blackberry in a bowl of milk*, she thought. This mental image was so depressing that she couldn't even enjoy herself anymore. Abandoning her teacup on a side table, she slipped into the room adjoining the salon.

The library.

Even larger than the drawing room, the walls here were covered from floor to ceiling with exquisitely bound books. With a single, sweeping glance, Belle knew: these shelves held the rarest, the finest works in the history of book-collecting. She stood frozen, dumbstruck. Monastic wooden-panel bindings. Fanfare bindings. Cathedral bindings. Bindings of ivory, silk, valuable textiles. Bindings of parchment, vellum, Moroccan leather, shagreen. Bindings with bronze corners and silver clasps. Bindings of precious metals, encrusted with gems and pearls.

Never had she imagined that such a collection could exist. Not even the storeroom at the Chancellor Green, not even the treasures of the Pyne had given her such a thrill.

Moving from one section of wall to the next, she circled the room, getting up on tiptoe to read the titles. After a time, unable to restrain herself, she climbed the first steps of the ladder and bent close to the spines.

"They're real, you know. The books, I mean. You can touch them. You can even pick them up, if you want to be sure they're not a mirage."

Surprised, she turned. There was a young man seated on the edge of the desk, one hand shoved casually into a pocket. His suit was lighter than those worn by the gentlemen in the salon. Though he was dressed with impeccable elegance, complete with tiepin and watch-chain, there was something oddly old-fashioned about his appearance. His neck was so long and his wrists so thin that they seemed to float in his wing collar and shirt-cuffs, and yet there was nothing scrawny about him. His even-featured face recalled the Belvedere Antinous, with the same marble-like pallor and strength of the famous statue. There was something romantic about him too, like Berlioz or Chopin, a feverishness that emphasized the intensity of his gaze. Belle, who always noticed men's looks—at least as much as they noticed hers, at any rate—thought that this was a man of remarkable beauty. The handsomest specimen she'd seen at Princeton yet.

"You haven't seen anything yet," he insisted. "Open the armoires."

"Who are you?" she asked, defensively.

"I should be asking you that question. Are you the governess?"

"Me? Certainly not. I loathe children."

This reply, so improper for a young woman, left him speechless. She was still perched on the ladder and showed no inclination of coming down.

"Well?" she persisted. "Who are you?"

"Arthur Upson, of the University of Minnesota."

"Belle Greene, of the Chancellor Green."

They nodded at one another.

"Ah, there you are!" Junius had come hurrying in, flanked by Aunt Lottie. "I should have known we'd find you both here. Miss Martins, do you remember Mr. Upson?"

Aunt Lottie, though normally endowed with the memory of an elephant, didn't seem to recall him. *Oh no*, thought Belle, descending the ladder, *she's gone all to pieces*.

"We have never actually met, Miss Martins," said Upson, coming gallantly to Lottie's rescue, "though we have corresponded for some years. I worked on the cataloguing of the Edmund Brooks collections."

"You're the antiquarian book dealer from Minneapolis?" Miss Martins asked.

"The very same."

"Goodness, I always imagined you were older! My compliments, young man. Your shipments have always arrived on time, and in excellent condition, which I don't think I can say about anyone else! If only everyone had your work ethic . . ."

Talking about books had turned Lottie back into herself.

"Mr. Upson is much more than a good book dealer!" said Junius enthusiastically. "Surely you've read his poems?"

"I didn't realize Mr. Brooks's assistant was a poet," Aunt Lottie confessed.

"I did," put in Belle quickly, sensing that her limelight was being stolen and judging it prudent to remind everyone of her presence. "I've read his poems."

"Really?" asked Junius skeptically, clearly convinced she was bluffing.

"Really, Mr. Morgan."

"And what did you think of them?" he asked, ironically.

"Mr. Upson's talent was the talk of every newspaper in New York last year. And I must say that I agree with the critics who compare him to Keats. But—if I may, Mr. Upson—your collection *Octaves in an Oxford Garden* is not the work of a colorist, whatever they say, nor even the work of a writer of exotic verses. Your sense of rhythm, your gift for harmony—they make you a melodist, more than anything, and your tones are much bolder than anything your rivals, with all their technical prowess, have produced."

Junius couldn't keep from exchanging a glance with Miss Martins. Their protégée was certainly rising to the occasion. The old lady was clearly thrilled. Mr. Upson, for his part, seemed deeply touched. Finally, a young woman who understood the meaning of his work!

"I missed those articles," confessed Junius. "What a shame."

"You were in Europe," Belle reminded him.

"My wife and I had already been struck by Mr. Upson's talent when we met him at a reading of his poetry in Oxford! It took him three years to accept our invitation and come to work in cataloguing at the library. Even now he can only give us a few months, as he's planning to return to Minnesota."

"Mr. Upson's going to be working with us at the Chancellor Green, then?" enquired Aunt Lottie, half-delighted, half-unnerved at the thought of having to train a new recruit who would not be staying long.

"No, Miss Martins—I'm speaking of *my* library. Speaking in confidence," he went on, addressing the company at large, "my collections would benefit greatly from your brilliance. How much do you earn, Miss Greene?"

The question was so unexpected, so stark in this sumptuous setting, so crass in being posed in front of a stranger, that Belle grew flustered.

"I—I don't know . . ." she stammered.

"Oh yes, you do. You know perfectly well."

It was Aunt Lottie who answered him. "Miss Greene earns the same as all our young ladies. Five dollars a week."

"Five dollars! Good lord, that's a pittance! A train ticket to New York costs twice that much!"

"Second class is cheaper, Mr. Morgan," said Belle, teasingly.

"And cheaper still in the Jim Crow cars for Negro passengers, I've no doubt. But—five dollars! Our friend Richardson is having a laugh, surely!"

It was a blow delivered straight to the heart. Was this an allusion to something? Belle had turned white with shock. Why would Mr. Morgan mention the Jim Crow cars? Did he know? "*. . . cheaper still for Negro passengers.*" The idiot. "Negroes" paid double! Of course he knew! And now he would humiliate her, throw her out. Fear ripped through her, stealing her capacity for rational thought. She could feel herself panicking, left with nothing but the instinct to flee, to save herself.

"Would you be terribly upset with me, Miss Martins, if I borrowed your pupil for a few weeks?" Junius was saying. "Mr. Upson can't possibly catalogue all of these books in three months. At least not alone. But I would very much like for the work to be finished by the time he leaves us. Lend Miss Greene to me until the spring, and I promise to return her as good as new!"

Mr. Junius Morgan's wishes were as good as commands. The old lady couldn't refuse. Still, she could negotiate.

"Just until Easter, Mr. Morgan," she said. "I'll need her after that. The Garrett collection is arriving in April, and we'll have our hands full with those Oriental manuscripts."

Junius turned to Belle. "You haven't been consulted, I know, but you will do it, surely."

"No."

A bomb exploding in their midst would have had less impact than this point-blank refusal.

" . . . thank you," she added, amidst the silence that followed.

*

"I thought your mother had *educated* you, Belle da Costa Greene," Miss Martins said severely as they rode home in the hansom cab. "I see that I was wrong. You were fed, but certainly not taught anything!"

The horse's shoes slipped on the ice, and the cab skidded downhill, throwing the women forward and forcing them to brace themselves against the partition that separated them from the driver to keep from sliding off the bench seat.

"I'm not accustomed to having other people decide my fate without me," retorted Belle.

"You should get used to it."

"He borrows us, loans us out, gives us away . . . he's treating us like servants—even slaves!"

"Preposterous. He was trying to be kind."

"And *I* was trying to be clear. I do not belong to anyone."

"Certainly not; you don't even belong to yourself—on that point, we're in agreement! You're incapable of controlling yourself!"

Belle looked down. She knew she had just missed her chance, knew it with despairing certainty. Working in Junius's library would have been an absolute dream.

"I thought you were cleverer than that," Aunt Lottie continued mercilessly. "You thought you'd won the game, and at the
last moment you cut your own throat. *Why?*"

"I don't know."

She could hardly muster the will to defend herself. She felt
completely overwhelmed, at a loss to understand her own mind.

"What got into you?" Aunt Lottie persisted.

"I don't know," Belle murmured again.

"Deep down, you're nothing but an empty vessel," the old
lady said bitterly. "A mere soap-bubble, but without a bubble's
grace!" She fell silent for a moment, then burst out again: "What
on *earth* got into you?"

Belle merely shook her head. Aunt Lottie turned away and
stared out the window.

"You're going to have to learn how to live, my girl," she said,
with an air of finality. "And fast!"

# CHAPTER 3

## THIS DIVINE ADVENTURE
## 1904–1905

Friendships can be formed at first sight that are every bit as intense as romantic love. Since their first meeting at Constitution Hill, Miss Greene and Mr. Upson had been together constantly. Their closeness was so apparent, and so potentially scandalous, that Miss Martins took it upon herself to describe them as engaged, though they had only known each other for two weeks.

The day after tea at the Morgans', Aunt Lottie had dispatched one of her nieces, a Miss Gertrude Hyde, to assist Mr. Upson with his task. Meanwhile, Belle's presence in the Pyne had become near constant as she tried to rectify the disastrous impression she feared she had made on Junius.

In truth, however, he appeared to have forgotten all about the scene that had taken place amid the books in his sumptuous library—including his notion that Professor Richardson's female employees should have their salary increased.

Miss Greene's refusal of his offer did not bother him much; he was perfectly satisfied with Miss Hyde's skills, and happy to leave the organization of the catalogue to Mr. Upson.

The day before Christmas vacation began, Junius left for New York with his wife and children, but not before ordering his steward to ensure that his new librarian would be comfortable in Princeton: access to the Morgan estate's billiard room, golf course, and stables; the use of one of his automobiles for trips into town; tickets to every entertainment held on campus.

Driving Miss Hyde home in the car after work, Mr. Upson

never failed to enquire after Miss Martins's health. This resulted in his regularly being invited to dine with the Martins-Hyde family.

Belle and Gertrude shared a bedroom in Aunt Lottie's house. They had worked together at the Pyne Library for nearly two years now, and they were thick as thieves. Though their characters were very different—Gertrude was shy and plain—Belle admired the young woman for her good heart and her quiet competence, while Gertrude, for her part, was spellbound by Belle's charm. Now, the sudden presence of Arthur Upson in their daily lives ushered in a whole range of new and undreamt-of possibilities.

If Aunt Lottie hadn't brought them back down to earth by forbidding them to step out unchaperoned with a young man after dark, the two girls would have spent every evening with him at the theatre. Fortunately, there were still plenty of opportunities for riding lessons at the Morgan estate on the weekends, games of tennis on the frozen court, and rambles through the New Jersey countryside in Junius's borrowed auto.

"Faster, Mr. Upson!" Belle would shriek.

"Shut up!" Gertrude always cried. "Don't listen to her, Mr. Upson—slow down!"


Arthur Upson and Belle Greene shared the same unquenchable passion for living, playing at existence as if they were going to die tomorrow. And yet their vitality sprang from very different sources.

At twenty-seven years old, Upson had already had nearly a dozen brushes with death. He had been a sickly little boy, often bedridden for months, and later his poor health had forced him to interrupt his university studies more than once. But he was so inquisitive, so well-read, and so brilliant in every discipline that his professors had agreed to grant him a Bachelor of Arts degree without requiring him to take his final exams. Neither did his extreme physical fragility prevent him from being a keen sportsman; it was as if horseback riding and tennis gave him the comfort of reminding him that he was still alive.

In Minneapolis, where his family lived, Arthur Upson's courage and fearlessness were legendary. Not only did he battle his illness as if it were nothing—when it was in fact a malady of the pleural cavity, every bit as serious as tuberculosis—but he bore with philosophical resignation the other blows dealt to his family by fate. His father had been ruined by a series of high-risk speculations, and Arthur had been obliged to work to finance his own university studies. He had spent a year crisscrossing the United States as a dealer in rare books before finding a job with the major bookseller Edmund Brooks, where his vast knowledge of literature and his refined bibliophilic tastes had quickly made him indispensable. In him, Edmund Brooks had gained a cataloguer of genius, and an expert able to estimate the prices of first editions with precision.

"Maybe this is what love is, deep down," said Belle, laughing. "A communion of souls. What more could we need?"

They were riding through the woods on the grounds of Constitution Hill.

Belle was astride the young Miss Morgan's pony, a gentle creature Junius had bought for his daughter. Unable to ride side-saddle, she was wearing a borrowed pair of Upson's trousers. Other than the stable hands, no one was likely to witness the transgression.

The woodland paths smelled of damp earth. The fog had been chased away by a breeze, and the branches of the towering trees rustled overhead. The silence filled them both with the sensation of being part of this forest, solemn and sacred.

It was only since she'd moved to Princeton that Belle had begun to discover the countryside, and she had come to feel a kind of reverence for nature. The soft murmur of the snow that, flake by flake, melted in the hoofprints of the horses and slid from the heather. The ebony flight of crows cutting through the winter sky. The beauty of a landscape. It was one more revelation accompanied by the lyricism of Upton's poetry.

She let out a sigh of contentment. He poked her playfully with his riding crop.

"A communion of souls? Knowing you, my dear, the soul alone will never be enough to satisfy you!"

"Whatever do you mean?" she teased back. "I'm perfectly capable of spiritual love."

"Nonsense! With your sparkle? Your radiance? You embody, all by yourself, this divine adventure we call life. And life, for you, is a matter of flesh and blood."

"I wouldn't rely so much on appearances, if I were you. Who says I'm really as happy as I seem? As pure? As young?" She was playing with fire, and she knew it. "How do you know that the person next to you is actually the girl you think she is?"

"You're so unrehearsed, my dear friend, so splendidly natural, that you're an open book."

"Hmm. You know what they say about books, Mr. Upson. They shouldn't be judged by their covers."

"You're as terrible at philosophizing as you are improved at horseback riding."

"Thanks for the compliment. I expect I shine in other areas."

"You *should* thank me, in fact. I'm working to turn you into a person capable of rising to any occasion. Tennis, golf, billiards. And riding. I'm transforming you into an accomplished young lady, polished enough to satisfy even the Morgans. Well—'transforming' is merely an expression, of course. Only Belle can decide what Miss da Costa Greene will become," he said, teasingly. "A mousy little librarian, like Miss Martins? A gracious wife like Josie Dear? A doting mother?"

"A mother? Never!"

"An old maid, then?"

"Independent."

"Are you nursing a secret passion, by chance, Miss Greene? An impossible love?"

"Not for *you*, at least! But you—*you* must be thinking of marriage. You're old enough for it. To Gertrude, for example?"

A shadow passed over Upson's face.

Belle had guessed that Gertrude was slightly in love with him, and had gotten it into her head to bring them together. That way she could keep both of them for herself.

"Gertrude is perfectly charming," he replied, seriously. "You're quite right about that. Unfortunately, though, I'm in no position to offer a future to any woman."

Belle said nothing. She was certain she knew what he was alluding to: his poor health, his lack of means.

"I figure you'll end up married to some Princeton fellow," he went on lightly, before the silence had stretched on for too long. "One of those moony boys ruining their eyes in the Chancellor Green in the desperate hope of catching a glimpse of you. I've seen your little game of merry-go-round with poor Ned Field; you're driving him mad, whirling him in circles like a top. I don't think he's actually read anything in months; he'll fail his exams, and it will be all your fault!"

"I don't give a toss about Ned Field. And I'm not going to marry anyone. Unless it's for money. Lots and lots and lots of money."

Upson whistled. "You're prepared to sell yourself, then?"

"To *give* myself, Mr. Upson. To give myself. To a man so rich that his fortune will set me free."

"You're already as free as that bird." He pointed at the tiny figure of a falcon circling high above the clearing, preparing to descend on its prey.

For an instant, a fraction of a second, Belle was tempted to tell him the truth. Upson would understand. There were shadowy places inside him, too. Behind his buoyant façade lay pain, a whole world of torments he never betrayed.

She came so close to explaining herself. To admitting to him that she couldn't marry, couldn't become a mother, without running the risk of bearing a Black child.

"Free to do what?" he insisted, bemused.

Spurring her pony into a trot, she dashed off ahead of him. "Free to get the hell out of here!" she called over her shoulder.

\* \* \*

The departure at Easter of her beloved Upson—"my soulmate," as she would always refer to him in her letters—left Belle with a sense of frustration that no flirtation could soothe. Though she wrote to him every week, nothing could fill the empty place created by his absence.

What was more, without him, all the physical activity stopped as well. The stables and tennis courts of Constitution Hill were closed to her now, and her prodigious energy could no longer find an outlet.

In truth, the spring weather was going to her head, awakening in her the desire for speed, for driving fast in automobiles and galloping hard through the countryside. She yearned to experience passionate emotion, not daring to admit that her need for physical exertion was simply her sensual nature asserting itself—though she did confess to the discomfited Gertrude that she thought Venus and Cupid had something to do with it, and that she wanted to dance every night like some Greek bacchante.

She tried to quench this thirst for action by flirting as widely as she could. Upson hadn't been exaggerating when he teased her about the many students competing for her favors. How marvelous it was to feel desired! And such fun to break hearts! Belle wasn't cruel; it wasn't that she wanted to make anyone suffer, just to enjoy herself a little. How glorious to imagine that anything was possible, to feel as if the future belonged to you!

There were so many things to discover, so many pleasures to indulge in at Princeton.

Didn't Arthur Upson say that a wise spirit always made a point of taking the best things life had to offer? And that choosing excellence could never be bad for the soul? Well, for now, excellence lay in spending time with brilliant men. Masters like Junius Morgan and Mr. Richardson, in whose company she could think, work, *and* learn. And as for the trivial side of life, excellence consisted of choosing the best-dressed and most charming young men as her beaux.

She willed herself to be satisfied by the attentions of a distinguished young lecturer, the intelligent banter of an associate professor, the eau de Cologne of a PhD candidate—but in every case, she quickly realized that she'd gotten ahead of herself, and the excitement would fade. And so she moved from one passing fancy to the next, with no illusions about either herself or the young men; they would soon find consolation elsewhere. Proud, and romantic despite her denials, she was aiming higher than simple infatuation, and was always careful not to push the flirtation too far.

Junius Morgan had left New York for London, and had not returned.

\*

"Come on, we're sneaking out! Ned's sending his father's car."

"What if Aunt Lottie comes in?" asked Gertrude.

"Aunt Lottie doesn't exactly make a habit of coming into our bedroom in the middle of the night," replied Belle dryly. "But, just in case, put your bolster under the sheets the long way. That was a trick of my brother's back when we lived with my grandmother in . . ." She stopped short. *In Georgetown*, she'd been about to say. ". . . with my grandmother in Virginia, the old biddy, with that irritating blue blood of hers. Anyway, come on!"

Gertrude hesitated. She was a wisp of a girl with a freckled little face, her fluffy, dark red hair twisted into a knot on top of her head. She seemed always to be on high alert, caught between her lack of daring and the desire to overcome her own timidity.

"Upson's abandoning us is no reason for us to languish at home. Ned's playing in the revue that the boys from the Triangle Club put on at Christmastime. I've heard they were all dressed as women, remember? It was all anyone could talk about! They called it *The Man from Where*, and it was a great success when they went on tour in Boston. They're doing it one more time tonight, for the students who missed it."

"Go without a chaperone to a revue at the Triangle Club? You're completely insane! Aunt Lottie knows the professors there—she knows everyone! She'll find out in a heartbeat!"

"Who says we're staying in Princeton? We're going to the theater in Trenton!"

"But that's so far away!"

"Not in a Pierce-Arrow. An hour at most. Ned's reserved the best seats in the house for us, in the front row—it's going to be fantastic!"

Belle was already heading for the stairs. Gertrude followed hesitantly. Seizing her hand, Belle pulled her along.

The car was parked a short distance from the house. The two young women dashed toward it and climbed in. The driver turned the crank on the front of the vehicle, then resumed his place in the front seat and started the car up with a racket that shook the whole street. As the Pierce-Arrow began to move, both Belle and Gertrude noticed that the man kept eyeing them over his shoulder, his gaze resting on their faces, their necks, their throats. Belle shuddered and shrank back into the darkness, while Gertrude reddened, instinctively pulling tighter the already-buttoned collar of her coat. What respectable single woman, what member of the weaker sex would go to a theater without a married woman to escort her? He must take them for hussies. The sort of creature midway between an empty-headed shopgirl and a tart whose company the male students sought for a single evening.

"Good lord, he must think we're . . ." Gertrude stammered to Belle, unable even to put her suspicions into words. "He's gotten the wrong idea!"

In truth, it wasn't the thought of being mistaken for a good-time girl that was bothering Belle, causing a film of cold sweat to break out on her forehead. It was the color of the driver's skin. He was Black. And one thing she knew was that Black people recognized one another. She'd heard it often enough in Georgetown. Fooling a white person was possible, but a Black one? The whites, those simple fools, only perceived what was obvious and unmistakable—but Blacks had an unerring instinct for spotting their fellows. Their sensitivity on this point was so well known, in fact, that theater-owners tended to employ only Black ushers, ticket-takers, and doormen, in order to filter out any faux whites attempting to occupy orchestra seats and banish them to the balcony, nicknamed "Negro Heaven."

The driver was still turning around to glance at her, not even trying to hide it. She couldn't see anything but those eyes, staring at her. Was he planning to give her away to his boss? In Georgetown, she thought, trying to reassure herself, the common wisdom was that Blacks rarely betrayed their own. They saw that person as a turncoat, yes. A traitor. They scorned him and spat on him. But they did not betray him. Not to the whites, at any rate.

But the Black doorman at the theater in Trenton, whose job it was to do that very thing? If Ned's driver had recognized her as a Negress, certainly the doorman would—and he would unmask her in front of the students!

Just as it had done in the Morgans' library when Junius alluded to Jim Crow railway cars, panic gripped her, overwhelming her.

"My friend doesn't feel well," she said abruptly. "Turn around, please."

Gertrude shot her a look of gratitude and squeezed her hand.

But the driver didn't seem to have heard. Belle repeated her instructions into the horn that allowed passengers to communicate with the front of the car over the engine noise: "Take us back home, please!"

She made sure the tone of that "please" was polite, but would clearly brook no opposition.

"That's not what Mr. Field said. Mr. Field told me to bring you to Trenton."

"Mr. Field didn't anticipate my friend's becoming unwell. Given the circumstances, he would tell you to take us back to Princeton immediately."

The driver slowed down, but didn't obey. Gertrude's grip on Belle's fingers tightened painfully.

"I'm *ordering* you to stop!"

He braked so suddenly that the young women were thrown forward. Putting the car in gear, he backed up abruptly and screeched back onto the road in the opposite direction.

Neither of the girls said a word during the entire ride home, keeping their eyes firmly down to avoid the driver's gaze.

Back at home, greatly relieved, Gertrude fell immediately into the arms of Morpheus. Belle, though, couldn't rest. She trembled inwardly, unable to calm herself even here, in this safe place. Finally she got out of bed and went to the window, propping her elbows on the sill. Her gaze went beyond the sky, beyond the moon and the trees quivering in the spring breeze, focusing on the night itself.

*Ridiculous,* she chastised herself, *absolutely ridiculous! What happened tonight? Nothing, actually! No more than happened in Junius Morgan's library. But all anyone has to do is stare at me or say the word "Negro" to send me into a ridiculous spiral. How have I let myself get here? How have I become such a coward? The whites and their idiotic prejudices are not the danger. Neither are the Blacks and their silent condemnation. The real danger is my own fear. That stupid, shameful fear that drives me to weakness, to errors in judgment . . .*

The missed evening in Trenton now set off an unprecedented crisis within Belle. She had crossed the color barrier four years earlier without a qualm, but this, her inability to assume responsibility for her own choices—*this* shook her to the core.

"*No man is any use until he has dared everything.*" The quote from Robert Louis Stevenson haunted Belle. She swore to herself, then and there, that this night would mark the last time she ever wasted an opportunity, the last time she deprived herself of pleasure. The last time fear would make her back down.

From now on, she would never shy away from a single risk, consequences be damned.

\* \* \*

"You are happy at Princeton, aren't you, my dear?" asked Genevieve affectionately.

"More than happy, Maman!" Belle assured her.

"Your brother and sisters seem to quite like what they're doing, too."

"How's Teddy?"

"Teddy . . . well, she keeps me on my toes, that one. Moony little thing. She's twenty years old, but she seems to have taken endlessly claiming to be fifteen a little too much to heart and acts like an eternal adolescent."

Mother and daughter were strolling arm-in-arm on a May Sunday in 1904, not far from the family's apartment. They shared the same youthful figures, the same small waists cinched by wide belts, the same long light-hued skirts, the same white blouses, the same flower-bedecked straw hats. They were walking slowly through Riverside Park, that great garden stretching along the banks of the Hudson. Without even being aware of it, they headed in the direction of the enormous granite and marble tomb of General Ulysses S. Grant, the one whose design had been chosen by Richard Greener based on the Mausoleum of Halicarnassus in Asia Minor. One of the seven wonders of the world. They gazed up at the pediment, the colonnaded façade, and went on their way.

"There's something I didn't tell you when you moved to Miss Martins's," continued Genevieve. "I didn't want to worry you. But you should probably know." She hesitated. "I don't know if you have any contact with the Black community in the city—"

"For the last time, Maman, no!" Belle cut her off. "None at all!"

"But you must see colored people there, don't you?"

"No. One doesn't see them on campus—or very few of them, at least. Only the domestic servants and housekeepers."

"Be vigilant anyway, my dear, because a cousin of your father's lives in Princeton's Black quarter. She knows you. She met you several times at the house. Maria Robeson is her name."

Belle didn't react, didn't give any indication of curiosity, or even that she remembered the name.

"Maria looks white, like us," Genevieve went on, "but she's married to a colored man. And the two of them belong to the activist group your father used to be a member of."

Belle gave an irritated shrug. Genevieve pretended not to see it and continued, her tone carefully neutral:

"The papers are full of nothing but the war between the Russians and the Japanese. They're especially anxious about what's happening on the eastern border—in Vladivostok . . . And also about the fate of the American community there, and our consul's role in protecting our commercial interests. Your father's name is everywhere. I'm afraid his presence in the papers will bring him—and us, too—back to mind for Maria, and others who used to know us."

"You have to stop thinking and acting like we're guilty of something, Maman! We're white, and we have nothing to hide. And as for the conduct of our consul on the Russian border, we read the papers like any other American citizen eager for news. Period."

\* \* \*

*Junius.* He was back. And with him, an air of London and Paris, a whiff of adventure. He'd returned from his European hunt with a prize for the library: three editions of Virgil printed in Venice in the fifteenth century, their typeface and illumination a perfect complement to the other trophies in his collection. He'd also come back teeming with new ideas for a joyous celebration marking the Roman poet's 1,975th birthday on October 15 of the following year. And, against all expectations, he had not forgotten his conversation with Miss Martins about the remuneration of the young women she employed, and had convinced Professor Richardson to pay them a salary twice as high as they had previously received. In this way they went from earning five dollars a week to making forty dollars a month, starting the day after Junius's return home.

"Soon you'll be able to travel first class, Miss Greene," he joked, when Belle knocked on his office door to thank him for his intervention.

It was almost impossible to make out Junius's silhouette in the dimness of the room. Light remained the greatest enemy of the manuscripts he studied.

"Undoubtedly," she replied, in the same teasing tone. "The Pennsylvania Railroad won't be able to refuse Princeton's great benefactor a thing. But before I board the very first car on the train—thanks to you—please allow me to express, on behalf of my colleagues and myself, our deepest thanks for your generosity."

Junius flushed and waved the compliment away.

"I merely acted as a relay. I didn't do anything, really."

Belle hesitated. *Don't lay it on too thick.* "Flattery is forbidden" was practically Junius's motto. She must proceed with caution.

She had taken advantage of the six months of his absence to learn all she could about Junius Morgan's character. Now she knew two things about him for certain: The first was that he was indisputably the greatest expert on Virgil in the world, but that he had absolutely no vanity about it. One of his many virtues was his discretion, even his modesty. He was proud of what he'd accomplished through his own hard work, yes, but being fawned over infuriated him. And that was the second thing she knew. He loathed flatterers. People said that, unlike his uncle, J.P. Morgan, who fancied himself another Lorenzo the Magnificent and loved to have praise heaped upon him, Junius had a horror of sycophancy in all its forms. As soon as a compliment fell from the lips of an admirer, he would change the subject. If the flatterer persisted, if he or she continued to gush over his learning or his largesse, Junius tended to launch, sardonically, into a speech that was complex to the point of absurdity—a situation that quickly became highly embarrassing to the sycophants, who invariably couldn't understand a word of it, and many of them came away with a memory of Junius Morgan's mockery that was all the more perplexing when contrasted with his typical politeness.

Those closest to Junius knew that this capricious game of his, this insolent behavior toward people who annoyed him, was a well-honed technique for protecting himself against their intrusiveness. And they knew, too, that Junius was not merely the scholar he appeared to be. A penchant for indiscretion and extravagance, a streak of madness flashed occasionally in that methodical mind.

Sociable by nature, a loyal friend, he retained a group of old pals from his Princeton youth, all good-humored fellows who, even in maturity, loved to indulge in schoolboy pranks and nights of drinking and carousing. Junius detested beer and cards, but he loved fishing and boating parties, and was, moreover, an accomplished yachtsman who took the blue ribbon at every regatta. The rigor of his intellect, it was clear, did not preclude any form of epicureanism.

When it came to the classical writers he read so assiduously, he had a decided preference for forbidden texts—precisely those that weren't to be found in the Chancellor Green: the erotic poems and fables of Antiquity.

And, then, the conventions of social life bored him to tears.

"It's the director you should really be thanking, Miss Greene," he said now.

"And we will," said Belle earnestly. "But I want to thank you, Mr. Morgan, with all my heart, for your *kindness*."

"I'm the one who should be expressing my gratitude to you, Belle," he said. He had the air of simultaneously weighing his words carefully and making fun of her.

Getting up from behind his desk, he opened the heavy green velvet curtains covering his windows. Daylight flooded the room. He covered the volumes lined up on his desk with a cloth, sat back down, and continued, in the same tone:

"I heard that you agreed to forget your regrettable antipathy toward my collections and that you participated in their cataloguing with brilliance and dedication."

"I simply typed out the index cards that Mr. Upson dictated to me. He, and he alone, is the author of your private catalogue. However . . ." she held out a binder. "I have been working on the materials you donated to the Princeton library. Your first donation to the Chancellor Green in 1896, I mean, and the ones that have come after it over the past eight years. This is an overview of the Virgils in the Junius Spencer Morgan Collection at Princeton, with their titles, year of publication, printer name, paper quality, binding type, and a timeline of their respective provenances. Also a brief summary of their contents and the subject matter of their illustrations."

Junius donned his pince-nez and leafed through the thick binder she handed to him, reading carefully, his face impassive. She stood there in front of them, considering all the ways she might have done a better job. Should she have organized the catalogue differently? Begun with the oldest works, rather than their date of acquisition?

But he gave a low, almost involuntary whistle. "You've put a great deal of work into this, Belle. To say the least."

"I don't know about 'work,' Mr. Morgan, but I certainly enjoyed myself. Before this, I'd known what a manuscript was, an incunabulum, a printed book. But the wonders of your collection staggered me. I felt a sort of . . . ecstasy, believe it or not! Untying the laces that held the bindings closed . . . undoing the clasps . . . breathing in the perfume of that rich paper, brushing a fingertip against the engravings, and deciphering the bookplates with the arms of the different owners down through the ages . . . it was extraordinary! Being able to take it all in like that gave me a real sense of your vision. All of these works, their beauty—their rarity—their provenance—they interact with each other in a way you can actually feel!"

Faced with such sensual enthusiasm, Junius smiled. It was an expression both indulgent and mocking. A glint in his eyes behind the pince-nez spectacles, almost lost in the reflection off the glass, made him seem incredibly seductive to Belle.

"May I ask you a question, Mr. Morgan?" she continued, her heart thumping with excitement. "Why are you getting rid of these marvelous things? I mean, why not keep them among the rest of your treasures at Constitution Hill? Why keep giving them to the university?"

"Why do you think?"

"I don't know. If I were you, I don't think I could part with these objects after I'd combed Europe for them. And why do you have other collectors—even your own uncle—buy rare manuscripts that you've discovered, when you could just acquire them for yourself?"

"Why do you think?" he repeated.

"Because they don't fit into your chosen area of research?"

"Precisely. And why else?"

"Because it's not the idea of possessing these things that motivates you, but rather the thought of bringing them together?" she ventured, a bit less confidently.

"Yes. Bringing together books, or objects, preserving them in order to form a cohesive whole in which each component interacts with another and all the parts are complementary—that's what I'm striving to do, as you described it yourself."

"Well then, I ask you again—why scatter them?" she asked, her voice rising passionately. "Why not keep them together, in *your* collections?"

"Rest assured, Miss Greene, I'm not giving everything to Princeton. And you're in a position to know that, since you were at Constitution Hill in my absence. I'm just donating what I feel can contribute to the edification of students, to American culture, and to humanity's collective wisdom."

"If I understand you correctly then, Mr. Morgan, possessing fifteenth-century volumes is a magnificent thing, but offering them to researchers who can extract knowledge from them is even more wondrous?"

"Well summarized. In the meantime, your catalogue is quite poorly done!"

She couldn't keep from flinching with shock. Aware of the abruptness of his criticism, he tried to soften the blow a bit:

"You've done a formidable job with very difficult material, certainly, but may I suggest some modifications? For example, try arranging the works by language: Latin editions first, then French translations, Italian, German, or English next. For the rest, your criteria—the dates and places of printing, the timeline of owners, et cetera, are applied methodically, with a formulation I find quite pleasing. Come back and show me your new plan at the end of the week—if you're willing to, of course," he added wryly. "I seem to remember that you don't do anything unless you've personally decided on it!"

*

Nearly a year of training with Junius Morgan himself: the dream! From then on, they were together constantly. And Junius's tutelage was not limited to the stacks of the two libraries. Like the philosophers of the Aristotelian School who walked with their pupils in the open air, he loved to instruct her during long strolls outdoors, the summer heat slowing neither their reflections nor their footsteps through the fields. Their conversations were unrestricted and rambling, untainted by dogmatism in any form, passing from observation of the birds to the basic rules of the hunt in an auction house:

"Target your prey. Keep your mind focused on the reason for your choice and the price you have determined to pay. Learn to distinguish the mere attractive object from the rare pearl, prettiness from beauty, and never privilege form over substance. The text, Belle—the *text*! A superb binding that encloses a dull text is worthless."

Belle listened avidly, soaking in Junius's knowledge, the way he thought and spoke, his mannerisms.

"I'm turning into a sponge on legs with you!" she joked.

"A siphon on wheels, you mean! You suck information as greedily as a vampire."

"Charming—thank you very much, Mr. Morgan!"

She was learning that he was as interested in the *Aeneid* as he was in modern literature; that the score of a football game between the Princeton Tigers and the Yale Bulldogs excited him just as much as a medieval psalter.

With him, she recaptured something of the bond she had shared with Arthur Upson. But, unlike Upson, Junius was never completely serious, nor completely present. At the Chancellor Green library she had once heard Miss Martins compare him to an elf—a curious image, but an accurate one. There was something ethereal about him, something almost uncontrolled about the way his mind worked. He had a certain tantalizing elusiveness. She had tried to pin down that aspect of his nature, to tame it with her charm, but it always flitted out of reach.

Without truly understanding her own frustration, she always returned from their walks in a state of agitation, often overwhelmed by her need to make him stay, her desire to touch him, to embrace him. But he never made the slightest move in that direction.

When he walked her to Miss Martins's doorstep, he never did anything more than tip his hat and grasp her hand briefly, lightly. He inevitably declined the offer of a cup of tea and walked away with his customary light step. She always closed the door behind him as if this mattered not at all—and then pressed her hand to her heart to calm its pounding, obliged to stand still for a moment, tamping down the tremendous surge of feeling he aroused in her.

At night she lay in bed, wondering about Junius's feelings toward her. Why did he insist on reminding her again and again that she was young, that she had her whole life ahead of her, that the world was her oyster? He used the difference in their ages as a barrier: *You're such a whippersnapper!* How could she make him understand that she was no naïve ingenue?

Unless it was really the difference in their social standing that kept him at a distance?

And yet, she sensed that he was bored in his world of bankers, of wives spending on Fifth Avenue the money their husbands earned on Wall Street. That the endless chitchat, the five o'clock teas, the charity balls and interminable dinners where all the women looked alike had become an ordeal for him.

But he had refrained from confiding in her on the subject so far and never mentioned his wife or children. Never a single word about his private life. Still, it was abundantly clear that he sought out her company. That he found her charming, and allowed himself to be charmed.

Why? Why was he keeping his distance from her?

Would he ever take her in his arms?

*She's so passionate,* he mused, with a kind of affection. *Dynamite—quicksilver! Her curiosity and impertinence—a true fountain of youth. Deliciously invigorating.*

He knew that all he had to do was make the slightest overture, and she would give herself to him. Body and soul, the way she did everything. But he couldn't do it.

Taking this petite, unmarried, young employee as his mistress would mean compromising her. Everyone knew each other in Princeton. There were already rumors . . .

Taking her for his mistress would mean turning her into a fallen woman, one New Jersey's Puritan society would forever condemn to the demimonde.

There was no doubt about it: bringing her into his bed would mean the end of Miss Greene. The end, for her, of any possibility of social advancement. She would be considered fair game for further seduction. She would lose her career. Her dream.

Belle was worth more than that.

Entering into a liaison with her would also mean betraying his wife. And Junius was not a man to lie. Leave Josie Dear? Perhaps. Be unfaithful to her? No. Especially not with Belle. It would be too . . . predictable. Banal, even.

But: being Pygmalion to her Galatea and transforming her into a master bibliophile *par excellence*? Providing Miss Martins with a worthy heir? And bequeathing to Princeton the most remarkable of librarians? That, *yes.*

\* \* \*

It was October 15, 1905. Toasts to Virgil's health were being drunk in the home of Mr. Woodrow Wilson, president of the university, at a sumptuous reception marking the anniversary of the poet's birth—and honoring Mr. Junius Morgan. The illustrious Mrs. Bertha, star of many a stage tragedy, had been invited from New York to declaim the most beautiful passages from the *Aeneid* in Latin during the dessert course. It was exactly the sort of thing that Junius loathed. An entertainment that was meant to be elegant but proved to be utter torture. How could this fat lady in her low-necked pink dress massacre Dido's lament with such aplomb?

Pleading an emergency, he abandoned his wife to her small talk, leaving her the car and driver, and crossed the campus to the Chancellor Green.

In spite of the late hour, there were a few students still hard at work. Bypassing the reading room, he made a beeline for his office. Extracting a key from his vest pocket, he opened one of his desk drawers and pocketed a small pistol. Out in the corridor again, he encountered Belle, who was closing down the stacks.

"You're not at the president's house?" she asked, surprised.

"I ducked out."

"You naughty thing!" she said archly. "Running away, Mr. Morgan! Didn't you like her, Mrs. Bertha, with her *At regina dolos—quis fallere possit amantem?—praesensit . . .*"

"You know the *Aeneid*, I see!"

"By heart."

"Well. My hat is off to you, Belle. I'd imagined you in many roles, but never that of Sarah Bernhardt."

"You haven't seen anything yet, Mr. Morgan."

"Neither have you, Miss Greene."

"You're quite the enigma . . . Just where are you off to now?"

"A place you've no idea exists . . . but one you might like."

"Where is it?"

"You'll know soon enough. That is—would you care to accompany me?"

The expression on her face, and the alacrity with which she finished locking up the stacks, were so eloquent that no words were necessary.

They could hear dogs barking in the distance.

They had traversed the series of open fields that bordered the town, a sort of no-man's-land where no one ever went. This was Princeton, too, these shadow zones everyone pretended not to know about.

Through the trees, she glimpsed bonfires illuminating the night. There was no other source of light, not even the moon. The ground and the sky were invisible in the October fog. But Junius walked with sure, quick strides. He knew the way. Next to him, Belle, wrapped in her shawl, hurried to keep up. Straight ahead of them was what looked to be some sort of camp.

"Are we going to visit the natives?" she asked, half joking, half intrigued.

"There are no Indians left in New Jersey, Miss Greene. But if our little adventure should get out of hand, leave it to me to act. These people are old friends; I've known many of them since my student years—but not all of them. Some can be rather hot-blooded and are invariably itching for a fight. Things can always take a wrong turn."

They had reached a clearing dotted with tents, horses grazing nearby. There was a thumping of drums now, and the sound of a guitar, and the cracking voice of an old man, singing. They picked their way through the colorful draperies to the caravans that bordered the clearing, where children played and chickens scratched beneath the placid gazes of squatting women tending braziers.

They rose and gathered around Junius the moment he appeared. All of the women wore long skirts, their hair covered with scarves bound low across their foreheads, heavy gold jewelry gleaming at their ears and necks and wrists. They spoke a strange language that Junius seemed to understand. The older women patted his cheeks, uttering cries of joy, the younger ones giggling beside them.

"We grew up together," he explained to Belle, sheepishly.

When they had finished fussing over him, they turned and looked at his companion. Belle could feel their eyes on her, taking in every detail of her anatomy, and she did the same thing unashamedly.

"Your wife?" asked one of the women in English.

"You're making me too young, Lalia. I'm far too old for this young lady. Where is Zanko?"

They pointed to the last caravan. A gaggle of children had already run ahead to announce the arrival of guests to the leader.

This large extended family of Roma had fled persecution in their Hungarian homeland and arrived at Ellis Island in 1880. The tribal patriarch, Zanko's grandfather, had spoken five languages, the oldest of which descended from Hindi. And it was this—the mystery of their languages—that had drawn Junius to their camp as a young student. Before giving in to his fascination with the people themselves and their traditions, Junius had been careful to always visit them alone, developing bonds over the years with those who were willing. He always went to bid them farewell when they moved on for the year and greeted them when they returned. It was a relationship that had lasted nearly twenty years. Zanko never failed to remind the young men of the camp, who would gladly have given Junius a good thumping and robbed him of his wallet besides, that this *gadjo* was the only American who had shown true fraternity with them—and that, if he hadn't spoken to the mayor on their behalf, they would not have been able to continue spending their winters in Princeton.

"Welcome home, my brother!" Zanko exclaimed now, embracing Junius.

He was a giant of a man with a face so deeply lined that it almost looked scarred. He wore a loose smock through which a number of large pendant medallions were visible.

"Welcome to you, Zanko! You arrived late this year. You'll stay until summer, I take it?"

"God willing!"

Zanko squatted down next to the wheels of his caravan, at a low table hastily set up by his wife and daughters. He invited Junius to be seated, and beckoned the other men to approach and partake of the tea his wife poured from an immense samovar. They launched into quiet conversation, paying no attention to Belle or the other women, who remained standing.

Several of these women now drew closer to the fire with their tambourines. The guitar, which had fallen silent at the guests' arrival, resumed its plaintive lament, the voice of an unseen old lady intoning a melody. Her husky tones, evocative of sobs, soon led to dancing. The tempo was slow at first, the women keeping time by slapping their tambourines against their hips so that their tiny cymbals jangled. Then there was a swaying of skirts, a sinuous undulation of shoulders, an arching of backs.

"Go on, little one," Zanko's wife ordered, pushing Belle forward.

She didn't need to be told twice. Fists on hips, head thrown back, she began copying the women's sensuous movements.

"You, too," the matriarch said to Junius.

"Let's leave that in my youth, Romica."

"You, too," she insisted.

Junius exchanged a glance with Zanko. The latter's expression was clear: one did not disobey an order from Romica. He rose and joined the circle of women.

It was almost beyond belief: a Junius Morgan caught up in the music, his whole body swaying to the rhythm of the singer's lament. Grace and sensuality, personified.

Belle, swept up in the moment, had fallen effortlessly into the rhythm of the dance. Looping the ends of her shawl around Junius and drawing him to her, she swayed her hips in a way that caused the circle to whoop approvingly. Zanko and the other men had risen in their turn, clapping their hands and chanting as the *gadjos* danced.

When the song ended, Belle and Junius, breathless, exchanged a look of triumph, clasping hands, laughing.

But before they could rejoin Zanko, the women descended on Belle and led her away.

"You are different. Who are your people? Where do you come from?" Belle stiffened. "Hold out your hand."

She wanted to refuse. The woman didn't give her the chance, grasping her hand. Belle acquiesced reluctantly. God only knew what this woman would see. Belle felt fear rising within her. The soothsayer's fingertips trailed slowly along the lines of her palm, palpating the phalanxes. A look of perplexity crossed her face. The other women fell silent.

"Do you see something?" Belle asked eventually.

The woman nodded, but did not answer.

Belle's old terror, the terror of being unmasked, seared through her. The silence stretched on.

"Well?"

The soothsayer looked up and, meeting Belle's gaze directly, said:

"I see a great future for you. With him . . . but not in the way you might expect."

\* \* \*

If Belle had thought that the episode among the Roma would

bring on a new intimacy with Junius, she was mistaken. Two weeks without a word. Without even a look. She tried to manufacture opportunities to cross his path, but he avoided her. And the rupture was complete when he departed for New York.

They said he'd gone to his uncle's house, for the inauguration of the library he had designed. He was gone until the Christmas holidays. On the last day of classes, Miss Martins came in search of Belle, who was manning the reception desk.

"Mr. Morgan wants to see you in his office," she said curtly.

Aunt Lottie had been worried on that evening of October 15, when Belle hadn't come home after the library closed. When her protégées worked late, they didn't have dinner together, but she always left a little something on the stove for them. But Aunt Lottie, coming downstairs at two o'clock in the morning, saw that Belle had turned off neither the gas burner nor the kitchen lamp. Just as she was considering phoning the police, she heard the young woman's soft footfalls on the stairs. Furious, she hadn't waited for morning to express her displeasure in a flurry of reproaches and reprimands, which Belle had endured without uttering a peep about where she'd been.

After a month of estrangement, relations between them had improved almost to the point of being normal again. But the severity of Miss Martins's tone, and the tragic expression with which she had relayed the order to report to Junius, spoke eloquently of her disapproval of Belle's relationship with him.

"Right away; he wants you right away!" she snapped.

Belle obeyed with alacrity.

Junius was standing in the dimness of his office, as usual. He began speaking without preamble the moment she entered the room.

"The expert I had hoped would direct my Uncle John Pierpont Morgan's library in New York has just accepted a curatorship at the Metropolitan Museum of Art. He's refused my offer. Would you be interested in the job?"

"Me? My God, I—"

"Nothing has been decided," he added hurriedly. "It's my uncle's choice to make. I think you're ready. I've spoken to him about you. Go and see him; he'll be expecting you the day after tomorrow at eleven o'clock, 33 East 36th Street. And Belle, whatever you do . . . don't visit the hairdresser's! Just be natural."

Belle emerged from this interview in a daze.

A single question dominated her thoughts: *What could it possibly mean to "be natural" with the most powerful man in America?*

# CHAPTER 4

## THE WHITE MARBLE PALACE
### 1905–1908

B elle, you didn't!" cried her brother Russell, when she returned from her appointment at the Morgan mansion. "Mind your own business! If I didn't take this risk, I would have no chance."

"You've shot yourself in the foot!"

During the forty-eight hours leading up to the fateful day, Belle had prepared for her interview with painstaking care, acquainting herself with the Murray Hill neighborhood in which the library was located and learning all she could about the man she was going to meet.

John Pierpont Morgan.

Through Junius, she knew he was president of the board of directors of the Metropolitan Museum of Art, as well as a sponsor and founding member of most of the other museums in New York.

She had also learned that "Uncle Pierpont," or "J.P.," as Junius sometimes called him, cherished a love for *objets d'art* that bordered on obsession. That he was interested in *everything*: furniture, jewelry, faïenceries, Chinese porcelain, Roman archaeology, Greek archaeology, Egyptian archaeology. And, of course, paintings and books. He was an insatiably curious collector who was passionately fond of art in *all* its forms. A knowledgeable bibliophile, he searched out early printed texts, original editions, and medieval bindings. In short, Uncle Pierpont coveted all the world's beauty, and bought so feverishly that he left himself no time to study the pieces he accumulated.

In this, he was very different from Junius.

J.P. Morgan was a compulsive amateur collector whose voracity had no limits. However—the excessiveness and disorder of his acquisitions aside—his aesthetic sense was unparalleled. His intent was clear: to harvest the finest of Europe's cultural legacy and build America's future with it.

Belle had found a treasure-trove of information about him in the periodicals at the Chancellor Green. Researching him had been easy; the newspapers talked only of him.

Born into a family of bankers—his father had founded the Morgan Bank—John Pierpont had multiplied the fortune he inherited a hundredfold by speculating on arms sales during the Civil War. He had then turned his attention to the most modern technologies, investing in railroads, electricity, oil, and steel. Now the possessor of a number of immense trusts, the entire United States economy was dependent on him. The press invariably described him as a fearful despot, surly and unapproachable, often irascible. His energy, his work ethic, and the violence of his rages, which were set off by the slightest provocation, exhausted those who worked for him. It was said that, during the construction of his library, he had driven his architect so mad that the man had ended up having a nervous breakdown.

Belle had spent the evening before her meeting with him reconnoitering the block of mansions whose crown jewel stood at the corner of 36th and Madison.

The Morgan Library.

It was a rectangular, one-story white marble palace extending majestically across the space between Pierpont's own mansion and that of his daughter, both of them red-brick houses teeming with doors and windows. Belle had been struck by the contrast between the new edifice and the sumptuous residences that flanked it, and pleased by the grace of the library itself, which evoked both a Greek temple and a Renaissance villa; its refinement down to the smallest detail spoke eloquently, she thought, of the nobility of its builder. It was clear that, in the eyes of J.P. Morgan, his library celebrated America's rightful place among the great cultures of humanity.

Things grew slightly more complicated for Belle on the big day itself, when her anxiety gained the upper hand over her usual orderliness. Though she had tried on ten dresses the night before, and consulted her sisters about what to wear, she ended up changing three times in the morning before finally going back to her original choice of outfit. This meant she had to run for her tram, and she spent the rest of the trip in a flustered rush.

Yet she managed to arrive on time for her interview and, summoning the appearance of calm, made her way up the five steps that led from street-level to a small wrought-iron gate. Climbed the staircase flanked by two lionesses on the loggia. Crossed the peristyle to the bronze double doors, like those of a temple. But here, disaster—there was no trace of a doorbell or a knocker to be seen. She searched among columns, next to statues, in niches for a button or a bell-pull that would allow her to signal her presence. Nothing. She was going to be late! The idea was horrifying. Just then, by some happy chance, a steward in livery opened the door to let out a man who passed Belle without looking in her direction, a bag tucked beneath his arm.

The steward now ushered her into an immense vestibule in the form of a rotunda. The splendor of the space was breathtaking. She had not expected such magnificence. It was a riot of lines, colors, materials. The floor was paved with multicolored marble, the walls and cupola covered with frescoes. It was the Italy she'd never visited, the Italy of Michelangelo and Raphael, the Italy of books and of her dreams, stretching away before her eyes.

As the steward took her coat, hat, and scarf, she stood still in the center of the porphyry rosette inlaid into the floor, gazing up at the ceiling, at the allegorical figures depicted in the lunettes above lapis lazuli columns. This décor, she sensed, was made up of symbols whose meaning she did not understand. Only the four female figures representing the Arts and Sciences were familiar to her; the rest was a mystery.

Wonder and curiosity had overwhelmed every other emotion. Her nervousness was forgotten.

Three doors opened off the rotunda. The steward had disappeared through the one at the far end with her coat and hat; it was the smallest and most ornate. Now he reappeared and knocked at the left-hand door, which was monumental, surmounted by a capital. Pushing this door open, he murmured "Mr. Morgan's *studiolo* . . ." before melting away again.

Belle went inside.

The only thing she could see at first were stained-glass windows, and a massive black desk that stood out against the purple damask hangings on the wall behind it, adorned with the arms of the cardinals of the Chigi family. The walls were crimson, the carpets crimson, the armchairs and sofas all crimson. And everywhere there were empty glass cases, paintings propped against plinths, busts and church candelabra in rows on the floor.

"As you can see, I'm in the midst of moving! Pardon the disorder!"

He'd emerged suddenly from a corner of the room, a cigar clamped between his teeth. Tall and powerfully built, grayhaired and gray-mustached in a suit cut in the English style, he waved her into a chair and sat down behind his desk.

He was just as the newspapers described him. A man of nearly seventy, irreproachably elegant: wing collar, spotted ascot with tiepin, cufflinks, pocket watch, and a camelia in his lapel. There was nothing elderly about him, and he might even have been handsome if his nose hadn't been grotesquely deformed by a condition that turned it purplish and bulbous. But Belle's eyes rested on that immense nose for only an instant, because

J.P. Morgan possessed another feature that instantly drew her full attention: his eyes. From beneath bristling eyebrows, he gazed at her with intensity. There was no malice in the look, but its ardor and concentration were terrifying nonetheless.

"My nephew has spoken of you a great deal," he muttered through his full mustache.

He stubbed out his cigar.

She smiled, summoning every ounce of her charm. "Good things, I hope?"

"He insists that you're a rare pearl and I shouldn't let you get away."

"Mr. Junius Morgan has always been extremely generous to me. He's been kind enough to take me under his wing for almost two years now. I might even go so far as to say that he's taught me everything I know. Techniques of illumination, how to differentiate authentic manuscripts from forgeries . . ."

"Have you seen this?" Morgan interrupted, indicating a large box of drawings at his elbow. "What he's just made me buy?"

He rose and opened the box with reverence. "Come and look. One hundred and twelve Rembrandt etchings."

Belle got up and came around the desk, bending over the plates with him. As Morgan carefully turned the pages, their emotions intensified in tandem. She couldn't hold back an exclamation.

"I've never seen more beautiful prints! How sharp even the smallest details are!"

"And you haven't seen anything yet," he said. "Look at the strength in that face."

"And that one—Rembrandt's mother," she murmured reverently.

They fell silent as he continued leafing through the etchings, neither of them needing to say anything now, their mutual joy at the beauty of each image bringing them together in a sort of intimacy, a shared ecstasy.

"These drawings . . . the delicacy of the expressions . . . absolutely splendid!" Morgan concluded. "It was Junius who found them. He found my Dürer engravings too, and my first-edition Gutenberg Bible, and my ninth-century Gospels, and the four original pages of Shakespeare that he's just brought me. My nephew is a genius—and if he's trained you like he says he has, like *you* say he has . . . well, let's keep talking, shall we?"

Belle returned to her chair, and he looked at her for a while without speaking.

"Junius says you're twenty-two years old. But you're quite a bit younger than that, aren't you? Barely an adult."

For the first time, Belle blushed.

She had dressed like a very young girl. "*Whatever you do, don't go to the hairdresser's!*" Junius had instructed. And so she'd worn her long hair loose and streaming down her back, held off her face by a ribbon tied in a large bow. For her outfit, she'd chosen her prettiest frock, but also her simplest—a striped navy-blue dress, a college-girl's dress. "*Be natural!*"

Clearly, she'd succeeded only too well.

She claimed to be twenty-two years old. She was actually twenty-six. And he thought she was eighteen.

Morgan noted her uneasy expression.

"Youth has never been a sin, my dear. But I'm looking for someone more experienced. The position here will involve taking receipt of all the crates of books stored in my home. I don't mean only the books in my personal library, but also the crates that are piling up in my attic, in my cellar, and in the stacks at the Lenox Library."

"I've worked at the Lenox Library—I know which crates you mean."

"Yes, but you haven't opened them! And neither have I. They will need to be inventoried, catalogued, and arranged in these cabinets." He gestured at the glass-fronted cabinets lining the walls of his office. "And not just in this room. In the reading room, too, where the galleries contain hundreds and hundreds of shelves. To accomplish a task like this, I will need not only a scholar, but someone with the stamina of a market porter. Actually, Mr. Kent, the librarian at the Grolier Club, has the physique for it . . . Do you know the Grolier Club?"

"The most prestigious club for bibliophiles in the United States," said Belle eagerly, pouncing on the opportunity to impress him. "Named in tribute to Jean Grolier de Servières, the great sixteenth-century French book collector."

Nodding, he continued:

"You will understand, I'm sure, that Mr. Kent's application is of greater interest to me than yours. He hasn't yet accepted the offer from the Metropolitan, and so I am still hoping that he will come to work for me. I'm sorry to disappoint you, but Mr. Kent remains my first choice."

His frankness shocked Belle into speaking boldly.

"You were speaking of youth just now, Mr. Morgan," she began, her voice firm and strong. "I have the enthusiasm and the energy. Your nephew told you that I learn quickly. Try me, sir. Try me for six months—unpaid!"

His penetrating gaze rested on her. This was the first time a potential employee had ever offered to work for him *gratis*. Normally, due to the enormity of his wealth, people demanded exorbitant salaries that were totally disproportionate to the job.

Most people were seeking to serve only their own interests in approaching him; he was well aware of that. He was nothing to them but a social springboard, the promise of financial gain. A way of enriching themselves, from top to bottom. His fortune lay at the heart of every single one of his human relationships, skewing and distorting even the most trivial interactions.

He changed the subject:

"My nephew tells me you live near Columbia University?"

"Yes, with my mother and my brother and sisters."

BELLE GREENE · 117

"And your father?"

She tensed. Was this a trap? Did he know something?

Junius had described his uncle to her as a shrewd and clever man with the memory of an elephant. And J.P. Morgan had met Richard T. Greener, when the latter was secretary of the Grant Monument Association—had known Rick Greener *well*, in fact, when both men sat on the committee's board of directors.

"My father is deceased."

"I'm sorry."

"I was very young; I hardly knew him."

"You grew up in New York?"

"Yes and no. I spent my childhood with my mother's family in Virginia. My grandparents owned a plantation there. But they lost everything in the Civil War. They were Portuguese, originally—aristocrats from Lisbon. My brother and sisters occupy high professional positions," she insisted; "they'll help me. I can work for you without pay for as long as you like."

"All work deserves pay, my dear. We'll see. I'll give you my answer after Christmas. In the meantime, have my steward show you the East Room."

The interview was over. They stood. J.P. Morgan escorted her gallantly to the door of his office. They shook hands, Belle noting the friendly twinkle in the tycoon's eyes. She'd read of his susceptibility to feminine charm and beauty. Though she knew she couldn't hope to rival the women that inhabited his world, she sensed that she was not unpleasing to him.

But when she stepped into the East Room and took in the full majesty of this reading room, with its grillwork-screened cabinets rising over three levels, its galleries and balconies, Belle's heart sank. Reigning over this world was very possibly beyond her skill. Creating it might well be beyond her strength.

". . . Offering to work for nothing? For the richest man in the world? He must have thought you were a madwoman, Belle,"

Russell exclaimed, aghast, when she described her interview with Morgan. "Some sort of nut!"

"Or an heiress, maybe," she joked.

She was trying to recount her brief jaunt to Mount Olympus with her usual nonchalance.

She was bluffing.

For, God knew—the thought of working among Mr. Morgan's Rembrandts and Dürers made her heart thump with excitement! It had rapidly become her life's dream. *The Morgan Library*. Entering that paradise, she'd felt the anxiety of any young woman showing up for a job interview. Leaving it, she had experienced the terror of being passed over for the role. Of not having impressed Morgan enough.

The answer came from Princeton, by telegram to her New York apartment, on December 31, 1905.

Three lines.

**You've got the job. Stop. Seventy-five dollars a month. Stop. Mr. Morgan's library. Stop. Tomorrow eight o'clock. Stop.**

**Happy New Year!**

**Your devoted servant, Junius Morgan.**

The war-whoops and wild dancing that greeted this incredible message resulted in strongly worded protestations from the Greene family's neighbors.

*Belle—J.P. Morgan's personal librarian!*

At seventy-five dollars a month, she would be earning almost double her salary at the Chancellor Green! And triple what Louise and Ethel earned!

The general euphoria was followed by equally intense consternation on Belle's part: *tomorrow?* Starting *tomorrow morning?* Without even saying goodbye to Aunt Lottie, and Gertrude, and all her colleagues. Without having been able to tell them, to thank them, to hug them. Without even having resigned.

But how could she jump on a train on this evening of St. Sylvester's Day—how could she go and see them, and explain, when they would all be at some New Year's Eve party or another, surrounded by friends and family?

On this first, fevered night as a Morgan employee, Belle experienced a pair of contradictory emotions that would stay with her through the years to come: the intoxication of feeling herself to be free, and the frustration of having to submit to the tyranny of her master.

\* \* \*

A beehive. An anthill. The white marble palace, the temple with its harmonious lines, the venerable sanctuary hummed with life that no one, not even its owner, could have imagined the previous week.

The bustle of movers coming and going with boxes and crates, the shouts of the workers prying out the nails that held them shut, the triumphant hoots of the apprentices when the lids came loose. And, rising above the hubbub, the imperious voice of the petite Belle da Costa Greene, warning everyone not to touch the books. She alone would unpack them, dust them, inventory them. She alone would arrange them in the East Room's cabinets, or those in the vault, if she judged them to be too rare or too precious for ordinary storage.

By the hundreds, the large wooden cases arrived from here, there, and everywhere: not just the Morgan townhouse and the Lenox Library, as he had told her, but from other New York institutions, as well—not to mention the tycoon's warehouses and his London residence.

Ten days of commotion that allowed J.P. Morgan to assess the magnitude of the task. Junius's protégée, as resourceful and

energetic as she was, could not possibly manage it on her own.
Morgan had admired Miss Greene's vivacity, her stylishness, and
her daring. He was not a man to shy away from risk, himself. Mr.
Kent's definitive refusal of the post had cemented his decision.

But time was running short. He was leaving for Europe at
the beginning of February and would remain there for six
months, as was his habit. The library must be ready by the day
of his departure. And so he quickly hired an assistant for his
librarian.

This turn of events dealt a nasty blow to Belle. She even felt
as if Morgan had stabbed her in the back. The new recruit, an
unmarried lady named Ada Thurston, was a hundred times
more qualified than she was—and twenty years older, besides.

Miss Thurston had been educated at the prestigious Vassar
Female College, the equivalent of Princeton or Yale for young
women from good families. She'd even stayed on for three
years after earning her degree in 1880, teaching gymnastics
and helping to develop the sports department, particularly the
baseball team. After that, she had taken a cataloguing course
at the Pratt Institute, graduating with honors. She was someone of real consequence, and the hierarchical relationship
between the boss and her subordinate seemed guaranteed to
be contentious.

Fortunately, Miss Thurston was rather plain-faced, with a
short, stocky body and, despite her muscles, an almost patho-
logical timidity. Mr. Morgan terrified her, and she lost her nerve
completely in his presence; indeed, her fear was so great that she
couldn't even remain in the same room with him. Whenever she
heard his tread on the underground staircase that linked his
house to the library, she invariably vanished into the nearest
storage room.

Belle, though, with her usual ease of manner, always went to
greet the Big Chief, as she called him in the privacy of her own
thoughts. She had no fear of his company. On the contrary. She

loved nothing more than sharing with him her vision for the organization of the galleries, and discussing inventory techniques.

Belle sparkled; Ada ran and hid. The result was that Morgan found the former charming and the latter uninteresting. On this second point, he was wrong. Despite their differences, the two women complemented each other perfectly, and both were devoted to the same cause: the Morgan Library. Two forces of nature, two workaholics operating in concert.

Within a month, they had formed a fast friendship. Belle began calling Miss Thurston "Thursty," while Ada referred to her as "Bull," for the way she always seemed ready to charge forward.

The cherry on the cake was the forthcoming departure of J.P. Morgan for England, France, and Egypt, which would leave them as sole mistresses of the library.

But before that happened, they had thirty days to prove to Morgan that he could leave without a qualm, entrusting them with the keys to the palace.

*

Top hat on his head as usual, cigar in one hand and walking stick in the other, J.P. Morgan stood on the threshold, between the bronze doors. In his long traveling coat that just reached the shining tops of his shoes, he seemed taller and more imposing than ever. More tense, too.

"If you need anything, Miss Greene, ask Charles King, my secretary—he knows everything," he said, not for the first time. "He'll arrange assistance for you."

On the other side of the street a crowd had gathered to gawk, a few journalists among them, keen not to miss a single detail of Morgan's departure.

The car that would drive him to the dock was waiting at the

curb, along with the six other automobiles in his retinue. The friends who were escorting him to the ship or traveling with him to Europe were growing impatient. They were going to miss the boat! His employees, Miss Thurston among them, had accompanied him to the loggia.

He couldn't seem to tear himself away.

The directors of his bank and his close business associates, who had come to bid him farewell as was customary, were grumbling on the stairs. It hadn't escaped their attention that J.P. Morgan had chosen, as the place from which he would depart America, not his Wall Street offices, not his own home, but his library. Or that he was addressing his final remarks not to his wife or daughters, but to a young woman to whom he spoke in an urgent tone, as if he were entrusting a nurse with his child. She looked very small next to him as she nodded reassuringly.

"Don't worry, Mr. Morgan. I'll think of you, and write to you, and tell you everything."

"Are you sure you have all my addresses?"

"I'll keep tabs on your location."

"Write to me every day, Miss Greene. Every day!"

\*

Peace, until July.

And freedom!

"Thursty, where did we put the delivery receipts for these books?" Belle hollered, waving a list of titles.

She had chosen as her office the third room leading off the vestibule, the one referred to as the North Room, and was frequently seen hurtling out of it through a door topped with a sculpture of the Madonna and Child, the staccato clicking of her heels echoing off the rotunda's marble floor.

"Mr. Morgan seems to have paid for them," she continued, "but never received them."

"The sellers probably never sent them," opined Thursty from her perch on a ladder.

"Then we'll have to conduct a new survey, to find out which books we're missing. Find me the names of all the European booksellers; we'll have to write to them and claim the books we've acquired. I want every single one of them here when the Big Chief gets back!"

\* \* \*

Mission nearly accomplished. By May 1906, the most precious manuscripts, the jewels of the collection, including two Gutenberg Bibles and the first printed editions of the *Iliad* and the *Odyssey*, published in Greek in Florence in 1489, were safely stowed in the vault, along with the Lindau Gospel, so named for the German abbey that had preserved it. A purchase of Junius's, whose encrypted telegram to his uncle she had archived: "*Tambales solmites* (I can obtain for you)," it read, "a famous ninth- or tenth-century Gospel, with a gem-encrusted gold binding. A treasure of great value, of unparalleled [ . . . ] interest. Description to follow." In fact, Junius coded all of his messages. The antiquarian booksellers of Paris, London, and New York were always watching greedily to see how he reacted to an item, and he couldn't display any enthusiasm without arousing covetousness and increased prices.

The splendid Lindau Gospels was the first of the six hundred and thirty illuminated medieval and Renaissance manuscripts to which Belle turned her attention. *MS M.1.* She kept it displayed on a lectern in the vault. She loved to be alone with it, losing herself in contemplation of the precious stones and gold reliefs that adorned its binding, her fingertips delicately touching the figure of Christ on the cross, the four angels, the sun in mourning, the inscription *Hic est Rex Iudeorum*, "This is the King of the Jews."

Whenever there was no chance of Thursty walking in unexpectedly, she would even kiss the manuscript reverently, like a priest with the Scriptures, before closing the vault door. Her emotion when among these immortal texts always ran high and boundless.

Exactly as she had suggested when discussing the plans for the library with Junius back in Princeton, the vault was located on the same floor as the Holy of Holies, accessed through Morgan's office, the magnificent West Room with its red silk hangings, where he had received Belle on the day of her interview.

The king's private domain.

Above the heavy, ornate mantelpiece imported from Florence, Belle had had the workers hang the *Portrait of Pierpont Morgan* by artist Frank Holl. She knew he loved the painting; so much so, in fact, that he had had photos taken of it for his friends. In the portrait, he was shown dressed all in black, enthroned in majesty like an aristocratic Renaissance banker; and the rhinophyma that deformed his nose had been discreetly brushed out.

On either side of the fireplace she had had installed, on two pedestals, the splendid pair of andirons from the workshop of a Venetian sculptor: two bronze sphinxes, dating from the 1530s.

More pedestals in the corners of the room contained Morgan's latest purchases, objects he had bought in Europe and sent back to the library via his agents. These included a sculpture of the Christ Child by Antonio Rossellino, and a large, full-length terra cotta statue of the Virgin Mary attributed to Donatello.

And, as if this side job as a decorator weren't enough, Belle had stocked the cupboard in Morgan's personal bathroom with the extremely gentle soaps he favored, as well as his preferred eau de Cologne, which she'd had delivered from Paris. She had ordered cases of the Cuban cigars that bore his name, the Regalia de Morgans, and the Morgan Tea, a blend of Earl Grey and Lapsang Souchong, that he would sip on his return to New York.

And then there were the books. She had chosen the most exquisitely bound texts for the shelves of the small glass-fronted cabinets that lined the walls of his office, rising partway up the cardinal-red walls.

"Well?" she asked Junius, who had come to have a look at the work in progress. "What do you think, Mr. Inspector of Public Works?"

"'Bull,' as I hear your long-suffering Miss Thurston calls you, you are irreplaceable!"

She laughed, delighted. "Already?"

"In Princeton, anyway."

"You can't imagine how much I miss all of you. I went out there to give Aunt Lottie a kiss the moment I had a chance!"

"And you've wrapped her around your little finger. She cites you all day long as an example of how things should be done."

Belle tucked her arm through his.

"And what about you, Junius?" she asked, coyly. "Do you miss me, just a little?"

"I am forever chasing your memory, praying all the while that my uncle doesn't become too deeply ensnared in your net."

The young apprentice's transformation into the grande dame of the library had not escaped his attention. No more Peter Pan collars; her blouse was now adorned with fine Brussels lace, a delicate amethyst brooch at her throat and a bunch of violets on the breast of her jacket. The blending of the shades of lavender and gray was subtle, but of considered elegance. The hat, shoes, and gloves clearly came from the finest fashion houses.

She noticed the way his gaze traveled over her. It was a look at once surprised and admiring.

"Just because you've made me a librarian doesn't mean I have to dress like one!" she said, smiling.

\* \* \*

J.P. Morgan's return was no picnic, to put it mildly.

It was a tempest, a tornado, a tidal wave that upended everything in its path. Thursty went back to hiding in storage rooms. And Belle braved the storm.

As lavish in his praise as he was ferocious in his criticisms, the Big Chief made no effort to spare her nerves. She hadn't doubted for a moment that he would be impressed by the amount of work accomplished, appreciative of the immensity of their efforts. And he was. Yet he couldn't refrain from a few obnoxious remarks.

"These sphinxes on pedestals in *front* of the fireplace don't belong there. They look ridiculous! They should be *inside* it; they're andirons, after all!"

"All the same, you *cannot* subject sixteenth-century objects to fire!"

"Why on earth not?"

"Because, Mr. Morgan, it would be an act of murder."

"I have not given you permission to decide what I do in my own home! Put those andirons under the logs!"

She tried to explain. "These sculptures only became andirons recently. When they were originally made, they were ornaments on a tool-holder placed next to the fireplace. They were connected by bars, which some later owner removed. I believe putting these objects directly in the fire would seriously damage them."

The explosion that met this speech shook the rafters. A barrage of profanity that terrified everyone in the building. It surely spelled the end of Miss Greene, Miss Thurston, and even Junius, who had brought these two harpies into Morgan's temple.

Belle withstood the torrent without flinching.

In contrast to the standard reactions of those close to Morgan, who cowered in the face of his rages, or of his employees, who babbled excuses and fled, Belle did not budge. She simply waited, and then said coolly, when he'd subsided:

"I will obey you and put these two masterpieces in the fireplace. But I still think you're making a mistake. *Sir*."

She turned on her heel and left the room.

Trembling, she stormed back to her office. The surge of fury that gripped her now was at least as intense as the one she had just endured. How *could* the man be so arrogant—so crass? His stupidity was enough to make one weep!

It took her a few moments to grasp the likely consequences of her behavior. One did not contradict Mr. Morgan, and she would pay dearly for this show of resistance. So much for the wonders of the Morgan Library. If she wasn't fired within the hour, she certainly would be by the end of the month. In any case, the bliss of the past six months was over now. And the worst was yet to come.

The sudden knock on the door, and the sound of the tycoon's voice, made her start with terror. She paled as he entered the room and rose from her chair.

"Sit back down, Miss Greene," he said.

Taking the chair on the other side of her desk, he began:

"The ocean-crossing, and my travels in Egypt, have tired me greatly. And there are family problems here at home that aren't helping my state of mind. I'm sorry for the scene I caused just now."

"I'm the one who's sorry," Belle stammered, shocked. "I do apologize for what happened."

"During my absence, you've accomplished everything I could have dreamed of for this library. I'm grateful to you."

She smiled at him, touched.

"And now," he continued, "we must begin thinking about cataloguing the acquisitions I made in London this winter."

She jumped at this opportunity.

"Indeed, Mr. Morgan—I've noticed that, over the years,

you've bought many objects in Europe that the merchants never actually sent to you. I've written to them all about it, and some of them have replied to me. Others haven't. If you'll allow me, I shall exert a bit more pressure on those recalcitrant sellers."

Morgan raised an inquiring eyebrow.

"What exactly do you mean by that, Miss Greene?" he asked. "Are you planning to send a few Sicilian assassins to Paris?"

She chuckled.

"I have other ways to make the merchants give up the goods. But knocking them around a bit for good measure . . . why not?"

This exchange sealed their reconciliation. A new era had begun.

Belle had no idea just what an era it would be.

* * *

The previous April, her father, Richard T. Greener, had returned from Vladivostok.

Suspended from duty and recalled to the United States, he had come back to defend himself against the accusations that had cost him his post.

The current presidential administration was unhappy with his poor management of the commercial interests of his compatriots in Russia. It was even more highly displeased with his personal conduct, which had shocked his fellow American nationals.

His weakness for flamboyant clothing (he was fond of rose-colored shirts), his taste for vodka, his passion for poker. His frequenting of brothels. And his public cohabitation with a Japanese woman named Mishiyo Kawashima, who had borne him two sons and a daughter during the six years of their relationship . . . all exploits that were unbecoming to a representative of puritan America. And an African American diplomat, to boot.

His return began to be reported on in the newspapers.

In them, he expressed his indignance at the injustices he was suffering, making noisy efforts to redeem his reputation. His detractors' complaints were based solely on racism, he insisted. He had carried out his mission faultlessly, and, during the two conflicts he had experienced while posted to Vladivostok, the Boxer Rebellion and the Russo-Japanese War, he had conducted himself with so much honor and bravery that the Chinese government had conferred the Order of the Double Dragon on him.

Arriving at the port of San Francisco on the morning of Wednesday, April 18, 1906, the very day of the great earthquake, he had lost everything—including the trunks containing his documents, books, and personal effects.

Now, in this month of July, he had reached the East Coast and settled in Washington, where he had once lived with his family, and was anticipating a meeting with President Theodore Roosevelt.

Richard Greener's presence in North America—and, what was more, so close to New York—posed a terrible threat to his wife Genevieve and their five children, all of whom dreaded his appearance at their 507 West 112th Street apartment. Belle more than anyone.

The prominence of her job with the famous J.P. Morgan meant that she, like Greener, had begun to arouse the curiosity of journalists. Indeed, this burgeoning interest in her extended to even the highest circles, where there were murmurs that Miss da Costa Greene's spectacular ascent to the head of the Morgan Library could only be due to family connections.

Who could this mysterious young woman be, if not the magnate's illegitimate daughter?

\*

However, J.P. Morgan already had plenty of children: three

daughters and one son, whose lives and movements he directed like an orchestra conductor.

His son, Jack Morgan, aged thirty-nine, was married with children and lived in London, where he headed up the English branch of the bank. Unlike his father, he had a happy family life and a reasonable nature—and he was no collector. Instinctively, Jack felt closer to his mother.

The girls, on the other hand, adored their father unconditionally—particularly the eldest, Louisa, his favorite. She had married a banker six years previously, and fortunately for everyone, Morgan got along well with his son-in-law. It was for this young couple that he had built the mansion next to the library.

Neither was there any friction with Juliet, Morgan's middle daughter, who had also married a banker.

The youngest girl, Anne, on the other hand, was a source of anxiety for her father. It was she, in fact, who was the "family problem" Morgan had mentioned to Belle.

After spending years serving as her father's chaperone on his peregrinations with Adelaide Douglas, his mistress—and with Adelaide's predecessor, Edith Randolph—Anne had recently informed her father that she refused to continue playing this role. She had even stayed in Paris without him, and then in London with two of her friends, a pair of young women who were from wealthy and respectable families but whom, it was whispered, were disciples of Sappho.

An openly homosexual Morgan daughter? The ultimate shame.

Yes, Morgan himself had a mistress, and so what? He *almost* never had more than one at a time, and the relationships were based on affection. And they were always with women from the upper reaches of society. Not actresses, or courtesans, or even young bits of fluff, but mature women, married or widowed, who shared Morgan's learning, his intellectual curiosity, and his aesthetic tastes. True traveling companions.

Moreover, he was always careful not to expose his wife to scandal or public humiliation.

Yes, he had taken Adelaide Douglas to Paris, and all over the world for nearly ten years, but she did not officially share his bedroom, or even the same hotel; while he stayed at the Bristol, he had reserved an entire floor for her at the Vendôme, duly keeping up appearances.

And yet, there was no lack of desire on his part to be rid of the peevish Mrs. Morgan. It wasn't that he blamed her for anything—except, perhaps, her fractious temper, their incompatible natures, and the crushing boredom of her company. They lived separately for ten months of the year, and he frequently sent her, despite her recalcitrance, to various European spas for treatment of her depression. He generally kept her as far away from himself as possible, and treated her with merely the outward appearance of respect.

But he would never saddle her with the shame of a divorce, or the social disgrace that would result from it. In the uppermost echelons of New York society, a divorcée, even through no fault of her own, would no longer be received by the city's hostesses. He would not inflict this living death on her. Mrs. Morgan she was, and Mrs. Morgan she would remain. On this point he was firm, and he made no secret of it. He had even fired a bank employee who had been surprised in adulterous *flagrante delicto*. When the young man had tried to defend himself by arguing that everyone did the same thing behind closed doors, Morgan had retorted that doors were made for precisely that reason.

Though he could seem hard, he was a deeply emotional man who was distressed by the misfortune of others, particularly the weakest members of society. His donations to charitable organizations numbered in the millions of dollars. He sympathized with the sufferings of women and was greatly interested in scientific research into female diseases and methods of contraception. He had even founded a hospital for unmarried mothers, where they could give birth safely, and with dignity. His political enemies, Southern conservatives who criticized the enormous J.P. Morgan trusts, had turned this act of benevolence into a joke, snickering that it took a whole hospital for the dozens of whores he'd impregnated to give birth to his bastards.

His sentimental nature, though, was known only to those closest to him. He felt, himself, that his private life was no one's business, and he required his friends to honor this code of silence—those true friends whose loyalty and discretion had lasted nearly a quarter of a century. These included his personal physician, James Markoe, an obstetrician who had made him aware of the deplorable conditions under which women who were struggling financially were forced to give birth; his old friend Charles D. Lanier, one of the most powerful bankers in New York; and William Laffan, owner of the *New York Sun*, a trustee of the Metropolitan Museum, and a great connoisseur of Oriental art. It was Laffan who had taken him to Egypt and convinced him to create a department dedicated to Egyptian art at New York's largest museum.

For years, Dr. Markoe's home had been the place where J.P. Morgan spent time with his close friends, going directly there in the evenings from his Wall Street office. After an informal medical consultation in the ground-floor clinic, Morgan and Markoe would go upstairs, where the rest of the group was waiting for them. There, Morgan would also find his mistress Adelaide, who was a dear friend of Mrs. Annette Markoe—with whom the tycoon had also once been in love. During dinner, Morgan would amuse the assembly with anecdotes about his encounters with the "cold fish" of high finance, skewering the pretentious and the puritanical alike with his wit. His hostess, Annette Markoe, would engage him, as the party indulged in liqueurs and cigars after dinner, in a competition to see whose knowledge of Bible verses was greater, as both of them were devoted readers of that text. Bets were made. The gaiety of these evenings had persisted during their travels, as they all journeyed through Europe together.

These days, J.P. Morgan had no further need to crisscross the world, or even New York, to spend time with his close friends. Now, he received them in his library, which had become his headquarters, where he invited not only the crème de la crème of society but the rank and file as well. The lettered came to admire his collections, the fashionable to take tea, and it was Belle's responsibility to receive them and to do the honors of the place. In they all streamed, in a constant parade that enabled her to rub elbows with members of the different worlds to which Morgan belonged. In this way she became known to his powerful associates, industrialists such as John D. Rockefeller and Henry C. Frick, newspaper owners, museum curators.

Morgan himself might show up at any time of the day or night and, whether he was alone or in company, he expected his librarian to stand to attention. To be by his side. He could no longer manage without her, he claimed. It was an exaggeration, but exaggeration was a character trait she understood.

Librarian, yes. And also hostess, secretary, factotum, reader, advisor, and confidante.

During the six months of the year he spent in the United States—normally the summer and autumn; he traveled in Europe the rest of the year—he expected Miss Greene to be wholly at his disposal. It was out of the question for her to do anything other than cater to his every need. And yet there was plenty of work to do at the library. Books continued to arrive from his London residence by the crate, hundreds of books, which Belle had to quickly inventory, catalogue, and arrange, which involved a complete reorganization of the East Room shelves. But he always summoned her to his side the moment he arrived and closeted himself with her in his office, so that she could sum up the content of that day's newspapers for him. He would listen to her read the stock reports while he played a round of solitaire, his preferred way to relax. It was a game that allowed him to concentrate and reflect, and he could spend hours at it, spreading the cards out on his desk, giving himself up to contemplating them, counting them, and shuffling them—all the while meditating on high finance, his collections, his library, his family and friends, his mistress, and his other conquests. On all the "Blondes," as Belle disdainfully referred to them, who were in constant, relentless pursuit of him. For, despite his age and his disfigured nose, J.P. Morgan was attractive. And he loved to attract.

He was perfectly conscious, of course, that power—his political and financial omnipotence—had something to do with his strength of seduction. But wasn't power the very essence of his personality?

Belle herself was no exception to this fascination with authority.

Every day, she allowed herself to be seduced by the Big Chief's intelligence, his aura, and the extraordinary confidence he displayed in her. He interrupted her endlessly, distracted her, drove her up the wall—but he never bored her. She enjoyed his company, and knew how to listen to him like no one else.

He confided in Belle his regrets, his weaknesses. He spoke to her unguardedly about his relationship with Adelaide Douglas. On Morgan's orders, Belle sent theater tickets to Adelaide for plays he thought she would enjoy, had flowers delivered to her—especially white violets, her favorites—and paid for the jewelry he had ordered from Cartier. And it fell to Belle to take delivery of the larger gifts for Adelaide, such as the red Morocco box once owned by Marie Antoinette.

On a sentimental whim, he systematically purchased everything that might have belonged to the notable Adelaides of history. These included a missal of 1739 with prayers handwritten by Madame Adélaïde, favorite daughter of King Louis XV, as well as one of her magnificently bound books of hours, and two dozen letters written in 1870 by Mary Adelaide, Duchess of Teck, a first cousin of Queen Victoria.

It was to Miss Belle Greene that merchants all over the world sent their invoices, she who was responsible for paying them. Morgan had given her carte blanche to withdraw exorbitant sums from the account he had opened specifically for this purpose.

He told her his most intimate secrets, which he did with no one else.

"I don't understand her attitude toward me," he lamented, speaking of his youngest child. "Anne has always done what she wanted. When she refused to marry the Marquis de Castellane, who I thought was an excellent match for her, I gave in! Between you and me, I've never imposed my will on anyone!"

A smile tugged at the corners of Belle's mouth, but she refrained from any comment.

"You know that, don't you, Miss Greene?" he continued. "I leave people completely free. Free to have their own opinions and tastes, to make their own choices. Particularly women, for whom I have the greatest respect. So why does my own daughter treat me so coldly?"

He affected not to understand anything. There was never any allusion to Anne's homosexuality, the true reason for their estrangement, or to the fact that he was the one who had broken off communication with his daughter. Only one thing was certain: he was suffering from it. And that suffering moved Belle. There was something innocent about him, an almost childlike sincerity, that she found appealing. Beneath the vital force of the man, she sensed a boundless loneliness. Royal and vulnerable. All-powerful and yet not untouched by pain.

He had talked to her about the death of his first wife, which had shattered him. They had been married just four months when she died of tuberculosis; he had been unable, despite all his efforts, to save the love of his life. He had never fully recovered from that failure.

Belle, for her part, was careful not to share even the smallest confidence. She pretended to reveal a teenage infatuation with one of her Latin professors, but never confided any true secrets. She sometimes mentioned her mother, the loving widow she adored, and her tall, blond-haired brother and sisters—who, she said, took after the Dutch van Vliet side of the family. She spun tales for him about her ancestor, the redoubtable Marquise da Costa, from whom she had inherited her dark skin and hair—all Portuguese traits, which she loathed. For the rest, she remained silent.

*

In this month of February 1907, on the day before his next trip to Europe, J.P. Morgan experienced one of his frequent depressive episodes. It was a true anxiety attack, which only Dr. Markoe was normally able to soothe. Today, though, it was his librarian to whom he turned for reassurance—as well as subjecting her to the standard barrage of instructions.

"Don't forget, Miss Greene, to send a very large bouquet of pink peonies from Thorley's to Mrs. Annette Markoe on Easter Sunday; she adores them. And add four bouquets of white orchids for her birthday. And remember the case of 1899 Château Lafite Rothschild for William Laffan."

"Of course I will, Mr. Morgan; you've already reminded me a hundred times. Don't worry about a thing."

"I'm counting on you to act as my representative here! You're my brain now."

"Your thoughts become flesh and blood. You can count on me."

* * *

*Evviva la libertà!*

At last, she could breathe.

Six months of intense work with Thursty by day; six months of diversion at night, in the company of her latest admirers: William Laffan, the scholarly publisher of the *New York Sun* and a specialist in Chinese porcelain, and the banker and Morgan associate Charles Lanier. Both gentlemen of a certain age—sixty and seventy years old, respectively—and both married men who declared themselves madly in love with this young woman in her twenties.

Flirtation, bon mots, pirouettes, laughter. Theaters, restaurants. She went out with Laffan and Lanier every night, allowing them to woo her, smiling at their old-fashioned compliments and courtly advances. She had no expectations concerning them. No concrete ones, at least. No material interest. Simply the joy of exploring the rich and vibrant life of New York City.

For her, the intoxication of knowing herself to be enchanting; for them, the pleasure of being enchanted. Each of them gained in self-confidence; each of them benefited.

She knew that these sophisticated men were teaching her the art of how to behave among the upper classes. She was a skilled bluffer, able to affect the poise of a *grande dame*, but in truth her understanding of social conventions was still limited. She knew nothing about wine or hunting or golf, and Laffan and Lanier introduced her to these pleasures and many others: the best tables in Manhattan's restaurants; the finest vintages; opening nights at the Metropolitan Opera. On February 11, 1907, she was their guest, in Charles Lanier's private box, at the Met's premiere of *Madame Butterfly*, in the presence of Puccini himself. After the performance, she dined with Enrico Caruso and Geraldine Farrar, the two brightest stars in the musical world. She had never had so much fun in her life.

Belle had been careful to impose three rules, though. One: she would never be alone with one of her admirers; her time spent with them must always be in the company of others—

preferably with their wives, in order to "reassure" those ladies. Two: she would never accept even the smallest gift from either of them. Neither gowns nor jewelry. A bouquet of flowers from time to time, at the very most. And they were not allowed to take physical liberties with her, ever. That was rule three. They were not even permitted to brush their lips across her fingers, gloved or not: "Since when, Mr. Lanier, has it been acceptable for a man to kiss the hand of a young unmarried woman?" She commanded respect, and they knew it. What was more, she "belonged" to Morgan. Exclusively. Her loyalty to him was manifestly clear in even the smallest details of her conduct—as indeed it was in that of her admirers' behavior toward her.

Despite Miss Greene's gravity, however, she still used the same blunt speech, the same slang, the same witticisms that she always had, and that both shocked and delighted her suitors. Neither did her virtue keep her from darting knowing glances at them from behind her fan, or going into coquettish raptures over their depth of learning. She remained the queen of flirtation, and her magnetism was irresistible. She questioned Laffan endlessly about Chinese art and Egyptian archaeology, Lanier about the intricacies of high finance. And their answers always thrilled her.

"It was J.P. who saved the United States Treasury from bankruptcy, did you know that?" Lanier remarked once.

"God! When was that? I'll bet I wasn't even born yet!"

He laughed. "It was twelve years ago, actually, Miss Greene. Morgan found the legal loophole that allowed President Cleveland to start issuing Treasury Bonds without the approval of Congress."

"And the Treasury was saved?"

"Yes. Thanks to him, the government was able to replenish its gold reserves. He's a great man, your protector. Willing to do anything to save America, even risk his own fortune."

Never had the two old gentlemen felt more interesting, more

dashing, more witty. Never had they met such a vibrant young person. She could have brought the dead back to life.

When J.P. Morgan returned from Europe in August, he found his circle of friends utterly conquered. In Belle da Costa Greene, they raved, he had come to possess a true gem. A miracle of intelligence and charm.

Their wives and daughters took a more nuanced attitude toward Belle.

Just where had this *miracle*, as the men called her, come from? From what background? What universe?

\*

"They're both such marvelous fellows, Ethel!" Belle exclaimed, flopping onto the bed she shared with her sister.

Ethel, younger by a year, fought off her sleepiness, eager to hear the story of Belle's adventures. Desperate not to miss out on a crumb, to hear it all first. But Belle never told her anything until she'd written a letter to her dearest friend first, her soulmate, Arthur Upson. He had to be the very first to know about her madcap nights, the people she met. She talked to him endlessly about J.P. Morgan and his liegemen, Laffan and Lanier.

"You're in love with Mr. Lanier?" Ethel goggled, propping herself against the pillow.

"Lanier's an old man! He's seventy! You can admire people without being in love with them."

"Morgan's seventy years old, too. And from what I can tell, *that* old man's had you all in a flutter since he got back!"

"Oh, the Big Chief, well, that's a whole different kettle of fish."

"Even with that nose of his?"

"I don't give a damn about his nose!"

"What if he tried something with you?"

"Let's hope he doesn't," Belle laughed. "When it comes to him, I make no promises."

Though her brother still disapproved of the modest wage she was accepting from Morgan, Belle's mother and sisters supported her enthusiastically, even adjusting their lives to fit the hectic rhythm of her social life and her feverish comings and goings.

More than ever, it was to Genevieve's creativity, her talent as a seamstress, that Belle owed the elegance that pleased Morgan and his friends so much, the instinctive chic that J.P., so dapper himself, appreciated in its every detail. Yet the salary of a librarian, as Russell kept insisting, would never have enabled Belle to buy the kind of wardrobe necessary for theater trips with Laffan and Lanier, or evenings at Delmonico's, the most fashionable restaurant in the city. And so Louise, Ethel, and Teddy spent whole nights leafing through fashion magazines, copying for her the styles featured in *Vogue* and *McCall's*.

Belle's success reassured them all that they had made the right choice in cutting themselves off from their past, breaking the vicious circle of segregation that clipped the wings of so many in the Black community. It soothed the pain of severing ties with their beloved family in Georgetown, and the anxiety provoked by Richard Greener's return to Washington. The sacrifice had not been made in vain. The gain had outweighed the cost. God only knew how far Belle might rise. Even Russell, with his endless grumbling about her passion for Morgan, was proud of her victories. Yes—God only knew how far she might rise! The idea was present in their every waking thought.

Belle's ascension was, in truth, the triumph of the family business. Genevieve and her children were all working to make the firm of Greene & Company a success—and its muse into a star.

\*

Every day from morning till night, the living room of the small apartment on 112th Street resonated with the echo of the parties, dramas, and intrigues that filled the white palace on 36th. But now, in this month of October 1907, the Greene household was no longer the only one paying attention to what was happening in Belle's temple. The rumors swirling around J.P. Morgan had reached a fever pitch, and the whole city seemed to be converging on the gates of his library. The very future of the country was being decided there behind those great bronze doors.

For several days now, Wall Street had been enveloped in a devastating panic that had already resulted in a series of bankruptcies and suicides. Banks and large financial trusts were collapsing. From east to west, the stock market crash was engulfing the nation in despair. Bankers, stockbrokers, industrialists, and government agents made a beeline for the Morgan Library. They had come to beg the man who had saved them from bankruptcy in 1895 to find a way to rescue America again, mingling in anxious crowds with the journalists swarming around the building. The carriages and automobiles of company presidents clogged every street in the vicinity. A continuous stream of bowler-hatted men in dark suits streamed up and down the stairs at a run. If J.P. Morgan didn't find a way to avert disaster, and fast, the crash would ruin millions of small investors.

The Greene family among them.

"I can't explain what's going on. I don't know, myself," said Belle, exhausted, when she came home to wash, change her clothes, and sleep for a couple of hours between two o'clock and five o'clock in the morning. "All I can tell you is that we're headed for catastrophe at a gallop. All of high finance is crumbling to pieces. Mr. Morgan set up a commission tonight to audit the largest financial trusts. As far as I understand it, he wants to identify the ones that are clean and the ones that are rotten. Let the hopeless ones go and save the others by giving them an infusion of money. The problem is that the amount of money he would need to rescue the trusts that still look solid is in the hundreds of millions of dollars. And in America, we don't have a federal bank that can do that sort of thing, just Morgan."

"Belle, you have to eat something," put in Genevieve, who had waited up for her all night. "You look absolutely dreadful."

"No time."

"Of course not," Teddy teased her. "Not while Junius Morgan's spending his nights at the library, too!"

Belle didn't even register her sister's crack.

"Mr. Morgan's car is downstairs—his driver's waiting for me," she explained. "I have to take care of the practical details, greet the company presidents, figure out where to put everyone. I know them all now—Mr. Rockefeller, Mr. Frick, Mr. Astor, Mr. King. They're all rivals—they hate each other. And they're afraid. I can't put them in the same room. Mr. Morgan needs me. I have to go."

"I would imagine that even Mr. Morgan's taking five minutes to eat dinner," persisted Genevieve impatiently.

"He hasn't eaten in days. Just smokes cigar after cigar, and he hasn't slept. How is he still on his feet? I can't figure it out! At his age, too—he's incredible!"

"That's no reason for *you* to go without food or sleep."

Belle wouldn't listen to a word of it.

"The city of New York itself is going bankrupt," she said sharply. "The mayor's put out thirty million dollars' worth of bonds, but who can buy them?"

"Your darling Big Chief, of course," said Russell, ironically.

The term finally got a reaction out of Belle. Glaring at her brother, she stood very still for an instant:

"How do you know? Nobody knows that! He did it, yes. He

saved New York from bankruptcy. Quietly. And he replenished the stock market out of his own pocket, to three times the level it was before. But even his generosity only stopped the market losses for a few hours. It's uncontainable."

She walked out of the apartment through the icy fog of early morning, disappearing into the back of the car and not returning until the middle of the following night. Pale and drawn, she tried to sum up in a few sentences the news of the day, which the press was reporting only with extreme caution.

The government had instructed pastors and priests all over the country to reassure their flocks. President Roosevelt had even allowed himself the luxury of a hunting trip in Louisiana, in order to put on a good face and soothe investors. When a journalist had questioned him about the panic on Wall Street, Roosevelt had responded, showing off his trophies, "We got three bears, six deer, one wild turkey, twelve squirrels, one duck, one opossum, and one wildcat. We ate them all except the wildcat."

"So the situation isn't as tragic as you've been describing it," commented Teddy.

"Says you," retorted Belle, taking the skirt Louise handed her. "It's a fiasco."

She dressed and put up her hair in ten minutes, wolfed down a sandwich, gulped a glass of water, and bit into an apple, talking all the while. Her agitation was so great, she could speak of nothing else.

" . . . one of the groups the Big Chief thought was most solid, the TCI—that's the Tennessee Coal, Iron and Railroad Company—collapsed this morning. Its shares dropped to a fifth of their former value. More rioting on Wall Street. The shareholders have stormed the Stock Exchange. And people are coming to blows in the banks, trying to get back their deposits. No one has any cash left. The only way to reassure the public and to stop the disaster would be for Mr. Morgan to buy up TCI's shares through his company, U.S. Steel."

"He can't," barked Russell. "He'd be violating the antitrust law if he did that. He'd have an absolute monopoly on steel, coal, railroads. He'd have the whole American economy in his hands. Roosevelt's been fighting trusts for years; he'll never let Morgan do it. I know your boss thinks nothing's off-limits to him, but . . ."

"But it would put a stop to the general panic! I don't have time for your nonsense, Russell. I'll see you tonight."

This time it wasn't a whirlwind of pleasure drawing her from the family home. It was the weight of History.

\*

Two weeks at an unsustainable pace. Each battle won leading to a new crack in the economy, a new hemorrhage, a new panic.

The marbles and frescoes of the Morgan Library, now transformed into a quasi-military headquarters, served as the backdrop for ever-tenser discussions of the chaos into which America was sinking. Tonight would be the last chance to come up with a solution. Enough to-ing and fro-ing, enough opinions and counter-arguments. Today, Sunday, November 3, 1907, the world of high finance would have to reach an agreement. The time for rivalry among the presidents of the various trusts was past; the survival of the country depended on the forgetting of personal interests. It fell to each company to put aside its own politics and policies for the sake of the nation.

J.P. Morgan had summoned the fifty most powerful businessmen in the United States to one final meeting in his library. Once there, he had separated them *manu militari* into two groups. On one side, Banking. Twenty-five presidents put in the reading room, among the ten thousand books that lined the walls and galleries of the East Room. On the other side, the Trusts. Twenty-five presidents in the West Room, Morgan's office.

He had given all of these fifty magnates the same order: "Do what you must, gentlemen, to save the national economy. Find a way to raise funds equivalent to twenty-five million dollars. I will see about rescuing the TCI. For the moment, the consortium does not wish to sell at the price I'm offering, and my advisors don't want me to buy at the price they're asking. On this point, too, we must reach a decision in an hour, or two, or ten—but it must be tonight. If we can successfully make an acquisition today that will save the consortium, we will still need to convince the government of the absolute necessity of this measure. My men and I are working on this project in the North Room, my librarian's office, at the far end of the vestibule. If you need me, speak to her. Miss Greene represents me. She will bring me your messages with your solutions. It's nine-thirty P.M. It's up to you, gentlemen; it's up to us all, to act so that tomorrow will be a new day."

Then Morgan closed the doors of the two rooms, one after the other, and, cigar firmly planted in his mouth, calmly crossed the rotunda toward the room where Junius, Lanier, the presidents of his own trust, and his attorney were combing through the accounts of the Tennessee Coal, Iron and Railroad Company. Belle, who was waiting for him in the doorway of the North Room, saw him stop, hesitate, and turn around. Walk heavily toward the rotunda entrance. Rummage in his pocket. Pull out a set of keys. And lock the three bolts on the front door.

He had locked the most powerful men in finance into his library—the kings of the railroads, the kings of steel, of oil, and of coal. Belle couldn't hold back an exclamation of surprise.

"Are you planning to hold them prisoner for long?"

"None of them is leaving here until we've solved the problem," he growled. "Not one. Not before everyone comes to an agreement. Have some coffee brought in to them, will you? It's going to be a long night."

"The TCI consortium has just accepted my purchase terms," exulted Morgan, when Belle returned from a trip to the West Room. "How are they doing in my office?"

"They haven't gotten anywhere. Same in the reading room. They're all so nervous that none of them can sit down, or stay on their feet, and they're all talking at the same time."

In contrast, Belle's office, the North Room, where J.P. Morgan had set up camp with his men, seemed like an oasis of tranquility. Junius and Lanier sat reading silently from a stack of files on a pedestal table, while Morgan's attorney was busily writing notes. The only signs of tension came from the two presidents of U.S. Steel, Morgan's own corporation, who had just hung up the telephone after a conversation with the White House. Now both of them hurriedly shrugged into their coats.

"Mr. Frick and Mr. Gary are on their way to the station to catch the midnight train to Washington," Morgan said, shuffling cards for another game of solitaire.

The mantelpiece clock chimed eleven times. Sweeping Belle's files off the desk with the back of his hand, Morgan dealt the cards.

"They're on a mission to wake up the President and convince him to let me buy the TCI," he continued. "Roosevelt will have to give his consent immediately. Before the stock market opens tomorrow morning. If he doesn't, it's all over. The Secretary of the Treasury is with us. But Roosevelt? To violate the laws he based his campaign on, to make a liar out of himself . . ."

"What happens if the president refuses?" asked Belle, remembering what Russell had said about the antitrust laws.

Morgan shrugged his shoulders helplessly. He drew a card and put the ten of clubs on top of a jack of hearts.

"If President Roosevelt refuses, he'll be killing America. Get

Mr. Frick and Mr. Gary on their way. Here are the keys. Be discreet, Miss Greene. Don't let anyone see them leaving."

"What should I do about the others? Mr. King and his colleagues tried to break the doors down when they found out you'd locked them in here. They're furious. I calmed them down with liqueur and cigars, but that can only help so much."

"They can come and find me when they've reached the twenty-five-million-dollar solution. In the meantime, send out for petits fours from the Waldorf Hotel."

"Already done."

"Good. Now we just have to hope they'll make a decision before breakfast. Go back in twenty minutes and see where they are."

He turned back to his game of solitaire.

She watched him turning over the cards, wondering how he was able to concentrate on the game at a time like this. He didn't even look up when she bustled in and out of the room, breaking off only to leaf thoughtfully through his latest acquisition, a set of volumes of Lincoln's correspondence, which sat at his elbow atop a stack of Belle's papers.

And yet, she had not exaggerated when she'd told her family how he bore the full weight of the crisis on his shoulders. He had hardly taken a moment to breathe, and no more than a couple of hours to lie down and rest. The result of this was that he'd awakened drawn and hoarse the previous morning, and Dr. Markoe had had to be urgently summoned to dose him with honey and cordials.

*And now here he is, playing cards!* she thought, caught between exhaustion and amazement.

She took a deep breath and ventured: "Why . . . don't you just tell them what to do?"

"Because I don't know."

"Give them the solution yourself. Without you, they'll never find it!"

"I don't know the solution, Miss Greene. When one is presented to me, I'll be able to judge whether it will work or not."

She made several more trips from one room to the other, the men shouting, smoking, arguing. And the later the hour grew, the less she believed an agreement was possible.

It was past four o'clock in the morning.

Returning to her office empty-handed for the umpteenth time, she found Morgan on his feet, cigar still clamped between his teeth, dictating a text to his attorney through a cloud of smoke:

"Since they're not capable of coming to a decision on their own, we're going to have to force them," he said. "Follow me."

He strode to the West Room and flung the door open. The room fell silent. The few presidents of trusts who were sitting down shot to their feet.

Morgan gestured to his lawyer to read the statement they had drafted. A mere few lines, stipulating that each of the owners of the trusts there present agreed to take out a joint loan of twenty-five million dollars, intended to protect the weakest trusts.

Morgan put the contract on the table and, pointing at it, said simply:

"Sign here, gentlemen."

No one moved. Morgan waited, scrutinizing each face in turn. No reaction. Nothing. Cutting through the group, he headed for the back of the room, striding so forcefully that the chandelier trembled. Toward the fireplace, where the most senior member of the assembly stood. Edward King. King cut an imposing figure, of a height and gravity to rival Morgan's, his snow-white sideburns giving him the appearance of an English aristocrat. His position as head of the New York Stock Exchange, and his election to the leadership of the Union Trust Company of New York, placed him squarely above the rest of the throng crowding the room.

Morgan took him by the sleeve and steered him unceremoniously toward the table.

"This is the place, King, and here's the pen," he said, holding out his Waterman.

King hesitated. Took the pen. Signed. On cue, the rest of the magnates filed to the table and followed suit.

At 4:45 on the morning of Monday, November 4, 1907, the bronze doors of the Morgan Library opened, setting J.P. Morgan's hostages free.

Two hours later, his associates Henry C. Frick and Elbert H. Gary had breakfast with President Roosevelt at the White House.

At nine o'clock, despite the protests of some of his advisors, Roosevelt gave his permission for the purchase of the TCI.

At ten o'clock, the stock market, notified of the president's agreement, announced that stock prices were rising. It confirmed its partial recovery when it closed at three o'clock that afternoon. The trend continued the next day, and for the rest of the week.

At eleven o'clock in the morning on the following Sunday, a jubilant crowd gathered beneath the windows of the Morgan Library, shouting: "Hurray for the old man!"

The economy had been preserved.

Lord Rothschild, in an open letter to the press from London, praised Morgan's selfless act: "Until now, everyone knew him as a great financier and a man of rare intelligence. His conduct in recent days has aroused the respect and admiration of all."

The triumph, though, was fleeting.

Only a few years later, J.P. Morgan would be put under investigation. Accused of having misled President Roosevelt and taken advantage of the crisis to merge U.S. Steel and the TCI. Suspected, even, of having created the banking panic of 1907 out of whole cloth for his own personal enrichment. He would be forced to defend himself in front of a Congressional tribunal, and to prove that these allegations were untrue.

A detail that his detractors were careful not to reveal, however, and one that Belle was among the very few to know—and reminded people of whenever she had the opportunity—was that J.P. Morgan's American companies had lost twenty-one million dollars in the venture.

For now, resting against the leather cushions in the back seat of the car driving her home, she gazed out the window at the New York skyline, the ghostly silhouettes of buildings flashing past. Lines, cubes, arrows. The thousand tiny windows, lighting up one by one. And above them, far overhead, billows of white smoke rising and dissipating in the dawn light. All around her, the first delivery wagons parking in front of the shops. The horses whinnying amid the tinkling of doorbells, the backfiring of automobiles, the metallic clang of the streetcars.

Closing her eyes, she slept.

\* \* \*

"Miss Greene, how would you like to spend a few days with us at Constitution Hill?" Junius suggested early the next summer.

The tension of the financial crisis, all the nights spent together at the Morgan Library, had brought the two of them close enough that the social gap between them no longer mattered—but had not led, for all that, to the liaison Belle had once dreamed of. She had long ceased to cherish any illusions on the subject. Junius's heart lay elsewhere. *Where*, exactly, remained a mystery. And so she had transformed her infatuation into friendship, and the path of camaraderie was one he followed her down happily.

"Our friend Arthur Upson will be gracing us with a visit in late August. Will you join us?"

Absolute happiness: Junius, Upson, and Princeton, back together again. The trio of her dreams!

There were no more comings and goings on the train. J.P. Morgan had given Belle the use of one of his Pierce-Arrows when he departed for Europe in February—and of his box at the Metropolitan Opera, too, on those nights when his wife and daughters were not in the city.

Belle saw little of the Big Chief's family. While she adored being wooed and flattered by his friends, she found the women in his circle excruciatingly dull. They, for their part, kept their distance from this petite librarian who had made herself a little too indispensable.

He had also left Belle with free rein over his checkbook, so that she could settle the expenses she incurred representing him. On this point she always exercised restraint, and was careful never to abuse the privilege—all the more so because Morgan had given her a generous Christmas bonus and showered her with gifts, including a diamond-encrusted cigarette case.

Her salary, now quite comfortable, had even enabled the Greene family to move, in the spring of 1908, to a new apartment at 403 West 115th Street. The place had a pretty view of Morningside Park and its own telephone number, 4893 Morningside. It also boasted the particular advantage of being divided into two parts, with two separate entrances: on one side, the five rooms inhabited by Genevieve and her children; on the other, a miniscule studio that Belle claimed for herself. This arrangement allowed her to continue presenting herself as a young woman from a good family who still lived with her mother.

*"My dear Upson and darling soulmate,"* she wrote to him one day in early August, as she had done every week for four years.

Despite the distance between them, their friendship had deepened until it became one long, ongoing conversation. Writing allowed them to be much freer in their language than they had been when they were together at Princeton. Their letters were filled with cheeky thoughts that made each other laugh, with all the sarcasm they would never have been able to express aloud. With time, they had even come to share their most private moods and feelings with one another.

"*I'm scribbling this note to you from my bed, while I wait for my breakfast to be brought to the exquisite room Mrs. Junius has assigned to me. Josie Dear really is much nicer than all the other 'Morganettes,' you know. A bit dull, maybe, like the rest of them, but kind. What joy, Upson, to get back in touch with my youth, and my dear Princeton! Today we're all going out in the car to have a picnic with the McAlpins—they don't interest me much, but they're great friends with Junius and his wife.*

*Last Saturday, Mr. Woodrow Wilson, the president of the university, gave a big reception at his house, and Junius got me invited. I'd met President Wilson a few times at the Chancellor Green, and recently at the Morgan Library. He came to talk to me one-on-one after dinner. I tried to make him tell me the title of his next book, which everyone here is talking about. He said he would tell me the secret, on the condition that I grant him a favor. I laughed—and accepted, of course! He wants copies of some manuscripts I have at the Morgan. An edition of Milton's* Paradise Lost, *in particular, and one of Goethe's* Faust. *I must say, the request surprised me, but I promised him I would see to it. He was quite thrilled by the idea of having wrapped me round his little finger!*

*You can't imagine, Upson, how impatient I am for your arrival! Who could have imagined four years ago, when you were working so hard to turn me into a person capable of facing anything—tennis and golf and billiards and riding, remember?—when you wanted to transform me into an accomplished young lady polished enough to please even the Morgans—who could have imagined, then, that we'd both find ourselves here this summer! How I've missed you! Our separation has seemed endless. Thank you for your three letters in June, which I received all at once, with your latest poems. You might say they aren't much good, but your collection* The Tides of Spring *is, in my opinion, worthy of Keats's most beautiful poetry. Come, come, come quickly so that we can discuss it! What on earth are you doing in Minnesota? You said you were taking a vacation there before coming to Princeton— what silliness! Get yourself here immediately!"*

There was a knock at the door. The chambermaid set down a tray laden with porcelain, silver, and a bouquet of tea roses in a crystal vase. Belle closed her eyes and sighed with pleasure. "How marvelous luxury is!" There was a note propped between the teapot and the cup, asking her to come downstairs as soon as she was dressed. Another splendid day in store!

Entering the library, she sensed immediately that something was wrong. Junius was there alone, and greeted her with a somber "good morning" without even inviting her to sit down.

"Mr. Upson will not be coming," he said flatly. "He has drowned in a lake."

Belle stood stock-still. Unaware of the effect his words were having, Junius went on:

"That boy was so talented. What a terrible tragedy this is."

She gripped the back of a chair, her lips white. She didn't cry. She made no sound at all. Eventually, Junius noticed how stricken she was. He hurried to her side, helping her to sit down, stammering apologies.

"I should have been more careful about how I told you. Forgive me. I know you helped him catalogue my books, but—"

"What happened?" she murmured, faintly.

"I received a telegram from the bookseller he worked for. Upson had just finished the play he was writing. He went rowing in the evening on Lake Bemidji, north of Minneapolis. His rowboat turned over. They found his body two days later."

"He killed himself."

"No! What makes you say that?"

"Mr. Upson was a superb sportsman. He could row perfectly."

"Belle, it was an accident!"

"He hid his suffering. But the truth is that he was tormented by illness."

An uncontrollable wail rose in her chest. The tears gushed. Belle couldn't contain the agony, couldn't hide it.

"His work—his poems—everything!—it all showed how hopeless he felt," she sobbed. "I didn't understand—I didn't see it coming!"

Bent double, she dissolved in tears, weeping silently, unable to compose herself, unable to stop.

Junius, surprised and uncomfortable, could come up with no soothing gesture except to extend his handkerchief. She didn't see it.

Belle's devastation shocked him profoundly. He had never imagined that she could be overcome by emotion. Not so violently, at least. She, who was always so detached. Always kept things light. Always behaved with such assurance, such panache.

He had never thought of her having a life outside of books. That was the only passion she ever expressed: *books*. No doubt there were many other truths she kept to herself. Deep down, he realized, he didn't know her at all. He knew nothing about her. He hadn't even been aware of the bond she shared with this boy Upson.

Bleakly, he watched her sob. He didn't dare take her in his arms.

Years later, Belle would admit that Arthur Upson had taken with him a great deal of her faith in life, and her confidence in herself.

She wrote:

"From the day after his death, I found genuine attachments almost physically terrifying. All of the deep relationships I formed ended that way—with absence, or abandonment, or bereavement. As if some implacable force beyond me, that I could not fight, caused me to lose the people I loved overnight."

Absence? Her father. The Georgetown family. Arthur Upson. So many beloved ones, lost without even a farewell.

Certainly, she was surrounded by affection. But with her family, and with J.P. Morgan as well, she lived under constant pressure. Everyone expected her to lead them, to guide them, to bring them along. With them, she could never display the slightest weakness. Any pause, even the briefest one, would put them all—herself, her mother, her brother and sisters—in danger. It was her pugnacity alone that kept them safe from the vagaries of fate. One wrong move, and the whole house of cards would come tumbling down.

Where was the flaw, if not in her emotions? In a lack of self-control? In her excessive honesty with others?

After Upson's death, she swore never to bind herself to anyone too intimately. Never again would she let anyone, any man, become so necessary to her existence.

Never again.

* * *

After nearly three years with Belle as head of the Morgan Library, J.P.'s collection had been catalogued, organized, and, above all, harmonized.

And now?

Belle began to toy with the dream of transforming the library, *their* library, into an institution of such excellence, such importance, that the Morgan Library would be rivaled only by the British Museum in London and the Bibliothèque Nationale in Paris.

One day, perhaps . . .

When the Big Chief was abroad, and not taking up every moment of her time, Belle voraciously read catalogues from auction houses and exhibitions and art books all over the world. She took classes in Italian, French, and German so that she could correspond with foreign curators, scholars, experts, collectors, and booksellers.

She worked, too, at disciplining Morgan's purchasing habit, and tempering the eagerness of his agents. Her employer was no longer allowed to buy further copies of volumes he already possessed, or books that didn't interest him, or that were too expensive. She demanded that sellers comply with market prices.

It was impossible to propose anything at all to the tycoon now without the *imprimatur* of the chief curator of his library. Impossible to circumvent the approval—or the veto—of *B. da Costa Greene*. Merchants unable to conceive of the idea that they might be doing business with a woman protested frequently against the diktats of Mr. Greene, that terrible killjoy.

Belle's authority and intellectual power fascinated Junius Morgan. She never missed an opening night at the opera and went out every evening, yet arrived at the library at sunrise. She never stopped to rest. "You are *tireless!*" he would exclaim to her, with a mixture of admiration and dismay.

He was thinking, himself, of stepping away from business— both his own and his uncle's. He had loathed his position as a banker during the crisis and yearned to change his life. His attachment to his children was the only reason he continued to spend part of his time in New York. For the rest, his wife Josie Dear bored him almost as much as his Wall Street colleagues. His marriage was a disaster. He dreamed of nothing but leaving her and settling in Paris on his own.

But before he took this great leap, he had to plan his departure. And Belle could help him by becoming his successor.

There was a major sale scheduled to happen soon in London, in which the library of Lord Amherst, an extraordinary collection that included the first books ever printed in English, would be put on the market. Seventeen rare incunabula published by

William Caxton in the fifteenth century, which would attract bibliophiles from England, of course, but also from France and Germany, as well as Morgan's American competitors. The auction would be held at Sotheby, Wilkinson & Hodge in early December 1908. Why not send Miss Greene?

The time had come, Junius thought, for Belle to meet in person her many correspondents, to speak face to face with foreign booksellers and collectors, and to put her charm to work on them, to obtain the books she wanted.

This suggestion, murmured in his uncle's ear, weighed heavily on J.P.'s mind. Miss Greene, purchasing in his place? Miss Greene, purchasing in *Junius's* place? Miss Greene, standing in for them both? It would mean giving her control of the very essence of the Morgan Library: power over acquisitions.

The real difficulty lay not in convincing Uncle Pierpont of Miss Greene's ability to represent him in England—he had complete confidence in both her skill and her loyalty, he had seen her at work during the crisis. No, the problem would be persuading Morgan to accept her absence for nearly two months when he, himself, was in New York.

And how could a single woman be permitted to cross the ocean alone?

For this question, at least, Belle had a ready answer:

"That's no problem. I'll take my mother! Who better than she to serve as my chaperone?"

\*

And so, on a November morning in 1908, Mrs. Genevieve van Vliet da Costa Greene and her attractive daughter arrived at the New York docks, their trunks firmly secured to J.P. Morgan's car.

Hats tilted rakishly over one eye, smartly gloved, parasols and reticules looped over their wrists, they had prepared their traveling wardrobes with extreme care; it was a trousseau worthy of two newlywed brides. Genevieve's skill as a seamstress, along with an array of beautiful accessories, had worked wonders. Belle's mother was in fine form, a lovely and charming widow with a little retroussé nose and hair in a thick golden twist shot through with only a few strands of silver. Her traveling outfit, a stylish confection of wide black and white stripes, emphasized her girlish allure.

The "girlish" Mrs. Van Vliet da Costa Greene, however, was now sixty-two years old, though she claimed to be fifty. Belle herself was twenty-nine, but admitted only to twenty-five. And both mother and daughter had only just begun turning back the clock; Genevieve would remain fifty years old for another decade, while Belle would grow younger and younger until, eventually, she had subtracted fifteen years from her true age.

Now, as guests of Mr. J.P. Morgan, they boarded the *Oceanic*, the finest of the transatlantic steamers offered by the White Star Line, of which Morgan was the principal shareholder.

With its two thousand electric lights, its glass-domed library, and its dining room lined with windows overlooking the ocean, the *Oceanic* incarnated—even in the eyes of the most demanding passengers—the ultimate in comfort and refinement. The Greene ladies would travel first-class, in the most luxurious of all the suites—the rooms reserved for Morgan himself.

The crossing to Southampton took six days. It was an idyllic voyage, which they whiled away bathing in marble tubs, dining at the captain's table, and waltzing with a variety of elegant dancing partners.

But all of that was a mere trifle compared to their arrival at Claridge's, the hotel people called the "Buckingham Palace's annex" because all of Europe's crowned heads stayed there.

As the heels of their boots sank into the patterned carpet of the opulent lobby, Belle and Genevieve exchanged a glance of complicity and triumph.

No Black woman had ever walked through the glittering doors of Claridge's.

No Black woman had ever paced these lily- and rose-scented rooms.

Now, beneath the astonished gazes of the doormen and porters and grooms, of the staff who, bowing and scraping, bid them welcome, they shared a hysterical giggle that nothing could stifle. They laughed and laughed, unable to stop. *If all these people only knew!*

# Book II

## She Had Swallowed the Sun
### 1908–1910

CHAPTER 5

THE TRIUMPH OF THE CENTURY
1908–1909

Genevieve, who had based her imaginings of what their sojourn in London would be like on the genteel pleasures of the *Oceanic*, quickly became disillusioned.

Their first three days in England were utterly grueling. It was a schedule better suited to a government official than a librarian. The truth, thought Genevieve unhappily, was that Belle thought she could complete several months' worth of work in just a few days. She had organized her trip so methodically that, as usual, she hadn't left herself a moment to breathe. The pace would be impossible to sustain. She was already meeting with a series of strangers on the very evening of their arrival, receiving them one by one in the sumptuous restaurant at Claridge's Hotel. In a brief gap between meetings she leapt into a carriage to fetch a bill here, a package there, addressed to the Morgan Library but overlooked by Customs or the post. Genevieve, for her part, took away nothing from these marathons but the impression of a dark city blackened by soot and crammed with wagons and hansom cabs. Fewer automobiles than New York, fewer electric lights, fewer advertisements in windows and on the sides of buses—but in the end, swept up in the hectic whirlwind of her daughter's itinerary, she really saw nothing, experienced nothing at all.

By now, the "London bookmen," as Belle called her visitors at Claridge's, knew that the most powerful banker in America was represented by a woman, and an endless stream of booksellers, experts, dealers, and curators—each more solemn than the last, and all of a certain age—came to pay court to her.

The ritual played out identically at every encounter. Breathless from their latest errand, the Greene ladies appeared together in the doorway of the restaurant, pausing for an instant beneath the chandeliers, then strode toward the corner table, nestled amid gilded plasterwork and green plants, where their guest had already been seated. This was *their* table, which corresponded to their suite number. Petite and slender, a bit eccentric in their feather-adorned pillbox hats, they joined their guest for an informal conversation over breakfast, lunch, tea, dinner, or even a late-night supper.

Rising to introduce himself and greet the ladies, the gentleman invariably addressed himself to the more venerable of the two— *Madame mère*, of course. The female director of an establishment owned by Mr. Morgan could only be the wife or the widow of one Mr. B. Greene . . . and yet how bizarre, to picture a lady in charge of a library! A lady whom one had just met in a hotel! Yes, it was Claridge's, the best restaurant in London, and a spot none of them usually had the means to frequent, and then only for this sort of meeting with their millionaire clients. And *then* to find out that Mr. Morgan's representative was the other one, the petite young woman with the rosy cheeks and fresh complexion, the perfumed *mademoiselle* who insisted on paying the bill, and did so by signing the tab with a flourish—well, it generally took the men a moment or two to get used to the idea. America was not England; that was certain! And the mores of American women never ceased to amaze the British.

Genevieve, in her role as chaperone, felt obliged to be present at every one of these encounters—but at the end of the tenth one, she had to admit that she was a bit bored. It was one thing to love literature, to adore Dickens, Keats, and Thackeray, but it was quite something else to listen to endless discussions of codices and incunabula. The conversations were only ever about rare books, and the auctioning off of that Lord Amherst's library mid-week. Belle returned to the subject again and again, gleaning new details from each of her visitors, her tried-and-true method of eliciting information.

Lord Amherst's story would have been interesting, thought Genevieve, if she hadn't heard it twenty times. He was an Egyptologist of distinction, and one of the greatest bibliophiles of all time, with a collection of nearly a thousand volumes whose beauty and historical value incited widespread admiration—and greed. Unfortunately, this ardent collector had been the victim of a swindle that was now forcing him to sell off the great passion of his life. His commercial representative and trusted advisor, the solicitor who had overseen his affairs, his lands, and his properties for nearly half a century, had used his name and his fortune to indulge his own vice of gambling. Roulette and poker, and then the horses, and finally the stock market, in the hope of winning back his losses. The solicitor had lost everything, and then he had taken his own life. All of this had happened two years previously, in 1906. The solicitor had left debts of nearly three hundred thousand pounds, about which his employer had known nothing at all.

But these debts had been taken on in Lord Amherst's name, and both personal honor and the law demanded that he pay them back. In addition to the treasures of his library, he was now finding himself obliged to part with his rich tapestries and most of his art, which were to be sold off at other auctions, planned for next January and March. If these sales did not fetch enough, Lord Amherst would then have to sacrifice the magnificent family seat, Didlington Hall.

To make sure that the two Greene ladies grasped the full enormity of the amount for which the Amherst family had been made liable, their guests had taken the trouble to convert the sum into American dollars: nearly one and a half million![1]

[1] Roughly fifty million dollars in today's money.

Lord Amherst had first tried to sell his library, including the early printed texts that interested Miss Greene, in a single lot to a public institution, entrusting the greatest rare book dealer in London, Bernard Quaritch, with the task of finding a buyer. But the asking price for the thousand volumes was so high that, in two years, no national institution or museum had been able to come up with the money. And so Amherst had had to resign himself to parting with his books one at a time.

His creditors were putting more pressure on Amherst by the day now. The auction would commence in three days, on Thursday, December 3, and last until Monday the 7.

Less than a week to break up a priceless collection.

"We have to get them, we have to get them, we *have* to get them," Belle muttered, leafing for the thousandth time through the lavish catalogue issued by Sotheby's.

Mother and daughter were in their suite, with its two bedrooms opening into a sitting room furnished with pink silk Louis XV wing chairs, inlaid wood tables, and a grand piano.

The mantelpiece clock chimed midnight. Belle, sitting crosslegged on her bed with the catalogue in her lap, hadn't even undressed yet.

"Have you started talking to yourself now?" called Genevieve from her own room, where she sat in front of the mirror at her dressing table, taking the pins from her hair.

She was already in her nightgown. She felt weary to the bone; the hectic events of the day had exhausted her completely. The pace Belle had set for herself was truly unsustainable! *Steady, Genevieve*, she told herself firmly, forcing herself to brush her hair the required fifty strokes and braid it tightly for the night. God, what a day! Besides the meetings with the usual bookmen, there had been the incredible visit to Mr. Morgan's private residence at 14 Prince's Gate. Climbing the steps to the house, you would have thought you were entering a rather ordinary dwelling—but once you were inside, the place proved to be a palace. The walls of the dining room, which was large enough to hold Congress in its entirety, were covered from floor to ceiling with masterpieces of English painting: Reynolds, Romney, Gainsborough. They had admired the magnificent *Portrait of Georgiana, Duchess of Devonshire* and a number of aristocratic likenesses by Van Dyck. The furniture had once stood in the palace of Versailles, and some desks and chests originally from the Petit Trianon had belonged to Marie Antoinette herself. Beauvais tapestries. Sèvres and Saxe porcelains. Venetian chandeliers. Chinese vases. Bohemian mirrors. And, in glass display cases, hundreds of ornaments. Not to mention the collections of miniatures and tobacco- and sweet-boxes that sat on countless tables.

Gazing at her reflection in the mirror, Genevieve tried to remember the objects that had impressed her most. There were so many! Too many. Mr. Morgan's eclectic tastes in art in all its forms left her at once dazzled and astonished. She had loved the Velázquez, and the Rembrandts upstairs. And the enormous Van Dyck painting of the woman standing, dressed in red, with a baby. And then there was the small sitting room entirely devoted to *The Progress of Love*, the series of four canvases by Fragonard, commissioned by King Louis XV for Madame du Barry.

Not even the Metropolitan Museum, which Genevieve had visited several times during her marriage to Rick, and still did with her daughter from time to time, possessed pieces of such quality. Belle had told her that Mr. Morgan was planning to bring it all to New York and exhibit it to the public, so that his fellow Americans could enjoy it—but for now, customs duties made that impossible. The United States taxed every imported object at twenty percent of its purchase price. And so Morgan was keeping his treasures in London until he was able to get the laws changed.

The visit to his residence had excited Belle beyond words. She had known her employer was a voracious collector, but now she knew he was a great connoisseur, as well. Of course, she had no doubt that, in the vast accumulation, there were phony pieces as well as genuine ones, pieces of great and lesser quality. But it had become clear to her today that he had a true eye, and good taste. That he was not merely curious and avid but had real aesthetic sense. She was still in shock. Her joy and exhilaration at the Big Chief's collection had reached a peak. Far from feeling the slightest fatigue, she was bursting with energy. She wanted more.

If Genevieve had thought that they might take a moment to breathe, she was wrong.

From Prince's Gate, they had gone straight to the Victoria and Albert Museum. Four hours on their feet amid the faïence and porcelain, listening to the interminable explanations of one of Mr. Morgan's great friends, a Mr. Fitzhenry, who had shown them the museum's collections of Delftware. Belle had been so enthralled by Fitzhenry's history of ceramics that she had bombarded him with questions for another hour.

And then, a visit to Bernard Quaritch's new bookstore at 11 Grafton Street.

Of everyone they had met so far, Genevieve had liked Mr. Quaritch the most. He was a composed young man who understood both the price of things and the importance of taking one's time—and yet he was the least senior of the bookmen, only about forty years old, tall and overweight, with slightly protruding eyes and a dark mustache which he wore waxed and tapered in the manner of Napoleon III. Indeed, people called him the Napoleon of booksellers, so kingly was his position in the world of book dealers. His father, Quaritch the Elder, had orchestrated every book sale of any importance during the second half of the nineteenth century until his death in 1899. It was he who had advised Junius Morgan and hunted down the Virgils in Junius's collection for him. Junius remained Belle's idol, and he valued both Quaritches, even counting the son as a friend. According to Junius, the younger Quaritch was even better connected than the father among European aristocrats looking to buy or sell. Beneath his courtly manners, he was a great hunter, his skill and pugnacity unequaled in the auction rooms of Sotheby's and Christie's in London, or Drouot in Paris.

Genevieve, for her part, had found young Mr. Quaritch wonderfully gallant. The enthusiasm he had displayed during their visit to his extraordinary shop had delighted her; he had just moved into the place, bringing with him two hundred and fifty thousand *tons* of books. He had also demonstrated remarkable patience in explaining to "Miss Greene's charming mother" the subtle qualities of some of the treasures he had on offer. His bookstore was a gold mine three stories high.

Young Quaritch loved women; there could be no doubt on that point. Belle had wrapped him around her little finger, and vice versa. And so, thanks to his vast network of connections, he had offered to escort them to the exhibition rooms at Sotheby's before other collectors descended on the place in a mob. With two days to go before the sale, the auction house was preparing to open its doors to the public.

Genevieve had gone along on this outing as well. She knew her daughter well enough to know that, under the pretense of ambling among the shelves on Quaritch's arm, her daughter was assessing, comparing, estimating the worth of Lord Amherst's incunabula, her face a study in absolute concentration as she examined the quality of the pages and bindings. Yet Belle displayed no unseemly eagerness, leafing through the volumes with reverence but never spending a particularly long time looking at any one of them. The talk in London was of nothing but the unlimited means of the American collector she represented; no one, not even Quaritch, could know which books the Big Chief had his eye on, for fear of driving bidding amounts ridiculously high.

Belle's leisurely stroll amid Lord Amherst's literary heirlooms had been the most stimulating part of her day, and certainly the most fraught. To Genevieve, though, it was the least interesting. For her, these old grimoires with their Latin titles—"The only ones like them in the world," as Quaritch had murmured in Belle's ear; "the only ones like them," a phrase that made both their eyes sparkle and their hands tremble—aroused no emotion whatsoever.

And now, at midnight on this Monday, "Miss Greene's charming mother" found herself utterly spent. She might look young, but tonight she was feeling the full weight of her years and admitted defeat.

Belle, though, was giving no sign that she intended to go to bed anytime soon.

"I can hear you all the way in here, my dear!" Genevieve exclaimed, getting up and going into her daughter's room. "What are you mumbling about?"

"I'm saying that I have to get them."

"Yes, that much was perfectly clear. You're saying it even in your sleep. This obsession of yours is becoming truly worrying, Belle. What do you have to get, exactly?"

"The seventeen Caxton incunabula."

Genevieve sank into the wing chair next to the bed.

"Honestly, Belle, you might as well be speaking Greek."

"The first books printed in English by the merchant William Caxton. You might not remember, but I showed you his portrait when you visited me at the Morgan Library; it's one of the lunette paintings in the rotunda. To Mr. Morgan, William Caxton's almost as important as Gutenberg."

*Steady now, Genevieve, steady. Just play along. Try to find out why these "seventeen Caxton incunabula" have got Belle so excited.*

*Take an interest. Ask questions.*

"I thought Gutenberg was the great inventor of printing," she said, carefully keeping her voice neutral. "That's what you've always told me, at least. That books were written, copied, and illustrated by hand before he came along."

"Yes—it took monks years and years to produce a single illuminated text. Psalters, breviaries, books of hours. But in 1450, in Mainz, Gutenberg invented the movable-type printing press, and was able to print several Bibles in just a few months. The Big Chief has two of those, and you can't imagine how beautiful they are. Gutenberg Bibles. Absolutely exquisite. But they're printed in Latin. Twenty years later, William Caxton had the idea to modernize Gutenberg's technique and print secular texts in a living language. The books he printed are landmarks in literature. They established English as a language, when before that point it was just a group of dialects. William Caxton changed *everything*. He's as vital to the history of books as Leonardo da Vinci is to art."

Belle paused for a beat, to let her mother contemplate Caxton's greatness.

"You know," she went on, "the fellow we had lunch with yesterday, that Franco-British cataloguer who inventoried Lord Amherst's library?"

"The one with the hodgepodge of a name?"

"Seymour de Ricci. He's tried to take a sort of census of all the Caxton editions in Germany, France, and England. They're extremely rare, and priceless. The Earl of Pembroke and the Duke of Devonshire each have several in their collections; they're the crown jewels of their libraries at their estates of Wilton and Chatsworth. The British Museum has two of them, and the Bibliothèque Nationale of France has one. Lord Amherst has *seventeen*. All of exceptional quality."

"Don't you have any at the Morgan Library?"

"Yes. But not enough. And they're not in as good a state of preservation. For Mr. Morgan's Caxtons truly to constitute a collection, we need *all* of them."

"Is that possible?"

"Not in a public auction. I might get two, perhaps three, and the competition will be fierce. Mr. Morgan's rivals are going to be at Sotheby's on Thursday, too: British Museum curators, scholars, book dealers—and our friends, the other American collectors, of course. They all want at least one Caxton, and everyone's going to be salivating after the wonder of wonders: the *Recuyell of the Historyes of Troye*. It's the *first* copy of the *first* book ever printed in English. It's going to go for some insane sum. If I get it, I'll have spent more than my whole budget for the others."

"If this book is the most precious one, maybe it's worth sacrificing the rest?" Genevieve suggested, amenably.

"It's never worth contributing to the dismembering of a collection!"

"Well, you'll figure it out. And now, my darling, it's time to put your nightgown on and get some rest."

Belle sat unmoving. She reflected for a second and then said, each word very distinct:

"I don't just want the *Recuyell*. I want all seventeen Caxtons. All at once."

"That's absurd. You're setting the bar even higher than Mr. Morgan is."

"We're working to bring together a collection worthy of the British Museum, to make his library the masterpiece of his dreams," said Belle obdurately.

Genevieve frowned.

"The masterpiece of *your* dreams, you mean," she said, her tone severe now. "As far as I know, Mr. Morgan has not asked you to get all seventeen volumes for him!"

"It doesn't matter. I want them."

"From what you've told me, you have no chance of doing that—so let this obsession of yours go, and come to bed."

Genevieve made as if to rise.

"I'll have to see Lord Amherst in private," persisted Belle. "I need to speak to him one on one. The problem is that he isn't in London. Quaritch says he won't be back until Wednesday. That's two days from now. The very last moment. The evening before the auction."

"Why so late?"

"Lord Amherst is going through a great deal, as we both heard. His financial ruin, and having to give up his library, have destroyed him. His family's afraid for his health and trying to protect him from his emotions. He has a wife and six daughters with him, keeping a close watch on him. They're all at Didlington Hall, their mansion in Norfolk, around forty miles north of Cambridge, and they're refusing to allow any visitors."

"That's a long way from here," observed Genevieve, yawning. "Now come, it's time for bed!"

"Three hours by train to the small depot at Brandon, and then six miles by car to the estate."

"You're not planning to go, are you?" exclaimed Genevieve, appalled.

She had leapt to her feet. Belle faced her defiantly.

"And why not?"

"Because it simply isn't done to show up at people's homes without being invited!" her mother barked.

"I don't give a damn what's done or not done."

"We're in *England*. Not among the savages. And even in the land of the Zulus you would have to have *some* manners!"

"You have to know what you want. I know exactly what I want. I want the Caxtons."

"I didn't raise you to behave like a roughneck ready to break down the door of a family in distress. Especially the family of an aristocrat like the Right Honorable Baron William Tyssen-Amherst!"

"I'm representing the richest collector in America, aren't I?"

Genevieve, on her feet, stared at Belle silently for a long moment.

"You've lost your mind, Belle," she said at last.

"Lord Amherst has met Junius, and they got along very well."

"How long ago was that? Two years? You said he isn't receiving anyone at the moment."

"I called the estate. Their chauffeur will come to fetch me at Brandon tomorrow afternoon."

"Oh *no*; you are *not* going to go there!"

"Not a word to anyone, Maman."

Genevieve tried to calm herself, to be reasonable.

"Let me remind you," she said coolly, "that Mr. Quaritch and the British Museum curators are giving a big dinner in your honor at the Savoy Hotel at six-thirty the day after tomorrow."

"I'll be back by then. Don't worry. If Quaritch or anyone else asks you where I am, just say I have a cold and am keeping to my room, so I'll be fit for the dinner on Wednesday. Just stay calm. Relax."

Genevieve conceded defeat. "But I'll come with you, darling. Of course I will. I won't leave you to make the trip without a chaperone; what would Lord Amherst think?"

"I'm going alone."

\*

Seated in the frigid carriage of a train wending its way across the English countryside, Belle didn't even glance at the landscape, even for a moment. Eyes closed, head down, chin nestled into her fur collar, she concentrated on memorizing the exact histories of the seventeen Caxtons. Amherst would only agree to sell them to her *before* the auction—for that was her plan, to buy them *all* before the auction even took place—if he judged her worthy of acquiring them. She knew how crucial it was, for a collector of Amherst's ilk, to pass his treasures on to someone equally ardent, someone who understood the importance of what they were receiving. Love and knowledge: they would be her tools in the negotiation to come. And so, it was vital for her to impress him with the breadth of her knowledge. To cite the dates of the books in the course of a remark, their size, the sort of paper they were printed on, the name of their binder—and, of course, their provenance. *The Recuyell of the Historyes of Troye*, for example. The list of its owners. She knew this by heart, but repeated it to herself now: "The volume remained in the possession of the Fairfax family until the middle of the eighteenth century, when in 1756 it was sold in London, under lot 2026, to Francis Child. The seventh Earl of Jersey subsequently inherited the book, and sold it in his turn on May 6, 1885 at Sotheby's. And the man who acquired lot 967 during this sale was none other than your own agent, my Lord, the father of your current book dealer: Bernard Quaritch the elder, who purchased it for you."

On the subject of the books, then, it would be impossible to catch her out in a mistake. But her studies wouldn't be enough to win the war.

Now to consider the price she might propose. An amount large enough to tempt Lord Amherst.

Quaritch had said that Amherst was anxious to reimburse a trust belonging to his wife's cousins, a matter about which he was desperately unhappy—but that this debt, undertaken in his name by his solicitor, could wait. There was another debt, also incurred by that swindler, that was far larger and more urgent: two hundred and fifty thousand pounds sterling, owed to creditors who were demanding that Amherst repay them before the year was out, under threat of imprisonment. If she offered the lord ten percent of that sum, or twenty-five thousand pounds . . . From her reticule, Belle extracted a small notebook already covered with scribbled figures and multiplications of pound values by three to convert them into dollars. The Caxtons, she calculated, would cost her one hundred and twenty-five thousand dollars.[2] A staggering amount—and yet it was less than the total budget Morgan had allocated to her. Even offering twenty-five thousand pounds, she could still buy a few other little gems at the auction on Thursday. And yet: one hundred and twenty-five thousand dollars! The figure was so enormous that she couldn't fully wrap her mind around it.

Suddenly, she couldn't hold back a giggle: here she was, preparing to spend a hundred and twenty-five thousand dollars in a single afternoon, and when she first arrived in Princeton she'd earned only five dollars a week.

She put the notebook back in her handbag and took out her checkbook. She wrote the amount on a check and slipped it into an envelope bearing the Claridge Hotel's letterhead.

Now to go over the personal information she'd been able to learn about the family. The temperaments of Lord Amherst, his wife, and his children.

Amherst was surrounded by an army of women endowed with strong personalities. His daughters could even boast of uncommon occupations; the eldest had excavated in Egypt with her father, discovering thirty-two tombs at the site of Qubbet el-Hawa, near Aswan. Another daughter raised Salukis—the magnificent Persian dogs bred to hunt antelopes for nomadic tribes—which she had brought back from the Orient. The fifth daughter had published several scholarly books on English gardens. God only knew what the others did!

There had originally been seven daughters, but the youngest had been carried off by typhoid fever in France on the very day of the arrival at Didlington Hall of a shipment of sarcophagi purchased by Lord Amherst at various auctions, along with mummies exhumed by his archaeologist daughter at Qubbet el-Hawa. Father and daughter both kept their trophies in a large

[2] Roughly 4.2 million dollars in today's money.

building known as "the Museum," which they had had constructed on the grounds of the estate.

Belle's source for all of this information, a British Museum curator, had smiled wryly as he told her of the murmurs among Norfolk's rural denizens that it was Lord Amherst's Egyptian mummies that had brought this spell of bad luck down on him. That, since the arrival of the cadavers at the Chapel of Saint Michael on the Didlington estate, the small church had been haunted, that the bells tolled at midnight without anyone ringing them, and that the vicar no longer dared to hold services there.

It was true that the text of one of Amherst's precious papyri called down death upon those who violated the sacred tombs. But from there to imagining that the man's swindling by his right-hand man and the ruin of his family were the product of a mummy's curse . . .

In any case, the daughters were extremely protective of their father, and some of them were claiming defiantly that he was not bound to honor debts that he had not undertaken himself. One of them was even furiously opposed to the sale of his collections—and that of his library in particular.

As for Lord Amherst himself, Belle had not been able to obtain a clear psychological portrait, yet she understood that he embodied the traditional values of the English aristocracy, with all its principles and all its prejudices.

Quaritch had taken extreme pains to make sure she knew that Milord's attitude toward Americans was one of both deep mistrust and total disdain. In his opinion, they were nothing but unsophisticated boors, Philistines, of which J.P. Morgan was a perfect example: vulgar and greedy, convinced that they could do anything they wished because they were rich, and determined to strip England of its riches for the benefit of their backward country.

In short, Lord Amherst reacted with visceral horror whenever he was in the presence of a Yankee invader.

*

There was no sign of the chauffeur who had agreed to drive her to the estate. No carriage or any other vehicle waiting outside the station at Brandon. The village was deserted. It took Belle half an hour just to find someone who could give her information on how she might reach Didlington Hall. A local peasant could drive her in his wagon for a fee, she was told—but it was December, and the road through the woods was almost impassably muddy, traveling the six miles to Didlington would take them the whole day. Belle was fighting down rage when the noisy arrival of an automobile solved the problem. The car belonging to the master of Didlington was occupied elsewhere, it transpired, and so he had sent a cab from the neighboring village of Swaffham rather than someone from his own household.

This vehicle, which had lost its top at some point, made slow progress along the forest road. Huddling in the heavy blanket she was sharing with the driver, Belle shivered. Despite the driving goggles, gloves, and cap the cabbie had lent her against the wind, the freezing air burned her throat, and the trees dropped gobbets of ice that melted and ran down the back of her neck.

If the extreme discomfort of her arrival was any indication of what was to follow, the day was promising indeed.

The car passed through the gates of the estate. Through the fog, Belle glimpsed a crenellated tower that reminded her of Princeton.

The manor house, rising up in all its splendor, likewise brought Constitution Hill to mind, with its bow windows and brick walls, its French-style gardens and green lawns sloping gently down to the lake. Here was the original of the residence Junius had constructed, the house he had seen and dreamed of living in, even more dreamlike in its English setting, more magnificent. This palace of the barons of Amherst boasted nearly eighty rooms, including the "King's chamber," a ballroom, and the opulent library, its ceiling painted with frescoes.

But the real shock for Belle was the sight of the black granite colossi that stood in a row along the house's façade, all of the cat-headed Egyptian goddess Bast, staring defiantly down at visitors.

Disheveled from the taxi ride, her hair in disarray, Belle was relieved of her coat. Without even offering her the opportunity to powder her nose, and in an authoritarian tone as cold as the air in the maze of corridors through which he now steered her, the butler asked her to follow him to the winter sitting room where Milord's family awaited her.

At one point, Belle froze momentarily in her tracks. Through a half-open door, she had caught a glimpse of the vast, ruined library, its walls lined from floor to ceiling with dark, empty shelves. For an instant she could not tear her gaze away from the tragic sight. It was a vision of desolation and death. A library stripped of its books.

At last they reached the winter sitting room, a cozy space furnished with ladies' writing-desks and embroidered sofas. Several women were sitting around the hearth, near the crackling fire. The oldest of them rose to welcome Belle. The others were content to examine her from the depths of their armchairs, a slight nod their only greeting.

Belle thought that the woman coming toward her now must be Lady Amherst. She cut an imposing figure, looking to be around fifty years old and dressed in what Belle thought was a rather old-fashioned style. She wore a velvet ribbon around her neck and an Indian cashmere shawl pinned with a large cameo.

"My mother will be down shortly," the woman said.

Ah. So this was the eldest daughter, the archaeologist with the thirty-two tombs: Lady William Cecil, who had just been made heir to her father's title by royal decree; she would become the second Baron Amherst of Hackney upon his death. It was a rare exception to the standard rules of English aristocratic lineage, in which titles were transmitted through the male line. But Lord Amherst had no male relatives, and so his baronetcy would pass to his eldest daughter, and from her to her eldest son.

"My father is slightly unwell," she continued, "and begs you to excuse him."

As she said this, she looked up at a large painting on the wall: a portrait of a man with intensely blue eyes and a neatly trimmed white beard, ensconced in a leather chair. In his lap there was an open book, an *in-folio* with gilded edges that Belle recognized immediately. It was the *Recuyell of the Historyes of Troye*. Lord Amherst, posing for posterity with the most precious of his Caxtons.

Caught off guard, Belle didn't know how to react to the collector's absence. She hadn't imagined the business taking place without him. Instinctively, she had even been banking on the warm feelings she generally aroused in older gentlemen—and particularly in a book lover whose passion she shared.

But a negotiation between women?

She could read nothing in the faces of her hostesses but vague curiosity, slightly tinged with disapproval. Were they surprised by her youth, like the London bookmen? Unless it was her outfit—too modern—that displeased them? Or her perfume?

In preparing for this meeting, Belle had thought of everything . . . except that. Her appearance. Unusually for her, she hadn't given it a second thought. And her outfit and hairstyle, compared to the tight updos and tweed skirts of these aristocratic English ladies, must seem to them outrageously extravagant. She found herself reluctant even to open her mouth, afraid of how discordant her American accent might sound in this place.

The arrival of old Lady Amherst completed the tableau. She was the image of her daughters, twenty years later.

Tea was served amid a welter of polite murmuring. There was no question of speaking about anything other than the frightful December weather, and train journeys made difficult by the frozen tracks.

Finally, Belle felt compelled to make the first move.

"When I spoke to you on the telephone yesterday, my Lady," she began, unsure whether to address the mother or the eldest daughter, "I told you that Mr. Pierpont Morgan had a proposition for you. I will be direct: he is offering you twenty-five thousand pounds—immediately—for all of your Caxtons."

One of the daughters, the youngest, who was seated closest to the fire, sprang to her feet:

"For all seventeen? But we'll get much more for them day after tomorrow!"

"Perhaps," said Belle, her tone deliberately neutral, "perhaps not."

It was at that exact moment that the Right Honorable Baron William Tyssen-Amherst chose to make his appearance, the door bursting open to admit his wheelchair, pushed through the maze of corridors by the butler.

The lordly gentleman in the portrait on the wall had become a shrunken old man, his legs covered by a plaid blanket. On his lap he bore, not a book, but an elderly dog that he stroked mechanically, a white-haired poodle whose fur was nearly as unkempt as its master's beard.

Yet the master of the house was still clear-eyed and sharp-tongued. He snapped out an order to be helped to his feet, assisted to his usual chair by the fire, and seated there comfortably. The women fluttered around him like a *corps de ballet*.

When the plaid blanket had been tucked around his legs again and the dog put back on his lap, his eldest daughter reminded him of their visitor's presence and the reason for this meeting. He listened to Lady William Cecil without a word, simply nodding in Belle's direction by way of greeting—and then settled back in his chair as if he meant to keep out of the conversation, to let the negotiation proceed without him.

His silence resonated with mistrust and hostility, the closed expression on his face making his thoughts on the presence of "the American's errand-girl" in his sitting room perfectly clear.

"They have just offered us twenty-five thousand pounds for your seventeen Caxtons, Daddy," said the daughter nearest to the fire. "We think it far below the price at which you've estimated them."

"Mr. Morgan is offering you this sum in cash," explained Belle. "Here and now. You wanted to sell your library as a single unit. In response to this desire, he is proposing to acquire and conserve all of your Caxtons together, rather than allowing them to be scattered to the four winds. He is paying cash," she repeated, "so that you will not be forced to part with the jewels of your collection one by one, at auctions where anything might happen."

No reaction. Lord Amherst simply stroked the dog, his face blank, as if the discussion had nothing to do with him. Undoubtedly she was so distasteful to him that he preferred to abstract himself. Belle felt compelled to press on.

"The truth, my Lord, is that if you do not accept Mr. Morgan's offer, he will not attend the auction. And his absence will not look well for Sotheby's. It will throw the value of your collections into doubt. People might think they don't interest him. And you are aware, surely, that the auction house is entitled to twenty percent of the costs of the sale. And that it is disposed to permit delayed payments by purchasers. Book dealers like Mr. Quaritch will have six months to pay; curators will have a year. If you accept the extremely generous sum proposed by Mr. Morgan," she said, taking the envelope from her handbag, "you will have access to it immediately. I am leaving you the check. You may tear it up if you wish to refuse the offer, or deposit it as early as tomorrow morning if you accept."

Belle put the check on the table.

This audacious move, and her speech, had left Lady Cecil, her mother, and her sisters speechless with astonishment. Lord Amherst was the first to react.

"Your employer will understand that I cannot accept this slip of paper."

He had become the proud aristocrat once more; the firm voice did not seem to belong to the broken man who had entered the room in a wheelchair.

"Keep your check for other purchases," he said disdainfully.

He had stopped stroking the dog, his hand resting on the animal's head. It fell to Lady Cecil to carry out the physical action her father intended. Rising to her full height, she picked up the envelope and held it out, her expression one of such coldness that Belle felt her heart lurch. Taking the envelope, she put it back in her reticule and rose in her turn.

"Will you please let me know your answer?" she asked, the words coming out a bit too quickly.

"Your employer will understand, once again, that I cannot make a decision of this sort without first discussing it with Lady Amherst and my daughters. Without having reflected fully upon it myself. And without consulting my book dealer, Mr. Quaritch."

Belle refrained from pointing out that Mr. Quaritch was also Mr. Morgan's book dealer.

"Of course," she said. "An unexpected last-minute offer—naturally you must think about it. But if you should accept, we will have very little time to act. To withdraw the seventeen Caxtons from the sale, I mean. To remove them officially from the catalogue. That would have to be done before one o'clock on Thursday, so it is fairly urgent."

"You shall have my answer in writing."

"In writing? But the sale is the day after tomorrow!"

"I don't like the telephone."

"May I ask you, then, to inform me of your decision by telegram at Claridge's Hotel?"

"My silence will tell you more than any telegram."

"There is no better means of avoiding a misunderstanding, as you said yourself, my Lord, than a written answer. A cable will suffice, with a simple 'yes' or 'no.' And now I won't trespass on your hospitality any further."

No one urged her to stay. Lady Cecil was at least courteous enough to see her to the door, not without reminding her that the Swaffham cab was waiting to take her back to the station.

What a disaster. On the train back to London, Belle chastised herself for the crudeness of her approach. Inexcusably vulgar. She had acted like a rug-merchant—she had all but blackmailed Lord Amherst, and Mr. Morgan would have been utterly ashamed of her. *"If you don't accept our offer, we won't attend the auction, and our absence will look bad . . ."*

Worse than vulgar. Pathetic.

She had wanted the Caxtons *too* much. She had never doubted, even for a moment, that she would get them. She had forgotten the limits that every buyer must set for themselves.

It was Lord Amherst's absence in the early part of the interview, she thought, that had ruined everything. *If I could only have spoken to him one on one. I didn't have a chance with all those women around him, those English biddies, so snobbish and stuck up. Cold fish. It's over.*

And Quaritch? With him, too, she had made so many mistakes. She should have taken him into her confidence, persuaded him to provide an introduction, gone to Didlington in his company.

In her determination to act alone on unfamiliar terrain, she had disregarded even the most basic rules of conduct. It was Bernard Quaritch whom Lord Amherst had previously entrusted with the task of selling his library off as a single unit.

And the book dealer had offered that unit first to Mr. Morgan, who had declined. Now, Quaritch was not only in favor of the auction at Sotheby's; he had orchestrated it himself.

As was customary, those clients of Quaritch's who were unable to attend the sale in person, or who wished to remain anonymous, had already given him orders to buy on their behalf. He was probably already in possession of a list of potential buyers for every volume, along with the maximum price he was allowed to offer. He would advance the amount at his own expense and then be entitled to a commission, eventually billing for his services based on the winning bid for the lot he had purchased: ten percent for occasional customers, and five for his most loyal clients, including Morgan. Belle, who had been paying Quaritch's invoices for three years, understood this arrangement perfectly well. Quaritch worked for the buyer and the seller at the same time.

And now, in trying to double-cross him, she had dug her own grave.

*It's all over.*

Despite her efforts to acknowledge and accept her failure, she waited for Amherst's telegram all the next day. Nothing.

*My silence will tell you more than any telegram.*

She tried to reach Quaritch, to explain herself to him. His assistant, one Mr. Dring, very kindly informed her that Mr. Quaritch was not in the store; he was at Sotheby's. She waited a bit and called back. Mr. Quaritch would be back later in the afternoon, Dring assured her, and he would be at the hotel to pick her up at six o'clock sharp.

When it was time to start getting herself ready for the bookmen's pre-auction dinner at the Savoy, being held in her honor, Belle could hardly muster the energy to bathe and change. She felt paralyzed with anxiety. It fell to Genevieve to dress her, do her hair, and drag her down to the lobby.

She refused to leave Claridge's until she had begged the door-man to send any messages that arrived for her along to the Savoy, in case a cable arrived. Fortunately, the two establishments shared an owner, and she was assured that any telegrams would be speedily brought to her.

There had still been no word by the time they set off. *It's all over. I know it.*

In the car, while Quaritch, with his usual courtesy, regaled "Miss Greene and her charming mother" with anecdotes about their hosts for the evening, admirers whom they would be see-ing again or meeting for the first time, Belle tried to sound the book dealer out. She turned the full force of her charm on him; admitted to him that she'd gone to Norfolk, and confessed her lack of success with the Amhersts. He didn't seem shocked, or even surprised. A rather daring approach, certainly, he said, but what was wrong with boldness? "Nothing ventured, nothing gained, isn't that what they say?" The price she had offered for the Caxtons was perfectly respectable, he assured her, and he was certain that Lord Amherst, if he did not accept it, would undoubtedly at least consider it. The aristocrat, he reminded her, was no stranger to sales and auctions; he even described him as a skilled negotiator. Amherst's poor health, Quaritch said, had had no effect on either his faculties or his nature; he knew what he was about, and he knew what he wanted—or did not want.

As for the rest, Quaritch claimed ignorance. He had seen Amherst briefly, late that afternoon, he admitted, when the fam-ily returned to their London home, but he said that nothing of any importance had been discussed. One thing was certain, though; there had been no change made to the order of the lots at Sotheby's.

"However, my dear Miss Greene, as you will have seen, I am by no means privy to all the secrets of the gods," he said with a sardonic chuckle. "All I can do for you is to cross my fingers and touch wood!"

If the Greene women had found Claridge's Hotel impressive, at the Savoy they were treated to the full measure of English pomp, where elegance flirted with ostentation.

With its red lacquered columns and gilded plasterwork, its dozens of chandeliers and frescoed ceilings and, above all, its tall windows overlooking the Thames, the Savoy's River Restaurant was more magnificent than any ballroom in the most luxurious palace. Newly renovated and designed like a theater, the hotel provided an opulent backdrop for all sorts of events. Its courtyard could even be transformed into a Venetian lagoon complete with gondolas, its grill and restaurant into St. Mark's Basilica or the Doge's Palace. The splendid costume parties held there by English aristocrats since the hotel's reopening remained etched into the memory of everyone who had seen their sumptuous décor.

As for the menu, *suprême de volaille Jeannette*, strawberries *à la* Sarah Bernhardt, peach Melba, Bombe Nero—the specialties created by Chef Auguste Escoffier continued to add to the hotel's renown. And every evening, one of the best orchestras in London filled the restaurant with the softly played strains of fashionable tunes.

In all her life, Genevieve had never seen so many jewels and feathers. In New York, no one wore diamonds in public so early in the evening, and hats were *de rigueur*. Here she was surrounded by plumes and plunging décolleté. Genevieve thanked the heavens above that she'd worn her plum-colored ballgown, and forced Belle to don the silver-spangled green gown that Louise had copied with such difficulty from a Worth design, and to add the white sable stole and string of pearls that Morgan had given her for Christmas.

The focal point of the spectacle was the long, flower-bedecked oval table in the center of the room, toward which Quaritch and the hotel's headwaiter now guided them. Thirteen men awaited them there, dressed in white tie with white camellias in their lapels. They were all on their feet, hands resting on the backs of their chairs.

Watching the two American women make their way toward the table of gentlemen, the Savoy's clientele couldn't hold back a murmur. They were well traveled, all of them—Saint Petersburg, Berlin, Venice—but this was a sight none of them had ever seen. Two women, presiding over a dinner attended by fourteen men who were neither their fathers, nor their husbands, nor their sons, nor their brothers. Unthinkable! Even in New York! Adventuresses? *Courtesans?* The words quickly made their whispered way around the restaurant. Unacceptable! Here at the Savoy, one did not consort with *demi-monde* from private rooms at the Maison Dorée or Lapérouse in Paris!

And yet the gentleman companions of these two creatures were of such respectable reputation, such an appearance of morality and dignity, that no one dared to do anything more than whisper. They were forced to make do with endless conjectures about the identity of these two strange women.

The moment Belle sensed herself to be in the limelight, she regained her poise. It was an instant reflex, an old habit, even an instinct: the lifting of her chin and the concealment, the instant she felt eyes upon her, of her every emotion, her every secret.

Turning on the charm, she greeted each of her hosts gaily, focusing her attention on the man seated to her right, the oldest of the bookmen—aged fifty or so—and the most important. The best-looking, too. The embodiment of a handsome Englishman, with his gentlemanly appearance and well-trimmed mustache. He was taller than average, and bent his shoulders slightly in Belle's direction, the better to listen to her.

With his striking looks and sharp intellect, Charles Hercules Read knew he was irresistible. He had a keen sense of humor and could be very funny. He was president of the Society of Antiquaries of London, and keeper of medieval antiquities of the British Museum. It was he who had told Belle the story of the curse of Amherst's mummies, and he who was supporting his friend and colleague Alfred Pollard in the purchase of the Caxtons for the British Museum's Department of Printed Books.

Neither Read nor Pollard normally made purchases directly from Sotheby's; rather, they gave orders to Quaritch, the official agent for England's public institutions, including the British Museum and the Society of Antiquaries. But in the case of the Amherst sale, for which Quaritch was acting as both judge and jury, they had decided it was more prudent to attend the auction themselves. And both Read and Pollard were wooing Belle, their most formidable adversary, whose means—or rather, Morgan's—far exceeded the sums they had been authorized to spend.

No one mentioned the next day's auction, but everyone was thinking about it. And Belle was not unaware of the potential threat posed by this coalition of hunters who were stalking the same prey as she. There was every likelihood that they had already agreed not to bid against one another, but to obtain the seventeen Caxtons individually at ridiculously low prices—a wholly illegal practice, and one in which London's bookmen frequently partook without a qualm. They would organize a secret sale at a later date and divide the spoils among themselves.

"D'you know, in France, no one reads anymore?" said the large man on Belle's left, Benjamin Maggs, Quaritch's main rival. "I was in Paris the other day, and they told me at Plon that the automobile had killed book sales. Partly because those appalling machines are so monstrously expensive, and partly because of the time and energy it takes to maintain them. These nonsensical new fads don't leave people with even an hour to read anything at all."

"How right you are," said Belle lightly. "Thank heaven for trains!"

Quaritch, on the other side of the table at Genevieve's right, watched them talk. He had no intention of having Mr. Morgan's lucrative business stolen by that weasel Maggs. He moved quickly to retain control of the conversation.

"It is true that, these days, 'there are books of which the backs and covers are by far the best parts', as our national author once wrote!"

"A quote from Dickens, if I'm not mistaken, Mr. Quaritch?" Genevieve ventured.

Read leaned over to whisper in Belle's ear.

"My dear Miss Greene," he murmured, "promise me you won't bid against the British Museum for the *Recuyell of Historyes of Troye* and the *Canterbury Tales*."

Belle, who was on high alert, was staring at a bellhop crossing the room toward their table, bearing a piece of paper on a silver tray. Her heart leapt in her chest.

The boy stopped beside her. "A cable for Miss Greene." The gentlemen had fallen silent. She forced herself to smile right and left, to say, coolly, "It must be my family's reply to a telegram I sent them." She added, with a bit too much detail, ". . . telling them of our safe arrival in Europe."

She unsealed the envelope and extracted its contents as calmly as she could manage, though she couldn't help tearing the paper slightly as she unfolded it.

Three words, quickly read.

*Offer accepted.*

*Amherst*

She caught her breath, unable to keep the emotion that flooded through her from showing on her face.

"Nothing serious, I hope?" inquired Read.

Refolding the paper with trembling hands, Belle slipped it into her evening bag.

"Nothing serious," she echoed. "Thank you. On the contrary—very good news."

She gave him her most charming smile. He responded in kind, matching his powers of seduction to hers.

"So then, Miss Greene, can you promise not to bid against me for those two volumes tomorrow?"

"Yes."

"Really?"

"Really, Mr. Read, I can." Mischievously, she smiled at him again, with an expression that left him completely under her spell. "I give you my solemn promise not to bid against you tomorrow."

Quaritch almost had to fight the other thirteen men for the privilege of accompanying the ladies back to their hotel.

It was clear to them both that he was burning with curiosity. What had the telegram said? Genevieve refrained from asking Belle the question.

In the car, Belle let the moment stretch out. Quaritch bore the silence for as long as he was able and then asked, his eyes gleaming:

"Well?"

She let out a delighted laugh. "You know better than I do, Mr. Quaritch—we've won. And I owe you—the Morgan Library owes you!—an enormous debt of gratitude."

"Now, let's not make too much of it."

"How could we not! You did what was necessary where Lord Amherst was concerned, and you saved the day."

"I didn't know how it would turn out."

"Without you—without your intervention—"

"Allow me to return the compliment, Miss Greene. Without your daring . . ."

"—nothing would have been possible. It goes without saying, Mr. Quaritch, that you have certainly earned your commission."

"Let's not speak of it any further."

"But I think we should speak of it! I will never be able to thank you enough. You've been wonderful!"

"The loyalty of a connoisseur such as Mr. Morgan is precious to me. His satisfaction is a priority. I've been in his service for so many years—and his ambassadresses are ever so charming!"

The car had pulled up beneath the awning in front of Claridge's.

Allowing Quaritch to kiss her hand in the lobby, Belle rose on tiptoe to whisper in his ear:

"Tomorrow, no one must know who the buyer is."

"Understood," he murmured. "It's our secret."

They had just sealed a deal—and a friendship—that would last until the book dealer's death.

*

13 Willington Street, on the Strand, the auction house of Messrs. Sotheby, Wilkinson, and Hodge, had never known such a turnout. Book collectors and agents, drawn to London by the sale of the Caxton volumes, crowded beneath the auctioneer's rostrum. There was Mr. Baer who had come from Frankfurt, and Mr. Hiersmann from Leipzig, Mr. Gilhofer from Vienna, and Mr. Rosenbach from Philadelphia. And, of course, representatives of the Bibliothèque Nationale de Paris and all the other major international institutions, who had, unusually, traveled for the occasion. England, for its part, was well represented, with numerous champions present including curators from the British Museum, the renowned Biblical scholar Mr. Ginsburg, the attorney and collector Mr. Justice Ridley, and the book dealers Mr. Maggs and Mr. Quaritch.

All of them knew each other, and all of them hated each other, and all of them greeted each other warmly. They might almost have been at a sophisticated cocktail party in a library; the walls were lined with books, and the room looked like a banquet hall, with two long tables running the entire length of the room from door to dais. The bidders were seated at these tables, the crowd of watchers gathered behind them. The auctioneers drew each book from the shelves as its lot number was called and displayed it in the open area between the tables.

On the podium next to the rostrum was a large red velvet armchair that Sotheby's had reserved for Lord Amherst. Though the directors of the auction house usually advised sellers strongly against being present during the sale of their possessions—their emotions made buyers feel guilty, and could bring prices down—they had made an exception for the baron.

His entrance on Mr. Quaritch's arm caused precisely the kind of commotion Sotheby's directors had feared. Amherst was the epitome of elegance, his chest laden with medals and his bearing of the utmost dignity. But the extreme difficulty with which he climbed the steps of the podium spoke eloquently, to those who had known him before, of the affliction that had befallen him.

The thought that this old gentleman was about to witness the dismantling of what had been the most important part of his existence—the loss, piece by piece, of his life's passion—made Belle's heart clench. Uncharacteristically for her, she sought to keep a low profile, to blend into the crowd.

And yet it was impossible for her to go unnoticed. The Greene ladies were, once again, the only women in the place— and everyone here knew that Belle was acting on behalf of the immensely wealthy J.P. Morgan. Her hosts of yesterday evening had all hastened to offer her their seats. Large numbers of extra chairs had been brought into the auction room, but it was still not enough, and more than one buyer was forced to stand through the whole sale.

Charles Hercules Read was particularly attentive, Belle noticed, all gallantry and knowing glances. He seated her authoritatively next to him at the bidders' table, drawing every eye to her—exactly what she had been hoping to avoid. Still, she gave him her most brilliant smile and accepted his solicitousness graciously.

She had lunched privately with Quaritch before the sale, and together, away from prying eyes, they had worked out the final details for the purchase of the Caxtons. Quaritch had agreed to muddy the waters regarding the identity of the buyer by drawing the lion's share of the attention at the Sotheby's auction to himself.

It was common for Quaritch to attend sales on behalf of multiple collectors at once, and the actual recipients of his trophies always remained anonymous. And so Belle had placed a purchase order with him. He would buy for her the final lot she wanted, the second highlight of the auction, the Cambridge Bible, which had been personally owned by King Charles I of England. The cover of this singular volume was thickly embroidered in silver thread with motifs including a lion and a unicorn, the arms of the Stuarts. Imagine, the king had likely kissed this very Bible on the scaffold before being beheaded by Cromwell . . . Belle wanted it for the Morgan Library. *But not a word.* For her part, Belle would make a show of buying a few other items—small game, mere "trinkets," as she called them, in comparison to the Cambridge Bible.

At one o'clock sharp, the auctioneer, Mr. Hodge, one of the partners in the auction house, took his place on the rostrum and officially declared the Sale of the Magnificent Library of the Right Honorable Lord Amherst of Hackney open.

Solemnly, he read out the statutes:

"To avoid any error in acquisitions, no lot may be withdrawn from the sale as long as it is underway.

"However, the following lots have been withdrawn by Messrs. Sotheby, Wilkinson, and Hodge at the express demand of Lord Amherst: 124, 179, 180—"

These words had thrown the room into an uproar, everyone leafing frantically through their sale catalogue. *The Caxtons!*

A few protestations were shouted up from below the dais. Hodge took no notice of them, and continued, in a monotone:

"181, 205, 229, 345, 395, 449, 542—"

The recitation was drowned out by angry voices.

"Shameful!"

"Unacceptable!"

"We crossed the Channel for those Caxtons, and now you tell us on the very day of the auction that they have already been sold!"

The crowd of bidders had risen to its feet, shouting, demanding to know the name of the buyer. Belle and Quaritch exchanged a glance.

Like a judge presiding over a trial, Hodge rapped the podium with his gavel. "Silence! Or I will postpone the sale." There was a hush. "607, 992, 996," he went on.

When he had finished reciting the list, he concluded:

"The library of Lord Amherst, which it has now fallen incumbent upon us to sell, represents the history of printing since its very beginning.

"Given the rarity of these books and the beauty of the manuscripts, certain of which belonged to King Henry VIII, Queen Catherine of Aragon, Queen Elizabeth, and King Charles I, it is our fervent hope that they will remain in England."

Belle had stopped listening, her eyes fixed on Lord Amherst, still seated above the crowd, his expression one of deep mourning.

"Is it you?" Charles Hercules Read asked, catching up with Belle outside Sotheby's. "The Caxtons? It *is* you, isn't it!"

Twilight was falling. The sale had lasted three hours and would continue the next day. The tension of the past few days had been such that Belle was as utterly drained as she was satisfied. All she wanted was to go back to the hotel.

They looked at one another appraisingly for a moment. A freezing December rain had begun to fall, but Belle took no notice of it. Genevieve waited beneath her umbrella a few yards away.

Chin raised, Belle looked Read straight in the eye, her frankness catching him slightly off guard.

"It is you, isn't it?" he repeated.

She did not deny it.

"And yet you promised me."

"I promised not to bid against you today. And I kept my word."

There was a silence. Read, who had not wanted the Caxtons for himself, sighed.

"My poor Pollard. I'd assured him . . . he wanted the *Recuyell* and the *Canterbury Tales* so very much for his Department of Printed Books . . ."

"I will have a set of perfect facsimiles made," she said seriously, "so that your researchers can study both the *Recuyell* and the *Tales* any time they wish. And, Mr. Read," she continued gently, "there will be other Caxtons on the market. And now the Morgan Library has enough of them that I won't have to compete against Mr. Pollard in any more sales."

He smiled. "I'm not sure I believe you!"

Read was familiar enough with underhanded business maneuvers to know that success at auctions depended on three things: determination, cunning, and self-control. It was clear that this young woman possessed all three in spades. He could only admire her. Moreover, J. Pierpont Morgan had always shown generosity toward the British Museum, even bowing to its curators' wishes more than once.

Read himself enjoyed a privileged relationship with the American tycoon and hoped one day to be among the guests invited on one of his luxurious Nile cruises. And who knew; one day, perhaps, Miss Greene's employer might donate—or will— his Caxtons back to England?

A solid understanding was worth more than any dispute. Read opted to bury the hatchet. The incident, as far as he was concerned, was a thing of the past. They set off arm in arm for

Claridge's Hotel, in the ever-agreeable company of *Madame mère.*

Charles Hercules Read—soon to be knighted, becoming *Sir Charles*—and Belle da Costa Greene continued to write letters to one another, in which they exchanged professional information, support, advice, and flirtatious remarks, for the next twenty years.

\*

Every one of the next day's newspaper headlines concerned the sale. It hadn't been an easy night. Though Genevieve had slept heavily, Belle had found it impossible to rest. She was intoxicated by her own success, with an exhilarating feeling of power, all her fears banished. Mission accomplished. She reveled in the thought that she had risen, body and soul, to the challenge of justifying Mr. Morgan's confidence in her. But she could not sleep. Her nerves were still too much on edge, her excitement refusing to die down. She kept replaying the scenes of battle in her head: the meeting with Lord Amherst at Didlington Hall; the dinner at the Savoy . . .

"'From the *New York Times* special correspondent in London,'" she read aloud over her breakfast tray, "'There are rumors that the Caxtons fetched a price of five hundred thousand dollars . . .'"

She rapped the newspaper with a hand. "These reporters will say anything! Five hundred thousand? That's insane! One hundred and twenty thousand is already a king's ransom. Poor Lord Amherst. If he reads this, he'll go through the roof!"

She broke off for a moment, musing. "'. . . though it wouldn't be an outrageous price for such a treasure, according to the book dealers at Sotheby's yesterday. None of them doubts for a moment that Mr. J.P. Morgan is the buyer.'"

"'During the whole of the afternoon, the most sought-after lots went to Mr. Quaritch, among them the volume that was the subject of the fiercest bidding, the Cambridge Bible belonging to King Charles I, for the sum of one thousand pounds sterling,[3] his Austrian competitor having withdrawn at nine hundred and eighty pounds.'

"'Mr. Hodge closed the session expressing his surprise and satisfaction. The total of this first day is in excess of ten thousand pounds sterling, not counting the price of the Caxtons. Most of the volumes fetched sums three or four times greater than what Lord Amherst paid for them. His Grace must undoubtedly be pleased.'"

"Let's hope, for his sake, that this pace keeps up all week," sighed Genevieve.

"In the meantime, there's nothing left for us to do here. We've got what we wanted." Belle leapt out of bed. "Let's vamoose!"

"My dear, just because we're alone doesn't mean you should talk like a sailor. Speak correctly, please."

"We're going to France."

"France? Impossible, darling. The *Oceanic* departs from Southampton."

"We'll go and come back. Three days, just until the end of the sale. We'll be back by Monday—we'll have to be; I have a meeting with the museum curator in Cambridge on December 7. But until then, just think of it, Maman—Paris will be ours, just the two of us!"

\*

A seventy-two hour jaunt to the City of Light. For two

---

[3] Around five thousand dollars in 1908, or nearly $170,000 in today's money.

American women at the dawn of the twentieth century, an unimaginable adventure. The noon train on the Southern Railway, from Victoria Station to Dover. From there to Calais, on a steam ferry called *The South* on the way from England to France and one called *Le Nord* on the way back. A crossing that took a night, each way. From Calais, the express train to the Boulevard de Magenta. And then back to London.

Though Belle could be exhausting, Genevieve had to admit that she found her daughter impressive. Even her more worrying qualities were infused with a sort of vital energy, and Genevieve viewed her enthusiasm, her curiosity about the world, with mingled fascination and resignation. She had experienced it before, this feverish passion for living, during her years of marriage to Rick. She had loved his intensity, before everything turned sour.

And now? After Claridge's, after the Savoy, came the Ritz.

But if she had hoped to enjoy the serene splendor of the Place Vendôme in tranquility, once again Genevieve was to be disappointed. They set off immediately in the direction of the rue du Faubourg Saint-Honoré and the office of Léon Gruel, Morgan's longstanding Parisian bookbinder, whom Belle hoped to entrust with the restoration of some of the Caxtons. She also wanted personally to collect the book of hours that had belonged to Madame Adélaïde, the daughter of King Louis XV, which Morgan intended for his mistress Adelaide Douglas. And finally, she wanted to purchase the Christmas gift she had always dreamed of giving the Big Chief: a large cigar box in the form of a book, an exact copy of an *in-folio* by Jean Grolier, that most elegant of Renaissance bibliophiles, whose bindings were still unsurpassed in their loveliness. A costly present, meant to convey all her gratitude and admiration to the man who had done so much for her.

From Gruel's they went to visit the art dealer André Seligman at his gallery on the rue de Lille, where Belle picked up a seventeenth-century enameled pendant watch and two bronze statuettes by sculptors from the Fontainebleau School. These she planned to smuggle back into the United States by concealing them among her underclothes, to avoid the twenty percent customs tax on works of art—an act of fraud that could lead to the permanent confiscation of Mr. Morgan's possessions, as Monsieur Seligman's fifteen-year-old son warned her gravely.

In his father's absence, the teenager was clearly extremely anxious about Miss Greene's illegal intentions. The customs officials in New York didn't joke around about these sorts of things. Upon her arrival in America, Miss Greene's trunks would be searched, just like those of all the other passengers, young Germain Seligman insisted, and this would be no perfunctory search. The customs experts knew what they were doing. They knew what sorts of items first-class passengers tended to bring back from Europe. Belle would be found out immediately, and not only would she have to pay the taxes, but a fine would be imposed on her as well, the amount of which—based on the value of the objects—would be astronomical. The statuettes were too large to go unnoticed, and the jeweled watch too spectacular. Better to have them transported by Seligman's official agents, along with a customs declaration that matched up with the billing statements.

To distract the boy, Belle bought a few souvenirs from him, which she had him pack with extreme care and stamp as fragile: three porcelain parrots and a few pieces of chinoiserie intended for the new family apartment on 115th Street, the sort of charming decorative trinkets—expensive enough, but without any real value—that Junius would have called *musica*, in comparison to the bronzes. Then she and Genevieve left the gallery, laden with boxes containing everything she'd bought, including the watch and statuettes.

To close out the day, they made a leisurely visit to Monsieur

Poiret's couture house on the rue Pasquier. A bit of frivolity, at last!

There, in the private suite to which they were ushered—the moment they uttered the word *Ritz*, they'd been taken for wealthy Americans who would order gowns by the dozen—the mother and daughter happily gave themselves up to the joys of fashion, requesting that every dress in the catalogue be modeled for them, and leafing endlessly through Paul Iribe's *Les Robes de Paul Poiret*, the album the couturier had just sent to the world's most stylish women. As Madame Vionnet, Poiret's associate and right hand, kept reminding her, Monsieur Poiret dressed Réjane, Isadora Duncan, and the Russian princesses, among other famous beauties.

Tea gowns for Belle's auctions and sales, evening gowns for Mr. Morgan's box at the opera . . . they indulged themselves like teenage girls, asking to see the accessories, to try on the designs themselves. Genevieve, who had fed herself and her children by wielding her needle, took an interest in even the tiniest details: cut, fabric, the draping of a skirt. Belle, for her part, was drowning in pure pleasure. Poiret's creations were perfectly suited to her figure, so slender that it had no need of corsetry, and indeed the elimination of corsets was Paul Poiret's most daring innovation, one that had brought down a storm of criticism and protestations from many a conservative mother. Genevieve welcomed it, however, and Belle even more so. High-waisted dresses cut slim and straight in the Continental fashion, silk chiffon fabrics with Japanese-inspired prints, kimono-style coats edged with fur . . . the specialties of the house were utterly ravishing.

No more peplum jackets, lacy blouses, and tiny garnet brooches. No more mauve and gray. Belle had found the perfect style to suit her, resolutely modern. Vivid colors and baroque jewelry. In the absence of Cartier diamonds, Lalique enamels: peacock feathers, dragonflies, snakes, bats. Materials and shapes inspired by nature, by animals and flowers.

And she would stop powdering her olive complexion pale and forcing her thick hair into submission, masking the exotic quality that marked her beauty.

No. She would play it up. Show it off.

No one would believe that a woman considered Black under the law would take the risk of wearing clothes in New York's high society that evoked Africa or Asia. Only a white woman could allow herself these Eastern adornments.

And Poiret had found the ideal celebrity to introduce his designs to the New World.

Neither of them had a moment to lose; Belle was checking out of the Ritz tomorrow, and so the business between them was quickly concluded. Going against the conventions of "made-to-measure" couture, Poiret agreed to sell her his prototypes without any additional fitting sessions, something that would never have been done by Worth or any other major designer. "Ready-to-wear" clothing, ahead of its time.

"Just because I'm a librarian doesn't mean I have to dress like one!" Belle's words to Junius during their visit to the West Room a few years earlier now took on added significance. She would return from Europe at the height of chic, modeling the latest fashions from Paris.

*

The last part of their stay in London fulfilled all the promise of the first week. Belle solidified the friendships she had made before the auction, putting the finishing touches on the network of literary connections that would serve her in the years to come.

"Mr. Morgan's book curator came to visit me in Cambridge today," wrote the renowned scholar Sydney Cockerell in his journal on December 7, 1908.

"First I showed her our Fitzwilliam Museum, and then the manuscripts in our collections. After that I took her into the stacks at the St. John's College Library, and Trinity Hall, and then Clare's College and King's [ . . . ]. Miss Greene is an extremely charming, highly intelligent woman with a great, great enthusiasm for manuscripts."

High praise indeed, coming from the world's foremost expert on illuminated codices.

On the voyage back to America in Mr. Morgan's personal suite aboard the White Star liner, the Greene ladies luxuriated once again in marble fixtures, concerts, bridge games, and suppers at the captain's table. A dream. Their European adventure had lasted less than a month, but their view of the world had been forever changed, the trip awakening in both of them a nostalgia that only the next journey would relieve.

They would see Paris properly, they resolved. They would visit Florence, and Venice . . .

Reality descended again the moment they arrived at the docks in New York. "Ladies and gentlemen in first class, please return to your cabins, prepare your papers, and open your trunks."

Like a good student, Belle hurried to obey. She was well aware of the risk she had taken by not declaring the valuable objects she was bringing back from Europe.

Genevieve was trembling from head to foot. What if Belle's conduct led to an investigation—and from there to the revelation of their false names, false ages, false identities, leading back to their relationship to Richard Greener—their roots in Georgetown's Black quarter?

Mother and daughter had discussed the possibility. Belle, normally so far-sighted, had refused to be cowed by that particular threat. "We aren't scared women anymore, Maman. Or colored women. You have to think like a white. Otherwise you won't be able to live. And anyway, fear never gives good advice."

She didn't fully realize the effect her reckless actions were having on Genevieve, however, until she saw her mother pale and terrified at the sight of the customs agents making their rounds. Telling Genevieve to wait outside their cabin, in the corridor or on the deck, she took charge of all of their baggage. Her mother didn't wait to be told twice.

Belle had prepared herself for the pressure of the customs inspection, but suddenly she felt herself quailing. Genevieve's terror at the thought that the search could lead to catastrophe had gained the upper hand.

She placed on a table Madame Adélaïde's precious breviary, the Cambridge Bible, and the few Caxtons she had not left with the bookbinder Gruel. She knew she had nothing to fear from the inspection when it came to the books; American law did not consider them objects of value, and they were not taxed. And so they would remain nestled safely in their silk-lined tin boxes, which protected them from humidity better than wood. These marvels, at least, were secure.

For the rest, though—the enameled pendant watch and the small bronzes she had picked up in Paris . . .

She had chosen to take the pendant from its box and put it with her own necklaces and bracelets and brooches, all of it messily entangled in her jewelry box. The two Renaissance statuettes had been stowed with her boots and shoes in the footwear compartment of her steamer trunk, in plain sight and without any wrappings.

The parrots and the chinoiseries, on the other hand, were meticulously concealed beneath her most intimate personal effects, each piece buried deep among the lacy layers of her underclothing.

When the two customs officials came across the small packages that young Seligman had wrapped with care befitting precious works of art, Belle allowed a look of alarm to cross her face. The men, accustomed to these sorts of emotions, had no doubt they'd found something important—a suspicion strengthened when she burst out, watching them handle the pieces:

"Be careful! Those are fragile!"

After extracting the parrots from their silken wrappings, they asked to see the bill for them.

"They're family keepsakes. They belonged to my grandmother."

They exchanged a glance that said plainly, "Not another one!"

"She left them to me years ago. Look, they're all broken," she insisted, pretending to sink into a confused muddle of explanations and lies.

"That would deduct nothing from their value, Madam. On the contrary, in fact. And actually, these porcelain objects look to be in perfect condition to me. Do you remember how much you paid for them?"

"I told you—I didn't buy them."

There was a silence. One of the customs agents left the room for a moment and returned with his superior, who greeted Belle and then said, politely but firmly:

"Unfortunately, Madam, I think we'll have to keep these porcelain objects of yours until we've had them evaluated by our experts."

"Keep my porcelains! You're joking!"

She made a show of growing breathless with indignation, then gaining control of herself and calming down.

"If there is a small fine to pay," she huffed, "I am prepared to do so."

"You'll pay it later."

She waved her arms in consternation. "Surely you aren't actually going to strip me of my grandmother's gifts!"

"Terribly sorry, Madam, but it's the law. If you can't produce a bill, we have to confiscate the items. We'll let you know when, and under what conditions, you can get them back."

As they were about to turn their attention to the bronzes, she cried out.

"Oh, *those* you can take! But *not my parrots!*" she shrieked hysterically.

Anxious to avoid a scandal and to spare themselves the ordeal of a nervous breakdown in J.P. Morgan's cabin, the customs officers decided it was best to withdraw, taking the Chinese porcelains with them.

*

"And that's how it happened," she finished.

She had just regaled the Big Chief with the tale of her performance for the customs agents—and laid out before him with great solemnity, on the large table she'd had moved for this express purpose, the splendid Caxtons and the Cambridge Bible.

The two of them were standing in the West Room, bent over their spoils of war. Now she set down the French princess's book of hours intended for Adelaide Douglas, the two bronze statuettes, and the watch in its antique box.

He forced himself to restrain his pleasure and to think about what she had sacrificed to bring him these treasures.

"But you—your porcelains, and all the souvenirs you bought for your family—you've lost them."

"The parrots? I don't give a toss about them! They're meaningless to me. I have the bill for them, with the description, and believe me, compared to your bronzes, they aren't worth much. Far less than what those cretins were thinking, anyway. Customs will have to return my possessions to me, with their humblest apologies."

"That's my girl!" he exclaimed, and roared with laughter. "If you aren't the cleverest little thing I've ever met!"

The thought of how she'd pulled the wool over the eyes of the taxmen who had plagued him for years, forcing him to leave his collections in London, filled Morgan with glee. It had always galled him that the American government preferred to deprive the nation of such fabulous objects rather than forgo its twenty percent import tax! And Belle had triumphed over those imbeciles! Morgan gave a Sioux war-cry and thumped his desk as if it were a drum, then broke into a victory dance around the room. Delighted, she joined in, whooping.

Miss Thurston could hear the racket they made all the way in the storeroom.

It was January 1909, and this moment of abandon, so out of keeping with J.P. Morgan's staid image, sealed their rapport forever.

An intimate bond. Unbreakable.

Despite their differences in age, background, fortune, and temperament, despite everything that separated them, theirs was a true communion of souls, the ideal love of which each of them, in his or her own fashion, had always dreamed.

\*

Belle, seated at her desk, was sorting through the enormous pile of correspondence that had accumulated during her absence.

"Have you seen this?" asked Thursty, holding out a copy of the *The Times* of London. "Lord Amherst is dead."

Belle froze. Staring straight ahead, her face sheet-white, she didn't even reach for the proffered newspaper. Thursty, who hadn't been expecting the news to come as such a shock, hesitated and then read aloud:

"*London, January 18, 1909*

"*We have been informed of the death of Lord Amherst of Hackney at the age of seventy-three. He was famously the victim of a swindle by his solicitor, and the sale of his library that resulted had a disastrous effect on his health and hastened his end.*

"*Last December, Lord Amherst attended the sale of the collection of rare and magnificent books he spent his life collecting. He then returned to spend the Christmas holidays at his estate of Didlington Hall.*

*"Last Friday, Lord Amherst came to London to conclude some business related to the sale of his collections by the auction house of Messrs. Sotheby, Wilkinson, and Hodge. He seemed unusually fatigued by the journey and retired early.*

*"He awoke feeling rested but collapsed at breakfast. His physician was unable to provide any aid. His heart had given out.*

*"William Amhurst Tyssen-Amherst, Baron Amherst of Hackney, died at his residence at 23 Queen's Gate Garden on the evening of Saturday, January 16. He was born on April 25, 1835. By special permission, his eldest daughter will inherit his title."*

Belle sat still and silent, her expression one of mingled shock and sorrow.

"A sad fate," remarked Thursty. "Let's hope the same thing never happens to us. To Mr. Morgan, I mean," she added awkwardly. Sensing that she was only shoving her foot further into her own mouth, she hastily changed the subject:

"Since the news broke in the papers of your triumphs in England, everyone who knows Mr. Morgan has been clamoring to visit his library. It's been one endless parade, a dozen scholars a day—not to mention the simply curious. You'll see for yourself when you look at the guest book."

Belle allowed herself to be distracted by the recital of everything that had happened during her absence. She leafed through the *Amicorum*, the large volume with gilt-edged pages which the library's noteworthy visitors were invited to sign. There were the signatures of the boss's daughters and their husbands, and those of his female admirers, former mistresses, or future conquests: his Blondes. There were the signatures of the Duke of Montpensier, the Countess of Galliffet, and other European aristocrats who had traveled to New York.

"Thursty," she said, pausing on one particular name, "am I seeing Bernhard Berenson's signature here?"

"Oh, don't talk to me about him. He arrived from Europe at the beginning of December and came to the library twice with his wife. And he was absolutely unbearable both times."

"Perhaps, Thursty, perhaps. But his writings are masterpieces. I've never read anything more brilliant on Italian Renaissance painting." Admiration brought a flush to her cheeks. "I was fifteen when I discovered his first book on Venice," she went on. "It fascinated me so much that, just because of him, I began spending entire weekends and school holidays at the Metropolitan Museum. The man has an incredible eye."

"Well, he certainly thinks he sprang from the thigh of Zeus! He's so . . . self-important, so pretentious . . . If you'd heard him . . . He criticized every one of the objects in Mr. Morgan's office, every one of them! And don't tell anyone, but he looked down his nose at our Italian pieces. He could *just* bring himself to appreciate the manuscripts and incunabula. Barely."

"He's a star, Thursty! And a genius! The greatest art historian in the world!"

"I appreciate his work, just like you do. That doesn't mean I can't find him terribly unpleasant."

Belle ignored this remark. "I don't suppose he left the address of his hotel?"

"Did he! Only about a dozen times. He's staying at the Webster; he'll be there until the middle of February. He told me over and over, in case I'd forgotten. Despite all his criticisms, he says there's only one thing he wants in the whole world, and that is to become Mr. Morgan's personal advisor, his own private art expert. He's traveled here from Florence for that express purpose—to build a client base of American millionaires and get rich off them. Well, he doesn't have a chance, as far as we're concerned; Mr. Morgan can't stand him. He only allowed him to visit out of politeness. But he doesn't like him and doesn't want to see him again."

"Call the Webster Hotel for me, please, and say that Miss Belle da Costa Greene, from the Morgan Library, is requesting the honor of speaking to Mr. Berenson."

"We're calling that horrible man? What on earth for?"

## CHAPTER 6

## MY HEART'S DESIRE
### JANUARY 1909–AUGUST 1910

A h, Berenson!" one of the guests exclaimed. "He's so gifted that he could've become anything he wanted. He could have been God, but he chose to be the devil."

Since the arrival of Berenson and his wife in the United States, the talk at New York's high-society dinner parties had been of nothing but the mad pace of their lives. The couple had met with every collector in New York, Boston, and Philadelphia, hosting five receptions a day where, beneath a surface veneer of pleasantries, they toiled to expand their network of potential clients. Lunch at the Astors', tea at the Laffans', dinner at the home of Henry Clay Frick and his wife.

Same hosts, same places, same frenetic social pace as Belle. She listened avidly to every morsel of gossip.

The great man's wife had left her first husband and two daughters without batting an eyelash, people said, to follow Bernhard Berenson around the world. Since then, she'd served as his secretary, assistant, nurse, agent—and punching bag. It was also said that, despite the way she seemed to allow herself to be mistreated, she knew how to protect herself, and that their union was an open marriage in which both partners were free to indulge in affairs.

A dyed-in-the-wool feminist, Mary Berenson gave as many talks on women's right to vote as she did on the history of Italian art. Anne Morgan, the tycoon's youngest daughter, had taken it upon herself to arrange for Mary a whole series of meetings at the Colony Club, to which she belonged, a high-society women's club of which Belle was now a member, as well. The event had been a success, and it was Anne who, in the absence of her father's librarian, had organized the Berensons' visit to the Morgan Library.

Though American-born, both Berensons affected to reject their Yankee roots for an exaggerated Anglomania, acting—even in private—as if they were tourists in some philistine land. Despite this mutual snobbery, however, they were in most ways as mismatched a couple as one could find.

Mary Berenson was tall and large-boned, at once secure in her intellectual power and self-conscious about her lack of elegance, now accentuated by encroaching plumpness. A caryatid that did not wholly lack beauty, but whose Quaker roots had instilled in her a disdain for fashion and frippery. She tended to use old-fashioned words—the pronoun *thee* instead of *you*—and occasionally wore a white bonnet in the manner of a seventeenth-century Protestant.

Her husband was of average height, very slim and well-groomed, fastidiously elegant—it took him an hour just to get dressed each day, people murmured. To choose his suit and overcoat for the day from among the twenty or thirty Savile Row ensembles in his wardrobe, his gloves from among the rows and rows of them he possessed, his scarf, his hat. Always a fresh flower in his buttonhole, replaced three times a day until he dressed for dinner. He was plagued by stomach problems, a tendency to hypochondria and depression, but in reality he was healthy as a horse, with the strength and tenacity of a jockey. He was a witty and sparkling conversationalist who prided himself on his ability to stimulate the minds of his listeners and expected the same in return. Though he loved a good argument, he was always determined to have the last word.

When it came to the fairer sex, he was an incorrigible flirt, with both the need and the inclination to please. This was a longstanding tendency; even as a child, his mother and sisters had lavished so much adoration on him that as an adult he could charm the legs off a chair—and in the rare event that the chair happened to resist him, he solved the problem by tossing it out a window.

Now, at forty-four years old, he sported short hair and an impeccably trimmed beard. His even features, slim frame, and air of distinction had lost none of their youthful impact. His dark hair was untouched by gray; he was blue-eyed, with a straight nose and full lips. His intellectual agility, when combined with his looks, gave him a charm that few—male or female—could resist. He was a man unlike any other, whose beauty made every heart skip a beat.

Beauty! It lay at the very heart of his life. He could go into eloquent raptures over a magnificent landscape, or the poetry of a painting; nature and art enchanted him in the same way. He saw no difference between them and was liable to be wholly swept up in the contemplation of either one, with the same intensity. Roaming across the hills of Tuscany or visiting a museum, he was, and knew himself to be, possessed by a sort of mysticism, a blend of quasi-religious reverence and awe.

He had cultivated this passion for paintings over many years, developing and refining his own personal method of looking at them. He had begun training his eye in Venice, studying the canvases of Giorgione, soaking in the tiniest details until he possessed the whole of a tableau's composition within him.

In this way, Bernhard Berenson's visual memory had become a thing of such power that he could recall at will each of the works stored in it and compare these to others. He retained not only a perfect recollection of the image itself, but the room in which it had been located, the angle, the light. This gift, combined with the boundless energy that drove him to travel to the most remote parts of the countryside to view church altarpieces *in situ*, had made him a great expert in the paintings of the Italian Old Masters, one capable of assessing the quality of a painted drapery, of recognizing a charcoal pencil-line or a paintbrush stroke as the work of a particular painter. His extraordinary ability had made him so knowledgeable that now, in 1909, the verdict of Bernhard Berenson—"B.B." to those closest to him—on a painting, and thus on the artist who created it, carried more weight than the actual signature at the bottom of the tableau. In cases where his attribution and the signature disagreed, Berenson's faithful believed only one thing—that the signature was false, as Berenson's eye was never wrong. His judgment was infallible.

An aesthete, a scholar, and a gentleman, Berenson viewed business, and businessmen, with pure disdain. While he recognized that the success of his books on art history financed the luxury of his existence, and while he made no attempt to conceal the fact that his Florentine villa had been purchased with his author's fees, he refused to admit that he owed his fortune to his expertise, and anyone who dared to bring up the subject became a target for his sarcasm and loathing.

The hidden truth was that his success was due as much to his skill as a businessman as it was to his intellectual genius. He received a commission on the price of every piece of art whose sale he contributed to—a double commission, in fact; twenty-five percent from the gallery owner, and five percent from the buyer.

However, Berenson's contract arrangements with his various clients remained a secret that his enemies suspected but had never managed to prove. A mystery, like his origins.

He maintained complete silence regarding his birth in the Jewish community of a small Lithuanian village. He never spoke about his family's emigration to America, or about his father, who had been a peddler in Boston's poorest slum. He was silent about his poverty-stricken childhood, his rise—a few years after Richard Greener—to become a brilliant scholarship student at Harvard, then a dandy whose world travels were paid for by his friends. Silent, too, about his successive religious conversions, first to Protestantism during a sojourn in England, and then to Catholicism in Italy.

Silent, above all, about his true birth name: Bernhard Valvrojenski.

No one knew the full truth of his troubled history, except perhaps his mother and sisters. Not even his wife, who had been born neither Jewish nor poor. Bernhard Berenson buried the shadowy parts of himself as deeply as he could, cloaking his past in impenetrable darkness.

Dissimulation, lies, and false identities: also the tactics of a certain Belle da Costa Greene. They shared the same quality of living disguised in broad daylight, of reinventing themselves in the glare of the limelight.

And as if this mutual rejection of their origins were not enough, they shared another aspect of their destinies: a career based entirely on the protection of an individual more rich and powerful than themselves. Two great collectors whom they served in the same way: in her case, J.P. Morgan; in his, Isabella Stewart Gardner, for whom he created the Boston museum that bore her name.

Miss Greene's first encounter with the Berensons had been fairly forgettable; she had come to greet them in the lounge at their hotel and to offer her services in any way that might make their stay as pleasant as possible. Unlike Thursty, Belle had not been shocked by the couple's arrogance; she was accustomed enough to Morgan's rages not to be cowed by anyone who put on airs.

But Bernhard Berenson himself had proved to be every bit as impressive as his books. His astonishing genius was immediately apparent; he was the most intellectually stimulating man she had met since her Princeton years. And so she set about the task of pleasing him, organizing a private visit to the Metropolitan Museum.

And though she normally didn't give a toss about wives, she also tried to charm Mrs. Berenson. Here was a remarkable woman, she sensed, and she resolved to win her over. Mary fell obligingly into the trap, writing to her daughter, who dreamed of visiting New York: "Mr. Pierpont Morgan's secretary—Belle Greene, a most unusual young person, absolutely EXTRAOR-DINARY—has invited you and your friend Elie to accompany her to the opera, in her private box, on Thursday March 4."

Belle's box was, of course, the best in the house, as it was owned by the Big Chief, who let her use it freely in his absence. She made sure to make the evening an unforgettable experience for the two teenage girls, who returned from the outing gushing about how they had "adored Miss Greene." Mary, wishing to repay the kindness, then invited Belle to spend a few days in Boston with her and her daughters.

Belle accepted the invitation initially, but then sent a note excusing herself: "Too much work, sadly."

In truth, B.B., who had remained in New York to attend to his professional commitments, had begun a correspondence with Belle that was of a different tone altogether. He had seen her several times in the public places he frequented, then invited her to dine in a restaurant tête-a-tête before an unforeseen inci-dent had forced him to cancel their plans. To the telegram he sent expressing the depth of his regret, she had replied, "I am so happy to know that you are going to become a true friend (a rare thing in this world). So happy that I can almost, *almost* forgive you for not having lunch with me! I must confess to being hor-ribly disappointed by the delay. I had so hoped to have a quiet conversation with you. I would like to think that, before you return to Europe, we will have begun a real friendship. This let-ter is very frank, but I think you will understand me. Do join me for tea at my apartment one of these days."

She could not have been more clear—or less proper. What young virgin desirous of protecting her own reputation would invite a married man to her home alone? Certainly, her mother and sisters could serve as chaperones and give an air of respectability to the proposition—but who would be fooled?

Certainly not Bernhard Berenson.

"Belle's in love! Belle's in love!" sang her younger sister Teddy, jumping on her bed.

"Shut up, you idiot. You have no idea what you're talking about."

"You didn't see your face when your B.B. stood you up."

"What are you talking about? I don't give a toss. But have you seen his flowers? You'll never get a bouquet like that!"

The vase sat majestically on a table, overflowing with a creation from Thorley's House of Flowers, the best florist in the city, and the one Mr. Morgan used to court his Blondes. There was nothing staid or conventional about this bouquet, however; no white lilies or pink roses as were traditional for young unmarried ladies, and none of the violets or red roses typically reserved for married women. It was a magnificent arrangement, worthy of a seventeenth-century Dutch painting, and Belle recognized its symbolism immediately. There were anemones, the Grecian windflower, born of the blood of Adonis, lover of Venus—an allegory of fragile beauty. Forget-me-nots, the flower of memory, an invitation to fidelity. Asian buttercups, representative of luxury and seduction. Narcissuses, a metaphor for self-love. Then tulips, symbols of power and wealth. And finally nasturtiums, with their brilliant, fiery colors, twining around the vase like a flame—the embodiment of passion itself ever since Louis XIV presented an armful of them to Madame de Maintenon.

It was a whole coded language, more eloquent than any declaration.

In the company of this man, every visit to a museum or a gallery or a private collection was an adventure as exciting as any physical voyage. Listening to him explain, demonstrate, why this painting could only be the work of Raphael despite being generally attributed to someone else, awakened in you a hunger for knowledge so intense that it made you dizzy. He knew how to lead you into the deepest depths of a work of art.

Belle had only had this sort of experience before with Junius, and even that was a faint foretaste of what she was feeling now. It turned her into a silly, starry-eyed girl, reading poetry in the hopes of finding a few lines that would echo her own emotions. She clipped from *Scribner's Magazine* a set of verses by a female poet, entitled "The Turning Point," which ended with:

> *I have traveled alone,*
> *So far.*
> *And now, suddenly,*
> *A turning point.*
> *And you.*

And because Belle was fearless, she sent these five lines to the man to whom she had lost her heart. He didn't need to appreciate the literary quality to relish the gesture.

The natural ease and intelligence with which she managed his visit to New York, her kindness in organizing encounters for him with the collectors he wanted to meet, her enthusiasm and her obvious admiration for him—he couldn't help but be flattered.

For a woman to appeal to Bernhard Berenson, she had to be well-educated, elegant, capable of delicacy and wit. Miss Greene fulfilled every one of these criteria. He had a taste for wealthy women, as well; romantic rendezvous in humble cottages did not tempt him in the slightest. Normally he selected his paramours from among the aristocracy—Italian princesses or English duchesses. He loved nothing more than an ardent embrace beneath the fresco-painted ceilings of a palace. Instinctively, he

preferred flirtation to passion, and games of conquest to the ultimate victory.

And when it came to games, Mr. Morgan's young librarian
possessed unmatched skill.

Yet he sensed that, despite her appearance of offering herself
unreservedly, he was only seeing the surface of her being—and
that her daring, and her marvelous sense of humor, concealed
other mysteries. In truth, Miss Greene's radiance intrigued him
as much as her secrets. What were her origins? How old was
she, really? How had she acquired her culture, her refinement,
her vast knowledge of books? These questions, which he never
fully articulated even in his own mind, fed his curiosity. And
then there was Miss Greene's sex appeal, which overwhelmed
him completely. None of his previous mistresses had ever unsettled him in exactly this way. He loved the way she held her
head, her erect carriage when she walked, chin lifted as if in
defiance. The amber perfume of her hair, the texture of her
skin, the twinkle in her gray eyes. That slightly husky voice of
hers, with its almost masculine timbre, imparted by the cigarettes in which she liked to indulge. And he loved the ornate
jewelry she favored, the golden serpent twining about her neck,
her strikingly modern clothing that invited the eye to embrace
the new and different.

The truth was that the cool and distinguished Bernhard
Berenson had fallen completely under the spell of this American
siren, a self-made woman who not only earned her own living
but had forged an extraordinary career . . . A unique and atypi-
cal creature who belonged to no known social class, who
enjoyed the benefits of wealth without truly having a penny to
her name. "Unusual," as his wife described her. Everything he
should have hated. Everything he adored.

The urgency of his need to possess her only increased his
desire. Their time together was drawing to a close. Berenson

would be leaving the United States in mid-March. There were
only ten days left to make her his.

*

On March 15, 1909, the room service employees of the
Webster Hotel were buzzing. A certain guest who was known to
be difficult when it came to food—invariably sending dishes
back to the kitchen as "too salty," "too acidic," "too sweet"—
had ordered a late-night supper in his room, specifying the menu
in great detail. A supper for two. And what was more, he had
asked, once it was delivered, not to be disturbed.

No one in the hotel kitchen had any doubt about the gender
of this guest, let alone the morals of the woman he had invited
to his room.

For B.B., as for Belle, however, minimal precautions were still
necessary. He couldn't openly receive a lover in the suite he
shared with his wife—though Mary, who was still in Boston,
would not have objected if he had. She considered this latest dal-
liance of Bernhard's a mere trifle, to which distance would soon
put an end. In fact, she thought Mr. Morgan's librarian the perfect choice for a night's indulgence.

Belle, for her part, had to be mindful of her reputation.
People were already suspicious of the extremely privileged status afforded her by Mr. Morgan. He paid her too much, allowed
her too much freedom. Miss Greene could only be his illegitimate daughter, they murmured—or else his mistress. She and
the Big Chief laughed together about the rumors—and yet they
were careful not to invite too much gossip. The only real ambi-
guity in their relationship lay in Morgan's excessive jealousy
where Belle was concerned. He considered Miss Greene his
exclusive property.

Until now, Morgan had been quite pleased with Belle's lack
of a love life; it meant that he remained the focal point of her

existence, the *deus ex machina* with ultimate power over her fate. But if he were to discover that she had entered into a liaison with a married man—and one, furthermore, that Morgan himself did not like, God only knew to what extremes his fury might push him. Would he fire her! Yes—he would surely fire her! A catastrophe.

Belle knew perfectly well that by accepting Bernhard Berenson's invitation to dine in his suite, she was agreeing to go to bed with him. She hadn't been born yesterday; despite her professed age of twenty-four, she would be thirty in November. Though she made a point of emphasizing her youth, of repeating that she loved her freedom and had no desire to marry, neither did she wish to wither on the vine; she had no intention of dying a virgin. Many men had tempted her, but none, with the exception of Junius, had affected her this deeply. And she had accepted her own desire, resolving to give herself to Berenson, body and soul. On this point, they were agreed. She would belong to him.

The initial approaches had been furtive. Long handshakes in greeting and farewell, knowing glances, a brushing of arms in which both of them sensed the skin burning with desire beneath the fabric of their sleeves. They were each aware of the giddiness they aroused in the other, the turbulent feelings each of them left in their wake. It was far more than a kindling of the senses; it was a promise of eternity.

An eternity that would last a single night.

Belle counted the moments remaining until she would see him with anticipation so intense it verged on agony.

She knew they would only have a few hours to love one another. And then? Nothing. Absence. Emptiness. But at least she would have had those hours. The opportunity would not repeat itself, not now and not ever. This was the eve of the day before B.B.'s departure. He was set to sail on the *Mauritania* on Tuesday.

She had prepared herself for the rendezvous with exquisite care, wearing her most elegant undergarments, her most intoxicating perfume. Cautious as always, she had made sure to give herself an alibi for the evening, going to the opera where she was seen by all of New York in the company of her longtime devoted admirers, William Laffan and Charles Lanier. Berenson, for his part, put in an appearance at a party thrown by the Astors and then returned to his hotel and went straight to his room, where Belle joined him a few moments later. And now, he carefully removed the long tulle veil covering her forehead and her hair.

He was so overwhelmed that he could neither offer her a seat at the table nor sit down across from her. He merely stood, dazzled. Eventually she sat down on the sofa and picked up the book lying on its cushions. Baudelaire.

"Read me the one that touches you the most," she said, struggling to keep her tone light.

"You really want me to?"

"'Les Bijoux.' Yes."

The request enabled Berenson to pull himself together. He knew his voice was irresistibly sensual. Reading Baudelaire's poetry to women was his favored tactic for putting them under his spell.

*My well-beloved was stripped. Knowing my whim,*
*She wore her tinkling gems, but naught besides:*
*And showed such pride as, while her luck betides,*
*A sultan's favoured slave may show to him.*

While the charm offensive worked, the poetry only heightened their emotions. Where in their previous, casual encounters they had managed to convey their full feelings to one another, to connect deeply, now they found themselves unable to do anything but utter rambling trivialities.

Dinner was marked by long stretches of silence. Berenson,

who normally drank little, tried to loosen his tongue with copious amounts of burgundy—but to no avail; Belle's presence stripped him of his panache. Likewise, she was drinking champagne in a deliberate effort to get tipsy—but tonight the alcohol seemed to lend her neither wit nor eloquence. Even the cigarettes they both chain-smoked failed to relax them.

Being alone together had turned these two otherwise fearless people into terror-stricken adolescents. Too far gone to indulge in their usual banter, they burned with the same desire, but neither of them dared to make a move.

And yet Berenson had been so sure that Belle had long ago thrown caution and reserve to the wind. She'd shown herself much too skilled at teasing him not to have been initiated into the art by others. It wasn't that he believed her to be an "easy mark," simply lighthearted and insouciant, like many of his aristocratic conquests had been. Of course, they were all married, or had been previously. They knew how to take the initiative. How could he ever have imagined that Belle, so sure of herself as a flirt, was too sexually inexperienced to give him the cue he needed?

All of a sudden he felt such modesty, such vulnerability emanating from this young woman, something so pure, so innocent, that he no longer knew exactly who was standing there in front of him.

"I remember every second of that evening so clearly," she would write three years later. "I even remember what I was wearing, and the way I had styled my hair, which you said you loved. I remember the way you stepped behind my chair, the way you pressed a kiss into my hair. I didn't move . . . I pretended I hadn't noticed your kiss . . ."

What she did not add was that their unquenched desire would drive them mad, that their frustration, exacerbated by distance, would soon turn into obsession. That their separation from one another would stoke their passion into white-hot incandescence. And that she would carry within her a deep and piercing regret over this missed opportunity.

The dinner ended with Berenson's having attempted nothing more than that single, stolen kiss.

Belle, at as much of a loss as B.B. himself was, had stammered during the dessert course that it really was time for her to get home. He'd escorted her back to her apartment without protest.

On her doorstep at the moment of parting, the same anguish enveloped them both. Mary was returning to New York tomorrow. She and B.B. would pack their bags, would bid goodbye to their friends. On Tuesday, it would all be over. Belle and Berenson would never see each other again. They fell into a desperate embrace, kissing with all the passion pent up in them both.

He clasped her tightly in his arms, unable to let her go.

"Swear you'll write to me," he murmured urgently. "Tell me everything you're doing, hour by hour. Down to the smallest details. Every day. I want to know everything about you. Swear it to me, Belle. Swear it."

"I swear . . ."

"You'll write to me every day," he repeated. "And I'll do the same."

"Yes. And you'll tell me about all your wonderful discoveries . . . everything that makes you happy in this world, until we're together again."

"I don't want you to hide anything from me," he insisted. "I want you—all of you—to belong to me. I need to know what you think, what you feel. I need to know your heart."

"My heart? It's already yours."

"Prove it, by writing to me everything I'm asking you for. Tell me who you spend your time with. Who you like. Who you find interesting. I'm starving for you—for your soul—for all your secrets."

March 17, 1909. The fateful day of departure. Belle would remember it for the rest of her life. "I felt as if the sun and the warmth of the world were forever behind me."

Unable to rise above her despair, unable to accompany Berenson to the dock, she shut herself in her room to write to him, filling page after page with her large, sprawling handwriting, just as she had promised him.

The first of her six hundred and eleven letters to him was dated "The night of the day you left me."

"My heart's desire, I'm trying to face what awaits me: the hours, months, years without you. Accepting your absence means accepting the prospect of endless grief. But I must accept it, and quickly, or go mad. The truth is, though, that I can't stop thinking of what might have been . . ."

\*

Belle continued to go to the library every day, to pay bills and receive visitors, but her enthusiasm had gone. Her appetite for life only returned during those hours of intimacy with him, with the satin-smooth pages of her stationery, stamped at the top with a single name: "Belle." Stationery that she had ordered especially for this purpose, that she used only for writing to him.

"I swear to myself that I won't dream of you anymore," she wrote in the privacy of her rooms. "Of us. Of what we could have done, could have said, could have been. I know that my flights of fancy will be my undoing. But I kiss your eyes and your mouth, and I break the promises I made to myself to forget your face. How I would love for you to swoop down and carry me away to the other side of the world, to a place where we could really know life—really know each other! But no—I am here, in my bed, awake for whole nights running, paralyzed by my own despair."

*

Berenson himself was equally miserable.

Shut up in his office in his Tuscan villa, he wrote letters of six or eight pages to her every day. A manic correspondent, he bombarded her with epistles both tender and vividly descriptive about his smallest act, his every feeling—and his skill at letter-writing was such that everything he said was interesting and moving. Descriptions of paintings he had seen, thoughts on books he had read, gossip about celebrities of the art world, stories of the Italian princesses he met in Florentine villas. Avowals of his devotion to her, and his suffering.

In Berenson, passion mingled with regret and fear with reproach, leveled at both himself (how—why—had he not taken Belle Greene, possessed her, during their rendezvous at the Webster?) and at her (how—why—had Belle not given herself to him, as she had with others?).

He saw his return to Italy as a failure, though in fact his American sojourn had been highly successful. The links he had forged with the country's millionaire collectors now enabled him to view the future with a sense of serenity, and while he hadn't yet signed the contract with Duveen Brothers, the renowned firm of art dealers with offices in New York, London, and Paris, that would eventually pay him a generous commission on every painting they sold thanks to his attribution, he was still earning enough to live comfortably, able to restore I Tatti, his opulent Renaissance villa in the hills of Fiesole, without worrying about the cost.

The spring of 1909, filled with the din of hammer-blows, dust, wet paint, and water shutoffs, was an utter nightmare. Mary was supervising the restoration work. Translation: Mary was making her husband's life miserable. And making the house uninhabitable. And the crowning touch was that she had fallen in love with their architect, a very young man with whom she had begun an obsessive affair. It was the sort of turnabout he could not bear.

For his wife to encourage his romantic adventures was one thing. She had been the first to indulge in a liaison outside their marriage, and he had had to tolerate her infidelity. But it was quite something else for her to stop looking after her husband's well-being, his comfort, his health—for her to neglect him in favor of a passing fancy for some young dandy.

Their marriage, which had been more of a business partner-ship than anything else for some years now, began to turn sour.

The hostility Berenson felt toward his wife tipped him over the edge into true depression. Ever since their trip the United States, Mary had seemed like an obstacle to his happiness. He could no longer stand the way she spoke, the way she ate, the way she moved. Her height, her weight, her voice. Mary exas-perated him.

He dreamed of Belle.

He hadn't been able to leave her without sending a magnifi-cent present: an eighteenth-century edition of the *1,001 Nights* in Galland's French translation, which Jacques Cazotte had completed by adding the erotic texts, with a mosaic binding signed by Padeloup *le jeune*.

"You can't imagine my joy when I gaze at these sixteen books from you," she gushed. "I was alone in the Morgan Library—my library—when I received them, and I sat down Indian-style on the carpet with all the books I could hold in my arms, and some others in my lap, and the rest all piled around me. Then I opened the first volume at random—*L'Attente*, it was—*Waiting*."

"A strange gift, the *1,001 Nights*," she wrote, a smile curving her lips.

His way of helping her pass the time? Or was he alluding to the night they would spend together one day, surely, somewhere, sometime in the future?

But when?

\*

In "her" library, relations were no less tense than at the Villa I Tatti. J.P. Morgan's emotional equilibrium had always been fragile, but in this spring of 1909 he, too, was living through a crisis he found himself unable to rise above. His daughter Anne had officially set up house with the woman she'd fallen in love with.

The lady was almost twenty years older than Anne, and her name was Bessie Marbury. A force of nature, Miss Marbury was at that time the most influential literary agent in the world, counting among her clients Sarah Bernhardt, Edmond Rostand, Victorien Sardou, and Oscar Wilde, whom she counted as a close friend. A theater impresario and producer, she was already living with another woman, herself a brilliantly successful interior designer: this was Elsie de Wolfe, who had decorated the drawing rooms of the exclusive Colony Club and the private apartments of the great collector Henry Clay Frick. Bessie and Elsie had just purchased the Villa Trianon in France, a folly just a few steps from the small palace belonging to Marie Antoinette. Anne was financing the renovation of this temple to opulence, and the whole of Paris was clamoring to see it. Miss Morgan, then, had become the third pillar in what artists and writers called "the Versailles Triumvirate," one of the Three Graces of Lesbos, holding court in gardens that had once belonged to a queen.

And as if this scandal abroad were not enough, Anne was actively encouraging a domestic strike, here in New York, by textile industry workers, using the power of her name to force the bosses to back down, and her wealth to support the unions.

If they had only managed to have a conversation, the father and daughter might have reached an understanding. They shared the same compassion for the troubles of others, the same energy and courage, the same pride, and the same tenacity in standing by their convictions. But this similarity in temperament also meant that neither would ever give way to the other. The result was fierce conflict and, ultimately, estrangement.

It fell to Belle to soothe J.P. Morgan's suffering and to fill the gap left by Anne's absence by being constantly available. Shut up with him in the West Room as was their habit, she tried to distract him. They talked about everything and nothing. Books, people, politics, the election of the new president, William Howard Taft. Belle adored her role as Morgan's favorite. But their master–confidante dynamic was beginning to weigh on her. It was a one-way relationship, in which he shared everything with her but she could confide nothing personal in him. She was careful never to let slip anything about her love for Bernhard Berenson. The Big Chief already took up her days, her evenings, all of her Sundays, and his vice-like hold on her was growing stronger all the time.

The final nail in the coffin of her liberty arrived in the form of three letters, three bombshells dispatched by Junius from Munich in June 1909. The first of them was sent to Josie Dear, who received it in mid-August at Constitution Hill. The second letter was sent to Junius's uncle on his yacht anchored at Newport, and the third was to the Morgan Library's head librarian.

He would not be returning to the United States, Junius announced in these letters. He was leaving his wife, his children, and his job with the Morgan Bank. He was cutting ties with his past forever and settling in Paris. He thought of them all with fondness, he said, but he did not want to see them again. For now, at any rate. And until further notice.

The effect of these wholly unexpected letters on their recipients was devastating. Why such a complete break? No one had the slightest idea. And Junius provided no explanation. His tone was cold. Calculated. It brooked no argument.

Josie kept the true depth of her pain to herself, but J.P. Morgan expressed his in the form of a Homeric rage. One did not act this way in his family! One did not leave one's wife in front of the entire world! If Junius had become smitten with another woman, he had simply to conduct the liaison discreetly. You couldn't prevent a man from falling in love, or seeking happiness. But this—*this!* This public abandonment! This scandal! The *shame* of it!

Morgan had always felt closer to Junius than he did to his own son, had, in fact, loved his nephew deeply. And he had believed that love was returned. They shared the same interests, the same tastes. Every book now residing in the Morgan Library had passed through Junius's hands first. He had been the first to see all the collections of sketches and engravings. Rembrandt, Dürer. Twenty years of fellowship. And now Junius had just walked away.

Morgan bombarded Belle with questions. She was forced to admit that she knew nothing, either, or very little . . .

Junius had grown bored with Josie Dear after eighteen years of marriage; of this, Belle had no doubt. For the rest, though . . . She'd always known him to be very close to his two children. What, then, had brought him to this point? What secrets was he hiding? She remembered his nocturnal ramblings through the fields around Princeton, a pistol in his pocket, going to spend time with the people he affectionately referred to as "my relatives, the vagabonds."

But what did that have to do with his current actions?

Deep down, she realized, she didn't really know him. She had probably never truly understood him. She had believed their relationship was special, but now she saw how superficial it had actually been. Who was Junius, really? A mystery.

And yet he had kept writing to her in recent years. Even Quaritch in London, even the bookbinder Gruel in Paris passed on his greetings after he visited their offices. And now, after this incomprehensible missive, his letters stopped. There was only silence.

Junius, her teacher, her first love, a man she considered a close friend, had abandoned her. His absence, added to Berenson's, brought Belle very low. Like Morgan, she felt utterly betrayed.

His nephew was dead to him, the Big Chief insisted again and again. Only Miss Greene was left now. His jealousy at the thought that she might develop an attachment elsewhere, and leave him in her turn, became fierce in its intensity.

"If I were younger," he said to her one day in late August, "would I be to your taste?"

He had never ventured into this territory before, never even brought up the subject of their affection for one another. Had he sensed the presence of a rival? An intruder in his private reserve? Someone—something—that posed a threat to his omnipotence?

She chose to treat it as a joke: "You? Younger? Lord, no, I wouldn't have touched you with a ten-foot pole!"

"No, but really," he persisted, "if I'd been thirty years younger—would you have . . . liked me?"

She laughed. "Certainly not! I'd have been forced to quit the library within an hour of meeting you; you would have been far too dangerous!"

He seemed pleased by the flattery. But his demands on her time continued to become more insistent.

Wariness. Deception. Determination. Belle found herself fighting a trench war against Morgan. She tried to convince him to send her back to Europe—mentioning neither Florence nor Italy, of course, but working ceaselessly to make him see that she needed to return to London, for another sale at Sotheby's.

"London? Again? But you just got back!"

"You always exaggerate, Mr. Morgan. I got back more than six months ago. And this sale looks even more interesting than Lord Amherst's; Quaritch has just sent me the catalogue."

He examined the titles she had underlined. "Hmm. You're right—this is an extraordinary list! Well, just give Mr. Quaritch your orders for the items we're interested in. He's a clever fellow; he'll be able to stand in for us perfectly well."

But Belle persisted. "Mr. Quaritch himself suggested in his last letter that we come and see the condition of the incunabula for ourselves. Before the autumn."

"I see. I'll go myself. I'll be staying at Prince's Gate then, anyway."

"Wouldn't you like me to accompany you, Mr. Morgan?"

"I'd love it, Miss Greene; I'd love it! But we can't both abandon our library at the same time."

"You're right, of course. Not together. Certainly. I could go in August, perhaps—or even now, right away, since you—"

Frowning, he changed his tone. "You have complete independence for half the year!" he barked. "I leave you free to do whatever you like in my absence. So when I'm in New York, kindly try to avoid giving the impression that you wish to be elsewhere!"

He was teetering on the brink of an explosion. She backed down.

*

"Oh, my desires—my fruitless desires!" she lamented as she scribbled her daily letter.

"I think of the thousands of miles separating me from you with pangs sharper than any I have felt before. You seem so far away. Unattainable. I cannot even send my soul to you through space to kiss you goodnight, so imprisoned do I feel. And so alone."

Genevieve, watching her daughter's spirits sink lower and lower, carefully avoided asking any questions or making any comments. And yet she could not simply close her eyes to it; meeting that Berenson gentlemen had clearly shaken Belle to the core. How could she not worry about Belle's inability to sleep, her frayed nerves, the obvious ill effects of unfulfilled passion?

But what could Genevieve say to lessen Belle's suffering? That her beloved Berenson was married? That, even if he'd been single, she couldn't have married him?

Genevieve knew that all of her children would always have two separate lives. The outer life, which they led with gusto, each successful in the field he or she had chosen—Russell as an engineer, the girls as teachers, and Belle at the Morgan Library—and the inner life, the one they led behind closed doors, at home together. With their secret.

Thank heavens, neither Louise nor Ethel had yet been forced to give up any important attachments—but what would happen when they, too, fell in love? And when they realized that it would be truly impossible for them ever to marry anyone, Black or white?

In Belle's case, it was fortunate that her swain lived thousands of miles away. Genevieve had no doubt that distance would extinguish their passion in time. But what about her other daughters? What about Russell?

Just after their return from Europe, Genevieve had learned some disquieting news. An attorney had published a wanted notice in the *New York Times*, seeking the heirs of a Black activist named Isaiah Wears, who had died in 1905. This man had been a Philadelphia barber whose estate now belonged half to his cousin, Richard Greener, and half to his second cousin, Russell Greener. The former had shown up to claim his share upon his return from Vladivostok, but the grant of probate could not be issued until Russell Greener appeared to officially accept or renounce his part of the inheritance. The newspaper notice requested that he make immediate contact with either the executors of Mr. Wears's will in Philadelphia or with his father, at the home of the Platt sisters, 5237 Ellis Avenue, Chicago.

"Pa still needs money, like always," Louise had fretted. "He'll try to get back in touch with Russell!"

The siblings had waited for Belle and Genevieve to get home before they discussed what to do. Family meeting after family meeting was held in the living room.

"The lawyer didn't say how much my inheritance would be," Russell pointed out. He brought up the subject again and again, and the debates grew more and more heated.

"Stop fantasizing," snapped Belle impatiently.

"Look who's talking! Since that B.B. of yours left, you never stop daydreaming!"

"It's not the same thing. If you think cousin Wears was a millionaire, you've got another thing coming."

"Maybe, but when Maman needed money, it was Isaiah Wears she borrowed it from. Who knows how much he's left to me?"

"Who cares about the damned amount!" Belle exploded. "You're not going there! Even if it's an absolute fortune, Russell, you have to forget about it. Let it go!"

Belle's tone, and the tendency she had developed to act like the head of their family, were beginning to seriously irritate her brother. Her salary, and her new social status, made her think she was now entitled to give them orders. Yes, she paid most of the bills. It was only reasonable; she earned the most, and so she paid all of their living expenses. But that didn't mean she could start acting like her Big Chief and tyrannizing them.

Genevieve set about smoothing things over, and she was successful; the bond between brother and sister remained strong. But living together in the apartment on 115th Street was becoming difficult. Would Russell accept that he had to forsake the unexpected windfall that concerned only him? Would he be able to resist the siren call of money, or would he fall into the trap of claiming his share?

The danger was so great that Belle, already exhausted by her own stresses, refused even to think about it. She was fighting too hard against her own desires to worry about the temptations facing Russell. Nothing mattered to her these days but the letters arriving from Italy by the dozens.

"I wish so much—but what does it mean to wish?" she lamented. "One can't wish for the mountains to fall! I wish so much that no other woman had any claim on you.

"You see, My Flame, *Fiamma mia*, I'm nothing but a poor jealous girl at heart, not at all certain that she means anything to you, no matter how much you tell her she does."

During the long sleepless nights, she tried to pull herself together, to reason with herself. *Come on now: think. How long did you know this man? Not even a month. And how many times did you see him alone—really alone? Three, counting the night you wanted to give yourself to him . . .*

The vow never to have children, the vow she had once taken with her brother and sisters, weighed on her mind now. She never spoke to them about it, but she knew it haunted them all. To take the risk of becoming pregnant by Bernhard Berenson? To have a Black baby with a man like him? The idea made her shudder with horror.

*You see, silly girl? It's a romance without a future. And you dodged a bullet at the Webster. You should be thanking your lucky stars, instead of feeling sorry for yourself.*

*Draw on your love for him to embrace all that life has to offer.* Choose the best, *as Upson used to say. No more, no less. No drama, no star-crossed tragedy. This man is the mentor you've dreamed of. There's nothing he can't teach you. Accept what he is able to give you; make the most of it—and throw in a bit of levity every now and then, for God's sake!*

But her sessions of self-admonishment were to no avail. In this autumn of 1909, the effects of the crystallization of their love à la Stendhal were being felt on both sides of the Atlantic.

Nine months.

He hated I Tatti, Berenson insisted over and over. He hated Florence, he hated Italy; he wanted to get as far away as possible and never see any of them again. Mary described him as bewitched, unable to see anything, to feel anything, obsessed by a single idea.

Jealousy tortured him. He refused to believe that Belle could not come to him, refused even to consider the idea that Morgan kept her tethered. She had explained to him many times that she was a working girl, that she couldn't travel to Europe every summer like all her wealthy friends did; that, as a *poverina*, she was bound to play her role of court jester, for fear of losing a position the likes of which she would never be able to find again. But Berenson saw Belle's reasoning as a collection of empty excuses. The truth was that she had no intention of making their relationship real.

"You ask me to send you my private diary by return of post," she wrote. "They're just brief notes that wouldn't interest you. I write in my diary what I don't dare say aloud—wrong things, impossible, horrible, scandalous things that amuse me. For, at heart, in everything I do, and in everything I think, there is always a tiny, secret smirk."

These "wrong" thoughts that amused her—did they have to do with his own frustration, his despair? He worried that they did.

He had dispatched his younger sister Senda on a visit to New York.

Touched by B.B.'s way of being present through such a close

relative, Belle took pains to be friendly to the young woman, and indeed the two got along so well that Senda described Miss Greene as one of the queens of Manhattan, a creature who went out every evening and seemed to know everyone in the world.

"I've just returned from New York," she wrote to her brother on January 28, 1910, "where I had such a lot of fun! And the person who made my stay so wonderful was your friend Belle da Costa Greene. She reserved a place for me in her box at the theater. I dined with her before the opera, and she arranged a supper for me afterward with her friends. She gave a lunch at the Colony Club in my honor, too, and invited me to so many other parties, though sadly I couldn't attend all of them. Her kindness in organizing all of this for me touched me greatly—she seems to be, as you have described her, very American. She is the liveliest, the gayest, the most energetic person I have ever met! She gave me a tour of the Morgan Library and showed me *Endymion*, and the manuscript of Keats's *Sonnets*—I was able to read the very last words written in the poet's hand to his lover, that stupid girl. When I saw the portrait of Ghirlandaio, with all the warts on his nose, I couldn't help but notice a striking resemblance to Mr. Morgan."

This letter, which Senda meant to be kind—to thank B.B. for introducing her to someone so interesting—instead set off the powder keg of his emotions. So Belle was gay, was she? Having all sorts of fun? There could be no doubt—she was thumbing her nose at him. He had always suspected it. How could such an independent girl claim to be controlled by anyone? Whatever she might say, she could surely travel whenever she wanted. Hadn't she gone to Boston to see Isabella Stewart Gardner's collections in the museum Berenson himself had created?

But Belle had made the journey to Massachusetts at the whim of her own desire, her need to see the paintings he had loved, all the works he had chosen and bought. It was a way of being with him, at least in spirit. And she hadn't tried to moderate her enthusiasm at the sight of his trophies, gushing over the beauty of "his" Velázquez, "his" Raphael, "his" terra cotta Madonna. Later, she had rhapsodized in a letter to him about the masterpieces he had obtained for Mrs. Gardner.

Isabella Stewart Gardner herself, in a letter written to Berenson in late 1909, recalled the Morgan librarian's visit quite differently. Though Miss Greene had indeed uttered cries of admiration at the Boston collection, once back in New York her tone had changed to one of criticism—and, not content simply to denigrate the works of art, she had gone so far as to ridicule their owner at a dinner party. One of the guests reported to Mrs. Gardner that the young lady had described her as a woman without taste, so dull and stupid that she had recoiled from Isabella's invitation to visit the rest of her home. *Impossible!* raged the *grande dame* of Boston. Her encounter with Miss Greene had not been like that at all—not at *all!* Mr. Morgan's employee was telling fish stories.

Mrs. Gardner ended her letter to B.B. with two questions: "What do *you* think of that young woman? Do you know her well?"

Apt though Belle's jibes concerning the Gardner collection's masterpieces may have been, they were hardly going to please Berenson, naturally. How had Belle dared to criticize his patroness publicly—the sponsor who showcased him and touted his talents, and on whose goodwill the lion's share of his career depended? J.P. Morgan was Mrs. Gardner's main rival in matters having to do with art in America, and the two collectors loathed one another. How had Belle dared to betray him— *him*—in this way?

Prudently, he had elected not to disclose to his correspondent just how well he knew "that young woman"—all the more so because Mrs. Gardner concluded her missive with the words: "It so happens that the girl is of mixed race, and as such, she's unable to keep from lying!"

Where had Mrs. Gardner gotten this information? It was a mystery. One thing was certain: when they wanted to tear her down, Belle's enemies latched on to the color of her skin. Miss da Costa Greene, a half-breed? It was a haphazard attack, and one for which there was no proven basis. But if someone were to investigate further, just for the fun of it, sooner or later her secret would be revealed.

Strangely, it was not this rumor about Belle's origins, this nasty whisper beginning to circulate, that struck Berenson. The possibility that she might be of mixed blood meant nothing to him. Baudelaire, before him, had loved Jeanne Duval. And he knew himself well enough to sense that the exotic quality Belle possessed played a large part in his fascination with her. No—what shocked him to the core was this confirmation of what he had suspected: Belle was a liar. And he was a fool who had allowed himself to be led on for almost a year. She had played the role of a smitten ingenue when, in reality, she did not love him. She had manipulated him. She didn't love him at all.

But instead of quenching his passion, his doubts only stoked the flames. And her responses to his accusations caused him exquisite agony.

\*

The letters he sent berating her, and the apology-filled ones that followed, the fire-and-ice torture to which he subjected her, forced Belle, for her part, to pull back somewhat from the tumult of their relationship.

"I am trying to emerge from my depression by reminding myself that you care about my existence despite everything, as do two or three other important people. I'm hoping that the quality and virtues of my friends will serve to remind me of my own."

It was a way of reminding him that she had to keep living. He had his wife, his villa, his business, his books, his travels. What did she have? Her library. And her own panache. If he insisted on insulting her, she would respond with defiance.

Yes, she tried to go out every evening. She tried to make new friends. She had even met one woman who delighted her, the kind of woman she liked: financially independent, not reliant on her husband's wealth for her existence. A woman who called herself amoral, but who in reality possessed a firm set of personal values that she refused to betray. A woman without scruples, but who played fair. A woman of rare cynicism and matchless humor. One who lived a life of luxury. Divorced. Remarried. The author of popular plays and books, who received in her Long Island mansion the stars of New York's bohemian scene: actors, journalists, publishers.

It was a sphere altogether more exciting than Belle's circle of aged admirers—especially since William Laffan's death the previous November of a cerebral hemorrhage, which had not only plunged J.P. into a fresh agony of grief, but also meant that she could no longer spend time in Charles Lanier's company, since it was improper for the two of them to be alone together.

In her letters to Berenson, Belle called her new friend "Ethel the White," to differentiate her from "Ethel the Black," a close friend of B.B.'s whom Belle disliked, and also from her own beloved sister, Ethel Alice.

Ethel the White's real name was Ethel Watts Mumford, also known to the world as Ethel Grant.

Together they had made the rounds of the city's modern art galleries. Ethel introduced Belle to contemporary painting, and they had attended the first New York exhibition of works by Matisse, who fascinated them. His gallerist Alfred Stieglitz had even suggested that he paint the two women nude on his next trip to New York, to which Belle had agreed—but only if she were shown from behind. What did B.B. think of that?

It was spring, 1910, and Belle had recovered fully from her

low mood. Berenson had demanded that she write to him the smallest details of her daily life, and this she did. But her fulfillment of his wishes did not have the expected effect. Rather, it proved disastrous.

"I received your telegram today, and the two letters in which you accuse me of being an abominable little minx," she wrote to him with mingled pain, sarcasm, and sincerity.

"You say I'm manipulative. And you are right. Because there is no one more constrained than I. I seem impertinent—I seem spontaneous and free—but it's only a façade. The truth is— would you like me to tell you? I have to keep constant control over myself so that I don't lose everything. You can't even imagine how tight of a grip I maintain!

"You say I think of nothing but pleasure, of amusing myself. You reproach me for it so harshly, so cruelly. That hardly seems worth the trouble. For my actions—what I *seem* to do or say— are of no importance.

"For me, what *isn't* seen—what *isn't* heard—they're the only things that count. And my real life, my true life, I lead in darkness. Inside myself, for myself.

"Behind the curtain of my soul."

It was a weighty confession.

But if she hoped to soothe him by acknowledging that she was not what she seemed, she didn't succeed. Her confessions horrified him. There could be no further doubt, for him, that she was hiding things from him, that she was slipping away from him.

Consumed by jealousy, tormented by his own powerlessness, Bernhard Berenson sank into a deep depression.

\*

A year and three months.

The Morgan Library. Nothing else mattered now.

"My employer is the most exhausting man I know. He claims to be fond of my personality—but he is stripping me of myself, as if I were a glove to be slipped off in his presence—to be taken off and given to him, because the glove pleases him."

She made every effort to keep him happy. She flattered him, gave him whatever he wanted, indulged his every whim. Sacrificed her own pleasures—weekends in Newport with the Vanderbilts, balls at the Astor mansion. Everything. All she asked in return was one month, alone, unchaperoned, on the other side of the Atlantic.

Morgan refused.

He continued, of course, to acquire treasures that sent his librarian into raptures, including a tenth-century manuscript of Aesop's *Fables* and a Bible from the same period, illustrated with three hundred tiny illuminations of extraordinary beauty. But would that be enough to bind Belle to him forever? While they still shared the common ground of their passion for rare books, Morgan felt that inevitably he would, if not lose her, at least somehow be deprived of the pleasure of her presence. He clung to her affection and tried to prove his own with a meaningful gesture.

He invited her to Hartford Cemetery for the dedication of a monument to the memory of his father—a highly symbolic inclusion of her that placed her at the same level as his own family. Miss Greene was no longer simply his paid assistant, but a close friend.

The ceremony in front of the Morgan mausoleum, where J.P. himself would one day rest, left him melancholy and brooding.

In the Morgans' private car on the train back to New York, he asked Belle to follow him, to sit down with him in a quiet corner. Everyone else was taking tea in the center of the capacious car, with its red leather seats, ship's clocks, walnut buffet, and green curtains at the windows, monogrammed with the initials J.P.M. The youngest passengers were absorbed in watching the countryside streak by from the rear platform.

He was silent, contemplative. She waited respectfully.

"My father left us at the age of seventy-seven," he said eventually, "and I'm about to turn seventy-three. We must prepare ourselves for my death, Miss Greene—yes, we must think about it." He pulled several folded sheets of paper from his vest pocket, unfolded them, and spread them out on the table. "I want you to help me draft my will. I've already written it, but I'd like you to read it, and for us to correct it together."

"I'm very touched by your trust in me, Mr. Morgan," she replied, slightly unsettled. She glanced at his wife and children, standing just a few steps away. "But are you sure this concerns me?"

"Absolutely certain. I want to know if what I've written regarding you is acceptable: '*Article XVII: I leave to Miss Belle da Costa Greene, my devoted librarian, the sum of fifty thousand dollars.*'"

Belle couldn't repress the shock that flashed across her face. Fifty thousand dollars![4] A staggering sum. He saw her surprise. His eyes twinkled.

"I'm not finished," he went on. '*Though I can have no control over the actions of my heirs, I ask them to keep Miss Belle da Costa Greene on as director of my library for the duration of her natural lifetime, and to pay her a salary that shall never be inferior to the one she is receiving at the time of my death.*' Is that agreeable to you?"

"Agreeable?" Belle was breathless. If she could have, she would have thrown her arms around him and kissed him. He was protecting her now, and he would continue to protect her in the future. Grateful warmth flooded through her. He had thought of everything for her security.

How could she ever thank him?

[4] Around 1.8 million dollars in today's money.

Her gratitude, her personal affection, her professional inter-est—he had them all. And his very generosity, his fatherly benev-olence, gave him *carte blanche* to control her completely.

\*

"I would very much like to get to know your family, Miss Greene."

In this summer of 1910, the second summer of separation, a scorching sun beat down on the few pedestrians to be seen on Fifth Avenue. New York was deserted. All of J.P. Morgan's Blondes had fled to the fashionable warm-weather retreats of Tuxedo and Newport. Ethel Grant and her husband had just departed for Europe and wouldn't return until the autumn. Even Thursty had gone off to visit family.

Alone in the library, the center of her life, Belle was taking advantage of the quiet to catch up on some work. She had thought Morgan was on his yacht, but now he stepped into her office.

"I know how close you are to your mother," he began. "It would give me great pleasure to meet her."

"My mother would be incredibly honored to meet you, Mr. Morgan. She knows how much I owe you, and how much you mean to me."

"Why doesn't she come and have tea with us?"

"She's not in the city. I sent my family to Tuckahoe for the summer."

"Well, then, let's go there!"

This suggestion froze Belle in her tracks. She tried to picture J.P. Morgan in the bungalow she had rented for her brother and sisters. He insisted:

"Tuckahoe's right nearby. Hardly more than ten miles. We can go in the car. We'll pick up Lanier on the way, take him to dinner with us."

Panic.

"That seems a bit complicated, Mr. Morgan."

"Nonsense, nonsense. Miss Greene, nothing is complicated for you—there's no problem you can't solve!"

Belle's telegram, picked up at the Tuckahoe post office, was greeted with a flurry of consternation. They were to have J.P. Morgan at the house for dinner? *Tonight?* In a wooden bungalow, in a tiny country village that bore no resemblance to a spa? They were to host J.P. Morgan when they weren't even in their own home, when they were living in shirtsleeves and bare feet?

*Everyone to battle stations!*

"It's quite charming here," observed Morgan approvingly, his gaze sweeping over the rocking chairs on the wooden veranda, the long table Genevieve had set up in the fenced garden.

Lanterns, wildflowers, and checked tablecloths. She had followed her daughter's instructions: *Be natural.* Junius's advice from long ago. They couldn't hope to rival the settings or the food Morgan was used to, so they would give him a picnic beneath the arbor.

"You never told me your mother and sisters were so ravishing, Belle," added Lanier gallantly.

What must her family really look like to these two wealthy men? What impression were they giving?

An idea was tormenting her.

What if J.P. Morgan's sudden desire to meet her family—here, right away, tonight—was because he wanted to be sure of the color of their skin? He had never brought up the subject before, directly or indirectly. Certainly he had spent very little time around Black people—and he had probably known only one well, a Harvard graduate. But even if he remembered him, he had had no reason to make the connection between Richard Greener and his own librarian in the past five years. Had someone tipped him off?

The question had plagued her all the way from Madison Avenue to Tuckahoe's Main Street.

She tried to look at herself and the others from the outside, as someone else would see them. To view them objectively.

Louise wouldn't be a problem. She was so sweet and mild that she couldn't possibly be unpleasing to J.P. Morgan—and she was blonde and shapely, two traits guaranteed to win his approval. And she was interested in literature, and a decent conversationalist. Ethel, with her long flaxen hair, which she wore loose so that it tumbled down her back, would probably be much to his liking as well. Ethel was Belle's alter ego, the sister to whom she felt the closest—not physically, for they bore almost no resemblance to one another; Belle thought her younger sister a thousand times prettier. But they had the same vivacity, the same energy, the same playfulness. And then there was Teddy. Well, Teddy was another story. Belle viewed her younger sister's upbringing with disapproval, and she was the least intellectual of the siblings by far.

As for Genevieve, she had absorbed London etiquette so well that she could play her role as the aristocratic daughter of a respectable Virginia family to perfection.

By some miracle, Russell was not present. He had always shown the most hostility toward the Big Chief; God only knew how he would have reacted to Morgan's casually inviting himself to dinner. And he was the most "Portuguese" of all of them, the one whose olive skin was most like Belle's own.

In their yachting outfits, Morgan and Lanier clashed sharply with their surroundings. Their clothing was impeccable, their brilliant white jackets glowing against the weathered boards of the fence, their shoes gleaming almost too brightly in the unmown grass.

Genevieve had hurried to offer them a seat, and they had lit their cigars. Amiable and curious, they allowed themselves to be served.

For the first time, Belle saw them as two strangers, two eld-erly men who did not belong to her life.

There were no fresh sea breezes in Tuckahoe, and the July heat was making them all perspire. The men took out their handkerchiefs and, still smoking, they mopped their faces and dabbed at their mustaches. Mr. Morgan's nose had never looked so swollen.

But Belle was finding that she could relax. The Greene women made a good impression, and the conversation flowed without too many silences.

Nothing spectacular, though. The talk remained on a surface level.

The truth was, simply, that Morgan was rather bored. He rose to leave the moment dinner was finished, Lanier on his heels. Without even a pretense of trying to prolong the pleasure of the Greene ladies' company, he and Lanier roared back toward Manhattan in his Rolls, leaving Belle and her family perplexed.

While the evening could not be said to have been a triumph, or really even a success, properly speaking, its results were all that Belle could have hoped for. Seeing Miss Greene in that bucolic setting with her family had reassured the Big Chief.

All of those women were worthy people. Belle included. Very worthy people.

The trip to England no longer seemed to Morgan like a dan-gerous idea to be swatted down.

Miss Greene had a great deal of business to conduct in London, it was true. And the many sales being held by Sotheby's were worth the travel. Perhaps she was right to insist on attend-ing them in person? Her nabbing of the Caxtons had been a masterstroke, proving how important it was for her to be physi-cally present at these events. Who knew, perhaps the treasures she brought back from her European hunt this time would be equally impressive!

On July 11, 1910, one week after their evening in Tuckahoe, J.P. Morgan finally gave Belle permission to travel overseas.

She would depart on the *Oceanic* in mid-August. Without *Madame mère*, and with only a maid to serve as chaperone.

"Victory, victory!" exulted Belle. "The miracle has occurred. I will be with you in a month!" she wrote, drunk with joy, to B.B. "Do you think we will seem much changed to one another? I hope not!"

They had been apart for a year and a half.

"I would like for us to be exactly as we were when we parted. And for us to pick up the thread of our lives where it left off. And yet I wouldn't be surprised if we had to begin all over again.

"Whatever happens, be patient with me.

"If you think Claridge's will be packed too full of Americans this summer, or people who might recognize us, then don't make a reservation there by any means. Choose somewhere more discreet. But if you think it's all right, don't hesitate; the staff at Claridge's are perfectly charming. The truth is, I don't really care where we stay, as long as I have a bathtub, a sitting room, and a separate bedroom for my maid.

"And a bedroom—a single bedroom for two. Oh, how *exciting!*"

# CHAPTER 7

## HOW EXCITING!
### AUGUST–SEPTEMBER 1910

For Bernhard Berenson, nothing—absolutely *nothing*—ended up happening as planned. For a start, the *Oceanic* docked late at the port of Southampton, and Belle's train arrived on the wrong platform at Waterloo Station.

The instant he spotted her in the crowd of disembarking passengers, he was surprised and disappointed. She didn't look like the image he kept of her in his memory. She was shorter, thinner, darker. Less elegant than the sphinx-eyed goddesses he frequented in the drawing rooms of European aristocracy.

He had even, he was forced to acknowledge, forgotten her smile. And her voice with its American inflections, which she had worked for so long to smooth out. And yet, he knew himself well enough to realize that he was moved by the sight of her.

She didn't leave him a moment to reacquaint himself with her exuberant personality. Or with that husky voice of hers, accentuated by her addiction to cigarettes, that he had found so sensual in New York. Or the scent of her perfume, a blend of musk and amber that he had noticed and loved at the Webster Hotel. Garrulous and lively, she seized his arm, chattering about her eagerness to rediscover London at his side, gushing endlessly about how elated she was to be back in Europe at last. He tried to be appreciative of her enthusiasm, but her frank and open way of speaking, which evoked both childlike naturalness and the crudeness of a cabaret dancer, disturbed him. He found himself totally overwhelmed by her presence. He had not expected such vitality.

Even in the cab on the way to Claridge's Hotel, he felt thrown by her. She seemed more interested by the spectacle of the city than by their reunion. Pressed close to the window, she watched Buckingham Palace and the Marble Arch go by, commented on the advertisements, remarked with amusement on the posters for Lipton Tea and Nestlé milk decorating the sides of buses.

He could understand, of course, that she was refraining from too much intimacy in front of her maid. No one was more observant than he when it came to etiquette and the behaviors required in polite society. He felt these to be necessary, and he had always complied with them easily.

But still! She should be showing more love for him. More *consideration*, at any rate.

The idea that Belle could be intimidated, ill at ease, and tense never occurred to him. How could he have guessed her anxiety at his remoteness and his rather affected manners? A dandy of forty-five, an aging playboy who no longer matched *her* memory of *him*, either.

He had proven his skill at being discreet by reserving two suites at the hotel rather than just one—particularly because his wife would soon be joining him. They had business to conclude in London together, but she wouldn't arrive until tomorrow. She had granted him this one night, alone with Belle. And he was realizing that he had dreamed of it for far too long to approach it with serenity now. Would he defer the fateful moment yet again?

Instinctively, he agreed with Belle on this point. It would be unthinkable for them to shut themselves up together in a bedroom right away, to fling themselves into one another's arms.

They had to get used to each other again first.

But they couldn't do that in public, either. Impossible to rekindle their romance over dinner alone in a restaurant. Without a chaperone to distract prying eyes, they were forced into cautiousness. Berenson certainly had nothing to fear where his wife was concerned; she was well aware of the situation and had given her consent to it. But Belle was taking an enormous risk. If J.P. Morgan knew that the first person his librarian had met upon stepping off the train was this individual he himself had refused to admit to his circle of agents and representatives—that she was dining with that very person on the evening of her arrival—he would feel himself to have been cheated, both emotionally and professionally. Betrayed.

It would have been catastrophic. The only thing keeping Belle in the position she occupied was the Big Chief's protection. Should he withdraw his support, she would vanish from the New York scene, never to reappear there or anywhere else.

Unlike her well-born female friends, Belle had neither personal wealth nor the security of a husband to permit her the freedom of taking lovers. She survived in this world of men only by means of her reputation as an "honorable woman." The slightest whiff of scandal would be enough to brand her a harlot. She was already the target of nasty rumors about her relationship with Morgan. Another whisper would end her career.

By mutual agreement, then, Belle and B.B. opted for high tea in the Claridge's tearoom.

He came away from those moments over cucumber sandwiches and scones more confused than ever.

Belle's brashness and unrefined vocabulary had caught him off guard at the station, and now she surprised him with a purely intellectual conversation: a masterclass on medieval illuminations and a series of scholarly questions about Italian Renaissance art. She kept the talk wholly focused on their mutual passions, describing the collections she wanted to see in London. She wanted to see so *many* things.

Parting company with her in the lobby, he had to content himself with a quick kiss on her gloved hand.

Returning to his room, he wrote to Mary despondently that ". . . she has shown herself to be far more cerebral than sensual. There is virtually nothing erotic about her, after all."

The next day promised to be as frenetically busy as the ones they had spent in New York. Belle had a meeting with her correspondents at the British Museum, including Charles Hercules Read, with whom she had built a solid epistolary friendship, their sense of humor turning them into fast friends despite the distance. They embraced affectionately. It was a far easier reunion than the one she'd had with Berenson.

B.B. felt like a stranger to her. She couldn't seem to reconcile the man she had dreamed of with the one who had been waiting for her at the station. Compared to the biting wit of his letters, their vitality and intellectual richness, here was someone she found all but insufferable. Could it be that Thursty, who had pointed out his smugness and arrogance, had been right after all?

And he was too old. Twenty years older than her! Well, all right: fourteen. The actual number didn't matter as much as the stark contrast between her own youth and the fussy pedantry of this gentleman, always huffing about people's vulgarity, always complaining about everyone's bad manners. Suddenly the chasm between them seemed miles wide.

What had gotten into her, to fall in love with him so desperately, to spend nearly two years pining for him?

Disappointment cut through her so sharply, so painfully, that she had to fight back tears, to shake off the grief of disillusionment.

She had to overcome this setback. She would enjoy her lunch with Read, whose easy nature she found so delightful. She would visit the British Museum's Department of Printed Books, curated by Alfred Pollard, from under whose nose she had stolen the Caxtons. Of course, she would meet with Quaritch, who had undertaken the restoration of the Cambridge Bible for her, along with a few of Amherst's other incunabula. And she would visit with the Blumenthals, a husband-and-wife pair of American collectors who were friends of Morgan's and were staying at the Savoy.

As for B.B., he would make the rounds of London's most prominent dealers and patrons in the company of Mary, who had arrived that afternoon. A tea, a dinner, and a late-night supper had been planned in their honor.

The art world in London was split into two camps: those for, and those against, Bernhard Berenson.

His stormy relations with England's collectors dated back to the autumn of 1894, when the New Gallery had held an immense exhibition of Venetian Renaissance paintings. Three hundred works, belonging mainly to collections owned by British aristocrats, the attributions of which—repeated down through the generations in English castles—had always appeared ridiculously optimistic in Berenson's eyes. And so he had taken the opportunity presented by the opening of the exhibition to distribute a pamphlet containing his own opinions, an action unprecedented in its audacity. Of thirty-three attributions to Titian in the exhibition, he had agreed with only one. Of the rest, five paintings were copies of known works; two, copies of lost works; and the twenty-five others, crude forgeries. As for Veronese, none of the eight paintings exhibited under his name was actually painted by him. And of the eighteen works by Giorgione—by whom, Berenson maintained, only thirteen signed pieces existed in the world—all but one were fakes—perhaps most egregiously the *Portrait of a Lady Teacher at Bologna*, owned by Lady Ashburton, which was "neither a Giorgione, nor a lady, nor a teacher."

Needless to say, the aristocratic owners of these paintings had not taken kindly to Berenson's initiative and had been frankly appalled by his belittling of their possessions. It was an undermining of their blue-blooded lineage; their ownership of works by the grand masters was a source of deep ancestral pride.

True connoisseurs, on the other hand, had recognized the incredible keenness of Berenson's eye.

The scandal provoked by his pamphlet had made Bernhard

Berenson, at the age of twenty-nine, the most famous art expert in Europe. It was a masterstroke that had propelled him to the very top ranks of art historians, a controversial figure whose contributions were vied over by journals and newspapers.

Since then, his presence had caused art dealers all over Europe many a sleepless night. Now, in 1910, his verdict on their paintings was worth its weight in gold—or could lead to total ruin.

In the restaurant at Claridge's, Mrs. Berenson was awaiting a guest. Her husband had not yet arrived.

Belle crossed the room with her quick, light step, preceded by the chief steward, who treated her as an honored regular guest by now, indulging her every whim. She had always had a knack for winning the affection of the staff at the hotels and private homes she frequented. Her hostess was equally capable; Mary, too, had the gift of knowing how to please.

Both women had donned their most elegant attire for this meeting. Though there was very little that was conventional about either of them, they almost seemed to have made a mutual agreement to wear hats so understated as to give them the same look of bourgeois conformism. Tall, blonde Mrs. Berenson, imperious as a statue of Juno, towered several inches over every other woman in the room, while Miss Greene, trim and lithe as a cat, seated herself gracefully in the chair across from her.

Mary reached both hands across the table to clasp Belle's, loudly expressing her pleasure at seeing Miss Greene again, and Belle responded in kind. They had quite liked one another in New York, though their paths hadn't crossed more than three times. And, since that time, Mary had been forced to endure B.B.'s foul mood, caused in large part by his one ill-fated night, his missed opportunity, with this young woman. She was determined, now, to restore peace in her marriage—not least because she would then be free to indulge her own passion for a certain young architect.

Her presence at the same table as Miss Greene, her clear and visible display of friendship, had one overriding purpose: to legitimize any future sightings of the librarian and her husband together. It was a way of protecting Belle's reputation and hushing up any rumors of an affair. Miss Greene would become, very publicly, a close family friend.

Belle, of course, was perfectly aware of every nuance of this situation.

"B.B. rhapsodizes about how intelligent you are, my dear," Mary said warmly. "And you know how much that means, coming from him."

"Oh, but my dear Mrs. Berenson, *you're* the great connoisseur of Italian art! Everyone says so!"

The compliment pleased Mary greatly. It galled her always to be seen as playing second fiddle to her husband. She did far more than simply collaborate with B.B. on his books; his first publication might bear his name alone, but the truth was that she had written just as much of it as he had.

"Oh, but he's the master. He taught me everything I know, Miss Greene. Would you mind if I call you Belle? I feel as if I know you so well already! When I met my husband, I didn't even know how to *look* at a painting; can you imagine? I'd been to plenty of museums, like everyone, but I'd always missed what was most important. 'You have to look,' he said to me, 'look and look, until you feel as if you're part of the painting. Until you *become* the painting. That's when you'll be able to feel it. And then, all your pessimism about life and the world, all your bitterness, all your doubts will be swept away by a torrent of happiness. You'll have a sense of total reconciliation with the universe.' That's B.B. He may seem cold, but he's deeply sensitive. Almost too much so. That heart of his beats almost *too* strongly. He's a man so very alive, such a mystery even to himself, that he doesn't always know how to express his feelings—his tenderness, I mean to say."

Belle was listening attentively. Mary was describing what she had sensed, herself, when she was with Berenson in New York.

"He had an absolutely dreadful childhood, you know!" B.B.'s wife went on now. "Not the childhood he deserved, at any rate. The truth is, he's never fully gotten over it. He comes from a noble Lithuanian family that lost everything. You knew that, I think? It's because of his Baltic roots that B.B. has such refinement, such distinction. And yet he pulled himself up by his own bootstraps, through pure hard work and iron-clad self-discipline. It's thanks to him that his mother and sisters have a good life today. They're very attached to him, and he simply adores them, sees to their every need. His is a magnificent soul that life has wounded deeply. He shares his knowledge generously, but most of all—most of all—he knows how to love."

By the time Berenson finally took his place at the table, Mary had painted a portrait of him that placed him among the ranks of heroes and gods. She maintained this tone throughout the rest of lunch, and by the end of the meal he had become, once again, the man that Belle had fallen in love with. A man with such charm, such depth of spirit, that no woman could resist him.

Mary, her mission accomplished, was now free to depart London for Oxford, where she planned to undergo a slimming cure in one of the region's health spas.

"I really was enchanted by Miss Greene," she wrote to her husband two days later. "And I hope you will be able to develop a stable relationship with her, of the sort that will satisfy our aging bourgeois souls. I know most gentlemen are more fond of a one-night passion, but you aren't that type. Do what you can to make this liaison of yours something enjoyable and lasting. I'll help you in every way I can—I'll do this for you, for myself, and for her, for I admire her youth and her spirit, and she is an extremely attractive creature.

"There's just one thing, dear friend, that I must murmur in

your ear: do not boast about yourself too much in front of her. Let her discover your moral worth and intellectual brilliance for herself. I have been the serpent in the garden by encouraging you to talk about your virtues—restrain yourself from doing it too much. You have generally been able to balance that quality with moments of humility—but it is a mistake, I believe, to make too much of either your own vanity or your own modesty. People don't like that sort of excess. And I have seen her notice it. For example, there is no use in telling her that, at home, we practice the art of conversation in a far superior way to most people (I'm not at all certain this is true, by the way!). Let her see it for herself when she comes to visit us at I Tatti.

"Forgive me for giving so much wifely advice, my dear. But I know how much these young people like to mock their elders' arrogance—and I want you to appear in the best possible light."

Mary had no need to worry, as it turned out. The die was cast.

On August 19, B.B. received one of the greatest shocks of his life, a discovery that filled him with unimaginable joy. Oh, astonishment—oh, miracle—the young woman who gave herself to him that night was a virgin. This revelation explained everything: Belle's behavior in New York, a mixture of flirtation and modesty; her letters, which said one thing and then contradicted it. And her attitude when she had first arrived in London.

He was suddenly, powerfully aware of how frightened she must have been. He knew, now, that behind the mask of a liberated woman who drank, smoked, and went out every evening, there was another Belle, even more fascinating. An individual whose depth he had never realized, loyal, sincere, and faithful to their love. He, who had been so tortured by jealousy, now reproached himself for accusing her.

How could he ever have suspected, imagined, that he would be the first man Belle had known intimately? The idea that no one before him had possessed her was intoxicating. He felt overwhelmed and flattered at once by the gift she had given him, and his passion for her grew by leaps and bounds. It seemed impossible to express the tenderness he felt for her. The appreciation.

In the massive bed in B.B.'s private suite, Belle let herself be caressed. The night had been a revelation for her, too. The fulfillment of desire that had lived up to all its promises. She felt completely, entirely happy—a happiness she had first tasted at the Webster, and that she now knew had only been a vague glimmering of what was to come. Nothing had prepared her for the dizziness of feeling his skin against hers, the softness of his neck, the tickle of his hair against her palm.

Her instinct had not been wrong. Bernhard Berenson was the love of her life.

\*

The newfound harmony between them extended to another front as well, one that they both felt was even more important than the pleasures of the flesh. A kind of spiritual communion, the existence of which was proved to Berenson on the very day after their first night together.

"Stay here," he ordered, as they stood in the doorway of a room in the National Gallery. "Don't come in. I want to tell you a story first, so you'll know what I'm expecting from you. The fable about the god, the bow, and the arrow. Do you know it?"

"No."

"A god was teaching his young son how not to miss his target. He took him into the woods and asked the child what he could see. The boy replied, 'I see a tree.' 'Look again,' the god said. 'I see a bird.' 'Look again.' 'I see the bird's head.' 'Again.' 'I see the bird's eye.' 'Again'. 'I see the pupil of the bird's eye.' 'Now, shoot!' It's the same thing when you look at a work of art. If you can achieve truly complete concentration when you're looking at it, you will need no more than an instant to recognize the painter's hand. The painting I'm about to show you is famous, and easily attributable. But I want you to discover it from the best possible angle. I'm going to blindfold you now. When I remove the scarf, you must describe to me what you see."

Belle, enchanted, went along willingly with his little game. He took her by the hand and positioned her diagonally in front of a painting—exactly as its original commissioner, Alfonso d'Este, Duke of Ferrara, had seen it when he entered his famous white-marble-walled study in 1523.

When she opened her eyes, she found herself looking at a large tableau, which she recognized immediately. It was magnificent. She gave an involuntary cry of joy.

"What is it?" Berenson asked.

"Titian. *Bacchus and Ariadne*."

"More specifically?"

"The moment in Ovid's text where Ariadne is abandoned by Theseus on the island of Naxos. She turns away from the departing ship and sees Bacchus, who leaps out of his chariot to meet her. He has fallen in love with her at first sight."

"What makes you think it's a Titian?"

She didn't hesitate for an instant. "The shimmering colors, the material effects, the transparency of the glazing . . . and also the arrangement in a frieze. Maybe Raphael's influence, too, in Bacchus's leap. And Michelangelo's, in the bodies of the satyrs."

He was impressed.

"Have you seen many Titians?"

"I spent some time in museums here on my first trip to London. And at the Metropolitan, in New York."

"You didn't tell me that when we went there together."

"I was busy listening to you. And you didn't ask."

"Go on. Tell me about the details in this painting."

"It seems to me that the landscape, with that blue horizon, foreshadows Titian's later style of backgrounds. Same with the light. And in the foreground, the flowers—irises, columbines . . . it's funny; they remind me of Dürer's plants."

He frowned. "Dürer? What are you talking about? Titian never met Dürer!"

"No, but Dürer spent time in Venice on two separate occasions. He left his mark there. It was perhaps twenty years before this painting, but Titian saw Dürer's work, and he remembered it when he was painting these flowers."

Berenson acquiesced. "You clearly remember Dürer, too."

"I *adore* him. We have a collection of his engravings at the Morgan Library. I've spent simply ages looking at them."

"I don't know who you got your eye from, but . . ."

He let the sentence trail off, unwilling to push too far. The rest of the visit confirmed what he had sensed. He came away from it perplexed.

She had surprised him. Yet again.

Belle, for her part, felt as if she were floating. Berenson was exactly the mentor she had always dreamed of. He could teach her *everything*. The best guide—the best master—with whom to discover Italy.

All she wanted now was to wrap up her business in England and in Paris, where she was due to attend two manuscript sales at the Hôtel Drouot—and then . . . on to Venice, Florence, Rome.

That evening, in his daily letter to his wife, Berenson confided his amazement. In falling in love with Belle, he had found the Holy Grail.

The visual sensitivity of this young American was astonishing. She had an extraordinary instinct for beauty. No one knew better than B.B. himself how much an eye needed to be trained; even he had had to see *all* the Titians, *all* the Bellinis, *all* the Giorgiones, *all* the Lottos to be in a position to compare them, to reason and deduce. Who had trained Belle Greene? He'd known her expertise was unrivaled when it came to rare books and illuminations. A professional of the highest caliber, capable of differentiating, by examining paper, ink, and calligraphy, an authentic manuscript from one that was not. But Renaissance and early modern painting was not her field.

Moreover, she had never really traveled anywhere. She wasn't familiar with France, or Spain, or Italy. She hadn't been exposed to any of history's great masterpieces, only to the objects brought back to America by Morgan—fakes, most of them, in B.B. and Mary's opinion. The *Madonna* attributed to Raphael for which the banker had paid a fortune? Raphael—poor, tragic Raphael— had never come near it, B.B. had ranted to his wife; he'd never touched that canvas, or even laid eyes on it. And if Belle had seen nothing but those sorts of paintings[5] . . . where, then, had she acquired her technique? She'd studied the collections at the Metropolitan, yes, and visited the ones privately owned by New York and Boston millionaires. She'd read extensively, yes, and had the memory of an elephant—but there was nothing that explained her reactions over the hours he'd just spent with her at the National Gallery. How could she have known that Bacchus's leap toward Ariadne in Titian's painting was inspired by an angel displayed in the Vatican? He had asked her, of course, but had not been satisfied with her answer. She claimed to have taken classes in Princeton with Ernest Richardson, the director of the library—but Richardson was a paleographer. *What could he possibly have taught her about art?* B.B. wondered, with typical disdain. Then Belle had mentioned the teachings of Junius Morgan, her mentor. Berenson truly wanted to believe that the nephew was better informed than the uncle, but collecting texts by Virgil, French furniture, and silverwork did not make one an art expert.

[5] Berenson was wrong on this point; the Raphael *Madonna* owned by J.P. Morgan is authentic.

There was no telling what Belle da Costa Greene's future might hold, of course, B.B. wrote to Mary in one of his last letters from London. But, if his own intuition was correct, and if what he sensed in his new mistress proved to be accurate, she had the potential to become—with his guidance, of course—one of the greatest art experts of the twentieth century. He concluded the letter with these words: "Or perhaps I am just completely under this girl's spell—or Belle is the most receptive person I've ever met. Excepting yourself, of course."

A deft and graceful way of putting his wife back at the center of his musings.

Yet Mary had ceased to participate, for now, in what B.B. called "the Great Adventure of my existence." It was indicative of this new detachment that she would not be accompanying him to the major exhibition of Islamic art soon to be held in Germany, which they had previously planned to visit together.

Miss Greene's arrival on the scene had changed everything. Mary would see Islam's marvels in the autumn instead, or perhaps later this month, alone—or with her lover.

Belle, for her part, would have to rein in her impatience. She and B.B. were not taking the Rome Express from Paris, but the Orient Express, and disembarking at its second stop: Munich.

Italy would have to wait.

It was unheard of. Eighty rooms and three halls covering every country, every era, every style of the "Mohammedan World," from India to Andalusia, as the exhibition's curators proclaimed with pride. Nearly four thousand objects of unparalleled quality: rugs, banners, and wall hangings, as well as furniture, ceramics, and miniatures, all loaned from the most secret private collections. Room after room of masterpieces, all impeccably arranged and grouped in an austere setting to emphasize the modern quality of Eastern forms and designs.

It was *the* event of 1910.

"I hate Munich, and I loathe Germans," Belle wrote to her sister Ethel, "but how can I possibly convey the magic of those three halls? I spend entire days there, from sunup to sundown. I cannot get enough.

"As you will understand, B.B. and I are pretending to be simply casual acquaintances. No more, no less.

"We're staying in different hotels, and we arrive separately at the exhibition halls and go off on our own. But Ethel, the strange thing is that we always end up in the same rooms, in front of the same piece! It really is totally bizarre! Of all the dozens and dozens of carpets, we're both drawn to a particular example, a particular pattern. Or to the beauty of this carving, or that saber. Out of all those thousands of works of art, the same one enchants us; the same one transports us both with delight. Don't ask me how such coincidences are possible. We both feel that this Eastern world, in which depictions of humans are taboo, expresses a harmony just as powerful as Western culture. An oh, so sophisticated ideal. I've suddenly stopped believing that only Greek, medieval, and Renaissance art are worthy of interest. If you saw the magnificence of those fourteenth-century Qurans! When I get back, I'm going to persuade the Big Chief to open our library to Islamic manuscripts. J.P. has an inquiring enough mind to understand the necessity. I'm certain that the splendor of the calligraphy on the firmans will touch him. And I haven't even mentioned my emotion—and B.B.'s—at the stunning sight of those Persian miniatures. Their geometry, the delicacy of their colors, are all of a piece with the secret lives of books, and if I had the money, I would definitely collect them! Oriental art has a rightful place in human history—more than that, it's a source of inspiration for modern art, B.B. thinks; he can see the clear influence on Matisse . . ."

The exhilaration of discovering, at the same time, a form of beauty with which neither of them was familiar gave both Belle and B.B. the sense of undergoing an almost mystical experience.

There was no master here, no pupil, merely a common insight that brought them dizzyingly close. It was a shock that would lead to new horizons for the Morgan Library.

There was only one flaw in the scenario: other people.

Art dealers, gallerists, historians, experts, curators—all of Europe was hurrying to Munich. The whole art world. Even some American collectors, friends or rivals of Morgan's, had made the trip: the Blumenthals, the Lydigs, the Huntingtons, even George Perkins, one of J.P.'s associates. A platoon of millionaires who all stayed in the same places, visited the exhibition together, dined together, and planned to invade Italy together. The wives, Rita, Florie, and Arabella, each possessed an eye capable of identifying objects of quality—and also a nose able to sniff out a romance at a hundred yards.

Back to reality. How to avoid them? How to get rid of them?

All three of the ladies knew Bernhard Berenson personally, and they were all simply mad about him—including Mrs. Rita Lydig, whose fiery temperament was worthy of a true Spanish aristocrat and whose maiden name was . . . de Acosta. What a coincidence! Da Costa . . . was Miss da Costa a relative, by any chance?

"I felt the bullet whiz past, very near," wrote Belle to her sister, "and fired back by boring her to death with the manuscript of the *Da Costa Hours*: 'Surely you know, Mrs. Lydig,' I said, 'that Mr. Morgan has just acquired that splendid object, which was the property of Alvaro da Costa, armorer to King Manuel of Portugal?' I was so tiresome about it that she was convinced I'd forced poor J.P. to buy the volume just because it had belonged to my family. Such a twit and a snob, that Lydig woman.

"B.B. quite likes her and wants to have dinner with her—while I dine with the Blumenthals and the Perkins."

The latter, who were close friends of Morgan's, were scathing in their criticism of the celebrity being feted a few tables away in the same restaurant: Bernhard Berenson. He was loathed by art owners whose illusions about the authenticity of their art he had shattered. Loathed by art dealers with whom he'd refused to ally himself. Loathed by historians of Italian art whose attributions he contradicted. Loathed by collectors he'd outwitted by buying the paintings they coveted right out from under them. Belle, who knew herself to be in the hot seat, having been spotted with Berenson in museums in New York and London, defended him tooth and nail: he was a genius, a victim of the jealousy of mediocre minds!

"I may seem dramatic," wrote Belle, "but really I'm only saying what I think. Anyway—who would ever guess? Broad daylight is the best place to hide."

Her gushing praise was a smokescreen. If she had *really* been having an affair with Berenson, surely she wouldn't speak about him in that tone; rather, she would stay conspicuously silent, or at least be restrained in her admiration, tried to hide it a bit. But she talked of him with such passion! If she could, she vowed at dinner, she would spend entire days with him, soaking in his knowledge, learning everything he had to teach her. Such a great man, that people were slandering this way! What a pity!

At the end of these outings there were amiable farewells, effusive niceties; they greeted one another politely, formally, in the restaurants where their paths just happened to cross.

It was irritating. Inconvenient. And yet amusing, too. They laughed a great deal. Beneath his air of sophisticated detachment, Belle discovered, B.B. had retained all the adaptability and mischief of his youth. He was like an elf, a faun. He loved the game of deceiving the people around him. And their secret only added to the piquancy of their coming together again. It was delicious, an extra bit of spice they both savored in its every nuance beneath the fluffy German eiderdown in Belle's hotel room.

"She has become a wonderful mistress," B.B. wrote to his wife. "She loves me even more, and better, than you ever did! A pure miracle."

In the face of such joy, of a tone she had not heard from B.B. in years, Mary knew he was ready to travel again the dusty roads that wound among the hills of Sienna. With that mysterious creature, Belle Greene, who had so bewitched him.

First the train from Munich to Verona, and from there, God only knew precisely where they would go.

But wherever they went, it would be in Italy, as Belle had pleaded. Italy, at last!

*

Tirelessly they roamed one city after another—cities so full of tourists that they were forced to hide from mutual acquaintances at nearly every turn. They'd had a dreadful near-miss in their very first stop, Verona. While Belle waited for B.B. in an open-topped taxi in front of his hotel (she was, of course, staying somewhere else), he had bumped into the renowned French art dealer Jacques Seligman in the lobby. The two men had emerged from the hotel together, passing right alongside the taxi, and Belle hadn't had time to do anything but duck down in her seat. Had Seligman seen her?

There were many other instances in which Belle and B.B. came within a hair's breadth of being discovered, as well. It almost happened again at the mausoleum of Galla Placidia in Ravenna. Fortunately, however, B.B. happened to be standing beneath the celestial mosaics of the domed ceiling—nowhere near Belle—and was able to flee, though she was forced to endure the rapturous cries of yet another set of friends from New York, who simply couldn't believe the lovely coincidence of finding her hovering in the shadow of an arch. It happened in Perugia, too, where Florie Blumenthal and Rita Lydig cornered her in San Lorenzo. There were invitations to lunch and dinner, interminable chatting. And Belle was obliged to be even more flexible socially now, since she was traveling without a personal maid. Wishing to live as intimately with B.B. as possible, she had sent the girl off to visit family in Switzerland, and she would not rejoin them until they reached Rome. It had been a mistake—and a scandalous one, as no respectable woman would visit a foreign country entirely on her own.

But Belle's happiness and her sense of peace were so total that she was able to bear these trials with lighthearted aplomb. The tension of potential discovery took nothing away from her delight in the buildings of Verona. Her wonder at the golden beauty of the *Procession of Virgins* in the Basilica of Sant'Apollinare Nuovo in Ravenna. Her pleasure in the walls and towers of Perugia. She was utterly, unshakably dazzled by it all.

And there was something else, too.

The question of race never came up here! The moment she had set foot in this country, the heavy yoke that had been crushing her for years was suddenly lifted from her shoulders. More Italian than the Italian women with her olive skin and dark hair, she blended into the crowd, melted into the landscape. The feeling of belonging to these streets, to this country, was as instantaneous as it was permanent.

Not even the nights of separation from B.B. could dampen her spirits; in fact, he found himself almost irritated by her forbearance. How could his lover, so passionate, so capricious, bear this inability to be together so magnanimously, when for him it was pure torture? He had played the game of secrecy in London and Munich; he had even thought it amusing. But not here! He wanted to take possession of both Belle and Italy with full freedom. He had never wanted anything so much in his whole life as to have her at his side in the Piazza del Campo in Sienna. No one knew better than he from which angle, in which light the beauty of Sienna—like that of Belle—shone most radiantly. Italy was his domain. And Belle belonged to him. Belle was meant for him. The social conventions that forced him to keep his distance from her, even for an instant, seemed a senseless waste. Their days, their hours together were numbered. The *Oceanic* would sail from Southampton on October 19. In a mere five weeks Belle would cross the ocean once more, and the nightmare of separation would begin all over again.

Berenson might have seemed like the most controlled of men, with his impeccably trimmed beard; his stiff, high collars and light suits; his tie perfectly matched to his silk pocket-handkerchief; and his soft felt hat tilted rakishly over one eye, or his straw hat pulled down to mid-forehead—but he refused to accept any rules other than the ones he imposed on himself. These, it was true, were both strict and numerous. But the frustration of his inability to be with Belle openly? He'd never felt anything like it.

His patience was stretched almost to the snapping point. How could he shrug off the burden of these idiotic conventions . . .

. . . if not by turning to Mary?

She could join them in Perugia immediately, and the problem would be solved. Her presence would drape a veil of conjugal propriety over their Italian travels. He wrote to her exhorting her to come, and Belle supported the proposition by writing Mary a letter of her own, inviting her to accompany them.

Mary, in no great hurry to be a third wheel, replied to them with her usual gracious effusions. B.B.'s newfound happiness delighted her. Such contentment, when he had been so miserable, would be of great benefit to their relationship when he returned to I Tatti this winter. As to Miss Greene's reputation, Mary felt, there was no need for concern—except perhaps in Tuscany, where Berenson was known to one and all. And of course there were the aristocrats, and the librarians, and art dealers who harbored an adoration of J.P. Morgan. If the Florentines were to learn—and they would, that was certain—that the personal librarian of *Babbo Morgano* was in the city, they would try to sell her every bit of old junk they had lying around, with the same persistence they would have applied to her boss. For this reason,

Mary suggested, they should avoid Florence and its environs completely until she was back at the villa to receive Miss Greene formally. In the meantime, she advised, better to stay away from the big hotels. Keep to small towns and rooms in private houses, where they could claim to be husband and wife. They could rent a car and drive to the isolated churches of the Quattrocento, which B.B. knew and loved better than anywhere else.

"Mary's always had this gift of organizing other people's lives whether they like it or not," Berenson commented sourly. "She thinks she knows what's best for everyone, better than they do themselves."

"It doesn't matter. She's right. To hell with the cities! Let's change our itinerary—go where no one will spoil our fun! *Evviva la libertà, Bibi!*"

\*

This time, there was nothing left but wonder. Who could see this place and not feel as if they'd found the land of their dreams? Truly, Italy had kept all its promises.

Breakfast in a café at sunrise, heads bent close over that day's menu.

Quests to view all the splendors on offer, all the beauty that revealed itself at every turn; searches for hidden treasure, for marvelous secrets: an abandoned church, a faded fresco, an altarpiece blackened by time.

Games of identifying the style of a painting beneath the soot; to guess the colors and pick out brushstrokes through the years of dust.

Long moments spent perched atop ladders, faces lifted to vaulted ceilings, expressions of wonder at the shapes in the plasterwork: "Describe it! Put what you're seeing into words!"

The thrill of formulating a theory from the rickety perch, of suggesting a name.

Ascending hilly slopes in a rickety wagon to reach remote chapels gilded by the rich September sun. Rambles through the verdant countryside. Mad dashes from one village to the next. Strolls on ramparts and through piazzas and down narrow lanes.

Father, teacher, lover. What Berenson shared with Belle was a perfect communion of body and soul. The sort of love a man experiences only once in his life. She enjoyed what he enjoyed; she loathed what he loathed. She saw what he saw. She looked at things in the same way he did.

He showed her the great works, the ones which, early in his own career, had stunned him, reshaped his whole perspective. And the miracle happened again. He could see it: she, too, could feel just how extraordinary they were. How? Why? It was a mystery. She was possessed of astonishing taste, and even a sense of authenticity, a real aptitude for telling the true from the false, and also—especially—what was more important than anything else: a sensitivity to nature. She could freeze suddenly, mid-stride, and fall speechless, gazing for long, ecstatic moments at a beautiful landscape. Just like him.

The phrase she had uttered the other day at the Baglioni Chapel in Spello! Just a few words, pronounced in front of Pinturicchio's *Scenes from the Life of the Virgin*: "In his *Annunciation*, eternity manifests itself exactly as it does in life: in broad daylight." He had said the very same thing himself, aged twenty-five, at the sight of Fra Angelico's *Annunciation*.

These reflections, these echoes of one another extended even to the tiniest details. Though Belle loved creature comforts and the world of society, she—like B.B.—could also live happily without luxury or frivolity. She adapted with perfect ease to pre-dawn awakenings, walks in scorchingly hot weather, bumpy wagon-rides, humble accommodations, and simple meals. The only thing she could not tolerate was dirtiness. And, once again, B.B. was the same.

It was a honeymoon without a marriage. It was all that either of them had ever wanted.

Never had Belle been at such total peace with herself. It was the first real happiness she had ever known. It was fulfillment, satisfaction.

It was oneness with the stones and the earth, with color and shadow and light.

It was a pure merging of souls with Bernhard Berenson.

*

The sun was rising over Orvieto.

Faces turned toward the Umbrian plains, they lay quietly together in the dark bedroom. The house had been built atop ramparts, and they had left the window and the curtains wide open. Wisps of fog still cloaked the hilltops and hovered low over the grapevines. Large, broad-horned white cows slowly descended the slopes toward the valley floor, pulling carts heaped with baskets, ladders, and barrels. Snatches of song floated up from among the silver-leafed olive trees, sung by women in long red skirts. The grape harvest had begun.

As the sun rose higher, the hills seemed to recede into the distance, forming a more and more remote curve against the plain but unable, now, to close off the horizon.

Lying side by side like two effigies reclining on tombs, they both kept perfectly still. Despite their lingering early-morning drowsiness, neither of them looked away from the scene outside the window. For long moments, they luxuriated in the same shared vision. There was no need for words.

When the sun's rays reached the bed, B.B. shifted his position, propping himself up on an elbow and pulling back the blanket so he could gaze at Belle. Naked, she gave herself up to being admired. She seemed to take a sort of pleasure in her own nudity, just as B.B. did. It was as if he were memorizing every inch of her marvelous body, her olive skin contrasting with the whiteness of the sheets.

"Belle," he murmured. She closed her eyes.

She felt the way she sometimes had as a girl, sinking into dreams, hearing the sound of her parents' voices murmuring in the other room. But it was B.B., now, whispering into her ear: "Women like you . . . You're made for hours of passion, hours of light . . ."

She shivered. *Women like you.* She remembered a phrase she had often heard during her Georgetown youth: "The body of a Black woman, no matter how light-skinned, can never lie." At trials, judges would force mixed-race women claiming to be white to undress themselves. "The thighs of women like that," they said, "the crooks of their elbows and the areolas of their breasts, reveal them to be impostors."

She groaned and curled her body around his. The walls of the bedroom, now in full daylight, shone blood-red, the tiles glinting like fire. She pressed her lips to his, a burning seal.

He nearly lost consciousness, so strong was his desire.

\*

"Are you finished yet?" Berenson asked.

Sitting at the table, he sealed a half-dozen envelopes with a bowl of water and a small sponge.

The shutters were open, but the rainstorm that had been battering Viterbo for two days now obscured the view. They had pulled one of the panels partly shut to keep out the wind, but the clock tower could still be seen, framed by the window, its reddish brick looking almost black in the rain. The hammering of raindrops on the tile roofs drowned out the murmuring of the fountains; there was nothing but the sound of the church bells to mark the passing hours.

This rainy interlude had not prevented them from making

flying visits to the Villa Lante, Tuscania, and then Bagnoregio, returning home soaked to the skin and making love all night in their bedroom with its high ceiling and whitewashed walls. They had stripped the room of its ornaments and taken down the prints and tapestries, leaving only a bed, a chair, and the table for writing letters. The chamber now looked more like a monk's cell than anything else.

"Well?" he repeated. "You're not still writing Morgan an account of your life, are you?"

"I have so much to tell him."

"You've been telling him things for ages. I've already written my two pages to Mary, and letters to some of my other friends besides."

Belle had learned how important these hours dedicated to correspondence—one in the morning and one in the evening—were to B.B. She knew what he expected of her at these times, as well. She was to do for him what Mary had always done: make sure he had his little traveling clock, his books, his ink and pens and stationery. Lay them out on the table in every hotel room they stayed in, exactly as they were arranged on his desk at I Tatti. This done, even in the most modest inns, B.B. felt at home. He had shown her how to perform the daily ritual, and she carried it out with pleasure.

Wrapped in a shawl, back propped against the headboard and knees drawn up, Belle was writing to Morgan. Pressed into service as a writing desk was a large album of prints from Signorelli's *Apocalypse*, a series of frescoes they'd been unable to see, as they were currently undergoing restoration in Orvieto.

"Letters to friends? Ha! To your lady admirers, you mean."

Smiling, she gazed fondly at his back, bent over the table at the window as if he were busy at his schoolwork: those shoulders, slim as a teenage boy's, the boyish back of his neck that she found so endearing.

"I've never known so many women to chase after an intellectual like this. The Countess Serristori, the Duchess of Thingamabob, Lady Doohickey. Those Blondes are on you like white on rice. God, how I hate them."

B.B. still had so much in him of the mischievous little boy he had once been! Hot-tempered, too. But Belle could always distract him from his rages, like a child from a tantrum, by offering him a new toy or proposing a new game.

"You've no idea how much I adore your letters! You're so funny in them, so sharp. So rude and yet so *vibrant*. They were like champagne for my soul that winter in New York. I'm no good at writing, and anyway I *loathe* it."

"Yes, I've noticed that," he said, chuckling. "But you seem to do plenty of it, anyway, don't you! I don't think I ever got as many letters from you as that old gentleman does. What on earth do you tell him?"

"Everything. Well—almost."

"Do you talk to him about me?"

"Of course not! I talk about what I see. Paintings. Landscapes. The Rembrandt engravings at the library in Ravenna."

"What would he understand about any of it?"

She frowned.

"*What would he understand about any of it?* What do you mean by that, exactly?"

He turned, his blue-eyed gaze boring into her.

"You know as well as I do. Morgan's mansion in London, on Prince's Gate? I've been there. It's like the lair of King Midas's pawnbroker. Except for two or three pieces that Seligman and Duveen sold him, it's a bunch of junk. How can you call a hoard of odds and ends like that a collection?"

She sat up straighter. "If you have any feelings of friendship for me," she said tartly, "I don't even mean affection, or love, but *friendship*—you won't say another slanderous word against Mr. Morgan."

He did not back down. He turned back to his envelopes, making a show of continuing to seal them. He added stamps, continuing to talk all the while. He expressed himself calmly, but the even tone of his voice only accentuated the ferocity of his remarks.

"I haven't said a single slanderous thing. Just that J.P. Morgan's eye is worthless. With or without his riches. Personally, I've always thought that people that rich shouldn't be allowed to own works of art. Not even the smallest painting."

"So that goes for your Isabella Stewart Gardner, too."

"Mrs. Gardner has taste. And she's very well advised."

"I agree with you," she said bitingly. "The great masters you made her buy keep her from being utterly ridiculous. But her house—trying to be a Venetian palace—is a grotesque joke, don't you think? I have to admit, it's painful for me—and for you too, clearly—to imagine those masterpieces decorating a place like that. In fact"—she let the Signorelli album fall to the floor with a thud—"*that* woman considering herself the owner of *The Rape of Europa* seems to me to be an insult to Titian. And let's not even mention that poor self-portrait by Rembrandt!"

He was on the point of snapping that, with all due respect, Belle Greene was not exactly on the same level as Bernhard Berenson when it came to judging the artistic sensibilities of anyone at all.

He managed to restrain himself, however, and said, in a tone straining to be reasonable:

"I'm not the only one who thinks that J.P. Morgan doesn't possess deep knowledge about anything. Or that he'll buy any old thing that strikes his fancy. I was just speaking about it the other day with an art dealer, who said how surprised he'd been by Morgan's ignorance."

"With an *art dealer?*" she cried, her face reddening with fury. "Who?"

"It doesn't matter. But to hear him talk, your boss knows

absolutely nothing. *Niente.* Not even about books. He only reads Walter Scott. I highly doubt that he's read even a few pages of a *fraction* of the manuscripts you've had him buy for his library."

She had leapt from the bed. Incandescent with rage, she stomped to the open window and seized the shutters, which were clacking in the wind, and wrestled them shut. Then she turned to face him.

"You're wrong, my dear B.B.," she said, her voice low and quivering with anger, all traces of humor long since fled. Her hair plastered wetly to her forehead, rainwater streaming down her neck, she advanced on him.

"You're wrong," she repeated. "*So* wrong. If anyone knows anything about the science of books, it's him. But your mistake doesn't matter."

She was standing over him now, her expression ominous. "What *matters* is that you were talking about Mr. Morgan with an 'art dealer'—part of that crowd you speak about with such contempt, that you claim to hate. That—*that*—shocks me to my very core. You—*all* of us—you, your art dealer, me—we're all much too far below Mr. Morgan's humanity, his generosity, to criticize his tastes, or what he does. Your disdain can't touch him; it can't hurt him—but it hurts *me*." She paused, and then said, more gently, "Because you are so very dear to me, your words have the power to wound me deeply. In slandering him this way, you're offending me personally. He's the hero of my soul. And so I will ask you never, *ever* to criticize him in front of me again."

"Forgive my lack of tact," he said icily. "I hadn't realized that you loved this gentleman more than me."

"My affection for him changes nothing about my feelings for you." She had climbed back into bed. "The subject is closed."

She picked up her letter and began scribbling again, writing to "the hero of her soul."

She had no way of knowing the effort it cost Berenson to

control himself, to stay silent. He had nothing against noisy arguments; in fact, he was rather fond of them—as long as he was the one who started them and ended them, and as long as it was he who had the last word. This time, he chose to submit.

This, it turned out, was the right choice—especially since, a few days later at the Grand Hotel on the Via Veneto in Rome, B.B. received news that would put a brutal end to his contentment.

*

"A telegram from Mary! My sister has just been hospitalized in Paris. Galloping tuberculosis. She's not likely to live."

"Your sister Senda?" asked Belle, horrified.

"Bessie. She's alone in France."

"You have to go, of course! Right away!"

"And leave you here? Certainly not. Go and wait for me at I Tatti."

"My maid is back with me now. And I have several friends in the city. Don't worry about me—go! But send me news. Take the Rome express tonight and wire me that you've arrived safely as soon as you can."

He let her act as his personal assistant, just as Mary had once done, and as Belle herself had already been doing with diligence and efficiency for three weeks now. She packed his clock, his books and pens, and his work materials into his suitcase and checked to make sure everything was there, down to his neckties and handkerchiefs.

When Belle had seen him off on the night train and emerged alone from the station, she finally allowed the tears to blur her vision, the sobs to rise in her throat. She had left him in the train car, worried sick about his sister, wild with sorrow at having to leave her.

Belle knew how much B.B. had wanted to show her Rome. It was all he had talked about during their travels: the Eternal City. Driving on the Via Flaminia, he had even stopped in front of one of its hidden gems: the tiny church of Sant'Andrea, closed to worshippers, to which he alone possessed the key.

She knew, too, how much he feared their separation, how he dreaded that exile that would, in a few short weeks, put them back on opposite sides of the ocean. And now they had been forced to part even sooner, and at such short notice. She admired him for having the strength to walk away from their happiness, to depart without hesitation for his sister's bedside. This man, who was always so impatient, had proven *in fine* to be capable of any sacrifice.

Bernhard Berenson truly was, in every way, a man and a genius worthy of her love.

Mechanically, aimlessly, she wandered the streets of Rome, trying to get back to the Via Veneto on foot. She noticed neither the indigo sky overhead, more luminous even than the mosaics on the vaulted ceilings of the basilica in Ravenna, nor the twisted trunks of the tall black pines on the Pincian Hill. Three questions dominated her thoughts. Would she see B.B. again before she had to leave Italy? Would she see him again before she had to board the ship at Southampton? Would she ever see him again?

She did not pause in front of the Fountain of Moses, or even think of going into the church of Santa Maria della Vittoria, where divine Love pierced the heart of Bernini's *Ecstasy of Santa Teresa*. Reaching the Grand Hotel, she went straight to her room and collapsed into bed. After a sleepless night, the telegram from B.B. that she had been hoping for arrived. Bessie's condition did not seem as catastrophic as Mary had led him to believe. Berenson would get his sister settled in a clinic and return to Rome as soon as he knew she was out of danger.

This relatively positive news galvanized Belle back into action. She leapt out of bed.

"Enough whining," she told herself, studying her tear-swollen face in the mirror. "He would hate all this sniveling. If he could find the courage to leave, you can be brave, too, and pull yourself together. He'll be back. It's only a matter of days. His sister will be all right. Come on, now. Show some spirit, for God's sake!"

Suddenly she realized how completely, since their first night of love at Claridge's, she had lost sight of herself, submerged in an ocean of feeling that subsumed her entire being. How she'd ceased to exist, except through those feelings of love.

"Wake up," she told herself sternly, "or you're going to miss everything—especially Rome, which you've wanted to see for so long! What if you never get the chance to come back? Who knows—the Big Chief might already have made up his mind to fire you!"

She hoped they had managed to keep a low enough profile, but really, how likely was it that they had completely avoided stirring up gossip? Surely Morgan had caught wind of her escapades with the famous Bernhard Berenson by now. Too many mutual acquaintances had spotted them in the same cities for rumors not to be circulating.

The first result of Belle's sudden snap back to reality was that she chose not to obey B.B. and go to I Tatti to wait for him.

Not immediately, at least.

Instead, she arranged a meeting in the Vatican with one of her German correspondents, Father Franz Ehrle, the Jesuit prefect of the Vatican Library. A specialist in medieval Christianity, Father Ehrle was compiling an inventory of the printed books conserved in the pontifical archive in the Borgia Apartments, as well as a catalogue of the manuscripts there—a corpus of such breadth and richness that he believed it would take nearly a century for the work to be completed.

For centuries, the popes and their cardinal-nephews had collected priceless manuscripts. Not just Catholic codices, but treasures from every religion. Ehrle had dedicated himself to their restoration and conservation, and the prospect of learning from Miss Greene about the state-of-the-art techniques she used at the Morgan Library, or those of the eminent Professor Richardson, who had catalogued the Library of Congress, was one he viewed with pleasure.

The understanding between them was immediate and total. She would do everything in her power to assist him by obtaining Morgan's financial support for certain areas of his research. In return, he offered to reveal to her the mysteries of the *Archivio segreto*, the Secret Archive, taking her on a personal tour of the temple of universal wisdom.

A dream come true.

In the end, Belle's stay in Rome was a much-needed breath of fresh air. Armed with her Baedeker, that famous travel guide to Italy so beloved of tourists, Belle acquainted herself with the Eternal City—first on her own and then, even better, with an American friend, an older married woman of unimpeachable respectability. She was the ideal chaperone, a proper Boston lady—and a deadly bore. Appearing with her at St. Peter's Basilica, the Coliseum, the Forum, provided Belle with a conspicuous certification of good conduct.

But this situation lasted a mere five days. B.B. wired her that he would be returning to Tuscany on September 19, and she hurried there to await him, as he requested. Despite Mary's repeated invitations, however, she did not go to stay at the Villa I Tatti. Claiming that she had business with local librarians, she checked into the Grand Hotel in Florence with her maid.

"Come to dinner, at least," Mary implored her on the telephone.

"Bernhard will never forgive me for not having you to the villa. I'll come and pick you up in the car at around five o'clock, and show you a bit of the countryside around I Tatti . . . The little village of Settignano, on the next hill, is particularly charming; you'll see. It was where Michelangelo was put out to wet-nurse when he was a baby. And then we can spend the evening together, talking about our dear Bernhard. The chauffeur will drive you home. How does that sound?"

It was paradise, in fact. A perfect haven.

The Villa I Tatti was an oasis of beauty such as any aesthete could only dream of.

And yet, Belle felt nothing. Neither pleasure nor admiration. Not even when contemplating the landscape that had sheltered Bocaccio during an outbreak of the plague, and not when shown the Renaissance garden recreated in front of the house by a young landscape architect, one of Mary's protégés, with its cypress trees and boxwood hedges, its double flights of stairs, its fountains and water lilies. She allowed herself to be ushered through this fantastical kingdom numbly, as if anesthetized.

She felt only mildly interested in the many paintings by Italian Old Masters that Bernhard had accumulated through the years, and the same was true of his collection of stunning photographs, reproductions of works of art from all over the world, which he used to compare and attribute paintings.

Nothing—no emotion—except, perhaps, a kind of unease. Penetrating B.B.'s private world in his absence made her uncomfortable. And Mary was trying too hard, though it was true that having met in New York and then again in London had certainly created a bond of friendship between them, and Belle truly appreciated the warmth of this tall blonde lady, this believer in free love.

But at the other times they had seen each other, Belle hadn't been her husband's mistress, not *really*. She hadn't lived with him, the way she had done for the past three weeks. And now, sitting next to Bernhard's wife in his own bedroom . . . She had thought herself free of the strictures of convention, but being here, hand in hand with Mrs. Berenson on the marital bed, felt very unpleasant indeed.

And the worst was yet to come. Dinner with Mary's lover.

Geoffrey Scott was, in fact, a very handsome young man of twenty-six, tall and slim with a flop of hair over one eye and a pair of spectacles perched on the end of his nose. He was witty, intellectual, highly educated. Complex, too. The sort of Oxford-bred Englishman that would have appealed to Belle herself, once upon a time.

She hated the way Geoffrey spoke of B.B.'s imminent return, as if he were a tyrant feared by the entire household. Hated his story about the poor chauffeur who had allowed his mustache to grow in B.B.'s absence but had shaved it off this evening for fear that the change would displease his master. Hated Mary's remarks about the disorderly state of the house, which would inevitably send her husband into a rage, and hated the knowing glances she exchanged with the other men seated at the table: the landscape architect, a partner of Geoffrey Scott's, who was working with him on the restoration of the villa, and the French artist René Piot, from whom André Gide had commissioned *Le Parfum des nymphes*, and who was now painting frescoes on the ceiling of the library. The library, of course. Piot's slowness, his colors that should have softened with time but seemed instead to grow more garish by the day—the artist was preparing himself, now, for Berenson's criticisms, certain that there would be a fearful explosion of temper.

If the charm of I Tatti failed to work on Belle, neither did Miss Greene's magnetism have any effect on her fellow guests at the villa. Her language, common. Her manners, common. What could have caused Bernhard Berenson to fall in love with this little American snippet? How could she possibly make him happy? He, who had always been sophisticated to the point of elitism!

"You described her to us as a fireball, Mary!" exclaimed Geoffrey Scott, when Belle had left the villa to return to her hotel in Florence. "A wandering star! A blazing sun! I've seen nothing but a dismal, plain little Midwestern thing!"

"Don't be so hard on her," Mary chided. "The child must have felt completely lost among us; we know each other so well. And besides, my dear Geoffrey, you're going to have to get used to her; we're going to Venice next week with her and Bernhard. He's asked me to reserve four rooms at the Hotel Europa, plus one for the maid. We'll have a little group tour, to spare her that ogre Morgan's thunderbolts."

The relief Belle had felt in getting back to her hotel was equaled only by her joy at seeing B.B. again two days later, and the intoxication of the following days spent alone together in Arezzo, in front of the frescoes of Piero della Francesca.

Bernhard hadn't spent even a single night at I Tatti.

Venice would be another story.

*

They reached the Santa Lucia train station in a violent rainstorm.

The Doge's Palace was a mere blur in the downpour, the quays submerged. A line of small black dots crossed the Piazza San Marco: umbrellas, swaying above their reflections in the gray water. But the windows of Berenson's second-floor room at the Hotel Europa, located next to the place where the Grand Canal emptied into the lagoon, boasted the most beautiful view in Venice: the clustered domes of La Salute, gleaming like pure silver through the curtain of mist.

The little group had not allowed itself to be discouraged by the bad weather, and its members now split up: Mary and B.B. went to the offices of the local art dealers with whom they had business; Geoffrey to the churches; and Belle, to everyone's surprise, to her bed. She was suffering from a chill, or perhaps a bilious attack; she'd been vague about it. Hands clasped over her belly, eyes closed, she went back over the last few days in her memory.

Traveling as a group of four wasn't as bad as she'd expected it to be, she had to admit. Geoffrey had shown himself to be an amiable fellow, even rather funny. Far friendlier than he'd been to her at I Tatti, at any rate. It was manifestly clear that he wasn't in love with Mary; in fact, Belle thought he would have preferred the company of men. Despite the nightly games of back-and-forth that went on between the four of them—no one ever slept in his or her own bed—she thought Geoffrey gave in to Mrs. Berenson's desires out of weakness, more than anything else. Mary was an uninhibited sensualist, and her lover's lukewarm responses to her mattered little. She was persuasive, enticing, and he allowed himself to be directed. She needed his affection, and he gave it freely. Intellectually, emotionally, he understood her. Yes, everything was fine.

*I'm fine, too. This is nothing*, Belle repeated to herself, shifting uncomfortably on the bed. *It doesn't mean anything for certain. Nothing at all. It could just be tiredness, or indigestion. I've taken every precaution—done everything that doctor in New York told me to do. There's no reason to jump to conclusions . . .*

In the late afternoon, during a brief sunny spell, Mary ordered tea on the balcony. Belle prepared herself to join the others. Rest and solitude weren't doing anything for her. A few of Geoffrey's jokes would do her good.

A round table, four chairs, and the magnificent view of the Grand Canal in the waning sun. It was lovely . . . until B.B. burst onto the terrace.

"Don't trust this woman," he spat, throwing a photograph in Mary's face. "She has a black soul."

Seeming almost drunk with rage, he was humiliating his wife in front of Belle, in front of Geoffrey, in front of the maid and the waiter and all the gondoliers on the canal beneath the balcony. But despite the seething violence of his anger, his jacket remained buttoned, his tie neatly in place. Even in his fury, he lost none of his elegance.

"Manipulator—hypocrite—liar—you're a snake in a skirt, working behind my back to ruin me!"

One might have expected him to be shouting, but no. He did not raise his voice. He spat his venomous words from between clenched teeth, his quiet tone somehow all the more threatening.

"Why have you been hiding this photo from me?"

"You're so sensitive, my dear," replied Mary, her hand trembling slightly as she set down the teapot, "that I can't—I really mustn't—tell you *everything*. Sometimes I have to keep the truth from you in order to protect you."

"Protect me from what? Your thoughtlessness?"

"From vexation. To shield you from how crass people can be, when you detest it so."

"Don't listen to this witch," he snarled, turning to Belle. "She pretends to be so kind, so generous, so devoted—but her intentions are foul! I've just learned that Andrea Bottacin, one of the most important art dealers in Venice, sent a photo of a painting to me at I Tatti last month, asking me to write on the back of it the opinion I'd expressed in his gallery, when I was admiring the original. A portrait, said to be by Tintoretto. But this letter—this photo—my *darling wife* never gave them to me!"

"I knew you hadn't seen that portrait at Bottacin's, because we were there together," retorted Mary. "And what's more, judging by that photo, it is not and never was a Tintoretto—and so I didn't think it was proper for you to answer him."

"What gives you the right to decide what's 'proper' for me

to do? Bottacin didn't let the matter go; he wrote to me again. And my wife, my colleague, my right hand, thought it 'proper' to keep *that* letter from me, too! She hid it from me that that swindler was claiming to have heard me attribute the portrait to Tintoretto, with his son and nephew as witnesses. And that, on the strength of my word, he sold the painting to an English lord, who is now demanding a certificate personally signed by me!"

"This happened to us once before, last April. With a Parisian art dealer, and a Moroni painting. The French dealer's allegations threw you into such a rage that you got ill. I thought it was best to keep the whole thing quiet—keep you out of another dispute."

"Well, you were wrong! Bottacin just accosted me on the Rialto with that photo, claiming in front of the whole city that he'd sent me a hundred and fifty thousand lire to write that certificate for him. And that I'd better give it to him, here and now, because I never denied admiring his Tintoretto."

"I never touched his check," she protested.

"But you didn't refuse—you didn't tear it up and send it back to him as confetti."

"I never deposited it!"

"*Silence means consent!* Don't you understand, you stupid woman? This is about my honor! My reputation! If anyone should think that an attribution by Bernhard Berenson can be *bought!* That sending him a check is all it takes for him to validate a painting he has never seen, to drive up the price with a bogus certificate of authenticity! It would be the end—the end of *everything!* It would finish me!"

He stormed back inside, leaving Belle more shocked than Geoffrey, paler than Mary. The three of them sat silently for a long moment.

Mary sighed. "It's his sour stomach."

Belle refused the cup of tea Mary held out to her. She had

seen B.B. angry before, but she had never seen him in a state of such fury. It was clear, now, how very mercurial his temperament was. And the violence—the crassness of his insults. She was trembling with indignation on Mary's behalf.

"No one has the right to act like that," she said.

"He won't even remember it by this evening," Mary assured her, sitting back down.

"I will."

"It doesn't matter."

"It's unacceptable," argued Belle.

"We're used to it. Aren't we, Geoffrey?"

Unable to swallow her tea, Belle rose and left the balcony, almost as angry as B.B. had been.

Mary couldn't hold back a smile. Bernhard's mistress was defending her now! She loved this sort of gesture. Feminine solidarity. A pretty victory.

The scene that followed between Belle and Bernhard left them both furious and ill. She gave him the silent treatment that evening and all the next morning. He left to go for a walk without a single conciliatory word.

But that wasn't the worst of it.

These repeated arguments were keeping Belle from telling him what was really tormenting her. The uncertainty, the anxiety. What had been causing her nausea since their arrival in Venice.

The fog had finally lifted, the sun banishing the party's black humors. But their sojourn in Venice ended with the melancholy sense that summer had gone, that the holiday was over. It was September 29. Mary and Geoffrey were preparing to return to I Tatti. B.B. would be traveling to Paris. And Belle was about to leave for London.

"Don't leave me alone. Don't go to Paris. Please."

They were standing together in the Church of Santa Maria

Assunta on Torcello, an island in the Venetian Lagoon to which few tourists ventured.

"Come with me to England," she whispered. "Please."

He tucked Belle's arm into his own and drew her tightly to him.

"I would like so very much to take the train with you tomorrow," he murmured. "But I have to make arrangements in Paris for Bessie to travel to my mother's in Boston. And I have several important business matters to wrap up in France, as well. You come with me!"

"I can't. I must finish what I've started with the curators at the British Museum. I was only allowed to come to Europe because I proved the importance of my work here. And I've done nothing for a month! Will you come to me, as soon as you can?"

"I promise. Or you'll come to me, won't you?"

She didn't reply.

Hand in hand, heavy-hearted, they roamed the waterfront, losing themselves silently in the depths of the island.

"We were so close that day," Belle remembered. "Thank God, so very close. We were like a single soul, in the silence of Torcello."

She didn't tell him the reasons for her tears a few nights prior. Why she had wept in his arms until dawn, unable to stop, sobbing over and over again that the worst had happened, that the walls were closing in, that the world was crashing down. He had put the episode down to grief at their impending separation and asked no questions.

They spent their final hours together entwined in Belle's bed, promising to meet again in a few days, when each of them had fulfilled their duty.

What was the cause of their despair? They still had nearly three weeks to be together in Europe, before Belle had to return to New York.

Berenson let her go to London without ever imagining that he was really sending her off to war, to the slaughter. How could he have guessed that she was pregnant?

And yet there could no longer be any doubt. Despite her solemn vow never to have children, Belle Greene was expecting a baby.

# BOOK III

## BEHIND THE VEIL OF MY SOUL
1910–1924

# CHAPTER 8

## THE DAY I LEFT YOU FOR LONDON
## OCTOBER 1910–AUGUST 1911

Welcome to Claridge's, Miss Greene. We've reserved your suite for you—number four, as always."

Despite the kindness of the staff, Belle's feelings on checking in this time bore hardly any resemblance to the happiness and excitement she'd always felt in the past. She forced herself to give the clerk her most beguiling smile and allowed the bellhop to lead her toward the elevator, sinking her umbrella gaily into the carpet of the familiar lobby with every step. *Home, sweet home.*

Inside, she was weeping. Parting with B.B. under these circumstances had been wrenching, terrible. Did he know what she was going to do in London? Sometimes she was sure he did, sometimes not. She had failed to broach the subject at every opportunity. She hadn't dared. And he had failed to hear it in her voice. Hadn't wanted to, perhaps.

Though she often seemed carefree, uninhibited, and direct, employing coarse language in everyday life, the truth was that her sense of personal modesty, for private and complex reasons, ran so deep as to be painful. This shyness—and her pride, too—had kept her from speaking with B.B. about her concern over something as intimate as a pregnancy. One simply did not discuss this sort of terror with a man like Bernhard Berenson—especially when he refused to pick up on her hints.

She hadn't been able to muster up the courage to say anything to him, in the end. And she couldn't write to him about her condition now. Impossible to discuss something so sensitive, so dangerous, in a letter that could easily be opened and read between England and France.

The die was cast. She would remain silent. He would be kept in the dark.

Belle stepped into the elevator. The operator greeted her warmly in his turn as he pulled the gate shut.

"Welcome back, Miss Greene!"

Another dazzling smile.

"Thanks, Billy. It's so good to be back with you all again."

*If he only knew,* she thought with bitter amusement. *A Negress and an unwed mother. He'd throw me out on my ear!*

Her fear, her sadness were so stifling that she felt as if she couldn't breathe. She fought a rising wave of nausea as the elevator completed its journey.

The sitting room of "her" suite. The same mantelpiece clock chiming the hours, the same pink silk Louis XV armchairs before the hearth. The immense grand piano in the center of the room, one of Claridge's five Steinways, standing ready to assist some visiting diva in practicing her role.

Under normal circumstances, she would have immediately picked up the telephone and called everyone she knew in London, announcing her return, receiving myriad invitations from the bookmen of whom she was so fond. But she only had the strength to take off her hat, standing there while the maid began unpacking her trunks, her mind whirling relentlessly.

Eventually she sank down on the stool at the dressing table, staring at her own face in the mirror without recognizing it. Her eyes were bleary, her gaze unfocused. She thought back to all the other evenings when she had examined herself in this very mirror before swanning out to some glittering English soiree or other. She remembered her triumphant expression in the glass after the dinner at the Savoy with Read, Pollard, and all the other men from whom she had just swiped the seventeen Caxtons. And the feverish night when she had prepared so carefully to give herself to Bernhard Berenson. So long ago, already.

One thing was certain; Venice had not done her any good.

She looked like an exhausted tourist, haggard and lost. A foreigner. She wished desperately to be back in the safety of the apartment on 115th Street with her mother and sisters. She couldn't remember the last time she'd actually wanted to go home.

On the other hand, perhaps being so far from New York was actually a blessing. She couldn't bring herself to think about Russell's withering sarcasm if he knew about her condition. Definitely a blessing. There was no Mr. Morgan to demand her presence in his office day and night. No worldly acquaintances to notice and murmur. The Big Chief's wife and daughters were hardly likely to look on her favorably, either; they were already jealous of her intimacy with the man at the center of their lives. Not to mention Morgan's mistresses. If a single one of them suspected her of being pregnant, she was dead.

It would be easier to keep the secret here. An abortion abroad? No one would be the wiser.

But who could she go to, to get the name of a doctor who would perform the procedure? Charles Hercules Read? Bernard Quaritch? *Excuse me, gentlemen, do you have in your address book, by chance, the phone number for a good baby-killer?*

Here, as in America, abortion was considered infanticide, a crime for which a woman could be investigated, tried, and put in prison, along with any accomplices.

Keep the baby?

Out of the question! B.B. detested children. He didn't even like Mary's daughters, whom he blamed for greedily draining his wife's heart dry, leaving nothing for him.

*The only truly vulgar words I have ever heard him utter were about the Italian children, aged between zero and ten, we saw so often in Italy: "Look, another brat getting in our way; another dirty, shrieking brat!" What if, by a stroke of bad luck, my own "brat" were to have dark skin? Would it become "Look, another colored brat; a dirty little colored brat in my way" . . .?*

*Don't be so paranoid, Belle! You're being unfair. B.B. has never shown even the slightest racism in your presence. Though . . .*

Certain things he had said came back to her now. Sometimes, in moments of passion, he would call her his "dark-skinned empress," his "Queen of Sheba," his "Indian maharani," his "fierce little Malay." All allusions that were meant to be tender and loving—but which showed how aware he was of the color of her skin. Did he suspect? Did he *know*? She had always chosen to play the game, to stay ahead of the curve, by emphasizing her own exotic "Oriental" looks, which set her apart from the fashionable beauties of the day—and, sometimes, by lamenting them.

"I've always been the ugly duckling of the family. Well, not always. When I was little, in Virginia, I had the same blonde hair and pale skin as my mother and sisters. But they still look like flaxen-haired Isolde or Melisande, while I grew into a Blackamoor!"

It was the old tried and true method: putting herself on display, flaunting herself, the better to hide.

But this tactic had never worked as well with B.B. as it did with others, and for good reason. He knew better than anyone how to use the spotlight—and its shadows—to conceal himself. She had always hated the way he teased her. Making fun of her Dutch ancestry, for instance. Suggesting that she was not the daughter of the aristocratic Genevieve van Vliet, but rather the child of her former slave, the Black nanny who had served in the household of her redoubtable Southern grandmother. It had been a joke, to which she'd hastily responded in the same tone, asking him laughingly which Polish rabbi he descended from, exactly. This was shaky ground, and he hadn't appreciated the innuendo. Vague rumors might well swirl, but he would never admit his origins. Neither of them would reveal themselves to the other. These were secrets to be denied, even to the person closest to you, dearest to you, in the whole world.

And now, if he were to find out that he'd fathered a Black child, on top of everything else . . .

Enough of this. It was pointless to speculate any further, she mused bitterly. He was married, and he wouldn't divorce his wife. And even if he did want a divorce—as he had told her many times—she would never allow him to leave Mary. *I'm not made for marriage. With him, or with anyone. I love him. I adore him. He's the love of my life. But I wouldn't marry him for all the money in the world.*

Keeping the baby, then, was out of the question.

She wouldn't admit it to herself, but B.B.'s absence now left her without options. Abandoned. She fought to stave off a fresh wave of the panic that had threatened to drown her throughout the journey from Venice to Calais. If only B.B. had wanted to come with her! If only he could have!

And he knew so many people in London. He would have known who to contact. How would she manage the situation alone?

"I'm here, darling!" sang a well-known voice in the receiver.

"Ethel!"

Ethel Watts Mumford Grant, her dearest friend, whom Belle had described in her letters to B.B. last spring as the embodiment of the twentieth-century woman: "*She's an absolute terror, and I adore her!*"

"You're here! Where, exactly?"

"Claridge's, of course! B.B. told us you were arriving! We saw him yesterday in Paris. Oh, I have so much to tell you! Peter's reserved a table for this evening at the Grill; there'll be ten of us. Theater people. They're putting on my first novel—*Dupes*, you know—at the Palladium. Meet us in the lobby at eight?"

Ethel and Peter Grant: the wildest, most uninhibited couple in Belle's New York social circle. She had introduced them to B.B. upon her own arrival in London last August, and their dinner *à quatre* had been an unmitigated disaster. B.B. had thought the Grants intolerable, the husband and wife both so very common that, he had shuddered, Belle could only be contaminated by them.

He had changed his mind, evidently, because he had seen them again yesterday. Without her.

\*

"My darling, he's told me everything. I know it all!"

The two women were enjoying a cozy chat, smoking English cigarettes and drinking *champagne sec* in the Grants' suite.

Slim, brunette, and thirtyish, Ethel belonged to the international bohemian set that frequented the luxury spots of the Old World between July and October—Saint-Moritz, London, Paris, Nice, Cairo—before settling for the winter in New York state, throwing liquor-soaked parties in their Greenwich Village townhouse during the week and at their spacious Hamptons retreat on the weekends.

The pampered daughter of a Wall Street financier, Ethel had been so indulged in her artistic aspirations that she'd been able to study painting in Paris at the only studio open to women: the Académie Julian on the boulevard des Italiens. Her appetite for world travel whetted by this French experience, she had journeyed to the Far East with her father before marrying an attorney named George Mumford and settling in San Francisco. There she had given birth to a son and published her first bestselling novel, *Dupes*, which an avant-garde theater troupe had now adapted for the London stage. Mr. Mumford, Esq., had found neither his wife's literary pretentions nor her biting wit to his taste, so Ethel had packed up her little boy, left the marital home, and sued Mumford for desertion, winning an enormous divorce settlement and then racking up a series of triumphs on the Broadway stage, penning vaudeville comedies that were as hilarious as they were immoral. Her extremely witty *Cynic's Calendar of Revised Wisdom*, rereleased in a new edition every year since its original publication in 1902, kept her a fixture in the spotlight. And, last but not least, she had remarried a Scottish Wall Street broker, the very rich Peter Grant—who, unlike her first husband, both approved of her success and participated willingly in her social hijinks.

This was the alter ego whom Belle had chosen as confidante and accomplice. A terror, indeed.

"What do you mean, he told you *everything*?" she asked Ethel now, warily.

She was well aware of Ethel's fondness for meddling in other people's love affairs and wasn't pleased with B.B. for mentioning their liaison in front of her—or anyone. It was already bad enough that he went into detail about their romance in his letters to Mary . . .

"Everything," Ethel repeated with relish, "absolutely *everything!*"

She fitted a fresh cigarette into her long holder, leaned in to light her Sullivan Powell from the one Belle was smoking, and went on dreamily, through a halo of smoke:

"Sienna, Orvieto, Venice . . . to tell the truth, I'm envious. With a mentor like that, you must have had a simply magical adventure! I've had a fair few boyfriends in my day, you know. Interesting fellows, for the most part, but nothing to compare with a man as exceptional as Bernhard Berenson! What a charmed life you lead, my dear, to be loved by such a specimen. Enjoy it, darling; enjoy it to the fullest! Life is short."

"Indeed," Belle murmured. "Ethel, I have a question for you. You know a great many people in London, don't you? I'm not talking about theater people . . . Medical professionals, I mean . . ."

Ethel's face swiftly grew serious. She looked at Belle closely. "Are you ill?"

"Not exactly."

Their eyes met. Ethel understood immediately.

"Shit," she said succinctly.

"Well put," said Belle, stubbing out her cigarette in the ash-tray.

"*Shit*," repeated Ethel, not without savoring the word, so wholly unacceptable in the mouth of a woman. "Shit. But I told you how to keep that from happening!"

"Sponges, diaphragms, douching—I did it all. And I did it right. But clearly none of it worked."

"Don't panic. You're not the first, nor the last. I've been through it three times myself. We just have to find the right person. Not to worry. And there's no need for that ghastly expression, Belle; it's not so serious as all that!"

That was the incredible thing about Ethel—her ability to take life so lightly. *Not so serious as all that!*

Becoming pregnant had always been Belle's worst fear. Since the day she had begun passing, the self-imposed ban on child-bearing had been a constant presence in her thoughts. She had taken care, before joining B.B. in Europe, to consult a doctor who had prescribed pessaries and douches. Throughout her travels with Berenson, the risk of pregnancy had haunted her. She had been so *very* careful, had used every contraceptive method she knew of—all of them, *at the same time*.

All of which made her current condition even more difficult to comprehend.

But there it was.

*It's not so serious as all that!*

Through the magic of Ethel's presence, the nightmare was suddenly transformed into a practical problem they would work together to solve. And when it came to problem-solving, both women were skilled to the point of genius.

The "right person." A midwife in Chelsea, a knitting needle, herbal infusions, and curettage. Ethel brought Belle back to Claridge's half-dead.

Abdominal pains that bent her double, vomiting, hemorrhages. Belle's maid thought her certain to die. A woman whose devotion and discretion were both total, she watched over Belle day and night. Ethel didn't leave her side, either, camping out in suite number four and keeping B.B. regularly informed about what she termed "a liver problem that's turned the whites of her eyes yellow." Hepatitis.

Outwardly, he acted as if he believed this diagnosis, frequently demanded news, worried, panicked, telephoned up to five times a day.

But he did not travel from Paris to London.

Belle remained dangerously ill through the whole first week of October. In her delirium, she called out for Bernhard Berenson. Luckily, no one was there to hear it, except the two women who already knew.

When her fever finally broke, her first words were for him. *Tell him I'm all right*, she instructed. She wanted a telegram sent immediately, then and there, informing him that the worst was over, that she would soon be back on her feet. And that the whites of her eyes were once again "as light as her skin." But the first part of this impulsive message, whose courage and humor he would be the only one to appreciate, did nothing to lighten the pathos of its final plea: "Please, B.B., please come!"

He didn't grasp the urgency of her summons, or pretended not to.

A strike by France's rail workers, he said, meant that there were no trains running between Paris and any ports of embarkation to England. But, he wrote, why not benefit from the fact that the Grants were taking their automobile on the ferry this weekend? Ethel had written that she would be in Paris on Sunday. If she wished it, Belle could be with him in three days.

Her response was immediate: her freedom had ended. Her time was no longer her own. She was still a "working girl," and the boss was expecting her to finish the work he had sent her to London to do. Between her Italian holiday and falling ill in England, she hadn't fulfilled any of these tasks. She promised to do everything in her power to join B.B., but she doubted that she would manage it in the end.

His reply was equally swift: So, Belle would rather serve the "hero of her soul" than entertain the possibility of spending these last few days in France with the man she called the love of her life? She was choosing to please her Big Chief, whom there would be all the time in the world to cater to in New York, rather than answer B.B.'s call and seize the opportunity to travel with the Grants? Even when the time remaining to them was so short! Belle's ship was due to sail, he reminded her, in ten days.

Letters traveled from one side of the Channel to the other, crossed, were lost. B.B.'s messages grew more bitter by the hour; Belle's, more caustic. She was careful not to reproach him, but her words dripped with sarcasm. And pain.

She was beginning to seethe with anger at him.

She congratulated him ironically on his wisdom in not undertaking such a tiring journey, one that was probably pointless, and practically impossible, given that damned rail strike. To hell with hollow gestures. She understood completely! She couldn't agree more with his decision to stay put and take it easy! Especially because she was so busy herself. She only had one more week, after all, just one short week to finish all the work that had brought her to Europe in the first place. She had to pick up some manuscripts from Quaritch; pack some paintings from the Prince's Gate collection in order to bring them—legally, this time—to the United States; and visit the special collections at the British Museum, where Charles Hercules Read—so charming, so amusing—was anxious to show her his recent acquisitions. And, most importantly, she had to complete the purchase of the Rembrandt engravings she had negotiated in August. So much to do, so many fascinating people to see!

She took on, again, the overtly provocative tone that used to drive B.B. mad.

. . . Who knew, in fact, if—in the midst of this last-minute whirlwind—she would have been able to find even an hour to dine with him, anyway? The frustration of knowing he was in town, and of having no time to spare for him, would have been too dreadful! Yes, he had certainly done the right thing by not coming to London.

She concluded this sarcastic letter with a very straightforward jab: "And I suppose my letters must not be so *very* bad, if you find them satisfying enough that you don't need to see me in person."

Slowly, she sank into despair.

However blind he'd appeared to be, however naive, however unwilling to be honest with himself, he must've known what she was suffering from when she left Venice. How could he not have realized, when she spent the whole night before her departure weeping in his arms, terrified, gasping that the worst had happened?

And if he hadn't guessed, it was almost worse. To find such ignorance in a man of such genius.

At the end of the day, perhaps it didn't matter whether he'd known or not. She couldn't deny the obvious truth: he had left her to face this ordeal alone. And now he was willing to risk never seeing her again, rather than disrupt his Parisian plans. Had their happiness during the past two months been a delusion? Did that happiness even matter in the end, when both of them were now proving incapable of truly risking anything— were, in fact, backing away the moment any real effort was required? If B.B.'s feelings for her had had any depth whatsoever, he would have borrowed the Grants' car, or someone else's, *anyone* else's, to catch that ferry.

Did he care for her at all?

"Your choice not to come to England," she wrote to him, "may be a sensible one, but it reveals a deficiency in our love that does neither of us credit, and disturbs me a great deal."

But B.B. refused all blame. There was not a single train to Calais or Cherbourg. He had no way of getting to Dover. But she—*she!*—could have traveled to France with Ethel. Why hadn't she done it, if she was indeed in good health, and loved him as much as she claimed? *Had she been using him?* he asked her now. Had she used him as a means of exploring Italy, before tossing him aside when she no longer needed his services?

He sounded out all of their mutual acquaintances in Paris. As Belle had feared, rumors were everywhere. B.B. dined with Florie Blumenthal and Rita Lydig at the Ritz; they had no doubts about the Morgan librarian's admiration for his prodigious intellectual qualities. Hadn't they heard Miss Greene claim, in Munich, that she would happily spend her holidays with the illustrious Bernhard Berenson in exchange for a few crumbs of his knowledge?

Mary, to whom B.B. confided his fears regarding Belle's indifference on a daily basis, acknowledged that she never would've expected Belle to refuse to join him in Paris, never imagined that she could leave Europe without saying goodbye. The truth, Mary confessed, was that she wasn't sure anymore what kind of person her poor B.B. was dealing with. What sort of woman was Belle Greene, really? A little American tart, priding herself on having gotten the world's greatest expert on Italian painting to squire her around Europe? An ambitious bluestocking who had pumped B.B.'s mind for information without ever loving him?

Ethel Grant, for her part, told B.B. that this was just the way her friend was: Belle always fell hard and fast for a man and then lost interest just as quickly. To hear Ethel tell it, Belle had simply repeated the pattern, lavishing B.B. with passionate adoration and then dropping him once her curiosity was sated.

B.B. himself believed that Belle had been sincere in her feelings for him during their travels together. But now, he thought, she had shown herself to be devoid of all sentimentality.

Such accusations, at a time when her final separation from B.B. was fast approaching, threw Belle into a state of desolation. "Your letter today made me want to burst out laughing—or crying. I will choose to laugh, at least until you come to me."

It was wishful thinking. He did not come. She was forced to sail without seeing him again.

And so it was in tears, but with her arms laden with flowers, that Belle left Europe on October 19, 1910.

No one, judging by the numerous admirers and well-wishers that accompanied her as far as the gangplank, by the kisses she blew them all from the deck, by the brilliance of her smile and the energy with which she waved her farewells, would have guessed that Belle Greene was returning home with a broken heart. She had made sure of it. Neither Read, nor Pollard, nor Cockerell, nor Quaritch doubted, even for a moment, that the time she had spent in their company over the past few days had been anything but delightful, the perfect end to her European sojourn. An idyllic stay.

And it had been half true.

"Whatever the future has in store for us," she had written to B.B. on the eve of her departure, "we gave those two stolen months as a gift to one another, and they can never be taken away from us.

"Nothing can alter this truth: I loved you as absolutely and completely as a person can love. And for that, I'm happy. Happy that that love was so natural, so sincere, so deep.

"You know I was never a flirt with you. That I never held back or refused you even an ounce of my immense love.

"I am sure you know that, and that you recognize it."

Words of wisdom. Words of peace. But not words of hope, even for a moment. He noticed at once that Belle had used the verb "love" in the past tense.

*

And so, for Bernhard Berenson, the regret began again for the days, the hours he had not spent with her. Regret at not loving her better, even though he could have, regret at losing her.

By not going to London, he thought, he had made the greatest mistake of his life. That weakness on his part, that failure, would remain an open wound, and Bernhard Berenson's passion for Belle Greene would not wane in the decades to come.

Belle, for her part, was still in the grip of too many contradictory emotions to realize how deeply the English abortion had scarred her soul.

She continued to answer B.B.'s letters, to tell him of her daily activities, as he wished. She dedicated an hour every night to writing to him, and then an hour each week, and eventually an hour each month, for thirty years. She supported him in every way she could, arranging meetings for him with collectors who might benefit him professionally whenever he was in New York.

Bernhard and Mary Berenson would make two more visits to the United States, and Belle, later—much later—would cross the ocean nine times. During her brief encounters with B.B. in America and in Europe, she believed the flame of their passion to be flickering still, but realized with the passage of time that their few nights of love had been a mere flash in the pan. He would blame her for her flightiness and inconstancy; she would defend herself in the half sorry, half provocative tone she had employed during their first separation. Banter, innuendo, shows of bravado, false confessions—her letters never failed to plunge

B.B. into the same old rage, the same old depression. More clear-eyed than he was when it came to the truth of their relationship, she cried out to him in a March 1914 letter that:

"You want me to live for you alone, *through* you alone? I have to believe that you're joking!

"Given our respective egos, our mutual need for money, and our taste for the frivolous things in this world—given your love of high society and my own paltry ambitions, your words to me about the 'exclusivity' of our love are pure nonsense.

"We may be truly, deeply devoted to one another. But experience has proven that we're incapable of living together on a day-to-day basis. And I'm simply not made for the *ménage à trois* with Mary that you propose.

"We can each lead our own lives in our own way and meet elsewhere, in a different sort of relationship, beyond contingencies.

"We can each be what is most important to the other, without being absolutely *everything*.

"I think that's the direction our relationship was taking anyway—that sort of importance. But you will contradict me.

"For my part, I am trying desperately to keep you in my daily life as a spiritual guide, a sort of beacon.

"And yet, I am honest enough to admit that I will not give up my lifestyle for you. And since I know you feel the very same way, why waste your time trying to convince me otherwise?"

Belle was telling the truth. Bernhard Berenson would remain the guiding light of her existence. The love of her life.

She would never reproach him for allowing her to go through the abortion in London alone. But, in the aftermath of World War One, she confessed to him that, on the day she left him in Venice, her own capacity to love—to love, body and soul, holding nothing of herself back—had died. She concluded, desolately, "Why—*why*—did we decide to send me to London?"

\* \* \*

But for now, in October 1910, the hurt was too fresh for Belle to understand just how deep it ran. Brooding, moreover, was not in her nature. She hated being sad.

To hell with heartbreak! No one could know the real nature of the trip from which she'd just returned, or with whom she'd been traveling. And, even more importantly, no one must know of the grief that dwelt within her. The grief of being separated from the man she loved, from whom she'd parted without knowing if she would ever see him again. But also the grief of having discovered that man to be emotionally immature. And the grief of having left Italy behind, and with it the communion of souls, the shared vision of beauty, the magnificent dream their love had been.

And really, what did such grief matter, compared to the splendor of the adventure! She was too familiar with the weight of destiny to let herself be mired forever in the tragedy of an impossible romance. She remained as determined as ever to seize every opportunity the future might have to offer. And the best way to forget her pain, to hide it from others—and from herself—was to *act*. Forward movement. A social whirlwind.

Stopping at Cherbourg on the way to America, the *Oceanic* had taken on board a crowd of American millionaires stranded in France by the rail strikes: Ethel and Peter Grant, the Blumenthals, the Lydigs, Anne Morgan and her companion Bessie Marbury, Oscar Wilde's agent. Not to mention a whole host of stars: Sarah Bernhardt's great rival, the actress Ellen Terry; the mezzo-soprano Marguerite Sylva, whom Belle had so admired with Lanier and Laffan in *Carmen*; and the diva Olive Fremstad, who had originated the role of Salome in Richard Strauss's opera and danced on stage at the Metropolitan with Saint John the Baptist's bloody head dangling from one hand. The performance had been the biggest scandal of 1907, and

Belle was in a position to know; another of J.P. Morgan's daughters, who was a patroness of the Metropolitan Opera, had convinced the Big Chief to demand that the show be canceled and prohibited from being staged again.

Enchanted by these legendary creatures who openly indulged in liaison after liaison, Belle spent as much time with them as she could, observing. Cocktails, cigarettes, and chit-chat in one siren's cabin; recitations of poetry in another. In all of these women she saw vitality, impulsiveness, drama, narcissism. Talent, a taste for success, a passion for power, and dedication to a profession. Like her. "Yes—I admire the type of woman who takes her pleasure like a man," she would later write, "who grows weary of her romantic liaisons like a man, and who cuts them off like a man. The type of financially independent woman who does not have to earn her living through marriage because she has a career of her own. A woman who is more or less masculine in her nature, but who is even more passionate than a so-called 'normal' woman."

Thanks to her exposure to these worldly queens, Miss Greene was reborn from her ashes.

Even Ethel Grant, who had taken it upon herself—without being asked—to act as the point of contact between Belle and B.B., alluded subtly to the former's spectacular revival:

*"Dear B.B.,*

*"In twenty-four hours, we will dock in New York, after a week marked by extremely high waves, very low troughs, and dreadfully billowy seas. Bilious Belle herself has railed endlessly against bloody Poseidon and his terrible mood swings—and you, too.*

*"I have passed along the adorable little sixteenth-century Italian painting you entrusted me with for her, just as you wished, and also the two Fortuny gowns you had made for her in Paris. She seemed touched, but claims that wearing the gowns or looking at the painting without you would cause her more pain than*

*pleasure. I defended you, of course, and told her again that it's all my fault, that it was I who convinced you not to travel to England, thinking she would join us in Paris—but she continues to repeat, 'It would have been so easy for him.'*

"*That being said, she is in fine form, more robust than ever, and both her eyes and her complexion have regained their formal glow. She has wrapped the four hundred and ten first-class passengers on this ship around her little finger, and they hang on her every word and laugh like hyenas at her every witticism. What more could one want?*

"*I must tell you, as well, that she put the time in London without you to very good use, and was very busy indeed. She's returning to the United States with paintings officially declared to be worth more than thirty thousand dollars—not to mention the other knick-knacks brought back from Prince's Gate, safely protected by the silk and lace of her unmentionables, which you, my dear B.B., are the only one to have had the privilege of admiring.*"

Ethel did not specify which "knick-knacks" Belle the Bilious had tucked among her silk underthings, nor did she mention the new scheme Belle had concocted to fool customs. She did not tell B.B. that Belle was planning to use his "adorable little sixteenth-century Italian painting" as a decoy to distract the agents when they made their routine search of the ship—or that she had made up her mind to let them seize B.B.'s gift—after much weeping and supplication, of course—for the sake of retaining her other treasures, the Prince's Gate ornaments intended for Morgan. The confiscation of the painting posed no risk, for, because it had been a gift and not a purchase, she could recover it with an affidavit provided by B.B.; he would simply have to go to the American consulate in Paris, the city where he had bought the painting himself, and attest to the date and value of the work. It was exactly the sort of administrative approach that drove Berenson wild with frustration, but, Belle figured, he owed her that much—to take a few moments of his precious time away from whatever business it was that had kept him in France, kept him from her. And, she knew, he would never willingly give up a sixteenth-century canvas to the American taxman without a fight.

Ethel Grant, half minx, half good girl, concluded her letter to Berenson with the following witticism:

"And so the voyage of our Bilious Belle will have its grand finale tomorrow, October 26, 1910!"

Well might Ethel refer to Belle's cunning plan as a "grand finale." It went off without a hitch.

Once again, the Big Chief gave his Sioux war-cry and danced around his desk, this time to celebrate the clandestine arrival of not two, but *three* statuettes to add to his collection of bronzes. Not the receipt of a single Louis XV watch, but an entire lot of baroque jewelry destined for the display cases of the West Room. And, finally, a small oil painting on copper he'd been coveting for an alcove in his own bedroom.

Besides this illicit booty, there were other treasures, including the three manuscripts purchased from Drouot and the Rembrandt engravings Belle had bought in England. The addition of the latter to the pieces previously acquired by Junius meant that the Morgan Library now held the largest collection of Rembrandt etchings in the world.

And all without paying the twenty percent import tax.

It was Belle's way of thumbing her nose at the government once again. And it was an act of madness, for less than a week earlier, the tax office had arrested and imprisoned Joe, Henry, Ben, and Louis Duveen, prominent art dealers in London and New York and frequent associates of Bernhard Berenson's. Accused of having lied about the value of goods they had declared, the Duveens had just been ordered to pay fifty thousand dollars in fines—a colossal sum, to which was added the surety on which their release depended. The fine posed no threat to their business; they had the means to pay it. But the scandal of the Duveen brothers' arrest delayed the repeal of the law on importing artwork, which Morgan had been working furiously to achieve. This ridiculous tax, which prevented him from repatriating the treasures he kept at his London townhouse, was a constant source of exasperation to him. And so he felt nothing but unbridled enthusiasm when it came to Miss Greene's fleecing of the customs office. He rewarded her cunning with a bonus of two thousand dollars, which enabled her to purchase, for herself and her family, the two adjoining apartments at 138 and 142 40th Street, in the glittering heart of Manhattan, just a few steps from the Morgan Library. Belle would soon become part of a highly exclusive club: the five highest-paid women in America, all the others heads of their own companies.

New York was Belle's oyster. She was among the lucky ones now, and for good. She belonged, at last, to the glittering sphere of real estate owners, Wall Street investors, fashionable beauties, heiresses, and stars.

\*

"Miss Anne Morgan, Miss Belle Greene, Miss Marguerite Sylva! Ladies, a smile, if you please . . ."

Reporters, sent by major press agencies and countless smaller newspapers, jostled and shoved one another on the dock, competing to catch the attention of the celebrities now disembarking from the *Oceanic*.

"The Three Graces together at the foot of the gangplank— thank you."

Belle turned her face away from the camera's popping flashbulb, presenting to the lens only the feathers in her hat.

She knew that the *New York Times* subcontracted its society pages to the *Washington Post*, the largest newspaper in the city of her birth, as well as the *Chicago Tribune*, the paper to which her father surely subscribed. If any one of those newspapers published a photo of her, everyone who had known her in the old days would immediately make the connection between Belle Greene and Belle Greener.

She kept moving, careful not to stand still.

"One more shot, Miss—just one moment, please!"

More flashes. More images that Belle made sure would turn out blurry. Unpublishable.

Beyond the pack of journalists, she spotted the familiar faces in the crowd of the friends who had come to welcome her home. The men she'd flirted with last year: Jack Cosgrove, editor-in-chief of *Everybody's Magazine*; Franck Pollock, who had already proposed to her twice; and the publisher Mitchell Kennerley, the most flamboyant playboy in New York—and her favorite. So many admirers to whom she hadn't given a second thought in the last two months. The only one missing was Junius. She had attempted to see him in Paris, in early September, but he had avoided her. And the Big Chief, she knew, was on his yacht until Monday. But she also spied, off in the distance, the angular silhouette of dear Thursty, who was waving frantically at her with one hand and brandishing a bouquet of daisies in the other. Belle's heart leapt, and she hurried toward Thursty—and then toward her mother, so slim and elegant beneath her parasol. And then Louise, and Ethel. Her family.

It was time to pick up the thread of her life again—and to begin weaving her net once more, but stronger this time, and longer, and broader.

Larger than ever.

*If you dream, dream big.* She had scrawled the phrase all over her school notebooks as an adolescent, and now it became the renewed focus of her life.

She would reconnect with the great dream of her life: to transform the Morgan Library into an institution of the same caliber as France's Bibliothèque Nationale and the British Museum. A daunting task, for even within the United States, rivals were emerging everywhere with a new goal—that of supplanting the Big Chief, and wresting from him the distinction of being the Owner of the Most Expensive Bible in the World.

It was late 1910, and America's millionaires were realizing that establishing libraries was as vital to their social status as amassing priceless works of art in their marble palaces in Newport or on 5th Avenue. That possessing manuscripts, medieval and early modern texts, and rare editions was a subtler and more sophisticated indication of wealth than owning paintings by Old Masters, and that books could be investments just as prestigious, as lucrative, as artwork. After Boucher marquise armchairs and Louis XV commodes, books had now become the trophies most sought after by the magnates who had built their fortunes in coal, steel, sugar, and railways.

This meant the end of the exclusivity of the private auctions in Paris or London, where all book sales had been held for nearly three centuries. There would be no more battles conducted between austere scholars around an oak table in a smoky room at Sotheby's or the Hôtel Drouot.

The battle for rare books now moved from one theater of war to another, from the exclusive world of the intelligentsia to the arenas of the tycoons. From the Old World to the New.

The fight for the Caxtons during the Amherst sale two years earlier seemed like mere child's play today, compared to another sale that would soon take place in the world's new capital of art and culture. The American press was referring to this event not as "the sale of the century," as the English papers had dubbed the Amherst auction, but as "the sale of the millennium."

The Hoe sale.

It was a matter of inheritance. The American Robert Hoe had numerous descendants, all of whom were expecting a share of his estate.

An industrialist who had become wealthy but not extremely rich, the late Mr. Hoe had been head of the family business, which provided rotary printing presses to newspapers. He had made his personal contribution to the Hoe family's success story by inventing a press capable of printing, in color, the comic strips in the *New York Times*'s Sunday supplement. The first president of the Grolier Club, the most exclusive bibliophiles' club in New York, Robert Hoe had belonged to the old school of collectors. Retiring and secretive, frugal and puritanical, he had acquired his books slowly over the years, making his first purchases with his own scant pocket-money. From early boyhood he had bought feverishly, stockpiling his treasures from the cellar to the attic, locking them away in closets and cabinets, avoiding all publicity.

After half a century of shrewd collecting, the result defied comprehension. Fourteen thousand, five hundred, and eighty-eight volumes, including two Gutenberg Bibles and four Caxtons of unparalleled quality, not to mention letters written by Christopher Columbus and Amerigo Vespucci; the first book published in Greek; sumptuously bound psalters; and prayer books belonging to practically every king in Europe's history.

The battle among auction houses for the privilege of hosting the sale had been titanic and bloody. Sotheby's and Christie's in England, and the American Art Association and the Anderson Auction Company in America had fought tooth and nail for months, trading low blows and reciprocal slander campaigns to discredit one another in the eyes of Hoe's heirs. The Anderson Auction Company had eventually won the day, after having exhumed an old article by an English critic that obliterated its American rival.

Since then, Anderson's experts had been busy compiling eight illustrated catalogues describing *The Masterpieces of the Hoe Collection*, some one thousand, six hundred, and ninety-one pages of text. Seventy-nine separate auctions were expected to be held with two sessions per day, beginning on Monday, April 24, 1911, and concluding on Friday, November 22, 1912— more than a year and a half to disperse the entirety of Robert Hoe's hoard.

As was to be expected, "the sale of the millennium" aroused a great deal of interest on the part of book dealers around the world. Quaritch, Maggs, and their competitors had already reserved their cabins on the ocean liners of the White Star Line and the Cunard Line. This would be the first time they had crossed the Atlantic in this direction with the new objective of *buying*; ordinarily, these men traveled to New York only to sell.

European curators and collectors, too, made their travel arrangements for the spring, more determined than ever to repatriate the treasures snatched from their home countries by Mr. Hoe.

\*

"To think, that scoundrel was stashing his hoard right under our noses," Thursty sighed, her gaze fixed on the unremarkable brick building at the corner of 36th and Madison, directly across from the Morgan Library, "and I never knew!"

"For once, you're the one exaggerating instead of me," Belle commented. "Of course you knew, and so did I!"

Standing together on the front steps of their marble palace, hatless, arms folded, the two librarians watched the parade of warehouse workers marching in and out of the building's red door, loading crates of books onto carts and wagons parked along both sides of the street. The vehicles' axles bowed beneath the weight of the cargo, the horses hitched to them snorting and stamping their hooves. The cortege would soon depart for the Anderson auction house, where the Hoe sale was scheduled to take place in a month.

The stillness and stiff postures of the women, both normally so active, spoke volumes about the tension they felt. Miss Thurston's chignon seemed tighter and grayer than usual, her waist thicker, while Belle was wrapped in her old Princeton shawl—not a garment in keeping with her typical elegance.

"No regrets, Thursty. You did nothing to let the Big Chief down by never visiting that place. Hoe never gave any indication, and he certainly never shared anything. His collections were always closed to researchers."

"He kept everything for himself, you mean!" Thursty exclaimed, fed up with reading the press's repeated claims that Robert Hoe's 36th Street library was far superior, in terms of both size and quality, to John Pierpont Morgan's collection across the street.

Unable to tolerate this denigration of her employer any longer—her loyalty to him was every bit as fierce as Belle's—Thursty ranted. "That *neighbor* of ours had nothing on Mr. Morgan! He didn't have even a shred of Mr. Morgan's generosity; at least people are allowed to visit our library, if they ask! That Mr. Hoe might have owned three hundred and fifty incunabula, but he kept them locked away behind bars, just like the cows on that model farm of his in Winchester!"

"At least our neighbor, as you call him, didn't have to watch his library scattered to the four winds during his lifetime, like poor Lord Amherst."

"Let's just hope we never have to witness anything like this, before or after Mr. Morgan's death," murmured Thursty darkly, jerking her chin at the wagonloads of crates, now being covered with tarpaulins. "I pray Mr. Morgan's heirs will spare us this kind of scene."

"Cut it out with that kind of talk, Thursty, will you? You'll bring us bad luck."

"We have to prepare ourselves for the future . . . Plan a bit, for whatever might be in store."

"All I ever do is plan!" Belle retorted, keeping her tone light.

She thought it best not to share her exact intentions. It was time, now, for her to decide not just which books from Hoe's collection she might wish to buy, but which ones she wanted to give the *appearance* of wishing to buy. Not just which items she would allow to get away, but which ones she would *appear* to relinquish to her rivals.

In short, it was time to develop her strategy. To reflect on her choices and form alliances. To propose exchanges. To reach an understanding with her English friends, so as not to become embroiled in a bidding war. To claim from Quaritch, Read, and Pollard a return of the favors she had done them over the years, for those prizes of Hoe's that she was determined not to give up. Not to them, not to anyone.

It was time to go through those eight blasted catalogues, to study the provenance and condition of every volume, to identify the ones she already possessed, and to pick out the ones that she absolutely had to have.

It was time for her to target her prey, the books she felt the Morgan Library could not do without, the pearls she would bring home at any price. To obtain *carte blanche* from the Big Chief to bid any amount she deemed necessary.

Miss Thurston knew her "Bull" Greene well enough to know that there was nothing the latter loved more than the rush of adrenaline on the eve of a sale. That she anticipated sales with a heart pounding with excitement, like a warrior before a battle. And that no one relished more than Belle the matching of wits with the foes who would try to deprive her of the four Caxtons and any other Hoe collection marvel on which she might set her heart. But Thursty also knew that one did not enter the arena without a plan. That there was method in the duels fought there, that they were orchestrated and calculated down to the slightest detail, like a game of chess—and that much of this maneuvering happened long before a sale even took place.

Thursty knew exactly what awaited them in the weeks to come: agonies of doubt over the lists of books. Hesitations. The anxiety that always accompanied the selection of their targets. She didn't need to hear Belle describe the magnitude of their task in order to sum it up herself: "We're in for whole days and nights of inventory—just like when we moved in here, five years ago."

"Yes, darling! Wear your oldest clothes and gird your loins, Thursty; we're setting up camp here until April 24. Starting that Monday, I need to know what we want. From that Monday onward," she repeated, "we must stand firm, and not give any ground, for nineteen months. Now, let's get to work!"

They went back up the marble stairs and vanished through the bronze doors of the Morgan Library, their heels thumping loudly on the tiles all the way to their respective offices.

Behind them, the long line of vehicles had begun to move, the carts creaking slowly down the wide, deserted street, swaying through each intersection along the four city blocks that separated their cargo's former home from the corner of 40th Street, where the sale would take place. Here stood the renowned Hyde Mansion, the foyer of which had been entirely recarpeted in red velvet by the Anderson Company. It was a private home that boasted on its top floor a glittering jewel: a small theater designed as a replica of Marie Antoinette's personal one at Versailles.

Glamour, glamour, glamour.

Four hundred and fifty chairs would be occupied by invitation-only guests with reserved tickets and assigned seats. The afternoon sessions would begin at 2:30 in the afternoon, evening sessions at 6:15.

There were liveried doormen, ushers, and waiters in Louis XV wigs, just like there were at the suppers held in the aristocratic homes of the Faubourg Saint-Germain in Paris. There were cocktails on the house, offered in the sumptuous drawing rooms before and after each session. Tuxedos and evening gowns were required for the open parties held every night of the sale. The Anderson Auction Company had done well, even importing the star auctioneer Sydney Hodgson from London, along with his assistant, so that the prices in dollars would be announced in a cut-glass Oxford accent. Elegance and refinement! Added to all this was a generous measure of social sleight-of-hand, for in addition to its theater, the Hyde Mansion possessed another advantage: two entrances. The main one, an ornate door facing Madison Avenue, for the members of the public who would be allowed in a week before the sale to ogle the treasures in the exhibition rooms—and the service entrance, which opened onto the narrow alley behind the building, for the evening visitors: these were the big cheeses, the ones who really mattered.

One of these VIPs was Mr. George Smith, Bernard Quaritch's domestic counterpart, "the king of American book dealers" with offices at 43 Wall Street—and an inveterate gambler often spotted placing bets at the racecourse. With him when he slipped inside the quiet mansion on several evenings before the auction was a gentleman he introduced to the two English auctioneers as a new addition to his distinguished client list: one Mr. Jones. Tall and powerfully built, still a handsome man despite his bald head and white mustache, "Mr. Jones" was, of course, the only person who believed he was traveling incognito. No one from Anderson's was fooled. The man was Henry E. Huntington, the Californian railroad magnate, so well known to Americans that the press had nicknamed him "Uncle Henry." A man worth fifty million dollars.

As he approached what might be termed a "respectable" age, Uncle Henry had been struck by a sudden case of bibliophilia. For the past two years, George Smith had been assembling for him a most magnificent library at his estate in San Marino, northeast of Los Angeles, purchasing indiscriminately and *en masse* collections that were put up for sale all over the world. Huntington himself did not travel to Europe; indeed, he had never even crossed the ocean. But making the trip to New York had not posed a problem.

A collection such as Robert Hoe's had proven too large, however, for Smith to buy the whole thing via backroom deals. The two men would have to choose together which pieces they wanted to acquire. "Choose"—such a distasteful little word. They wanted it all.

So, each evening, the chandeliers in the exhibition rooms were relit so that Mr. Smith and Mr. Jones could examine the books in the company of the sale's organizers. As Smith went on about the rarity of the pieces, Uncle Henry wandered among the shelves, drifting from one incunabulum to the next without leafing through them, his left hand ceaselessly jingling the coins in his pocket, his right hand pointing at the bindings: "Okay, Smith, get me that one . . . and that one, yeah. And that one. And that, too. And that. And that. And that."

Each "that" was music to the ears of the auctioneers, who wrote *H/S* next to each catalogue number as "Jones" rattled them off. Two letters that joined another set of initials peppering the margins of their notes: *B.G.*

*Belle Greene* vs. *Huntington-Smith*. It promised to be quite a showdown.

*

On the spring Monday when the sale began, Daumont carriages and state-of-the-art automobiles vied for space at the corner of Madison and 40th Street. Elegant ladies in wide-brimmed hats emerged from their vehicles as if arriving at church for an aristocratic wedding, taking the arms of their top-hatted husbands or sons and gliding up the red carpet that led from the sidewalk to the stairs. A society columnist stood by noting the most glittering arrivals: Mrs. John D. Rockefeller, Jr.; Mrs. John Jacob Astor; Mrs. Reginald Vanderbilt.

On the top floor of the mansion, in front of the theater doors, it was a free-for-all. Doormen and ushers, tickets in hand, didn't know which way to turn.

There were protests and huffs of indignation. No one seemed to think the seat they'd been allocated befitted their social standing, and everyone wanted to change. The foreign guests complained at having been dispersed throughout the room, far from one another, as if to weaken their chances of successful bidding. Madame Théophile Belin, the widow of the most renowned rare books expert in Paris, and Dr. Bauer, the famous Berlin book dealer, who were staying in the same hotel, were insisting on being seated next to each other. Mrs. Ethel Watts Mumford Grant, the well-known author of *Dupes* and *The Cynic's Calendar of Revised Wisdom*, demanded not to be separated from her friends in the Morgan clan, who occupied the first rows on the right-hand side. Mrs. William K. Vanderbilt, who had arrived with her miniature King Charles spaniel tucked beneath one arm, its bell-laden collar jingling incessantly, loudly asserted her claim to the two front-row seats she had reserved on the left-hand side—for herself and the dog.

Off to one side, the stocky silhouette of George Smith could be seen at the foot of the rostrum, smoking a fat cigar and giving instructions to his assistant Mr. Bowden. Uncle Henry stood next to them, very distinguished in his black tailcoat (too formal for the afternoon session, really; evening dress was typically not worn until after sundown), lavishing compliments on the ladies who had accompanied him to the sale.

Also present on the left side of the center aisle was the group of Philadelphia book collectors: the fabulously rich Wideners, Joseph and Harry, father and son—true gentlemen, and true bibliophiles. And the great librarian, holder of a doctorate in literature from the University of Pennsylvania, Dr. Rosenbach— "Rosie" to Belle and his other close friends.

On the other side of the aisle sat the emperor, the man himself:

Bernard Quaritch, eyes half closed, hands folded across his middle, his pockets full of purchase orders from every monied book collector in England. Surveying the room like an unbothered tomcat, supreme in his familiarity with the business at hand, he awaited the opening of hostilities calmly and quietly. The seat on the center aisle directly behind him was still unoccupied: this was the one reserved for Miss da Costa Greene. She arrived soon enough, striding through the crowd, completely at ease in her role as J.P. Morgan's representative and giving every appearance of being mistress of the manor.

Those visitors who had not previously spent time in Miss Greene's company were taken aback by her obvious power, her clear popularity. How had she attained this degree of success? Looking at her closely, they noticed that the features of this "ebony-haired beauty," as the New York press had dubbed her, were not wholly regular; that her olive complexion clashed with the piercing clarity of her gray-green eyes; that her smallness and slenderness were at odds with the proud way she carried her head. In short, nothing about her quite seemed to go together with the rest. And nothing exactly fitted the conventional standard of beauty. Was she merely pretty? The way every man in the room responded to her provided the answer: *she was far more than that!*

Miss Greene may not actually have been beautiful, but she made everyone believe that she was. And that was enough.

Wasp-waisted in a close-fitting silk jacket and wearing creamy, buttoned-up leather gloves and a feathered astrakhan hat, she cheerfully accepted the compliments of acquaintances and well-wishers. All the while, she took care not to meet the eyes of the Black ushers assisting other guests to their seats.

As her friends approached to wish her good luck she introduced them to one another, making sure everyone was comfortably settled, blowing kisses, shaking hands, laughing, joking.

Every eye and ear in the room was focused solely on her.

Only Miss Thurston, occupying the seat next to hers, could read the truth in Belle's eyes: she was nervous. Afraid, in fact.

The Big Chief never came to auctions. Normally he would have sent Quaritch, with clear instructions on the limit of the price he was willing to pay. But for America, for this, he had chosen Belle.

Currently in England, Morgan had been received by King George V on the eve of his coronation and was planning to travel to Belfast next, for the christening of the new flagship of the White Star Line, which he now owned: the *Titanic*. He was feeling so pleased with himself, so relaxed, that he had given Belle *carte blanche* to buy whatever she deemed worthwhile, at any price. It was a dangerous sort of license for any intermediary, to be completely without instructions from the purchaser. No rules, no limits. Belle was free to let herself be carried away by her own desires. By rivalry. By the game. And by the hunger to *win*. She knew it. And she was afraid. With the Morgan bank as a guarantor, everything was possible. She could buy exactly what she wanted.

With mingled anxiety and self-assuredness, she eyed her rivals. The heavy hitters were all seated in the first row, near the auctioneer. Choosing a seat behind them meant that she could observe them, while they would have to turn around to watch her bid.

She had no doubt, deep down, that she would win the hundred or so texts that she wanted—and at more or less the prices she had determined to pay.

Thursty sat straight-backed in her chair, handbag in her lap, while the handsome Charles Hercules Read tried laboriously to engage her in conversation. He was beginning to regret making the trip to America, especially because he hadn't been able to secure Belle's formal promise not to bid on *Le Morte d'Arthur* by Sir Thomas Malory—the pearl of English literature, recounting the exploits of King Arthur and the Knights of the Round Table.

And the rarest, most beautiful, and most complete of all the books ever printed by William Caxton in 1485. Alfred Pollard, Read's colleague at the British Museum, had been working for years, along with the whole team in the Department of Printed Books, on facsimiles of fragmentary versions of the text. They wanted the original. And Read had come to get it. Yet he dreaded Belle's passion for Caxtons. She had agreed, on behalf of Mr. Morgan, and for the sake of the friendship she and Read had formed in England, not to bid against the Museum. She would enter the fray only if Read dropped out of the bidding. Still, he feared the worst: the money provided by the British Museum was, in fact, extremely modest compared to the American magnate's wealth. Would J.P. Morgan's librarian keep her word, despite having unlimited funds at her disposal?

When it came to the unpredictable Belle Green, who could tell?

He felt uncomfortable, as well, in this so very un-British setting. He found himself amazed, and even slightly unsettled, by this well-heeled crowd, half composed of female millionaires. Were all these sophisticated ladies really serious book-buyers? Ridiculous! What could they possibly know about rare manuscripts!

A few seats away from Read, the head of the New York Society for the Suppression of Vice, which had maintained a disapproving presence at every major social event in New York for more than a quarter of a century, was thinking much the same thing: the weaker sex had no good reason to be there.

And indeed, this was also the silent opinion of the auctioneer as he took the stage.

After seating himself at the lectern, with his two appraisers at adjoining tables; after calling for silence, and referring to the late Mr. Robert Hoe as the American genius of book collecting, the greatest bibliophile of all time (praise that visibly annoyed Thursty); after neatly arranging his notes, groping for his monocle, and letting his gaze sweep over the expectant audience, he said in his deep bass voice, as severely and condescendingly as possible:

"Would you be so kind, ladies, as to remove your hats, so that your feathers do not obstruct our collectors' view of the marvels we are about to present? Thank you."

Laughing, Belle was the first to obey, removing her pillbox hat and resting it in her lap.

All of the other ladies present followed her example in a great rustling of taffeta, except for three: the elderly Madame Belin from Paris, whose flowered concoction remained firmly in place on her head; Mrs. William K. Vanderbilt, who was no more willing to doff her wide-brimmed hat than she was to take off her spaniel's bell-adorned collar; and the redoubtable Miss Rose Lorenz, representative of the American Art Association, Anderson's main competitor, which was determined to ensure that the auction would be a flop.

"Right, then. As you are all doubtless aware, we will proceed in alphabetical order by author, starting with the first volume in the catalogue. We shall begin, accordingly, with lot 1: *The Letters of Abélard and Héloise*, revised edition, corrected and expanded by Monsieur de Beauchamps in 1721. A very lovely edition bound in red Morocco and marked with the coat of arms of the Comte de Maurepas. Ten dollars . . . Twenty, on my right? Thirty? Thirty-two . . . Thirty-two fifty? Any more? Thirty-two fifty. Going once, going twice."

The hammer struck.

"Sold, to Mr. George Smith of New York!"

Belle had not moved. Smith hadn't either. But by the time the next twenty lots had been sold—all to Smith, and all at exorbitant prices, without his appearing to lift a finger—she had figured out the code: a wink for *yes*, at every bid.

He kept on winking.

"How ghastly he is, with that twisted smirk and winking eye,"

Belle murmured in Thursty's ear. "If the woman next to him flutters her fan too hard even once, his face will get stuck like that! He's like a one-eyed bulldog, wrinkled and slobbering. Disgusting."

"Why are you letting him get away with it?" Thursty whispered back. "I thought you wanted lot 25, *Aesop's Fables*, and lot 56 . . ."

"Too expensive. The fellow has no idea what he's doing. He's paying absolutely ridiculous prices."

"Still . . . we have the money . . . and you said—"

Belle shrugged.

"Fifteen hundred dollars for a copy of *Recreations with the Muses* old Hoe paid fifty cents for last year? Absurd! We're not budging."

"But lot 76—the Anacreon—"

The hammer had just struck.

"Lot 76, sold for one thousand, five hundred dollars to Mr. George Smith."

"Good God!" Belle's neighbors heard her exclaim under her breath. "What nonsense!"

There was a stirring among the other spectators, as well. The foreign visitors in the room, who had made the journey to bring back a few prizes, were beginning to realize that they would be going home empty-handed. Smith was systematically, relentlessly driving up the prices, without any regard for the actual value of the books.

Winning in order to win.

Even Bernard Quaritch, who was the only other bidder to have won anything, and had had to follow Smith's example and pay absurd prices to do it, was angry at himself for falling prey to the other man's tactics. There was no glory in being fleeced.

Behind Quaritch, Belle had begun fidgeting, blowing her nose, rummaging in her handbag, sighing, and rolling her eyes with each blow of the hammer.

"Ha!" she scoffed, shaking her head. "Absolute nonsense!"

Thursty could hardly contain herself. One hundred and forty lots had been sold, and Belle had let every single one of the books they'd wanted go to Smith. Had the weeks they'd spent preparing their selection been in vain? Those titles, carefully chosen, those volumes whose intellectual, historical, and aesthetic value they had debated over, those rare books they had deemed *necessary* for the Morgan Library . . .

"Bull" had attempted nothing. Bought nothing.

She hadn't bothered to lift a finger even once—wasn't even pretending to play the game. Why?

The rest of the crowd seemed equally confused. Even the auctioneer, who looked at her inquiringly each time a lot marked in the catalogue with the initials *B.G.* came up for auction, was pausing, giving her opportunities to outbid Smith. So far, she had not reacted.

Ethel Grant, sitting behind Belle, had leaned forward several times to hiss in her ear: "Come on! Wallop them! What are you waiting for? Come *on!*"

The journalists in the room were watching Belle closely as well, observing her reactions, taking note of her frowns—which seemed to be increasing in number, but that was all.

"Lot 142: Saint Augustine. *De Civitate Dei.* A superb edition on vellum, illuminated by a Venetian artist in the year 1470 . . ."

Miss Thurston stiffened. This incunabulum was the fourth book ever printed in Venice. Thursty wanted it. "Bull" wanted it. They had designated it as one of their priorities.

Would Belle let Smith and Huntington make off with it, as they had with so many previous lots?

Thursty cast a beseeching glance in Belle's direction. No response.

When Madame Belin, and then the book dealer Maggs, and then Rosenbach, and finally Bernard Quaritch dropped out of the bidding, the Huntington-Smith team believed they had won the prize.

Two thousand dollars. The largest bid of the day. An astronomical price for such a book.

"Twenty-one hundred!" a husky voice rang out.

Miss Greene had taken the field. Had taken up the challenge. The tension in the room grew thicker.

In the front row, Smith winked.

"Two thousand, two hundred from Mr. Smith, on my right," announced the auctioneer.

An almost imperceptible nod of agreement from Belle.

"Two thousand, three hundred, to my left, Miss Greene!"

Another wink.

"Two thousand, four hundred, to my right, Mr. Smith."

"Two thousand, five hundred, to my left, Miss Greene."

Two winks.

"Two thousand, *seven* hundred, on my right, Mr. Smith!"

Silence.

"Do you wish to bid, Miss Greene?"

Silence.

The crowd held its breath.

"Two thousand, seven hundred, Mr. Smith, on my right. Do you wish to bid?"

Thursty looked at Belle, who took a deep breath, gathering herself with visible effort. She looked up at the auctioneer and gave the minutest shake of her head.

No.

"Twenty-seven hundred, going once; twenty-seven hundred, going twice. Miss Greene, still no?"

Another shake of the head.

The hammer struck.

"The Saint Augustine, sold to Mr. Smith for two thousand, seven hundred dollars!"

Applause.

The *New York Tribune* did not fail to note Belle's vexed expression.

The truth was that it took everything she had in her not to stand up and walk out of the room. And she could not keep from exclaiming, as she descended the stairs after the session: "This auction is a disgrace!"

Belle, like J.P. Morgan, was not accustomed to losing. This was, in fact, the first time she had ever returned from a "hunting trip" empty-handed.

"But why—*why* on *earth* didn't you go higher?" Miss Thurston lamented as they waited in front of the Hyde Mansion for the car sent to pick them up. She was on the verge of tears.

"Leave me alone!" Belle snapped.

The day's failure—a public failure in front of the whole of New York—was making her feel physically ill. She wanted to throw up. Disappointment. Fury. But now she needed to get hold of herself. To turn the page. To come back here in a few hours in evening dress, as charming as ever, for the six-fifteen session.

Thursty would not stop pestering her, however, and Belle's temper was growing dangerously short. It was bad enough that she had harassed her all through the sale, but she would not stop even now. One more word, and Belle thought she might slap her. Thursty sensed this, but still she couldn't let it go. She wanted to understand.

"You could have bought it all," she insisted, climbing into the car with Belle when it pulled up. "Mr. Morgan gave you free rein. He's a hundred times richer than Huntington!"

"Exactly."

"Why did you give up without a fight?" persisted Thursty, accusingly.

"I didn't give up!" Belle struggled not to scream. "If Mr. Morgan gave me free rein, as you say, it was because he knows I won't spend his money on bullshit!"

"*Bullshit?*" repeated Miss Thurston, her face white. She had never said a word like that in her whole life. "The *Saint Augustine?*"

"There are seven other copies of that volume."

"None of which are on the market."

"But they will be, one day. And they won't cost twenty-seven hundred dollars. You know as well as I do that *De Civitate Dei* is worth five hundred at most. We even estimated it at less than that. It's a very pretty book. Not a unique piece." Belle paused, then went on, more calmly: "The worst part of it is that those two rubes, with their ridiculous prices, are preventing national institutions from buying books that they need—that they *deserve*. The British Museum might as well pack up and go home already. Read doesn't have a prayer here, and neither do any of the university librarians. There isn't a single researcher or student in the world who will ever see even one book from the Hoe collection on their worktable. And that's a real shame."

"All the more reason for us to buy them!"

"Yes, I could throw the Big Chief's money around for the sole pleasure of beating Huntington. But it would be a waste of ammunition. The real treasures are yet to come, the ones without equal anywhere in the world. The unique pieces. For those books, Thursty, I'll fight those fellows to the bitter end. For those books I'll go up and up and up . . . as high as it takes."

\*

"Have you seen the papers?" Russell barked, throwing a stack of newspapers down on his sister's bed. "*'Fifty thousand dollars for that book!' cries Miss Greene, triumphant. The costliest sale of the auction to date!*"

Curled up among her cushions, her lips curving in a smile, Belle caught up a few of the papers and spread them out with relish on the counterpane around her.

Clearly stunned by the enormity of the figure, Russell repeated: "Have you *seen* them?"

The question was purely rhetorical. There were papers piled

on Belle's dresser and all over the apartment; Russell had taken only a few from the top of one stack. Not a single morning had passed in more than two months without the readers of the *New York Times*, the *New York Tribune*, and *World Magazine* being informed of the previous day's battles in the theater on the Hyde Mansion's top floor, of the titles of the volumes that had been fought over, and of the outrageous sums paid by the combatants for "those old books." From Washington to Chicago, Atlanta to Palm Springs to San Marino, the stories were picked up and reprinted by every newspaper in the country. From coast to coast, all of America was following the two daily sessions of the Hoe auction.

Russell, who up to this point had had little interest in the vagaries of his sister's triumphs and defeats, had suddenly registered the magnitude of the affair. Now he read the headlines aloud:

"*The all-time record in the history of book mania was set yesterday by Miss Greene . . . A victory that earned the young librarian a standing ovation. The applause lasted so long that the sale was suspended until calm could be restored.*"

She rolled her eyes, feigning modesty. "Oh, those reporters. They always exaggerate. '*The slightest quiver of the feathers in her hat strikes fear into the hearts of the other bidders . . .*' Ridiculous! The others—those two raging idiots—they outbid me for a Gutenberg Bible, though only just. But still! And anyway, I don't shell out fifty thousand dollars at once . . . only forty-two thousand, eight hundred.[6] A bit pricey for one book, I grant you—but it was for a Caxton!" She scrunched up her face in thought. "Let's see . . . what did I pay for the other seventeen— what was it, two years ago? About half that much. And even then it was a fortune. But how could I let *Le Morte d'Arthur* end up in *California*? Look, you missed the best headline. Listen to

---

[6] Approximately $1,062,000 today.

this: "*"The most intelligent girl I've ever met!" exclaims Mr. Morgan about Miss Belle da Costa Greene.'* That was nice of him, wasn't it? And this interview, where I tear into Huntington and his henchman? Not bad, eh? Look here—I accuse them of artificially inflating the market and preventing university institutions from acquiring the texts they need. Here's what I said: *'I am not speaking of the true rare pearls of bibliophilia. Those are not typical. And in truth, pearls have no price. Rather, I mean the books that are useful to the public, vital to the study of history and literature.'* A five-column interview, brother of mine!"

". . . with your photo everywhere. Here, and here, and here. On the front page! Putting yourself on display—exposing yourself this way—you've completely lost your mind."

"Glory, my dear. Glory. But I will admit that perhaps front-page photos aren't the best idea. Look at this one—I look dreadful. Unrecognizable."

"You always say it's Teddy and me, or the others, who are putting the family in danger. But if Father sees this . . ."

"Stop calling him 'Father'! If *Greener* sees this, yes, he'll know where to find me. And you. And I'm sure he'll order you to claim your share in that cousin's fortune, so he can get his, too—or order you to renounce your right to it, so he can have *both* shares. It's just a pittance, in any case, not worth your bothering with. Because—big news—your career is made! I've gotten you the job of your dreams: an engineering post with the Mexican Petroleum Corporation, at a princely salary! Everything you've always wanted! There's something to be said, after all, for having a famous sister in the oil kings' newspapers, wouldn't you say?"

\*

Glory, indeed. However much she might pretend to mock it, Belle loved it. The most fashionable portraitists in New York were now begging her to pose for them. Belle Greene, queen of New York.

The miniaturist Laura Coombs Hills painted her on ivory, dripping with her trademark Eastern-style jewelry and draped in a filmy orange sari that she held closed with one hand, seemingly nude beneath it. The photographers Ernest Walter Histed, Theodore C. Marceau, and Clarence H. White sold her image to their friends in the press—and to Miss Greene's many admirers, for twenty-five dollars apiece.[7] These included Mitchell Kennerley, a man who had conquered countless female hearts, who called Miss Greene "his muse" and kept a photo of her in full view of the Manhattan social elite who streamed endlessly in and out of his office. The aristocratic baron Adolph de Meyer, the most famous of all society photographers, exhibited her likeness at the Ritz along with other fashionable beauties of the day. And the French artist Paul-César Helleu told the newspapers that, during a three-month sojourn in the United States, he had made a point of sketching the subjects he found most interesting. The *New York Times* printed his breathless remarks:

"Miss Belle Greene—ah, there, *there* is the epitome of an American woman! A female librarian? Ha ha ha, what is that? In France, we have never known the like! Typical, so typical of this country! *Parfaitement américaine.* Do you see that profile? The arch of that eyebrow? The line of that nose? So vibrant, no? And the cigarette; do you see the cigarette? When I drew her, Miss Greene said to me, 'Do you really think it's a good idea to show me smoking? Leave this cigarette out of my hand, Monsieur Helleu!' And I replied, 'Forgive me, Mademoiselle, but I shall not. I cannot leave it out. The cigarette is part of the portrait. It pleases me. And it will remain between your fingers!' And so it has."

A mistake.

---

[7] Roughly six hundred dollars in today's money.

Genevieve, in whose bedroom Helleu's pastel portrait resided, and who thought it inappropriate for Belle to be smoking, asked her oldest daughter Louise to erase the cigarette. Louise, who had taken art classes, obliged, and Belle's whole arm was gone in a few strokes of her pencil.

More seemly, nonetheless, for an immortal portrait of "a female librarian."

Laughing, Belle let them do as they liked.

Her only concession to decorum.

Her friends in the world of rare books, who had admired her *sang-froid* during the ordeal of the Hoe sale, who had praised her gravity and her integrity, no longer recognized her. She began spending all her time with playboys and party-seekers. Not even Ethel Grant, who was no prude, could keep up with her. Belle drank like a fish, smoked, danced, and indulged freely in God knew what other pleasures, every night until sunrise.

In terms of her professional life, there was no change. She continued to rise at seven in the morning, arrive at the library at eight, and work until six, always lunching with associates and colleagues in her field. After that, it was back to her new friends. And then . . . Genevieve didn't want to know, didn't want to hear—didn't want to *imagine* what went on behind the door separating their two apartments. She could smell cigar smoke wafting over from the other side, and even that was quite enough. Her concern mounted as it became clearer and clearer that Belle was exhausting herself, losing her way, losing her*self* in a whirlwind of success and money.

Belle's salary had grown to almost nine hundred dollars a month,[8] an enormous sum that she split into three equal parts. One third was saved for a rainy day, invested in shares recommended by

---

[8] Almost twenty-four thousand dollars in today's money.

her employer. One third for her personal expenses. The rest was for her family's needs. She was paying for Teddy's studies at Barnard College, the female branch of Columbia University. And she had rented a summer house for them all—which she hadn't visited herself, never having any time off. And Russell was happily established in the new job.

In practical terms, there was nothing for Genevieve to complain about.

But morally?

She had never dared to ask Belle any personal questions about the trip with Bernhard Berenson. Her daughter had returned from those two months in Europe raving about the wonders of Italy, and extolling the wisdom of the great art historian who had shown them to her. But on the subject of her own feelings, she hadn't said a word.

Belle was still writing to that man, Genevieve knew. And letters from B.B. arrived almost every day—a fact which did not please her. She had had Berenson to tea during his stay in New York and, with all due respect to him, she hadn't liked him. Still didn't like him. What kind of future was he offering her daughter? Genevieve couldn't help but think that, one way or another, he was responsible for the endless pleasure-seeking that had come to fill Belle's nights. And she resented him for it.

If only Belle could settle down. Despite how firmly she had convinced herself that she was very young, forever claiming the same age, she wasn't twenty years old anymore. In fact, she would soon turn thirty-two.

If only she could meet someone!

A husband who would take care of her . . .?

The idea seemed incongruous, and Genevieve never mentioned it aloud. But inwardly she raged against the vow that bound her five children, condemning them to eternal singledom. Enough, enough, *enough* of this ridiculous, dreadful determination never to marry!

Genevieve knew that Louise was very much in love with a young man she didn't dare even to mention to her sisters, for fear that Belle would laugh in her face and remind her that she was forbidden to wed. Yes, the young man was white. As was Russell's lady-love. And Teddy's sweetheart. And yes, they all ran the risk of having Black children. But wasn't it better to take that risk, rather than die of loneliness and frustration?

No one understood the fear of discovery better than Genevieve. The possibility of being unmasked haunted her day and night. But at age sixty-five, she felt that each of her children had the right to live their lives, and to let the four others live theirs, too.

And as for Belle . . .

Belle owed everything to Mr. Morgan's protection. Her salary, her social status, the respect she enjoyed in the eyes of the world. But Morgan would not live forever. And as far as Genevieve knew, his wife and children did not share his passion for his library—much less for his librarian.

When the "Big Chief" was gone, Belle would quite probably lose everything. *Everything.* It was time, Genevieve thought, for her to start thinking about a future outside the Morgan Library.

It was with these things weighing on her mind that Genevieve knocked carefully on the door of her daughter's smoke-saturated room that Sunday. The curtains were drawn, the bed a heap of disheveled blankets.

Even before she could open her mouth, Belle cut her off:

"I know exactly what you're going to say, Maman. And I agree completely!"

Naked beneath her Japanese kimono, hair loose, eyes twinkling, she wrapped herself up in her sheets, lifted a hand, and thrust it close to her mother's face.

She was wearing a ring on the third finger of her left hand. A diamond solitaire.

"Congratulate me! I'm getting married!"

## CHAPTER 9

### LIVE AND LET LIVE
### AUGUST 1911–MARCH 1913

Who's the lucky fellow? Is anyone going to be kind enough to introduce me?"

Ethel Grant, a bottle of champagne in one hand and her long cigarette-holder in the other, elbowed her way through the crowd of guests. Drunk and without inhibitions, she made no attempt to hide her sarcasm. She'd just learned of Belle's matrimonial intentions and was irritated at not having been taken into her confidence before tonight's little soiree. She could sense that Belle didn't fully trust her, was holding her at arm's-length. And Mrs. Grant was not accustomed to being left out. She was hurt. Still: *vive l'amour!* That was her philosophy, regardless of any vexations!

The problem was that she was also a nasty drunk.

Belle almost never received her friends at home. She tended to return a year's worth of invitations in one fell swoop by inviting everyone whose guest she had been to a large party at the Colony Club. The only exceptions to this rule were the small lunches she hosted in tandem with Genevieve, to show anyone who doubted her morality that she really did live with her mother. Or, perhaps, a private supper *à deux* every now and then with some dashing gentleman or other who might also doubt her morality but was, in this case, appreciative of the fact. Genevieve was not present on these occasions.

All in all, however, there were very few who knew what the inside of Belle's home looked like. And fewer still who had met her brother and sisters.

Tonight, though, on an odd sentimental whim, she had

decided to throw a housewarming party at the double apartment she shared with her family—though they had lived there for a year already, and she was not only moving out soon herself, but planning a wedding, as well. She had even taken the risk of allowing the very different, highly compartmentalized spheres in which she moved, day and night, to mingle: the world of libraries and museums with that of theaters and nightclubs and parties in Greenwich Village—and the world of her family, more cloistered still.

So it was that Teddy, dazzled, set eyes for the first time on her sister's famous friends, the actress Ellen Terry and the dancer Isadora Duncan, while Miss Thurston met with dismay the band of *bon vivants* with whom Belle had been spending her nights. The only one missing from this motley group was the Big Chief, who, fortunately, was not expected to return to New York for a few days yet.

Hard alcohol and cigars in the two bathrooms. A buffet set out in Genevieve's sitting room. A small foxtrot orchestra in Belle's. Ethel Grant roamed from room to room, targeting their mutual admirers as she went.

"Kennerley darling, are *you* our dear Bilious Belle's betrothed? No, of course not. You're still married to that rich woman who finances your publishing house, aren't you? Too soon, far too soon to marry Belle. Is it you, Cosgrove, perhaps? No, not you either. Still not divorced. So then, gentlemen? Which one of you is it?"

Ethel was obviously drunk and clearly furious. Hysterical, in fact.

Photographers, actors, singers, scholars, journalists, and publishers trailed her through the corridors as she pretended to lead a tour, pointing out the modern lines of their hostess's desk in the library, its walls papered with gray-green chintz the same color as her eyes; the pale lavender of the armchairs in her bedroom, its floor carpeted in white to brighten the space. Living on the ground floor of a building was never a good idea, Mrs. Grant proclaimed; both apartments were lacking in natural light. She pointed out the collection of Han vases and Chinese pottery on the bedroom shelves, Belle's latest fancy. And on either side of the bed, several paintings from the Italian School, including Bernardo Daddi's *Virgin and Child*, newly arrived from Florence, and the left-hand panel of a triptych, *Angel of the Annunciation*, recently bought at Christie's. Both offerings from an admirer of Belle's, Mrs. Grant explained to her curious audience. "Bernhard Berenson, do you know of him?" Expensive gifts, which showed just how attached the great man was to Belle.

"But the Renaissance is ancient history!" Ethel Grant continued, dismissively. "Of course, everything has changed now, with the appearance of a fiancé on the scene! Find him for me quickly, my darlings, I'm simply burning to meet him! Oh, goodness gracious—could it be that swarthy ephebe there, at the end of the hall?"

She pointed at the tall figure of a man in evening clothes whom Belle was introducing to a group of guests.

"But how old is he? Fifteen? No, impossible! That fellow with the look of a gymnastics instructor? That shepherdesque boy with the brown curls and athletic shoulders? Harold Mestre! Could it be *he?*"

"Yes, that's him," said Ethel Alice, Belle's younger sister, who detested Mrs. Grant. The Marquis Harold de Villa Urrutia Mestre, son of the Cuban financier Alfred Mestre, who had offices on Wall Street. "Handsome, isn't he?" she continued. "And nice, too! Very, very nice! A real gentleman. Madly in love with my sister. And someone who doesn't pounce on anything in a skirt—unlike so many others!"

That last remark stung: Peter Grant, Ethel's husband—also a Wall Street Banker, and competitor of Alfred Mestre's—had a reputation for bedding his friends' wives. He had even once tried to kiss Senda Berenson, Bernhard's sister, cornering her at the dinner Ethel had given in her honor. Senda, ordered by B.B. to report on Belle's social activities and connections during her second trip to New York, had told her brother of the incident, which had not exactly cast Belle's friends in a stellar light.

But what Senda didn't know was that Peter Grant was also paying court to Belle. And that Belle had allowed herself to be seduced.

They had spent a single night together.

And Mrs. Grant knew about it.

She had a score to settle with Belle.

Pushing past Ethel Alice, she swooped toward the couple.

"How *delighted* I am to make your acquaintance, Mr. Mestre!" she exclaimed, holding out her hand. Backing up a step, she made a show of looking him up and down. "So this is the man who has managed to make our Belle change her mind!"

Harold Mestre bowed politely.

Ethel continued to examine him, not bothering to hide her look of surprise. How old could he be? Twenty-five? Belle claimed to be the same age, but spiritually, compared to him, she was an old woman.

And her lover, a mere child!

"Do you know, Mr. Mestre, that Belle has always said she wasn't made for marriage?"

Ethel swayed slightly on her feet, but she smiled graciously, her eyes never leaving the young man's face. He was handsome, she had to admit. A splendid specimen, in fact. Tall and athletic, with a rather old-fashioned elegance about him. And there was something soulful in his eyes, his smile.

A good lover, undoubtedly.

But young, young, *young*. This boy could be no match for Belle. Anyone could see that at a glance. This was madness! To go from Bernhard Berenson to . . . this? What had gotten into her?

Belle leaned against the wall next to Mestre, hands in her pockets, dressed in an outfit of breathtaking modernity. A "sultan's robe" from Paul Poiret's latest collection, inspired by the *Arabian Nights*, featuring a black bolero jacket, broad white belt, and a pair of pantaloons that narrowed at the ankle, like harem pants.

She'd known that Ethel would put Harold to the test. Eyes twinkling, she read her former confidante's thoughts like an open book—and let her proceed, wondering with amusement how far this little game would go.

Would Harold be able to defend himself? Would he be spirited enough to do it? Could he match his opponent's wit? How would he measure up against the terror that was Ethel?

The ball was in his court. Either he would make a fool of her, or she would make one of him.

He seemed paralyzed.

". . . yes, yes, yes," Mrs. Grant went on, "our darling Belle has always said she would never marry—unless there were a great, *great* deal of money involved. So much that her husband would be able to support her family forever. Yes, that's what she said. And *voilà*, here you are! And you have turned all her noble resolutions upside-down! I have just one word for you, Mr. Mestre: *bravo!*"

Embarrassed by the sarcasm of this woman, whose hostility he could feel but not comprehend, he replied that he certainly hoped that Belle, in becoming his wife, would be able to rely on him, to stop working, to give up her duties at the library.

This last remark put the crowning touch on Ethel's mirth.

"You know our Belle very well, I imagine? And have done so for a long time? What a secretive little minx she is—I've never heard her mention you!"

He flinched. Nodding stiffly at her, he said, with icy politeness:

"If it's any comfort to you, madam, she has never mentioned you to me, either. Now, if you'll excuse us . . ."

Taking Belle by the hand, he led her away.

"How *can* you associate with that horrible Grant woman?" exclaimed Louise, flopping down next to Belle on the sofa.

The last guests had just departed, Harold—not wishing to impose on Miss Greene and her mother in the wee hours— among them.

After seeing her prospective son-in-law to the door, Genevieve had declared herself exhausted and gone to bed.

Packed together on the same sofa the way they'd done when they were children, the four sisters were sharing their impressions of the evening. Maids bustled around them emptying ashtrays and plumping cushions, while the waiters packed away the dishes.

Each of the girls had kept her champagne glass, and they were finishing off the dregs of the remaining bottles. Russell, sprawled in an armchair across from them, was nursing a cognac and puffing on a final cigar.

"Mrs. Grant's antics might be amusing on stage," continued Louise, "But here . . ."

"But she did so much for me in London," Belle cut her off, draining her champagne in a single swallow.

"She was awful tonight, though," commented Ethel, without enquiring further about just what Mrs. Grant had done for Belle in London.

Well might she refrain from asking: Ethel already knew everything. She was the only one in the family Belle had told about what had happened after her sojourn in Italy. Nevertheless: "A real hussy, isn't she?"

"She was drunk," Belle muttered.

Ethel shrugged.

"She's always drunk. Did you see your poor Harold's face when she started in on him?"

"I saw."

"He looked petrified."

"Unnecessarily. It was a game."

"Don't tell me that viper managed to—"

"She didn't 'manage' to do anything!" Belle snapped.

"The good thing about Harold," put in Teddy, "is that he's so tanned that, even if your children come out Black, no one'll know whether it's your fault or his."

Belle frowned. "Stop being stupid, Teddy! Nothing has changed for me. I'm not going to have children."

Deep down, Belle couldn't help but see her engagement as a breach of the contract ensuring the safety of all of them. A deviation. An error.

Yes, she had given in to temptation by accepting a proposal of marriage. But that didn't mean she would renounce all her commitments, or embrace parenthood.

"No children!" she repeated firmly.

"And just how are you going to manage that?" interjected Russell. "Does your fiancé know he's never going to be a father?"

"That's a good point," observed Louise. "Have you told Harold about this?"

Belle didn't reply. Russell sighed. "Your future husband *does* know that you've decided to stay barren, doesn't he? He's fully aware, the Marquis Harold de Villa Urrutia Mestre, that his noble line will end with his marriage to Belle Greener?"

*

Impossible.

Belle couldn't sleep.

Impossible to bring up her African roots with Harold. The Cuban Spanish were known to be even more racist than Southerners in America.

Impossible, on the whole, to admit her secret to a lover, much less to a husband. Her sisters would do well to remember that, too, and to keep mum around their beaux. Who knew what those young men might do with such a confidence! The Greene family's survival depended on silence.

So how on earth had she, Belle, gotten to this point?

It was something of a mystery even to her. And this was the first time in months she had questioned her own conduct at all.

Why had she fallen in love so quickly and so deeply with Harold Mestre? Why—how—had she allowed herself to be tempted by the thought of a life with this man, so much so that she now found herself entangled in this impossible situation?

She tried to sort it out in her mind.

She had met him . . . when?

At a time of victory. And frustration. In the spring. Just after having outbid Huntington and Smith for *Le Morte d'Arthur*. A mad time, when the newspapers were full of nothing but her exploits. She had been certain the Big Chief would be reassured by her gravity and focus during the Hoe sale, and would thank her by letting her return to Europe that summer—a trip made all the more necessary, in Belle's mind, by another major sale set to take place in London, the Huth auction at Sotheby's. She would need to be there, surely, to fly the flag for the Morgan Library.

He had refused.

Had he heard rumors of her liaison with Berenson? More jealous than ever, he was going to trap her forever in New York, even as their friends booked their passage to Italy and she dreamed of another Tuscany trip with B.B. She had fought tooth and nail against Morgan's veto, conjuring up the most specious arguments in an attempt to convince him. If Mr. Morgan was so fearful for his librarian's reputation, why not have her accompanied by an unimpeachably respectable chaperone? Her mother, for example? She had been so sorry not to be able to travel with her last year!

To B.B., too, she had emphasized the benefits of having Mrs.

van Vliet da Costa Greene at her side. Her mother's presence would allow them to travel together without being forced to rely on Mary. Genevieve wouldn't bother them. She would look the other way. She would do whatever they asked.

Total failure. Both men hated the idea.

So much for the dream of another odyssey through Italy.

After that, Belle had gone off the rails. This was nothing new, of course; the month of June had always aroused this sort of feverishness in her. The need to move, to dance, to ride horseback, to gallop, to drive fast. To love and be loved. To live! Venus and Cupid always besieged her with their arrows as soon as the flowers began to bloom. It happened every year. Even back in the Junius era, she had compared herself to a Roman bacchante, awakened by the first rays of the summer sun.

Where had she met Harold Mestre? At Princeton, of course. During the regatta. He'd been part of the judging panel for the opposing team, from Columbia University. "His" university.

Like Harold, Belle had remained loyal to the university of her youth. She returned to Princeton often, lending her support to the committee for the creation of a new library and religiously attending the festivities surrounding each year's graduation. Paying visits to Aunt Lottie, with whom she was still very close, and to her old friend Gertrude, and all her former colleagues. Even to Josie Dear and her two children, now living alone at Constitution Hill.

. . . A romantic meeting at Princeton. One interesting detail: Belle had first noticed the beautiful young man at a dinner party in Junius's former home.

She had always been affected by male beauty, and Harold Mestre's looks were spectacular. He had the bearing, the elegance of a Spanish nobleman. That dark, velvet-eyed gaze. He was a Latin lover incarnate, almost to the point of cliché.

It was she who had approached him first.

Another detail: he had fallen under the spell of her charm without even knowing who she was.

Trained as a scientist, he had studied engineering, and despite agreeing to work with his father as a stockbroker on Wall Street, he hated finance and dreamed of becoming a physician. Belle, who was unaccustomed to this sort of ambition among bankers, found him startlingly different from the norm. More touching still was his obvious personal integrity. It was clear that he cared nothing for glory or riches. In fact, his eventual plan was to leave his father's employ, attend university on scholarship, and work in a research laboratory.

In many ways—his walk, his athleticism, his laugh, the dreamy quality he possessed—he reminded her of Arthur Upson, the beloved friend she had lost.

Harold might be as dark as Arthur was fair, Cartesian where Arthur had been poetic, but he shared the same ideas, used the same phrases, the same words, even, both to tease Belle and to woo her. "You're the embodiment of this divine adventure we call life." It was exactly what Upson had said to her in the woods at Constitution Hill. "I bet you'll end up married to some Princeton fellow," Upson had predicted, "one of those moony boys ruining their eyes in the Chancellor Green in the desperate hope of catching a glimpse of you . . ."

Harold was not a Princetonian, but he belonged to the same class of boys.

He'd asked her to marry him one month after their first encounter, at a ball in Newport on a moonlit evening. The sea breeze had been filled with the strains of *The Blue Danube* and the rumble of waves crashing on the rocks, and Belle's head was giddy with the champagne she'd been sipping all evening. "Why not?" she had said. She could just as well have said no.

She knew it was madness. But how could she resist the need to know how far this madness might take her? How could she resist the curiosity, the emotion, the risk that made her heart pound with excitement? How could she turn her back on the pleasure of living?

Falling to one knee, Harold had taken a small box from his pocket and opened it to reveal the ring. The die was cast. She had allowed herself to be swept away by his resemblance to Upson, seduced by his faith in the future, intoxicated by his promises of happiness. Yes, yes, yes! Happiness. Didn't she have a right to that, like anyone else?

Why shouldn't she and her sisters be able to behave like every other woman on earth? Love one man—just one. And find a safe haven in marriage to him?

The future . . . shouldn't she think about it?

Genevieve talked endlessly these days about Mr. Morgan's advancing age and his eventual death, about Louise and Ethel's sweethearts, about the terrible vow that bound them, and about the eternal solitude that awaited them all if they didn't renounce this vow to remain single that would end up destroying them.

Speaking of singlehood, Harold had the immense advantage of not being married, unlike Belle's other suitors. And his Mediterranean ancestry, unlike her own, was real. An ancient Spanish noble family, versus a false Portuguese one. The parents' origins would indeed explain the skin color of any Villa Urrutia Mestre children, as Teddy had remarked after the party.

But the whole plan was nothing but a mirage. There could be no children, without the mother's ruse coming to light.

And so there could be no marriage.

But how would she explain to Harold that the lovely dream was over? That she could not be his soulmate, as they had both believed she was?

It wasn't that she had stopped loving him, or loved him any less. He had lost none of his appeal in her eyes; he still affected her just as much as ever. She adored his purity. She respected him. She admired him. But she didn't belong to his world. She wished she were different. She would have loved to prove, in the long term, a loyal wife and doting mother. She would have loved to fall in line.

Impossible.

That party at which all the different people in her life had been brought together had shown her just how incapable she was of changing the direction that she, herself, had given to her own existence.

And then there were those words of Harold's, that Belle would be able to "give up her duties at the library." Terrible. Where had he gotten such an idea? Nothing was more exciting to Belle than the library.

On that point, Ethel Grant had been right. No man could make her as happy as the Morgan Library did. The books were her flesh and blood. Without them, she would die, right then and there.

The rest of the world counted, of course. Her mother and sisters, Russell, B.B., and Mr. Morgan. And . . . Harold?

Harold wasn't even on the list, she realized now, to her horror. God, how had she let things get to this point?

She had to talk to him. Admit that she had been wrong. End the engagement.

She would tell him the truth. That everything was her fault. That he shouldn't forgive her. That he should *hate* her. She deserved to be hated, and even insulted. Accused of what B.B. always said she was. A tease and a whore.

All of a sudden: hard, cold reality.

\*

"Dear B.B.," wrote Ethel Grant from New York in the early winter of 1911.

"Haven't seen Belle. The truth is, she's avoiding being alone with me. She's far too afraid I'll make fun of her. But she *has* answered my question: she's not going to marry Harold Mestre anymore.

"I must admit that the battle isn't *entirely* won; she feels lost, doesn't know what to do. Ah, my dear B.B., is there anything more painful than tangled emotions?

"If I've understood matters correctly, she's already broken it off with Mestre, and gone back to him, several times. Really, she's playing chicken with the idea of marriage, which fascinates and terrifies her all at once. She romanticizes this man who could make marriage a reality for her, mixes up dreams and reality, realizes that she's been fooling herself, and then backs away. I don't believe she will ever marry—and if by some mischance she actually goes through with it, the marriage won't last ten minutes.

"I wish so much that you could simply enjoy her personality, without expecting anything of her in return. Indeed, that's the attitude I've adopted myself. You asked me if your case was different from the others—if you mattered more in her life than anyone else. To answer your question, I believe that she shares with you the sort of intellectual affinity that she desires most in life. But I fear that she never conducts herself, when it comes to you, with the sort of faithfulness that you have every right to expect from a woman. I know this isn't at all what you want to hear. Honestly, my dear B.B., I don't believe that any man exists who will be more than a passing fancy for Belle. Her feelings simply never last for very long. Only the present matters. Tonight, this moment. But never tomorrow. You were able to draw her attention and hold it; that is already a great deal. Most people cease to interest her, sooner or later. Myself included.

"As for Harold Mestre, don't worry yourself too much about him. He confided his heartache to me as soon as she admitted her doubts. I'm not at all sure he likes me very much, but he wants an explanation. And believe me, I give him all the enlightenment he may desire about the scandalous life of our Bilious

Belle. If she doesn't manage to end things with him, he may well take matters into his own hands.

"In truth, she hardly has any time for him. Since his return to the city, Morgan has been keeping her at his beck and call, overwhelming her with things to do and not leaving her a moment free for gallivanting. I doubt very much that he will allow her to return to Europe this year. Or ever.

"And that is the state of things here, my dear B.B.

"Peter joins me in sending his fondest wishes to you and Mary.

"With all my affection, your devoted Ethel"

*

"Mr. Mestre is out front; he's asking for you."

Thursty had burst into Belle's office, babbling this message far more quickly than was usual for her. Belle looked up.

"What on earth is he thinking? I've asked him not to come to the library when the Big Chief is here."

"He seems quite agitated. You'd better go and see him."

"All right. Take these letters to Mr. Morgan for him to sign."

"Me? Oh, no—you can do it in a bit. I daren't—he's in a simply thunderous mood. It's this weather. Take your umbrella; it's raining cats and dogs!"

Belle put on her hat, seized her raincoat, and ran for the bronze doors.

"Harold! Are you all right? What's the matter? I've asked you not to—"

The young man was pacing the slippery marble floor of the porch. Bareheaded, his raincoat dripping with water, he appeared to be in a none-too-pleasant mood himself.

"I have a few questions for you."

"I'll be happy to answer them. But can't it wait until tonight?"

"No! For once, it's going to be you who listens to me!"

She smiled. "That's all I've been doing for weeks—listening to you. And letting myself be convinced by your arguments."

"Have you broken things off with that man? Or do you plan to continue your affair after we're married?"

Belle darted a glance at the window of Morgan's office in the West Room. She took Mestre by the elbow and steered him down the stairs, out into the rain.

"What affair?"

"With that art historian."

"I know hundreds of art historians, and I have heaps of affairs with them."

He saw her smiling beneath the brim of her hat. Her flippancy infuriated him.

"Don't play stupid. Your lover in Florence. The famous one."

"Oh, Mr. Berenson? He's eighty years old, and he has a wife! No, I'm exaggerating—he's not quite eighty. But almost! And wherever did you get the idea that we're having an 'affair,' as you call it? He's my spiritual guide, my old teacher. I'm constantly writing to him for advice. Otherwise, I've only set eyes on him three times in my life."

"Answer me: will you keep corresponding with him after we're married?"

"After? How would I know what's going to happen *after*, when I don't know what's going to happen *before*—or what's going to *happen*, period?"

"What did you do last year in England?"

"Worked, my dear. Worked."

But Harold would not be dissuaded.

"In London, last October—what did you do, that made you so ill?"

She stopped walking. Her face paled.

"I can guess where you've just come from."

Belle's voice was low. She fixed him with a hard gray stare and said, her voice steely, "I don't want to know what horrors Ethel

Grant has told you. Don't say anything—I refuse to hear it! Just know that whatever she told you is false. However, you have chosen to believe her. And that says it all."

Drawing her raincoat more closely around herself, she started walking again.

"Belle, I am prepared to forgive you, but—"

"*Forgive* me?" she laughed bitterly. "You have *nothing* to forgive me for."

"—ready to believe you, if only you would explain yourself!"

She shrugged and kept walking, lips pressed in a thin line. The rain continued to fall heavily.

Sensing that he had gone too far, he retreated into silence.

They had made a complete circuit of the block and were now back on the corner of Madison and 36th. Harold took her elbow, forcing her to stop.

"You're right," he said, more calmly. "Mrs. Grant is a vicious woman. She and her husband, their friends—their whole social group—they'd corrupt anyone's mind. Cut your ties with all those people, Belle, and come with me. I've been offered an engineering job in San Francisco. A consultancy with the California Welfare Commission. It's nothing spectacular—but let me take you away from this place where you're losing yourself. We'll move there together and start over from scratch!"

She hesitated, then said, trying to keep her tone reasonable:

"I have my mother here. My family. How would I support them without my salary from Mr. Morgan?"

"I know how much you love being among books. I have realized it, believe me. And there are so many municipal libraries in California. Until we have children, you can work in some local branch. I won't keep you from doing it."

"Keep me from doing it? Listen, Harold, I think you've just answered all *my* questions at once. I've been trying to explain to you, for days and days now: I'm not the right wife for you. And if there's one thing in the world I hate, it's jealousy. Let's part as good friends. Don't you want that? I've already given back your ring. Let me try this again . . . Go west. Follow your calling. Become the researcher you've dreamed of being. And let's meet again in five years, to compare our notes on life. All right?"

They stood there in the rain, between the lionesses, in front of the Morgan Library gates. She walked rapidly up the stairs. He didn't try to hold her back. She vanished through the bronze doors.

"I've heard, Miss Greene, that you're going to be married?"
Her hand on the doorknob of the West Room, Belle froze.
*Warning: danger!* she thought.
Mr. Morgan hadn't set foot in her office all day. He hadn't called her into his own office, either, though he had probably heard her voice in the corridors. He hadn't even looked up when she'd knocked at his door with the letters to sign.
Arms spread wide, palms flat on his desk, he kept his eyes down, stone-faced.
Quickly preparing herself to soothe one of his rages, from which she knew she would emerge exhausted, Belle tried to stave off the eruption by stepping toward him lightly, a smile on her lips.
"Married? Me? What a ridiculous idea! Who told you that?"
"I've been told you're getting married," he repeated, his voice menacing.
She laughed.
"First I've heard of it. To whom?"
"I saw you with a man on the porch."
"If I were to marry every errand-boy who rings the door-bell . . ."
"More than one person has told me you have plans to marry," Morgan repeated a third time.
"More than one person is wrong."
"I'm warning you, Miss Greene."

His face had flushed dark red. Here it was. He would start shouting at any moment.

"I'm telling you right now that, on the day you marry, you will never set foot here again—do you hear me? *Never!* If you marry, I will never see you again as long as I live. If you marry, I'll strike you from my will! You'll have nothing! *Nothing!* Not one cent of the fifty thousand dollars I'd planned to leave you. I've warned you. Now, you may go."

The violence of this attack, coming on the heels of the scene with Harold, was too much for Belle. She was trembling. It took her a moment to process her shock.

"I have no intention of marrying anyone, Mr. Morgan," she said finally, her voice toneless. "But if I did, your threats to cut me out of your will would not change my decision. I am free to love whomever I choose. Free to start a family, if I wish. Free in myself, and free in my feelings. The time I share with you—the evenings, the Sundays, the summers, every national holiday, every vacation—I choose to share, of my own free will. I care for you very much, and it's a gift on my part. Because I could leave here at any time. Contrary to what you believe, you have no rights over me. I am not your *possession!*"

Overwhelmed with fury and humiliation, she had screamed the last sentence.

Pausing, she gathered herself, and went on with the same vehemence:

"You can buy many things and many people with your gold, Mr. Morgan, but you can't buy me, or my affection. When you treat me this way—like an object, something you've bought and paid for—you lose my love, and all my respect!" She shuddered. "I would rather leave—lose my job—than let you speak to me in that tone, as if I were a servant, or a slave!"

She turned on her heel, slamming the door behind her, and stormed back to her office.

The telephone mounted on the wall near the front door of their apartment rang endlessly. Belle, huddled on the sofa, stone-faced and steely-eyed, had forbidden anyone to touch it. Ethel, not daring to question her, was keeping to the kitchen.

"It might be Harold," Genevieve suggested timidly, moving toward the phone. "Don't you want to answer it?"

"Harold's moving to San Francisco."

Genevieve bit back an exclamation of surprise.

"For good," Belle added, cutting her off.

Genevieve was silent. So they were well and truly finished. Perhaps it was for the best. She knew Belle had had her doubts about the union. For her own part, she had liked Harold, but he was so different from her daughter. And Genevieve had been extremely anxious about Belle's determination not to have children. Unworkable in a marriage! She'd had seven children herself; her own mother had had six, and her grandmother had had eight. There was every reason to believe Belle and her sisters would be equally fertile. They simply had to abandon this ridiculous pact of theirs! Russell, too.

The telephone had stopped ringing. Belle didn't even seem to notice. She sat unmoving, her mind clearly elsewhere. And, judging by her expression, her thoughts were not pleasant ones. Genevieve stood frozen, torn between her desire to ask questions and prudence, which commanded her to keep quiet and wait.

The phone rang again.

"Your friend Ethel is trying to reach you, surely?" Genevieve couldn't resist saying, at length.

"Mrs. Grant is a foul-mouthed whore. Writes with sewer-water, not ink."

"I know she disappointed you on the evening of the party, but still—"

"I don't want to see her or hear from her ever again."

The telephone was still ringing shrilly.

"It's Morgan calling," Belle admitted finally.

"Mr. Morgan! And you're not answering?"

"He can go to hell."

"Belle! How can you say that? He's your employer! He's tried to reach you dozens of times—ever since you came home! He has some emergency, something important to tell you—he obviously needs to speak to you right away."

"Not outside work hours. I'm not some dog who'll come running when he whistles at all hours of the day or night. I'm not his Pekingese—or his house slave!"

"What is that ridiculous statement supposed to mean, Belle?"

"That he can wait."

"You are not going to let that great gentleman keep calling and calling with no answer!"

"Why not?"

"Because it isn't done!"

"Don't start again with all that about what's done and not done. And he's not a 'great gentleman'; he's a vulgar tyrant!"

"You've always told me the opposite. That you admired Mr. Morgan, cared for him more than anyone else in the world."

"I was wrong. He's a brute."

"What if this brute fires you?"

"He'll regret it, because I'm the one who's quitting."

"But the Morgan Library is your life!"

"I'm not so sure about that."

Leaping up, Belle seized her coat and announced to the room at large:

"Go on; answer it, if you like. And tell that old fool I'm on my honeymoon!"

"Are you crying?"

Ethel Alice, who had listened to the conversation between Belle and Genevieve from the kitchen, had just caught up with her sister in the street.

Though one was dark and the other fair, from the back, in their long raincoats, the sisters could have been mistaken for twins. They were both small and slender, their diminutive forms dwarfed by the tall buildings surrounding them.

Ignoring the downpour, they headed west on 40th Street, Belle setting a punishing pace in her sadness and rage. It was five o'clock, and the streetlamps weren't yet lit. All the windows were dark, and their faces, hatched with shadow, disappeared beneath the men's hats they'd stolen from their brother to spare the feathers in their own Sunday best. Hands buried in their pockets, hat-brims pulled down, they strode grimly together, silently side-stepping the enormous puddles that had formed in the squall.

"Are you crying?" Ethel asked again, trying to overtake Belle so she could see her face. Belle kept her head resolutely down.

"No."

"You are!"

"It's the rain."

"Are you sorry you left Harold?"

Belle shrugged. "I'm not the one who left. But this isn't because of him."

"Morgan?"

"I don't understand why he treats me with such disdain! I keep him company—I'm always with him—I do everything I can to reassure him!"

"He's jealous."

"He's sick, is what he is. Sick with his own power. So used to people bowing and scraping before him. I've seen him at work; he has no concept of any limits. If I let him treat me disrespect-fully . . . if I let him do to me what he does to everyone else . . . it'll destroy me."

"But if you *don't* let him do it, he'll fire you. And no one else will pay you what he does."

Before Ethel could go on, a car pulled up at the corner, and its liveried driver emerged, his hat in one hand and an open umbrella in the other, which he held over the heads of the two young woman. It was Charles, J.P. Morgan's chauffeur.

"Mr. Morgan sent me, Miss Greene. He would like you to return to the library immediately."

The sisters exchanged a glance. They backed up a step. The umbrella followed them.

"Mr. Morgan's asked me to bring you back to his office. Now."

"You see?" Belle murmured to Ethel. "You see how it is?"

Ethel nodded. "Yes, I see." She nudged Belle gently with her elbow, toward the waiting car. "But go anyway."


"I do not like it one bit when you speak to me in that tone, Miss Greene."

Morgan's voice was deliberately calm, reasonable.

In truth, he had no idea what the outcome of this meeting would be. Would he fire her? Would he forgive her? Would he . . . apologize?

"I don't like that tone either, Mr. Morgan. But you leave me no choice."

He flushed, seeming to reflect. When he'd sent his chauffeur to fetch her, he had been certain that she would arrive shame-faced, and that the reason she hadn't been answering her telephone was that she was sorry for her behavior and feared he was calling to terminate her. Well might she be afraid, he'd said to himself.

And so he had been waiting for her in his high-backed chair like some medieval lord, or perhaps a martyr. Judging by his expression, he considered himself the victim in this situation.

He had chosen, as the setting for their reconciliation—or their final break—not the North Room, Belle's domain, nor the West Room, his own kingdom, filled with the loveliest paint-ings in his collection and adjoined by the armored storeroom filled with his most precious treasures, but a room that was neutral ground: the vast reading room with its galleries of books rising up toward the sky, dwarfing any visitor with their magnificence.

He indicated a small armchair across from his, in front of the fireplace. Tight-lipped, she shook her head. Her hat was still in her hand; she had not even taken off her raincoat, but remained standing, as if ready to leave again in an instant. Strands of wet hair straggled across her forehead, making her look even more surly.

"That tone," he murmured again, faintly, as if overpowered by the magnitude of his outrage.

He knew he tended to phrase things poorly, both in literary and scientific discussions and in personal arguments. Belle knew it, too; he had bemoaned that quality to her before. Tonight, he was regretting every weakness he had ever confided in her. If he had no natural gift for eloquence, though, he was brilliant when it came to presentation. His solid common sense, the sincerity of his heart, and the depth of emotion that thrummed in his voice remained his greatest weapons. He followed his instinct, and it almost never led him astray. Now, true to form, he began with an expression of feeling.

"How you *do* try my patience, my dear. You have become so maddeningly sensitive! It's impossible to say anything to you these days, without you immediately leaping onto your high horse! That whole business today about being a slave, and my so-called tyranny . . . completely undeserved, when you think of how much freedom I give you here. How am I a despot? You order me around at will! You wanted me to buy those Coptic manuscripts . . ."

"It isn't about that," she grumbled.

Her expression remained stony. This time, he sensed, she would not back down. She wasn't even trying to lighten the mood, the way she usually did when they found themselves in conflict. Her mood wasn't going to make things easy for him now. Was she going to force him to fire her?

He hated feeling cornered. He tried to shift the battle to another field.

"Oh, no? Maybe you didn't want those tenth-century manuscripts I acquired for you?"

"The Coptic manuscripts from that Egyptian monastery are the most extraordinary discovery of the last ten years. But they have nothing to do with your . . ."

He cut her off before she could say the unthinkable, the insult that would force him to remove her from his employ:

"'Nothing to do'?" he repeated, as if it were just those three words he found shocking. "*Nothing to do? You* wanted to buy them; *you* wanted to have them shipped here; *you* wanted to study them; *you* wanted to photograph them—and I let you do it! *You* wanted to withdraw them from the American laboratories and send them to Rome because, according to you, our own experts wouldn't have the skill to restore such ancient paper. And I let you do it! And now you want to turn them over to that friend of yours, that German prelate from the Vatican Library, because you think he's the only one capable of restoring and preserving them! And I'm letting you do that, too! How exactly am I a despot? Enlighten me, please! *I'm* starting to become afraid of *you*, you're becoming such a dictator! While I . . . I—" his tone changed, and he suddenly brought up another subject. "Have you read the papers?" he asked, his expression tragic. "No—of course not, you're too concerned with your own little dramas to worry about what's happening in the country! You haven't read, I imagine, that President Taft—for whom we all voted—is accusing me, *me*, of having tricked Roosevelt into violating antitrust laws during the 1907 crisis? Or that the committee questioning Roosevelt had the audacity to ask him if he had allowed himself to be manipulated by me—and even *paid off* by my men—so that I would be able to buy out the TCI? You haven't read that my associates Gary and Frick have been summoned to testify, have you? Or that I'm suspected—I!—of having ruined not just my rivals, but the shareholders and the ordinary people, *deliberately?* And even of having caused the banking panic on purpose to get richer? That is where we are. That's where I am. Threatened by the disgrace of a trial, for having saved America."

Belle's heart clenched. The accusations were so unfair! J.P. Morgan had every flaw known to man, Lord knew; he was jealous, manipulative, cunning. But he was not so Machiavellian as that. Ever. She could testify to that. The articles that had dominated the front page of the *New York Times* every day for weeks now were shameful, and she didn't hesitate to say as much.

"I have read the papers, Mr. Morgan. And I can't tell you how appalled I am."

"Appalled? Really? Yet you're ready to join the mob shouting against me—to abandon me in such circumstances?"

"I'm not abandoning you!" Belle couldn't keep from protesting.

"No? What would you call it, then? At the first sign of difficulty, you desert me!"

He didn't leave her enough time to react. Like a wise sage who could tolerate anything, understand everything, even a betrayal by his underlings, he made a show of softening:

"If you're having personal difficulties, my dear, all I want is to help you. But don't treat me with this indifference!"

Like a solitary, wounded animal, he rose painfully from his chair and crossed the room slowly to his desk, talking all the while, his voice deliberately even:

"You're rejecting me. And my country is accusing me of being a con man. But I am still trying to serve that country by bringing the rest of my collection here. I've just gotten permission from the head of customs at the Port of New York: any works of art older than a century can enter the United States freely, with a tax of only five percent."

Belle couldn't hide her shock. Five percent instead of twenty? A triumph! Astonishing!

He pretended not to notice that her ears had perked up, that she had begun to follow him, to make her own way across the room behind him.

"A customs agent will visit the house at Prince's Gate before the art is shipped," he continued, keeping his tone neutral, factual, "to estimate the period of each of the paintings, the miniatures and furniture, the silver and sculptures. He will oversee the packing of everything, which should mean the crates won't have to be opened in New York, and will reduce the risk of anything being broken. But there will still need to be an art expert on site. Can you recommend anyone? You seem to have a great deal of esteem for that art historian in Florence. Your friend . . ." Morgan pretended to search his memory for the name. ". . . Bernhard Berenson?"

A final ruse. A rather clumsy attempt at trickery that drew a smile from Belle at last. The old fox! Would he never stop? He was still so suspicious that he felt compelled to set this trap for her. Far from angering her, as it would have done even a few minutes earlier, Morgan's play-acting was suddenly amusing again. And his sentimentality had regained its ability to touch her heart.

As for his plans . . . they were interesting, even exciting. Bringing his collections to New York in their entirety? A project of unprecedented magnitude! Exhibiting them to the public at the Metropolitan Museum? Thrilling! To give America such a treasure!

"As far as I understand it, Mr. Berenson's expertise is confined to Italian painting of the *Cinquecento*," she said, treading carefully. "Furniture and precious metals are not his forte, I'm afraid. You would need an expert with broader knowledge. One of the leading art dealers, probably."

The Big Chief's dark eyes twinkled. He had her.

"An art dealer. Yes. But whom, Miss Greene? Which one?"

"Not Duveen. Too many problems with the tax office. And certainly not any English firm! If Britain should start protesting the removal of its treasures to America, we'll never hear the end of it! What do you think about Jacques Seligman, in Paris? His knowledge in all areas is unmatched."

"Seligman. Noted. Contact him. Arrange for his travel and accommodations in London. Take care of him. Take care of everything. It's quite a task, Miss Greene, quite a task . . . the inventories, the packing, the paperwork, the handling. Everything must be ready to sail on the *Titanic* when she makes her maiden voyage in April."

And so the hatchet was buried. On both sides.

Back to work.

It was only when she rejoined Thursty in the back room—poor Thursty, paralyzed with anxiety at the violence of the scene between Belle and Morgan, terrified of losing her leader—that Belle realized just what a near miss she had had. Indeed, the bullet had whizzed past so close to her that she was still trembling.

In the intensity of her relief, in her overwhelming happiness, Belle knew, now, how very afraid she had been that God was about to cast her out of Paradise.

\*

Belle and Morgan had not simply forgiven one another; they had discovered another mutual interest. The Coptic manuscripts the Big Chief had mentioned during their summit in the reading room now bound them in a new intellectual adventure that transcended all grievances.

These manuscripts, discovered in the ruins of an ancient monastery by men from the village of Hamouli, had barely escaped destruction. After spreading the word about their find, the peasants had sold off their booty to traders from Cairo, hawking the manuscripts one by one in the best-case scenario, breaking them down into individual pages for sale in the worst. On their belated arrival in the village, the Egyptian police had seized what remained of the haul: seventeen volumes, dating from two centuries earlier than any other Coptic manuscripts previously known. These seventeen books included both the Old and New Testaments, in a set more complete than that possessed by any library in the world and featuring Byzantine illuminations such as had never been seen before, as well as exquisite bindings.

These were the manuscripts that Morgan had acquired at Belle's insistence.

Now she set about finding the right man, the right priest, to study them, translate them, and publish a critical edition of them. She also took it upon herself to screen the international visitors who came to her office to admire them, or sometimes to contest their validity.

By happy chance, the expert she found turned out to be none other than her friend from the British Museum, Charles Hercules Read. Even better, he had just certified the authenticity of the manuscripts, officially refuting the other scholars who had called them fakes.

A resounding success for the Morgan Library.

Things returned quickly to normal. Belle remained at the Big Chief's disposal day and night, allowing him to disturb her at all hours, sharing his indignation at the ongoing judicial proceedings against him, and reassuring him, with grace and ease, of her own affections.

Everything went smoothly in the lead-up to Morgan's departure for Europe just after Christmas.

In truth, she saw him off with a feeling of liberation that far exceeded her usual relief. The turbulence of the past autumn had continued to make itself felt, and this time both she and Morgan viewed his departure as a much-needed reprieve. Belle because her adoration for him had lost its spontaneity, and she felt she had to restrain herself constantly in his presence, and Morgan because he was hoping to forget about the congressional subcommittee investigating him. London would provide plenty of distractions, of course, as would a subsequent cruise on the Nile, stopping to visit various archaeological digs he was financing along the way. Next there would be a stay at the Grand Hotel in Rome; he had bought land on the Janiculum Hill and was planning to develop, at his own expense, the campus of the American Academy there. And then, finally, a rest: a spa cure at Aix-les-Bains in France, his yearly constitutional.

As for Belle, J.P.'s ocean liner had hardly vanished beyond the line of the horizon when she made straight for the Pierce-Arrow automobile manufacturer and ordered herself a ruby-colored Model 36 roadster, to be delivered in the spring. She was determined not to spend her summers trapped in the city anymore, if Morgan continued to refuse her permission for the European travels of which she and B.B. still dreamed.

Miss da Costa Greene's red Pierce-Arrow, roaring at breakneck speed along the roads of Long Island, would soon become one of her trademarks, along with the quivering of the plumes in her hat, a sign of either pleasure or impatience, and the powdery scent of the tuberose corsage she always wore pinned to her breast.

Everything else remained business as usual. Worse than ever, in fact.

Lists, appraisals, waybills, invoices, and letters to the art dealer Jacques Seligman. Correspondence with transport and insurance companies and with the White Star Line, the only shipping line Morgan trusted. Unsinkable, because he owned it.

Belle was expecting more than one delivery. The Renaissance bronzes would leave London in a first shipment in late February, rather earlier than originally planned. The paintings—the magnificent Van Dycks, the Rembrandts, the Raphael—would sail on April 10, as Morgan had said, on the inaugural crossing of the *Titanic*. For the rest, it remained to be seen. There was one non-negotiable condition: all of the crates with their priceless treasure destined to enrich and educate the American public, their contents valued at more than fifty million dollars,[9] must be safely stowed in the Metropolitan Museum's stores before the autumn. And that battle was far from won.

The transport of the J.P. Morgan Collections had become a diplomatic matter, an affair of state between the United States and Great Britain. The London museums the Big Chief had been allowing to display his bronzes and porcelains for years were now insisting that the pieces had been donated, not loaned, and were furiously protesting the removal of the most spectacular objects in their display cases. The National Gallery, too, which had exhibited several Morgan-owned paintings, was expressing outrage at the stripping of their walls. Public opposition to the "pillaging" of England's treasures was growing fiercer by the day.

As if that weren't enough, the American customs official dispatched to Prince's Gate, Michael Nathan, had added fuel to the fire by gushing to the press about his awe at the splendor of the objects Mr. Morgan was sending to New York.

All of this meant that letters were arriving on both sides of the Atlantic by the sackful.

Entreaties from Belle to Charles Hercules Read to remind his country's press that Mr. Morgan had donated princely sums to the British Museum. That Mr. Morgan had always intended to bring his collections home. And that Mr. Morgan had to protect his heirs from the monumental inheritance taxes associated with the presence of his collections in England.

---

[9] Nearly 1.8 billion dollars in today's money.

\*

Late in the afternoon of Monday, April 15, 1912, Belle walked the short distance up 40th Street from her home to the Morgan Library, fresh from a long weekend in bed with her friend Mitchell Kennerley—a way of relieving the endless series of frustrations that the first half of April had brought.

Mr. Nathan, the customs agent overseeing the transport of Morgan's collections, had suddenly—for "personal" reasons—returned home, leaving the inspection and packing of the treasures unfinished. How could they repatriate the crates without the approval of a duly sworn customs officer? If Morgan disregarded the requirement, he would be violating his agreement with the director of the Port of New York. Too risky. But to wait for Nathan's return, or a replacement's arrival, would mean a delay *sine die* of the transport—with the additional headache of having to cancel all the reservations on various White Star liners. What to do? Belle had had no choice but to handle the matter herself, and stop everything. Jacques Seligman was en route to Aix-les-Bains even now, to discuss their next moves with the Big Chief.

After such a trying episode—six months of work, ruined—Belle had decided that three days of rest and recreation in the arms of Mitchell Kennerley was just what the doctor ordered. Kennerley, the most exciting self-made man in the world. Thirty-four years old, handsome, crazy about literature and old books, a fast driver, and keen photographer. Born in England under very modest circumstances, he had married a Cleveland heiress who had supported his dream of starting a publishing house, where he published avant-garde writers and discovered talents disdained by the self-righteous mainstream press. The easy rapport he shared with Belle provided a respite for both of them from the turbulent relationships they had with their other partners. There was nothing she enjoyed more than their stays in the seaside bungalow he rented in the Hamptons, and his wild parties where writers and photographers rubbed elbows into the wee hours. It was a liaison worlds apart from her passionate one with B.B. and the melodrama with Mestre.

Reaching the intersection of 40th Street and Madison Avenue, Belle had her first glimpse of the commotion. Paperboys were shouting the news on both sides of the street, waving the latest editions with their blaring headlines at passing pedestrians. A crowd had gathered in front of the block of houses between 36th and 37th Streets, the private homes of J.P. Morgan and his son Jack, who served as his business manager. People were also milling in front of Morgan's daughter Louisa's house, Belle saw. And, worst of all, in front of the library. The front steps and the wide porch were crowded with gawkers and reporters.

What was happening at the Morgan Library? Alarm swept through Belle. She quickened her steps toward the marble palace.

"The biggest boat ever built by John Pierpont Morgan's shipping line hit an iceberg last night! Rescue ships are on the way!"

The paperboys' voices rang out sharply.

"J.P. Morgan's *Titanic* sank last night!"

Belle started running.

"Mr. Morgan's *Titanic* hasn't sunk! It's being towed to Halifax! No lives lost!"

"*Titanic!* Disaster! Countless deaths!"

Pushing through the horde of journalists, Belle reached the bronze doors, behind which were the Big Chief's personal secretary, his steward, and Thursty.

Even inside, they could still hear the shouts of the newsboys.

"*Titanic!* Disaster! Countless deaths!"

"Where have you been?" gasped Thursty. "We've been looking everywhere for you since this morning!"

Belle made no mention of the fact that she'd been in the publisher Kennerley's bed.

"The radio transmissions stopped coming at two o'clock in the morning," Thursty went on breathlessly, without waiting for an answer. "Since then, no word. Nobody knows anything. Mr. Morgan was informed this morning in Aix. Mr. Jack went to the White Star offices right away. Apparently a ship has been sent to rescue the . . . we hope that . . . Mr. Jack said there were almost nine hundred crew members and more than thirteen hundred passengers. A lot of people we know—people who've visited the library. Your friends. Mrs. Astor's son, and Benjamin Guggenheim, and the Wideners—"

"Harry Widener?" Belle cut her off.

"Yes, the book collector from Philadelphia, and his father, too. There are so *many* people on board. The families are all storming the White Star offices on Broadway for news; it's like a riot. No one knows anything," repeated Thursty. "Mr. Jack's waiting for you in the West Room."

Jack Morgan never set foot in the library if he could help it. Belle knocked on the door.

He was on the telephone, sitting behind his father's desk. Physically, he was a near-replica of the Big Chief. Belle had never realized just how alike they were, and it shocked her now. Jack was almost an exact copy, but without the ugly nose—or the charm. From a distance, anyone who didn't know them would have struggled to tell them apart. They were both tall and corpulent, with the same complexions, same face shapes, same gray mustaches, same dark eyes. The only difference was in the intensity of their gazes. Jack's wasn't stern like his father's, only serious, and far blander. There was no fire, no spark. His were not eyes that drew you in, but merely judged you and categorized you. According to his moral criteria—honest or dishonest. According to his social standards—well born, or poorly brought up. At forty-five years old he was a man of principles, obsessed with propriety, decorum, and "true" values. A hard worker. Honorable. Reasonable. The embodiment of the upper class at its best and its worst. The best? He was ardently devoted to his wife and children, tender with his mother and sisters, full of respect for his father. The worst? He was deeply, virulently anti-Semitic and a stereotypical banker, utterly lacking in imagination.

Deadly dull, in Belle's view.

He hung up the phone. Visibly stunned by what he had just heard, he sat, lost in thought. A few moments passed before he was even aware of Belle's presence.

"Ah, Miss Greene . . ."

Jack stood up slowly. He reached for his walking stick and his hat.

"You're here—finally. I was waiting to speak with you before I return to the White Star offices."

He approached her, the emotion clear in his face, hesitating a moment before he spoke again. He had never quite known how to act toward her, or even how to greet her. Charcoal's esteem for this young woman—"Charcoal" was the affectionate nickname he and his sisters had given the *pater familias*, an allusion to his dark eyes—and his enthusiasm for his librarian suggested that she should be treated with politeness and respect, and why not? Unlike the women in his family, he felt no particular hostility toward her. Even Anne, the rebel of the family, who almost never agreed with the others, didn't like her any more than the rest of them did. Jack, however, liked to think of himself as more moderate than that.

But to say that he appreciated Belle's constant presence at his father's side would have been an exaggeration. He could not help but be irritated by their closeness. Vaguely scandalized, even. Such familiarity between a female employee and her boss seemed improper.

This was not the time for personal antipathies, however.

"Please send my father hourly updates on the situation. I will keep you updated on what happens at White Star. Keep in touch with him constantly by telegram. But try not to excite him too much—his condition is fragile as it is. You will relay his wishes, please, regarding financial support of the bereaved families."

"It's true, then?" she asked, her voice quavering slightly.

He nodded.

"There's talk of a thousand victims. Maybe more. We're awaiting a list of survivors, but the rescue ship hasn't sent one yet. There appear to be around seven hundred survivors, but the rest . . ."

Jack's voice trailed off, his distress obvious.

"Let in the *Times* reporters and tell them what little you know. Tell them what I've just told you. The truth. The ship has sunk. And the unfortunate souls who have lost their lives . . . we don't know the figures. Their names will be made public as soon as possible. The director of the White Star Line is trying to prevent a panic, screening the information that's coming in, but his silence is worse than anything. *Worse than anything,*" Jack repeated heavily. "Holding back news only encourages false rumors. Vile untruths, on top of the ones some malicious people are already spreading, about . . ." he hesitated before pronouncing the word: ". . . my father. We must avoid . . . there have already been . . ."

He couldn't finish, and left the room. Belle could hear the shouted questions, see the popping of flashbulbs that greeted his passage. She needed only a few minutes to understand what Jack had was alluding to. There had already been a great deal of negative press that month suggesting that J.P. Morgan had been personally responsible for the financial panic of 1907. He was unpopular already . . .

. . . and now this.

\*

"He really was born under a lucky star, your boss," commented Russell, when the family gathered for dinner as usual that Sunday. "He'd reserved his personal suite on that beautiful ocean liner for the maiden voyage, then canceled just two days before it departed. What a coincidence . . ."

"What are you implying?" Belle snapped. "He never intended to be on the *Titanic*! I'm the one who canceled the reservation—but not for him. For the crates that were meant to be on board. It was *me!* At the beginning of April."

Caught up in the emotion of the last few days, she hadn't even thought of the art at first. Some of the greatest masterpieces ever painted had come within days of rotting on the ocean floor. In that sense, yes, the Big Chief had been lucky. As had all of humanity, for that matter. Belle wasn't hiding her relief . . . The collections had escaped oblivion by a hair's breadth.

But her obvious joy at the survival of the artwork exasperated her brother and scandalized the rest of the family. The sitting room of their flat fairly crackled with tension. And the tragedy of the *Titanic* had spurred them to other arguments, somehow, revived other disagreements.

"Really lucky, your Morgan!" repeated Russell. "Only two days before the trip!"

"He never comes back before the summer," Belle retorted. "He was scheduled to attend the inauguration of Saint Mark's Campanile in Venice, which he paid to restore, on the twenty-third of April. How could he have traveled here and back in less than a week, if he'd returned to New York on the *Titanic*? It's idiotic! The papers will say anything!"

"My God, Belle, open your eyes! Your Morgan *knew* the *Titanic* was going down! Maybe he didn't order the sinking directly, like some people are saying, but he *knew*! And here's the proof: he doubled the insurance on that ship, just before the crossing. Just *coincidentally*, of course. Not only is the sinking of the *Titanic* not going to cost him a penny, but he's going to get twice what it cost to build the ship as an insurance payout! But it's all a *coincidence!*"

"That is false, false, *false!* All of that about the insurance! Just another story, just made-up news to sell papers!"

"That doesn't change the fact that there were only twenty lifeboats for two thousand people," put in Louise. "It's a scandal. Monstrous. And your Big Chief *is* responsible for that."

"Just like he was responsible for the banking panic he created himself in 1907," agreed Russell. "He's a criminal, and he needs to be tried. And if that con man doesn't end up in prison . . ."

Belle was on her feet.

"Only a mediocre mind like yours could believe such hideous rumors!" she said fiercely. "May I remind you that you're living off him—that we've *all* been living off him for seven years! Without Mr. Morgan's protection, without his generosity, I wouldn't exist. And let's not even talk about you! Show some gratitude, please. When that 'con man' is gone, you'll see what happens to us. It'll be the end of the good life, Russell. You'd better hope that sweetheart of yours at the golf club comes with one hell of a dowry, because without Mr. Morgan's money, no one will want you!"

"Please, Belle," protested Genevieve, sensing that things were about to be said that could not be taken back.

But Belle kept on. "If you're all so determined to bite the hand that feeds you, then you're no better than any idiot in a lynch mob, howling lies and filth! But when he's gone, everything will end. And if you think Jack Morgan will respect his father's wishes and keep me on at the Morgan Library, you're kidding yourselves. His family—his daughters, who are waiting for my downfall with bated breath—they all know it. When Morgan dies, the library is finished. So, if I were you, I'd show some tiny shred of dignity and shut my mouth!"

Incandescent with fury, she threw down her napkin and left the table.

Genevieve's heart clenched until she felt as if she couldn't breathe. She couldn't even summon the courage to demand that Belle sit back down.

She stacked the plates and cleared the table silently.

An argument like this would never have happened with their Georgetown family—never!

They had to remain united. Their survival depended on it. All the more so because a major event was approaching: Louise's wedding to a speech therapist she'd met at the public school where she taught. White and Catholic. In order to marry him, she'd been baptized on Easter Sunday, April 7—the night before her thirty-fifth birthday, though the conversion register listed her age as twenty-eight.

Ethel, too, had just announced her intention to marry a Catholic. She would be thirty-two in December, but claimed to be twenty-five, a year younger than Belle.

No matter how many lies they told the civil registry, however, time was marching on. Who could blame any of them for wanting to live their lives?

Even Russell, thirty-four years old at home, but twenty-seven to the outside world, was starting to talk about a future with a well-born young lady from New Jersey, his boss's daughter. He'd met her at the local golf club, a highly exclusive establishment that, before accepting Russell as a member, had required him to show both his annual earnings and proof that he wasn't Jewish. The possibility that he might be *colored* had never arisen, however. Impossible, naturally, for so skilled an engineer, and a Columbia University graduate, no less, to belong to the Black community.

The conservative industrialists Russell frequented those days absolutely loathed J.P. Morgan, as much for his economic domination of an America governed by Wall Street as for his political leanings. Morgan was a liberal who supported the Republican party of Roosevelt and Taft against the more right-wing Democratic party,[10] the party of Southerners and opponents of

[10] Simply put, the Republicans of 1912 were "liberals" and the Democrats "conservatives," the opposite of the modern situation.

the trusts and monopolies of the North. And the *Titanic* disaster had provided the Democrats with plenty of ammunition.

Belle, for her part, couldn't bring herself to approve of her two sisters marrying men she felt were their intellectual inferiors. And Catholics, too, which meant they would want to have children, lots and lots of children. How would they react when one of those children came out Black? While Frederick Martin, Louise's fiancé, wasn't an imbecile—he'd developed a method for helping the sons of immigrants rid themselves of their foreign accents and was planning to found a school for children with language problems—Belle could not in good conscience accept Ethel's choice of husband, a mere wholesaler.

True to form, she'd expressed her opinion of her sister's fiancé loudly and frequently: her dearest Ethel, her "blonde self," had chosen a "good-for-nothing."

In truth, she blamed herself. It was her engagement to Mestre that had opened Pandora's box, had made all of her siblings feel free to pursue their own dreams of matrimony.

Louise and Ethel, of course, were furious at Belle's opposition to their marriages. What right did she have to meddle in their romantic affairs? Especially when her own love life was such a disaster? They were well aware of Belle's frequent dalliances with married men, liaisons which, as future wives themselves, made them extremely uncomfortable. They knew that her favorite lover was Mitchell Kennerley, the philanderer *par excellence* of New York high society, and that she was still engaged in an emotional affair with Bernhard Berenson. Married, both of them.

And so they had both joined with their brother in condemning Belle's amoral behavior.

Genevieve, greatly distressed by the discord among her children, had tried to smooth the ruffled feathers of each one in turn, but had been unable to restore the peace. Family dinners together had long since ceased to be a source of pleasure for her.

The Greene clan, together against the world? Not anymore! These days, it was more like a civil war.

And there was something else, too. The news that Belle had commanded her to keep quiet about, the catastrophe that was keeping them both awake at night. Genevieve was staying silent, as ordered, but the business concerned—and threatened—them all.

An envelope addressed to *Mr. Russell Greener c/o Miss Greene, librarian*, had arrived at the Morgan Library. Belle hadn't needed to turn it over to see who had sent it, but if she *had* had any doubt, there it was on the back: *Professor Richard T. Greener, 5237 Ellis Avenue, Chicago.*

Recounting the scene to her mother, Belle had admitted that the sight of those words had made her feel as if she were dying.

Even though the letter wasn't addressed to her, she had opened it.

Greener hadn't wasted any ink on unnecessary words. The letter consisted of a single paragraph, ordering his son to contact him immediately about the matter of the inheritance. Or else . . .

It was that *or else* that had made Belle's blood boil. *Or else.* One did not give in to blackmailers. One did not quail in the face of attempts to intimidate. One didn't even dignify them with a response.

And above all, one did not become ensnared in the trap!

Russell didn't need to know this letter existed. Bitter as he was, he would still have agreed to the meeting, to get his money. And that would have opened the door to all sorts of disasters— all the more so because Richard Greener's many failures since leaving his family had made him no less bitter than his son. "For my part," he had written in one newspaper, "I would rather be a citizen of despotic Russia than a pariah in this ignoble republic." The vehemence of his writings against his former white friends, the politicians who had deserted him during his travails with the people of Vladivostok, provided clear proof of his anger.

The letter and its envelope had been immediately torn into confetti and discarded in the North Room's wastebasket.

And now, to forget them. And the memory of Greener would be consigned to the wastebasket as well, with that ominous *or else* of his.

Nevertheless, fear had returned to the Greene house. What Belle and Genevieve had never stopped dreading, since the moment they had stepped over the color barrier, had happened. Their Black father, their Black husband, had found them.

\*

"A lovely gift indeed! *Who* bought you this automobile?"

Standing at his office window, J.P. gazed narrowly at the Pierce-Arrow parked in front of the library. His European sojourn had done nothing to lessen his jealousy. Had he heard more rumors in London, or Florence perhaps, about the *amours* of Belle and Berenson?

Letting the curtain fall shut, he repeated his question.

"Who bought it for you?"

One look at Belle's expression told him he had offended her. She turned on her heel, about to storm out.

"Please answer me, Miss Greene!" he barked. "Who gave you that automobile?"

She faced him, her expression thunderous. "Contrary to what you seem to believe, I am not some kept woman. And you're the first man who has *ever* had the cheek to insult me that way!"

He was silent for a moment, reflecting. "You're right, my dear," he said finally. "Please forgive me. The thought of testifying in Washington is driving me crazy."

She bit back the retort that the Washington testimony next week was a likely excuse.

"I don't have to explain anything to you. But if you must know, I bought the auto for myself."

"Forgive me," he repeated.

He was so anxious, she knew, so distracted—so suddenly old, she felt—that she let the subject drop.

That didn't alter the fact, though, that Morgan was easier to love from afar these days. She no longer had any patience for his interrogations.

Especially not after last Sunday, during the long Labor Day weekend, when he'd been on his yacht at Newport and she, arriving on Long Island in her roadster, had received a telegram from him. BE AT THE LIBRARY TOMORROW MORNING. MONDAY. NINE O'CLOCK. WITHOUT FAIL. IMPORTANT. She had risen at dawn and driven at breakneck speed back to the city, sick with worry that something terrible had happened.

It had been nothing of the sort.

"The important matter was that I wanted to see you, Miss Greene," he had announced, with a grin. "I missed you!"

She hadn't spoken to him for the rest of the day.

But she couldn't really blame him. She could feel that he was faltering, losing control. His obsession with proving to the world that he had never been deliberately dishonest in his business dealings was haunting him day and night.

Certainly, he had been criticized before over the years, particularly when he had sold arms during the Civil War or speculated on the gold market. But his unshakeable belief that he was acting for the public good, and his habit of cutting ties with anyone who did not share his vision, had made him deaf to dissenting opinions. Those rare individuals to whom he had confessed his fears, described his feeling of failure and his long battle against depression, had always tried to reassure him, Belle most of all. Except for the times when they fought, that was all she had ever done: reassure him and urge him to ignore his critics. But his vulnerability had increased with age. Rampant conspiracy theories in which he had been the instigator behind the sinking of the *Titanic* had floored him. He had already been horrified by so much loss of life, but that anyone could think him *responsible* for it had destroyed him. And now, just as Woodrow Wilson, a Southern conservative and fierce opponent of trusts, was elected president, the humiliation of having to justify his actions of five years ago in front of a hostile Senate committee . . . it was too much, and he was crumbling beneath the weight of it.

The Pujo Committee's report on his industrial and financial empire had proven devastating, lingering on the fact that, at the time of the 1907 crisis, Morgan's associates had sat on the boards of directors of one hundred and twelve major companies listed on the stock market. The result of this, the report had implied, was that the panic had been fabricated by high finance to weaken trust companies for the benefit of the banks. And that J.P. Morgan had taken advantage of the crisis to merge U.S. Steel with the Tennessee Coal, Iron and Railroad Company. Accordingly, the Pujo Committee had just subpoenaed Morgan to testify publicly before Congress, a hearing that would take several days and would be led by a conservative prosecutor who was out for his blood.

On the morning of Tuesday, December 17, 1912, Belle accompanied the Big Chief to Grand Central Station. Alone together in the back of his car, she could feel him shivering with cold and anxiety. He had hardly slept and was suffering from a heavy cold. He blew his nose again and again, and that poor feature had never looked more purplish and swollen.

Sitting stiffly in his long black coat, his walking stick between his knees and his top hat in his lap, he stared straight ahead. Belle, who was as nervous as he was, didn't speak. She had already given him words of comfort, told him how much she cared for him, how much she admired him. All the things he was still receptive to hearing. One word more, and her assurances would ring false.

The Big Chief's depression had infected Belle, too. She

couldn't help but share his dark thoughts. The cortege of automobiles that followed his car, carrying his family, was like a line
of hearses. It was as if he were going to his own funeral.

She had been struggling with her own dark mood for some
time. Louise had left home to marry, and had settled with her
new husband hundreds of miles from New York. Ethel was in
the hospital with peritonitis, hovering between life and death.
Genevieve was prostrate with worry. Somewhere, Richard
Greener was lying in wait for them all. And now, the "hero of
her soul" was going off to the slaughter.

Morgan had decided that he wanted Belle at his side until he
reached the train station, but that she would not go with him to
Washington. He would already be accompanied by some twenty
people: his son Jack, his beloved daughter Louisa, his son-in-
law, two of his business partners. And fifteen attorneys.

Watching him board the train with difficulty, clinging with
both hands to the door-handles of his private car, Belle was seized
with a sudden sense of foreboding. *Please, let him get through
this.* Superstitiously, she crossed her fingers behind her back.

She returned to the library with a heavy heart, gripped by fear
of what might be about to happen. Foremost among her emotions was guilt. She cursed herself for being so irritable with him
over the past year. Unable to keep from being impatient. And yet
he had given her endless proof of his attachment to her. Had
tried to, at least.

The Big Chief's absurd rages, his jealousy, his tyranny, were
all simply clumsy ways of expressing his affection, and his fear
that she did not love him for himself, but for his power, and his
money.

Belle's compassion, her sympathy for this man of seventy-five,
who had served his country and was now being accused of trea-
son, made her ill with shame and anxiety. The giant of a man that
was Morgan, struck down.

She was wrong.

He was indestructible.

He returned from the three days in Washington in fine fettle, relieved that the ordeal was behind him, and certain he had answered the congressional committee's questions clearly, despite his habitual trouble expressing himself. Proud of his performance, which his family and the lawyers had deemed brilliant.

He told Belle how he had put an end to the questioning himself, how he had stepped forward to shake hands with the committee members, thanked them for their courtesy, and told them how pleased he was to have given them his testimony. How he had left the Congress chamber to a round of applause.

He spent the next week on cloud nine, sending bouquets to all his female conquests: Lady Sackville-West, his newest London flirtation, and her friend Margot Asquith, wife of the British prime minister. And his legion of Blondes, of course. He busied himself enthusiastically with arrangements for the arrival at the Metropolitan Museum of the first part of his collection, and began to plan his next trip abroad. And he gave his librarian a diamond-encrusted Cartier watch as a holiday gift, along with a miniature portrait of himself, and a substantial check.

On Christmas morning, he arrived at the library singing a hymn at the top of his lungs that he had just heard in church, gaily tossed his hat and cane into the nearest available receptacle—which happened to be an extremely ancient porphyry sarcophagus—, hugged Belle tightly and kissed her on both cheeks, wished her a merry Christmas, gave her his final instructions for the coming months, expressed his regret that she couldn't accompany him to Egypt, and set off for Cairo.

Two months later, he settled into the Grand Hotel in Rome. But by then, depression had caught up with him again. Too much anxiety, too much pressure. He suffered horrific nightmares about the *Titanic* and the Washington interrogation.

Unable to eat or sleep, he started to imagine that he was the target of a conspiracy, that America was barreling toward ruin, that his heirs wouldn't survive, that his whole life had been a disaster. Receiving any news from New York sent him into a panic, but *not* receiving news terrified him even more.

To avoid unwanted attention from the Roman press and a stock market crash on Wall Street, Morgan's daughter, his physician, and the people close to him concealed or minimized his worsening health. No one at the library was aware of the true gravity of the situation until Louisa's telegram to her brother Jack, on March 31, 1913.

"Charcoal died today at five minutes past noon."

The shock was so great that Miss Greene, who had never been prone to the vapors, had never fainted even once in her whole life, collapsed on the floor of the North Room.

As she came to, she was heard to murmur: "He was my father. And my child, too."

# CHAPTER 10

## MY HEART AND MY LIFE ARE SHATTERED
### APRIL 1913–JANUARY 1914

Welcome home. On Thursday, April 10, 1913, Belle prepared for the Big Chief's arrival. There were no grand gestures, no bursts of emotion. No theatrics. She did not cry. Thursty could hear her heels clicking along the marble floors as usual. Moving briskly from one room to another as usual. The only difference was the silence. Belle, normally such a chatterbox, whose rapid-fire speech echoed constantly through the halls and rooms of the library at a million words a minute, had gone quiet.

That silence, and the deep mourning she wore, had turned Belle into a somber little figure. Gone were the plumed hats, the ornate jewelry, the chic outfits. In her black garments she had finally come to embody the character she had always refused to be: the drab, invisible librarian.

For ten days and nights, since Louisa Morgan's fateful telegram, she had been busily tidying the library, setting it to rights, mechanically repeating the same actions she had always performed when the Big Chief's return was imminent.

How many returns had there been, in eight years? She tried to count them, struggling in vain to wrap her head around the fact that, after this one, there would be no more.

"My heart and my life are shattered," she had written to B.B., announcing the death of the "hero of her soul." And yet she could not fully grasp the magnitude of the loss. Not really. If she had seen Morgan ill, tended him, sat at his bedside, she might not now be feeling this unreal sensation of floating. "I feel as if I'm enveloped in a thick fog. I can't imagine the future, can't even begin to picture it. Even you, B.B., you don't know all that he meant to me."

Despite referring to him in the past tense, Belle was still talking to Morgan in her head.

The grief was too sudden. And the emptiness too distant. She couldn't accept his absence.

He was still so *present!* He had planned his own funeral down to the smallest detail—chosen the hymns they would sing at the mass, requested to be buried alongside his father in the Hartford cemetery.

Well, he would find everything in order at the library.

She made sure that his bathroom cabinet was stocked with his favorite soap and cologne. That his letterhead and a stack of bills to sign were ready on his desk.

Letters of condolence were arriving from museums all over the world, museums that owed so much to his generosity. She sorted them *for him*. Sorted, too, the messages from the countries to which he had rendered service. Letters from George V of England, from Victor-Emmanuel III of Italy, from Kaiser Wilhelm II of Germany, from French President Raymond Poincaré and countless other heads of European governments, from so many thousands of others to whom his family would have to respond. She arranged the wreaths *for him*, the floral crosses and sprays and bouquets arriving by the dozens. She organized—*for him*—the police cordons that would keep away the reporters whose lack of discretion he hated so much, and the security guards who would keep away the whispering, murmuring throngs of admirers and enemies alike who had already crowded around his casket as it was carried out of the Grand Hotel in Rome.

She'd heard how the Italian army had treated him like a king, escorting his coffin, accompanied by a funeral march, to the train that would take him to Paris. How the French soldiers had seen him off with full military honors at Le Havre. How the ocean liner *France*, which was bringing home his remains, would find New York's flags at half-mast, how the stock exchange would remain closed on the morning of his funeral. How, after the humiliation of his Washington questioning, there were endless tributes pouring in now, tributes that he would have loved. But for Belle, none of it was real.

She knew, too, that he would not be taken from the ship to his home, as was customary. Nor would he lie in state on the legendary premises of his bank at 23 Wall Street, nor in his daughter Louisa's house, nor his son and successor Jack's. No—he would be where he had most loved to be in life. At the Morgan Library. With her.

He would receive the final farewells of his friends among his books and paintings, among the thousands of roses Belle had ordered from Thorley's, his favorite florist. White roses, like the flowers he'd always sent to his Blondes, and red ones like the silk that covered the walls of his office, adorned with the arms of the Chigi princes. It would be here, in the West Room, near his Caxtons and his Gutenberg Bibles, that he would play solitaire and talk with Belle, up to the last moment.

It was only when Belle stepped aside, taking a back seat to the family as the bier was borne through the double bronze doors, that it finally struck home: never again would she hear the Big Chief's Sioux war-cry or watch him do a victory dance. Never again would they rejoice together at the end of a successful treasure hunt.

*The magnificent life we shared is going with him to the grave.*

*

Belle's fate was now in the hands of J.P. Morgan's children, more specifically those of his son Jack. She had no idea what his intentions were toward her, but she feared the worst from this man who'd always struck her as boring. As it turned out, that was a mistake. In these tragic circumstances, he showed extraordinary tact and kindness, not only inviting her to ride to church in the same car as his close friends, but urging her to sit in the family pew and to join him after the mass, along with his mother, wife, and sisters, in the private train carriage that would take them to Hartford, the historic seat of the Morgan family.

She was reluctant to accept the latter invitation. Wasn't the graveside ceremony reserved for family? But Jack insisted.

When the train pulled into the station at Hartford, the immense firefighter's bell tolled seventy-six times. Belle's heart swelled. The Big Chief would have turned seventy-six in three days.

That morning in New York, nearly forty-five thousand people had paid their respects to his coffin in the forecourt of St. George's Episcopal Church on the corner of 16th Street and 2nd Avenue.

Here in Hartford, the whole population was in mourning. Schools and shops, banks and the post office: all were closed. Crowds lined the streets three deep and followed the cortege of automobiles as it wound slowly from the station to the Cedar Hill Cemetery, just over three miles away.

Belle rode in the third car, with Josie Dear and her children: Sarah, Junius's daughter, now aged sixteen, and Alexander, thirteen. No one spoke, but they were all thinking the same thing. How could anyone fail to notice the glaring absence of their husband and father?

The line of cars passed the house, now draped in black, in which J.P. had been born.

They reached Cedar Hill, dark clouds hovering low over the tombstones. It was threatening to rain, so the family gathered beneath an enormous tent that had been set up on the crest of a hill.

Belle hung back. She felt uneasy, as if she were intruding. She should never have agreed to come to the cemetery.

The distant figures grouped among the tombstones made her think, with cutting irony, of the members of Georgetown's Black community, at her grandmother Hermione's funeral. She thought back, as she often did, to that afternoon at the Freedmen's Cemetery in Alexandria when, standing at the open grave, she had made the choice to cut ties with her family history. Made the decision never to belong anywhere, ever again.

She didn't belong here, either.

She let her gaze sweep across the monuments of the Morgan family: the porphyry mausoleum of J.P.'s parents and the tomb he'd had built for himself, just across from them. On the western side of the plot, like his office in the library.

" . . . and so we commit his body to the earth, ashes to ashes, dust to dust, in the certain hope of Resurrection."

At the end of that dreadful day, Belle couldn't summon the courage to go home.

On the pretext of tidying Mr. Morgan's office—but which Mr. Morgan did she mean?—she had herself driven back to the library.

In the evening air, the red petals of the roses that had covered J.P.'s casket still fluttered across the front porch. Head down, face swathed in her black veil, Belle nudged the petals aside with her boots as she climbed the steps, banishing them methodically, angrily, as if cleaning away spots of blood that were sullying her marble palace.

A thousand terrors nipped at her heels.

What would become of the Big Chief's work now? What of the twenty-one thousand volumes he had gathered beneath this roof? Would this temple of knowledge and beauty, which she'd dreamed of transforming, alongside him, into a wellspring for researchers, be reduced to an empty shell? Would the Morgan

Library, which she had imagined as a hive buzzing with scholars from all over the world, become a dead place to which no one was granted access?

Reaching the shelter of the loggia, she finally gave in to her grief. Incapable of taking another step, she sank to the floor, sobbing noiselessly. She stayed there for a long time, weeping in front of the closed bronze doors. At last she pulled herself together, and rose, and vanished inside.

\*

"I feel as if the rug has been pulled out from beneath my feet. I can't bring myself to feel the slightest interest in life. Everything I touch, everything I see, everything I do reminds me of him. The image of his casket in the library haunts me day and night. I can't stop comparing the silence—the stillness—with the noise and commotion of his presence, when he was pacing around his office . . ."

Belle, if her mother were to be believed, would never recover from J.P. Morgan's death, and her gratitude to him would only grow with each passing day.

Despite their stormy relationship in recent years, Morgan had not changed a word of the will he'd read to her on the train returning from the ceremony in Hartford honoring his father. After his widow, his children, his lifelong friends, and the charitable institutions to which he had bequeathed generous amounts of money, Belle stood to inherit the highest sum.

The inheritance was so large, in fact, that the press got wind of the news and published Morgan's last will and testament in the newspapers. *FIFTY THOUSAND DOLLARS FOR THE EFFICIENT AND LOYAL LIBRARIAN,* trumpeted the *New York Times.* The rumor that Miss Belle da Costa Greene was the illegitimate daughter of J.P. Morgan gained new life.

Far from displeasing her, however, the resurrection of this

particular rumor delighted Belle. She promptly told anyone who would listen that she would have been proud to have such a man for a father. The hypothesis appeared all the more plausible because Morgan had ensured Belle's future, recommending that his heirs provide for her *ad vitam*, for life, with a salary equal to or greater than what she had been earning at the time of his death.

But would she—*could* she—remain at the library without him?

She knew she was at a crossroads.

What to do?

Take advantage of her new freedom? Freedom she had dreamed of having?

Should she join B.B. in Italy? Travel? Study? Settle in Paris, like Junius had?

Buy herself an automobile a hundred times more powerful than her red roadster? Order a ninety-horsepower Mercedes? Why not? She loved to go fast.

So many possibilities!

Fifty thousand dollars would enable her to live as she pleased to the end of her days. Alone.

But all six of them?

No.

She never forgot for a moment that she had a family to support. Or that the addition of the husbands, fiancés, and sweethearts of her sisters—all those good-for-nothing young men— would rapidly drain the coffers of the Greene clan.

Once again, she opted for prudence. She would protect her whole family's future by investing her inheritance in the stock market shares suggested by the Big Chief's friends. And by forgetting about the ninety-horsepower Mercedes.

Her own future, though, remained a mystery.

She felt lost.

The letters of condolence sent to her by her beloved London

bookmen assured her of their esteem and offered their services in helping her find a suitable post in England. American collectors wrote that they would be proud to employ her here at home. This evidence of so much admiration touched her immensely.

And yet it made her uncomfortable, too. The same discomfort she had felt at the cemetery in Hartford.

"Read, Pollard, Cockerell, and the others seem to be acknowledging me for what I am," she confided to B.B. "For myself, personally, and not just as a satellite of Mr. Morgan.

"Bizarrely, they seem to find me more acceptable now than they did when he was here. Their praise is very pleasant to read. But I have the feeling of playing a role, of being a usurper . . . as if I were cheating and had no right to their respect."

It was a strange and devastating confession, and she knew B.B. would not really understand it. Only her mother might have, perhaps.

"I feel like a fugitive Negro," she added, "hiding in the woods. With something suspicious about me. Something illegitimate."

Genevieve had no doubt about the magnitude of the damage that had been done. The loss of the Big Chief resulted in more than just the intense grief Belle felt; it was also making her question everything about her life. A true identity crisis. Without the protection of her chosen father, that shield against society, she didn't know where she belonged in the world. She no longer knew who she was, or what she should do with herself now.

"Nothing," Genevieve suggested. "Nothing. Don't do *anything*. When you don't know, you don't move."

This message was echoed in a letter from Junius that arrived the day after the funeral. A letter from him, at long last! It was his first sign of life in three years.

He hadn't even made the journey from Paris for his uncle's funeral, which was frankly unbelievable—but so was the Big Chief's failure even to mention him in his will, when he included absolutely everyone else. What had happened between them? What drama had torn them apart? Belle lost herself in conjecture. Had J.P. been so utterly unable to bear Junius's departure for Europe? Had his sense of betrayal run that deep? Had he felt every bit as abandoned as Josie Dear, perhaps? Belle had asked Morgan about the rift more than once, but he had never wanted to talk about it.

She, herself, had never given up on Junius. Despite his silence, she still thought of him as a dear friend. *My mad, bad, beloved Junius.*

In his letter, he said nothing about himself.

What sort of life was he leading in France? With whom did he spend his time? Where was he living? With whom? Silence.

Keeping strictly mum on the sentimental front as well, Junius confined himself to acting as Belle's mentor. It had always been his way of showing the affection he felt for her. And his guidance was worth its weight in gold.

Junius described his cousin Jack as the unloved child of a giant of a man, the misunderstood son of a force of nature. And Junius was in a position to know. He himself had been the favorite son, by choice rather than blood. And, in the end, a traitor.

Jack might not be a genius, wrote Junius, but he was intelligent, courageous, and highly capable. And a sentimental man, as well.

Far from resenting Charcoal for his lack of fatherly compassion, Jack had worshiped his father to the point of irrationality. He had utterly adored him, and now he was willing to do the impossible to live up to Morgan's example. He would respect his every wish and work tirelessly to exalt his father's memory. To hear Junius tell it, however, Jack now found himself in an extremely complicated inheritance situation. Morgan might have left him nearly everything—the bank, the companies, houses, and collections, but he had also left debts. And, as it turned out, the Morgans were not quite as incredibly rich as the world had been led to believe. Jack would have his work cut out for him, to stabilize the family fortune.

*Be very careful*, Junius implored Belle. She was to wait, to bide her time. And never to confront Jack directly. If she played her cards right, if she showed herself to be pliant and amenable, he said, she had every chance of carving out a plum position for herself at the side of the new Mr. Morgan.

\*

In early May, Mr. Jack Morgan entered the North Room, his step heavy and deliberate. There were no thunderous eruptions of temper, no outbursts, no scenes. A boss utterly unlike the one Belle and Thursty had always known.

They had thought him particularly kindly disposed toward them in the days preceding the funeral, but now it seemed they had been wrong. Jack had not set foot in the library in the three weeks since the ceremony. There hadn't been a single word from him; he hadn't even spared them a glance. And his indifference was beginning to weigh on them. It was even worse than the Big Chief's tantrums—even Thursty agreed with Belle on this point. Under his stewardship, the Morgan Library had become a ghostly place. An empty shell, just as Belle had feared.

They both knew he had no taste for books—or at least, no particular love of them. Though he had been educated at Harvard and was known to be a top-notch financier, he was neither a scholar nor a collector. The only books in his father's library that he had ever shown an interest in were those of the great English writers of the nineteenth century: Scott, Dickens, Thackeray—precisely the ones Belle and Thursty found least intriguing. In Jack's eyes, the Morgan Library was little more than an attractive outbuilding, an extension of the private mansion where his mother lived.

Solemnly, he asked Miss Greene to step into his office. Thursty watched "Bull" vanish into the West Room with a terrible feeling of dread. Belle would emerge from the interview without a job, she was certain of it. And then it would be her turn.

Belle, too, was fairly sure of what was about to happen. The bell had tolled for her; this was the end. Yet she felt neither fear nor regret, and, anyway, she found the sight of this man sitting in the Big Chief's chair, this man who looked so much like J.P. but was not him, disturbing and even irritating.

Unbearable. A usurpation.

She sat down opposite "Mr. Morgan" now, as she had done so many times. Her final moments in this room where her destiny had taken shape eight years earlier. Back then she had bent eagerly over the Rembrandt engravings that Junius had just acquired—an unthinkable act today, in the presence of this heir who was wholly without artistic taste, utterly impervious to beauty.

Elbows resting on the desk, Jack had steepled his fingers in a classic banker's pose. He hesitated. Searched for words. He seemed almost as incapable of expressing himself as his father had been.

"I know, Miss Greene," he began with difficulty, "the great affection you had for the late Mr. Morgan. And I do not doubt your devotion to his memory. I don't know what your intentions are—your personal desires, I mean—but I am asking you now to forget them."

She couldn't keep from flinching.

"The fact is," he continued, "we have run up against . . . unexpected financial difficulties."

*Poor Jack*, she muttered inwardly. *Poor, poor Jack Morgan, who has* only *inherited sixty million dollars!*

". . . and so we're going to have to economize rather drastically," he was saying.

*Fire me if you must, but don't try to convince me that you don't have the money to pay me! Enough of this nonsense!*

"In order to calculate the inheritance taxes, it will be necessary to identify and evaluate every *objet d'art* acquired by my father. I'm speaking of the pieces stored everywhere, in Prince's Gate and at the Metropolitan, as well. And the collections of drawings, engravings, books, and manuscripts here at the library. Many of the works were acquired before your arrival; you may not even be aware of their existence. Someone will have to find out their purchase prices and provenances, and from whom they were bought."

"I wish them courage indeed," she said, not bothering to keep a bitter edge from her voice.

"I need an exhaustive inventory. And so it will be necessary to search deep in your archives to find the invoices. If any information is missing, the person who conducts the inventory will have to write to dealers, experts, and curators to confirm the attributions and the current value of the items."

*What fun Mr. Jack's "person" is going to have,* she thought sourly. *Every single item in the library is exhaustively documented. The rest will be quite a job, though . . .*

" . . . and so I must ask you to agree not to leave us for the next two years."

Belle couldn't hide her shock. She waited silently for him to continue.

"With adequate compensation, of course," he said hastily, mistaking her lack of a response for reluctance. "A bonus of two thousand dollars in addition to your regular salary."

Jack's character might have been very different from his father's but, like J.P., he had the ability to surprise you.

"Any new pieces purchased by my father but not yet paid for," he went on now, "particularly the books and manuscripts, will have to be returned to the sellers, and the transactions canceled."

"Canceled?" she echoed, horror-struck.

All thoughts of the offer Jack had just made her were completely wiped from her mind. "Canceled, Mr. Morgan?" she repeated, her voice rising. "Impossible! Never! Our last manuscripts were fiercely negotiated, and hard won! Just like all the others! And you want to simply let them go? Perhaps you don't know how much your father wanted these masterpieces!"

He shook his head. "We have no choice. All we can do is try to get our accounts back in order, and limit expenditures. Once the inventory is finished, I shall ask you to draw up a list of books, paintings, and ornaments we can part with."

"*Sell* them?" she gasped. "But—"

Jack cut her off. "Yes, they will have to be sold. I have no other option but to sacrifice entire sections of the collections."

He fell silent, giving her time to absorb the news she had just been given.

She sat frozen, unable even to protest.

"You know how seriously I take my father's wishes with regard to his library," he went on in the same even tone. "That is why I am so eager to secure your presence and your support." He paused for an instant. "Thank you, Miss Greene. I bid you good evening."

The abruptness with which he terminated the interview took her by surprise. He had risen. She rose, too. He walked around the desk, as if to accompany her to the door. She hesitated. Shouldn't she give him a response to his offer of collaboration? Her agreement? Her refusal?

She hadn't even made her mind up yet, herself. But he seemed to consider the matter settled.

At the door, he paused again, his hand on the knob. It occurred to Belle that his hesitations—and his eagerness to conclude their exchange—were masking something else. Timidity? Anxiety? A dislike of conflict?

In his eyes, she saw a kind of plea.

The truth was, Jack Morgan was afraid. He didn't dare ask her the question outright. Didn't dare say, *Do you accept my offer? Will you help me?*

In those dark eyes, in the intense way he looked at her, Belle suddenly saw a little of the Big Chief. The torso bent slightly forward, the heavy body, waiting, as if suspended above her, powerful and helpless at the same time. In that moment, Jack looked so very much like *him*.

Overwhelmed by a sudden rush of feeling, without thinking, she heard herself murmur: "Of course, Mr. Morgan. I'll do my best."

She emerged from the West Room shaken. It wasn't the same sort of emotion as she'd felt when the real Mr. Morgan was there, but it was everything but indifference. It was a thousand warring sentiments. It was something between fear and fury and stubbornness. It was devastation at the news of the dismantling of the library's collections, and determination to preserve as much as possible.

The die was cast. Destiny had decided for her. She couldn't abandon the library now. She would stay and fight for as long as it took.

And, almost incidentally, Belle da Costa Greene had now become the highest-paid woman in America.

Yet her passion for the Morgan Library would cost her dearly. Farewell to her own dreams and desires; farewell to the hopes of freedom she had cherished for a brief moment.

Travels to Europe to be with B.B. seemed more unrealistic than ever, though he was now the sole light of her life. She needed his love. But he would have to wait—or come to her in New York.

Their eternal debate.

What could she do? She had taken on a herculean task: that of preventing Jack Morgan, who knew nothing about books or painting and had no aesthetic sense of his own, from making the wrong choices. Assisting and guiding him.

Just as she had in the good old days of the battle to build the Morgan Library, she bent her steps determinedly toward the storeroom where her comrade in arms was hiding. Though Miss Thurston no longer needed to flee the boss's rages—unlike his father, Mr. Jack did not intimidate her—it was still her habit to take refuge in the tiny room. She was there now, gathering her things, waiting mournfully for "Bull" to bring the news that they had both been fired.

Without taking the time to knock, Belle opened the door and, thrusting her head through the gap, gave the familiar rallying cry:

"Come on, Thursty, let's get to work!"

*

If Belle had feared accusations of using the late Mr. Morgan to climb the social ladder, of manipulating him into leaving her money in his will, and of publicly mourning his death merely to further her own interests and ingratiate herself with his successor, those fears could now be put to rest. No one doubted the sincerity of her affection and devotion. Even her devil-may-care bedfellow, the publisher Mitchell Kennerley, who respected no one and nothing, was astonished by the depth of her grief—so much so that he dared to ask her the question that all their friends were desperate to ask: had she been J.P. Morgan's mistress? His daughter? *Both?*

In short, had she ever slept with him?

Enigmatic and provocative as ever, she refused to answer *yes* or *no*; merely winked and said coquettishly, "Attempts were made!"

What she didn't tell Kennerley was that, among the "adorable" letters of condolence sent to her personally, there was one that had left a bitter taste in her mouth. In it, the writer made no attempt to hide his sarcasm, musing ironically about the fifty thousand dollar inheritance and the filial bond between "Miss Belle Marion Greene" and the deceased. Next, he repeated the demand made in his previous letter, to which no one had deigned to reply: for his son Russell to claim or formally renounce the money left to him by Cousin Wears.

Professor Richard T. Greener, whose address was written plainly on the back of the envelope, did not need to conclude his note with an "Or else . . ." for it to be threatening. His pointed use of Belle's middle name, Marion, as given on her birth certificate, without the da Costa patronym she had invented, clearly conveyed his anger and his intentions. He knew that Belle Marion Greene was solvent. He knew that Belle Marion Greene had far more to lose than her brother did. He knew that she had the power to settle family disputes, even those that didn't directly concern her. And he was not going to let the matter drop.

This letter, like the first one, was torn to bits and thrown away.

But how could Belle be sure that he wouldn't send a third?

Not replying, not making a move, as she had originally planned, was becoming dangerous. What weapon would he use in his next attempt at blackmail? It was clear that he wouldn't stop now.

The Big Chief, had he discovered her true origins, might have shrugged them off. *Perhaps.* And really, who was to say that he *hadn't* guessed her secret at some point? She had wondered about that more than once. Had he ever made the connection between his faithful librarian and the treasurer of the Grant Monument Association, one of the very few Black men with whom he had ever spent any time?

She knew J.P. had considered individual merit to be far more important than circumstances of birth. Knew, too, that his affection for her could have overcome anything, except abandonment.

But Jack? To judge by the vehemence of his anti-Semitism, it was a safe bet that his prejudices extended to other areas, as well.

If he hated Jews, he hated Blacks, too.

\*

"Going to meet your father in Chicago?" exclaimed Genevieve, aghast. "But that's madness!"

"A nightmare, you mean," murmured Belle.

Mother and daughter were in the living room of their new home.

Following Louise's marriage, they had left their ground-floor apartment at 142 East 40th for a place just down the street at number 104. It was smaller, but homey and comfortable, and boasted a lovely view. Nothing had changed in terms of their living arrangements: Belle and her personal maid lived on one side; Genevieve, Russell, Ethel, and Teddy on the other. The living room served as a sort of antechamber between the two apartments, and it was there that Genevieve frequently acted as mediator.

Now aged sixty-seven, she had lost none of her charm. She was still slim, petite, and even-featured, and if her blonde hair was mixed with gray and laugh-lines marked the corners of her eyes and mouth, her complexion was still remarkably fresh, and no one would have questioned the fifty years of age she claimed.

Genevieve had been sitting contentedly at her sewing machine when Belle had announced the arrival of another letter from Greener. The news had come as such a shock that the loud purr of the machine had stopped abruptly. The thought of her husband reappearing in their lives was horrifying. Even more than her children, Genevieve had dreaded Greener's return every day for years.

Anything was preferable to seeing him again, ever.

"Going to Chicago," she repeated. "Have you lost your mind?"

Ashtray in one hand and cigarette in the other, Belle was slumped in a chair. For once, Genevieve didn't tell her to sit up straight.

Genevieve was on her feet now. "You said yourself that we weren't to respond to that kind of intimidation!" she said hotly.

Belle shrugged.

"Greener knows where to find us now. If I don't react at all, he'll keep harassing us."

"And you think you can stop him by talking to him?" Genevieve shot back. "You don't know your father!"

Belle sighed. "I don't see any other way. I'll try to reason with him. So things don't get any worse, at least."

"He'll try to blackmail you."

"He already has."

"He'll ask you for money."

"Maman, we don't have a choice!" Aggravated, Belle crushed out her cigarette in the ashtray. "We've been afraid of this very thing happening for the past fifteen years. Let's resolve the problem once and for all. We can't live in fear of that man. We need to put an end to this."

She rose. Mother and daughter faced one another.

"What are you going to say to him? You have nothing to offer him!"

"I'm going to try to convince him to leave us the hell alone."

"Belle, don't do this. Talk to your brother and sisters about it, at least. Russell's the one it has to do with the most. All he has to do is let 'that man,' as you call him, have the whole inheritance, and that will be that."

"You've said yourself that Greener will never be content with just that. And Russell's too spineless to confront him . . ."

"Your disdain for your brother is only equaled by your recklessness," flared Genevieve, cutting her off. "You think you're invincible, Belle, but you're no match for Professor Greener, believe me. Don't go to Chicago to see him!"

Genevieve might seem mild-mannered, but none of the children dared to defy her will. Though she expressed it only rarely, when she did have an opinion, she did not budge from it. And they all respected her views.

Belle had written to Berenson more than once that her mother was the ideal chaperone, that her mother invariably bowed to her will, that she was free to do whatever she wanted. She was deluding herself. She had far less influence over Genevieve than Genevieve had over her.

The truth was that if Genevieve put her foot down and ordered Belle not go to Chicago, Belle wouldn't go.

So much the better.

In any case, the idea of a meeting with Greener was repellent to Belle. She had resolved to do it only for the sake of her family's survival. Driven only by reason and caution.

*Leave us alone.*

She had other troubles, besides. Other sorrows to overcome. Her beloved Quaritch had just died. He had fallen ill during the second part of the Hoe sale, with a case of influenza from which he'd never recovered.

Quaritch had been the only librarian Jack trusted. Without him, Belle had no one to back up the advice she gave her new employer.

So far, in that autumn of 1913, the books and manuscripts of the Morgan Library were still safe. Jack couldn't sell them until the matter of Morgan's will had been wholly settled. But what then? Art dealers were already circling like sharks. There could be no question of parting with *Le Morte d'Arthur*, or Lord Amherst's seventeen Caxtons—or any of the masterpieces Belle had collected over the past eight years! As long as she was still working on the inventory, there was no danger. On the other hand, the works of art were under immediate threat. She had to find an expert to protect them! She had suggested Jacques Seligman, the man chosen by the Big Chief to assist with the Prince's Gate collection. But Jack's reaction had been appalling: *A Jew?!* So she had proposed Bernhard Berenson next. His reply to this had been even worse. *That dirty kike?*

Jack saw Berenson as a corrupt historian who worked for the Duveen family of art dealers and was rewarded with a percentage of every transaction in which he participated. A man to be avoided.

Combating his prejudices was utterly exhausting. Steering him toward other opinions required immense effort. And keeping him from making mistakes, without angering him, demanded so much skill that Belle had forgotten that Richard T. Greener even existed.

Until the third letter arrived.

Greener was stepping up his efforts to intimidate her; this envelope was addressed to Belle Marion *Greener*. Even Thursty, delivering a stack of mail, noticed the error. Who *was* this professor that kept sending them letters and couldn't even write the name of the recipient correctly?

As bad luck would have it, the latest missive from Professor Greener landed on Belle's desk just as she was receiving some extraordinary news from B.B. He was coming to the United States. Belle wrote back to him immediately that she would be waiting joyfully to welcome him.

They had not seen one another in three years.

He would arrive in America in late December 1913, he wrote. He would not be staying in Manhattan, because he had business in Boston with his patron Mrs. Gardner, but he would return to New York in the first week of January. And then he would be all hers.

Richard Greener was demanding a meeting in Chicago that same week.

\*

Bernhard Berenson, accompanied by his wife, settled at the Hotel Belmont, where Belle had reserved them a suite with a sitting room and two bedrooms, just a few blocks from her own apartment. Entering their rooms, husband and wife each found a bouquet of orchids accompanied by a calling card. Mary's contained the single word *Welcome!*, while B.B.'s was slightly longer:

"*Daaarling,*

"*I have to go away tonight, to meet a man I haven't seen in more than twenty years. I'll be back as soon as possible. Don't try to come after me. If anyone learned who I am going to see, it would be disastrous for more than one person.*"

The sight of these words made B.B. feel he would lose his mind.

At that very moment, Belle was boarding the New York–Chicago train at Grand Central Station. The high-speed express train belonged to one of Jack Morgan's companies. The platform was carpeted in red, and there were three sleeping cars and a restaurant car. True luxury. She would travel 911 miles in twenty hours—with no idea of what to expect once she arrived.

She had replied to Greener's last letter with an unsigned telegram—it was imperative to leave no trace of any link to him—in which she agreed to meet him the next day, and said she would let him know when she arrived in Chicago. She specified neither a time nor a place for their encounter.

She'd thought of staying at the Palmer House, the most expensive hotel in Chicago, and inviting Greener to meet her at the bar. But then it had occurred to her that it might not be the best idea, given the nature of this meeting, to make such an ostentatious display of her wealth. Nor was it a good idea to leave herself open to the possibility of being seen with *that man* in a place frequented by many of her well-heeled acquaintances.

Who knew what state Greener was in now? Had his failures made him look worn and haggard, or was he still as handsome as ever? How old would he be now? Seventy. He must have aged a great deal.

Should she offer to meet him at his residence? The house he shared with his Platt cousins on Ellis Avenue? That wasn't a good idea, either. Better not to negotiate on his home turf.

In a restaurant?

She spent the whole night on the train trying to figure out a place for them to meet, and yet she absolutely could not picture the scene.

The closer she got to him, the more her fear and anger gave way to a sort of curiosity, even excitement. The idea of seeing him was less unpleasant than she'd expected. Though she had thought him banished from her memory, a thousand memories were assailing her now—and some of them were good ones.

She gazed absently at the green porcelain globe of the lamp fixture, wobbling with the train's movement. She remembered those winter evenings in Georgetown when her father's tall figure would round the corner of T Street after months of absence; remembered, too, how her little's girl's heart had thumped with excitement as she awaited that first glimpse of him. She saw him as he had been then, tall and slim, divinely elegant in his overcoat. She had always dressed up as if for a church festival to greet him, tying white ribbon bows on the ends of her pigtails and helping herself to Louise's best hat. She always ran through the snow to meet him, like a fiancée hurrying toward her sweetheart.

There on that train rocketing through the night, Belle realized that she remembered everything. The sound of his voice, his scent. His short, curling, perfectly trimmed beard, redolent of hair oil and lavender. He had always been so careful with his appearance.

So arrogant, too.

She shook herself.

*No dreaming. No illusions.*

She must not forget his coldness to Genevieve, or the way he had treated them all. The man had talked about nothing but Knowledge and Freedom, but he had tyrannized his wife and refused to pay a penny toward his children's education. He'd left for the other side of the world without saying goodbye, and without worrying about how his dependents would survive in his absence.

*No. Don't forget that.*

Behind his idealistic façade, Greener was nothing but a self-indulgent *bon vivant* who lorded his high-flown principles of equality over his family and the whole Black community. He loved power. His brothers in arms had certainly reproached him enough for it over the years.

And he loved money, which was always in short supply. But when it came to his own pleasure, he knew how to spend! After all these years of abandonment, what was he hoping to gain from this meeting, if not money?

She stepped off the train onto the platform at Union Station on Monday, January 5 at 9:26 A.M., even more confused and agitated than she had been when she left New York. The icy wind blowing off the river cut her to the bone. She quickened her steps in search of a hansom that would take her to the ladies' guest house recommended by the ticket inspector.

At the sight of the modest room, she recoiled. She had forgotten the dampness, the chill that reigned between walls like these.

The washbasin and jug, the old quilt on the bed, the hideous wallpaper. How long had it been since she'd slept in such a dreary place?

The luxury of her existence in Manhattan had made her forget how normal people lived.

She sat down gingerly on the stained armchair.

*What on earth am I doing here?* She thought, looking around the room. *What the hell am I doing in Chicago? To think that I sacrificed the joy of seeing B.B. again for this—to meet that bastard Greener. I must be losing my marbles!*

She shivered and lifted her overnight bag into her lap, hugging it to her body as if it would warm her up.

*What if I turned around and went home now?*

She pulled the rail schedule from her purse. The next train back to New York was that evening. She could take care of business and be back in Manhattan by tonight.

Or she could forget about business and leave now.

*Come on, buck up. You're already here. Telephone him, at least . . . But what will I say?*

Genevieve's words came back to her: "You have nothing to offer him!"

*I could tell him that Russell is dead. That the whole Wears inheritance is his. But I could have telegraphed him that from New York. No—don't write anything to him, ever. No traces. And anyway, the Wears inheritance will never be enough for him.*

She tried, as she always did before a sale, to calculate a budget for the operation. How much was Professor Richard Greener's silence worth?

*I need to set a limit for myself, like at an auction. How much am I prepared to offer him, for him to leave us in peace? Hard to tell . . . I have no idea what he's going to demand. How high am I willing to go?*

At length, she went down to the front desk and asked for the telephone directory.

Her heart thumped in her chest. She stood for a long moment before summoning her courage and picking up the receiver. The thought of speaking to her father was suddenly terrifying.

She turned the crank and gave the number.

Professor Greener was out, a woman's voice informed her.

Belle, who had been girding her loins to hear her father's voice, was both relieved and disappointed. He would be back late that afternoon, the woman continued. Who was calling, please? Belle hesitated, then murmured, low:

"His daughter."

There was a silence.

"Louise?"

"No."

"Belle? Ethel? Teddy?"

Belle didn't answer. She couldn't bring herself to give her name. Fortunately, the woman didn't wait for a response. She went on, volubly:

"This is Cousin Mary! Your father will be so happy to see you again! Is your mother with you? You must all come to the house for tea! The dear professor won't be back before five."

"I'm alone, and I don't have much time. I'm leaving Chicago tonight."

"Come earlier, if you like! We can have a nice chat while you wait for him."

"Thank you. I'll do my best."

Belle hung up, chagrined. How very typical of the "dear professor" and his ego, to demand a meeting in a distant city and then vanish until the evening of the appointed day!

And to force her to meet him in his own home, on his own territory, which was precisely what she had wanted to avoid.

As for Cousin Mary, who seemed to be on such intimate terms with the family and knew the first names of all the dear professor's children, Belle had never met her. She'd heard that Greener had moved in with four sisters, relatives on his mother's side, all of them widowed or unmarried. But there had only been one name listed in the telephone book for the address on Ellis Avenue: Ida Platt, Attorney at Law. Belle knew *her*, if only by reputation.

During the years that Greener had lived with them, he had

endlessly cited his cousin Ida as a paragon of perfection. Mixed race like Genevieve, but twenty years younger. She was enchanting, he said. A great musician, as well, and a skilled pianist.

Like Genevieve. *Better* than Genevieve.

Ida had been admitted to the bar in Illinois: an extraordinary triumph for the Black community! She was the first Black woman to earn a law degree in that state, having studied in Chicago, and the first to open her own law office. The only one in the United States with a large and important roster of clients. Greener considered Ida to be a model of success for all African Americans. A prodigy, like himself. His alter ego.

Greener had always been a champion of female emancipation and the equality of the sexes. In theory, at least.

The fact that he had chosen to spend his sunset years living with Ida was a testament to their affinity. And at any rate, he couldn't live without the adoration of women. He'd always been surrounded by admiring females endlessly singing his praises. And the prospect of seeing the impressive Cousin Ida in his thrall irritated Belle tremendously.

Nor did she have any desire to set foot in the Black quarter— the "Black Belt," as they called it—of Chicago, which was said to be overcrowded and dangerous. She had done what was necessary to leave and never look back. And now, sixteen years later, her father was drawing her back in.

She shuddered at the thought of returning to that world, of which she wished to know nothing. Shuddered, too, at the idea of being seen. Even though she knew she would not cross paths with anyone of her acquaintance there, she didn't trust random chance.

But how to extricate herself?

Getting out of the cab in front of the attractive Queen Anne-style house on the corner of Ellis Avenue and 52nd Street, Belle thought she must have come to the wrong address. These upscale homes, some of them with tall Christmas trees still visible through their bow windows; these broad white-frosted lawns; these tidy white fences . . . She questioned the driver, and he confirmed that there was no other Ellis Avenue in Chicago. So this was indeed the Hyde Park neighborhood. And she had had no need to worry about the denizens of the neighboring Black Belt. The residents of Hyde Park had imposed very strict laws protecting the white community from any intrusion. Any real estate agent daring to sell a house in this part of the city to a Black person would have paid for it with their livelihood.

She couldn't believe it. Greener, the famous Black activist, was living in the most racist white neighborhood in the city—an area directly adjoining the ghetto but which absolutely prohibited any race-mixing. It was surprising, to say the least.

The sun had gone down, and a freezing wind was blowing off Lake Michigan. Her shoes slipping on the icy pavement, Belle made her way carefully up the walk that led to the Platt residence. All the windows were brightly lit, and she saw a shadow move behind the lace curtains in the turret on one corner of the house. She had to cling to the railing to climb the slippery porch steps.

At the door she hesitated again, taking the time to smooth her long fur coat and adjust her hat before ringing the bell. Hardly had the chime sounded when a petite woman opened the door. They eyed each other. Cousin Mary? A servant? The woman did not introduce herself. She was perhaps sixty years of age, and plump. And white.

"Tea is ready in the professor's study in the turret," she said, her tone neutral.

This was a very different tone from this morning's telephone call. No more familial congeniality. The "dear professor" must have given other instructions. *No warm welcomes, please!* The woman did not offer to take Belle's coat.

"His office is this way."

Belle followed her hostess up two flights of stairs, noting the

piano in the living room on the way, as well as the air of comfort
that prevailed in the whole house. But she was too tense to register any more detail than that. On the uppermost landing, the
petite woman indicated the door.

"Here it is." She gave Belle a nod and vanished.

Before Belle could knock, she heard her father's voice.

"Come in."

She pushed the door open and stood there on the threshold.

He was writing. He sat very straight at his desk the way he
always had, his back not even touching his chair, the surface of
the desk covered with a collection of Chinese vases and Japanese
bowls and bronze Buddhas, piles of books and papers.

Unchanged, except for one thing: his hair and beard had
turned completely white. Belle found herself shocked by it. Not
that he looked older. On the contrary, he was more handsome
than ever. But he had lost the only trait that spoke of his African
American origins. His hair, in changing from ebony-black to
snow-white, made him look like a nineteenth-century statesman.
With his trim white beard, his combed and waxed mustache, his
English-style wing collar and silk necktie, he might have been an
aristocratic member of the House of Lords, or an American con-
gressman.

Though seated, he looked down his nose at his visitor. It was
a proud look, without a hint of tenderness.

"So *you've* come, have you?"

His voice had not changed either. It was still the deep, powerful voice of an orator who knew how to wield his eloquence
and modulate his inflections.

"I'm the one you wrote to," she said, coolly.

She was still standing in the doorway, struggling to rein in her
emotions. The sight of her father was far more unsettling than
she had expected. She felt as if she were turning back into a little girl. That unappreciated little girl who always tried so hard to
please him.

As incapable now as she had been then of the slightest ease in his company. No humor, no lightness, no insolence.

Constant tension. In his presence, she didn't recognize herself.

"I was expecting Russell," he said.

He had always preferred the company of his son. He must be disappointed.

"Sorry," she said ironically.

"I suppose your brother has given you a message for me?"

"May I sit down?"

He gestured at a chair across from his own.

She feigned interest in the tea tray sitting on a low table. "It's even colder here than in New York. I'm frozen. Would you like some? I'm going to have a cup."

Without waiting for his answer, she poured two cups and handed one to him. Their eyes met, and they both looked down hastily, as if fascinated by the color of the tea.

The only sound in the room was the clinking of spoons against the fine china. Neither of them took sugar, so the stirring was pointless, serving only to betray their mutual unease.

*Make small talk*, she ordered herself. *Don't get right to the heart of the matter. A bit of casual chit-chat before the attack.*

But she couldn't think of a single thing to say. Eventually she ventured, "I suppose the Chicago climate must seem absolutely tropical to you, after Vladivostok."

"After Vladivostok, I find everything tepid," he muttered.

*Get him to talk about* himself, she thought. *Only about himself. That's the only thing that interests him.*

"Did you enjoy your life there?"

"My life, no. But the adventure . . . Russia, China, Japan." He fingered the five-pointed star enameled in blue that he wore on his lapel. "In thanks for my actions during the Boxer Rebellion, the emperor of China awarded me the Order of the Double Dragon."

He fell silent, momentarily lost in memories. She noticed that he was puffing his chest out slightly, as if the medal made up for everything else that had happened. She smirked inwardly. He was still as immature, still as naïve and vain as always. Had he worn the decoration to impress her? Undoubtedly. Though, in all probability, he wore it every day. His need for adulation, to feel himself important, was so great!

She knew he'd been dismissed from his diplomatic post for unbecoming conduct. That he'd been accused of overindulging in drink, gambling, women. Of having a big mouth and meddling in political matters that didn't concern him.

Hadn't he been recalled to the United States in a humiliating manner, and against his will?

What Belle did not know, and would never learn, was that "over there" he had lived for eight years with a Japanese woman in what was for all intents and purposes a marriage. That she had borne him three children. That he had left those two sons and a little daughter without resources, forcing their mother to raise and support them alone.

He had always planned to go back and live with them again.

Now, however, he knew that was impossible. And his Japanese "wife," left forlorn by his abandonment and the silence that had followed, had just written to him that she wanted nothing more to do with him.

Instinctively, Belle sensed that she needed to show herself to be amenable now, to reassure him and comfort him in the image he was trying to project.

"The Order of the Double Dragon?" she marveled. "An immense honor for a foreigner! You must have done extraordinary things."

"I protected tradesmen and helped the Chinese citizens to survive in extremely difficult conditions."

He was growing more animated now. She let him continue.

"But it wasn't only the Chinese I helped. I also protected

Japanese civilians during the Russo-Japanese war. The emperor of Japan wished to decorate me, too. And what did that racist bastard Roosevelt do? Instead of sending my name to the emperor, he gave him the name of my replacement—and it was that fellow, who arrived in Vladivostok three years after the war, who was decorated in my place. And can you guess the name of the usurper? The ultimate impostor?"

Belle shrugged her shoulders, wide-eyed.

"*Greene!*" he barked.

The accusation was so clear—he had spat the single word with such disgust—that she couldn't refrain from protesting. "That Greene has nothing to do with us!"

"*Roger Greene*, instead of Richard Greener. Funny, isn't it? And Russell Greener—or Russell *Greene*, rather—is robbing me of my due now, as well."

There it was. The first shot had been fired; the battle was underway. Belle jumped in with both feet. Enough of this.

"Russell Greener is dead. He no longer exists. And Mr. Russell da Costa Greene, a young engineer who has no connection to you, is never going to come here to claim an inheritance that doesn't concern him. I suggest, therefore, that you have your son officially declared dead and claim the entire legacy for yourself."

"You've thought of everything, I see. But what guarantee can you give me that the late Russell Greener won't ever come back to life?"

"My presence here. And my word, which I'm giving you."

"The word of a person who's betrayed her own blood? You'll forgive me if that doesn't mean a great deal."

She leapt to her feet.

"I haven't betrayed anyone!"

"You've disowned your own people."

"The Black community was never my people!"

He thumped his desk with a fist. Greener was well known for the violence of his rages.

"In taking on the prejudices of whites," he declaimed, his hand coming down on the desk with each word, "in vindicating their claims of superiority, you're shoving us all down, keeping us from advancing. It's because of people like you that the Blacks of this country are farther from equality than ever."

"I don't see how my success harms anyone else," she shot back.

"The success of a single Black individual lifts up all the others and proves that all men are equal. Your pride in your roots should be stronger than your shame. If you weren't a coward, you would own your successes—not as a white woman, but as a Black one!"

"And if *you* weren't a coward, you wouldn't be living in Hyde Park!"

Both of them had abandoned any attempt at self-control.

He acknowledged the jab. "If I live in a white neighborhood, ride in a whites-only railcar, dine in a white restaurant, it's because I refuse to stay behind the fence that separates Blacks from whites. There is no concealment on my part. I'm not trying to deceive anyone, like you are; I am resisting. I refuse to obey any Jim Crow law, period. I refuse segregation in all its forms. I refuse to accept that our people remain in chains, while other Americans talk of nothing but the glorious liberty that reigns in our country. Unlike your mother and the rest of you, I do not lie. I have never cheated; I have never tried to pass myself off as what I am not."

"Wrong! Dead wrong!" Belle's cheeks were scarlet. *The hypocrisy of the man!* "Do you know why you can get away with defying the Jim Crow laws? Because you look white! But what would happen if your neighbors on Ellis Avenue learned the truth?"

"I've never hidden it from them."

"Nonsense! If they knew your origins, they'd drag you out of this house by force."

"That's their problem, not mine. I sign my own name to the

articles I write, calling them out for their ignorance and their cruelty. I rail against the passivity of Blacks who accept their oppression. And I give my address to anyone who asks. Without hesitation."

"And you live off your four mixed-race cousins who also pass themselves off as whites. As I understand it, the very successful law office of Ida Platt, Esquire only handles cases for white clients."

"I don't live off anyone, and I pay my own rent here."

She had hit a nerve. Both were silent for a moment.

Belle flushed. She hadn't come here to insult him.

How could she fail to be touched by the rage of this old lion who continued to stand firm against persecution? She recognized the greatness of his fight. His battles were just and had cost him dearly.

"I understand your bitterness toward us," she said, not without a hint of sadness. "Who wouldn't be bitter in your place, given the many injustices you have faced? Everything's been taken from you. Because you were a colored man. Everything. Your professorship at the University of South Carolina, your law office in Washington, your position as secretary to the Grant Monument Association, your consulship in Russia, and now the decorations that were rightfully yours. Because you were a colored man, your energy, your talent, and all your hard work have earned you nothing in the end. And you admit yourself that the situation of the Black community is more desperate than ever. How, then, can you blame your family for wanting to escape this curse? Why come after us with your threatening letters? Why don't you leave us in peace?"

He had risen and was standing over her, tall and fearsome.

"You are living proof of my failure," he ground out, his voice full of hatred. "Of the failure of all my beliefs and all my struggles. You embody the death of my dreams."

"I embody the existence you would have liked to have, yes!"

she retorted, matching his hostile tone. "I am leading exactly the life you wanted, the life you worked for. Didn't *you* want to study art history, write books, visit Italy? Didn't *you* want to live among books and paintings, and travel? Oh, and one more thing: I'm supporting your wife and all your children on my salary. A family whose most basic needs you could never meet."

He turned away from her abruptly and went to the window, pulling aside the curtain and gazing out into the night.

"I recognize that you have done what very few people not born into wealthy or powerful families ever manage to do," he said, wearily. "And moreover, you have done it as a woman. I commend your strength. Admire it, even, as it should allow you to endure what your people endure every day. In owning your origins, you would be showing the world what a Black woman is capable of. You would embody the fight for liberty. You would be part of this glorious work. You would make history."

He walked slowly back to his desk and sat down. "My own life might have been a failure, as you say, but at least I chose the honest path. You have opted for the selfish road: individual success. I believe that the real fight, real progress, consists of raising oneself up as a colored person. That person is building not only the history of the Black people, but that of humanity."

"In a word," she said tartly, "you belong to the category of men who change the world, and I to the category of those who succeed."

"Your words, not mine. Change the world. For if we do not—like Esau, who lost his soul in selling his birthright for a bowl of stew—we choose the less worthy path. If you are content with that, so much the better. Yes—if it has allowed you to vanquish your fear; if you feel free, truly *free*, at last, so much the better."

Once again, they were both silent.

He picked up his pen and resumed writing, as if his work had never been interrupted.

She sat, listening to the scratch of pen against paper. She couldn't bring herself to leave things this way.

His final "so much the better" had contained none of his previous anger, but rather a kind of resignation. And even forgiveness. She wanted to tell him that she accepted his choices, too, that she understood them. But how? He was no longer paying any attention to her. It was as if she no longer existed for him.

And yet, in his last words to her, she had sensed a desire for peace.

She rose. Looking at the curve of her father's neck, she was gripped by a rush of emotion. He seemed so vulnerable, suddenly.

But she couldn't muster the courage to ask him the questions whose answers she wanted most desperately to know.

*If it wasn't to talk about money, why did you want me to come?*

He remained silent, merely continued writing. The look they had shared, it seemed, had been enough for him.

*If it wasn't about the inheritance*, she cried in her head, *why did you want to see me?*

Something moved across his face. The shadow of a smile. A hint of affection. He looked up. Considered her with softness, now.

And there was something else, too. A kind of mutual admiration that soothed them both.

As if she recognized her father's excellence. As if he saw, in the elegant woman standing before him, his own flesh and blood. His daughter.

He had always been appreciative of feminine charm, of beauty and intelligence. In these areas, his eyes said, she had achieved perfection.

*Father*, she begged him in her heart. *What do you want from me?*

Sidestepping the questions he read in her eyes, he said, "I don't think there's anything for either of us to add, is there?"

She shook her head, breathless.

Both knowing that this moment would be the last they ever shared, they had no need of farewells to say goodbye.

She left.

Outside, she realized that she had never even taken off her hat and coat.

She returned to New York that very night. The interview had lasted less than half an hour. Nothing about it had gone the way she'd thought it would.

She came home shaken to her very core.


Richard T. Greener had raised questions that she didn't know how to resolve. Incited doubts that she could no longer ignore.

One thing was certain: he had become a man of worth in her eyes once again.

A deeply flawed man, to be sure.

But a person of integrity, and magnificent courage. A father whose daughter she was proud to be.

Brave, and good, the way she liked them.

What had he said, exactly: that she had sold her soul for the illusion of immediate pleasure? That, to be free—*truly free, at last*—she would have to have the courage to be who she really was?

Could she find the strength in herself to tell Jack Morgan her true origins?

Claim her own history, and reveal her secret?

Her father had awakened in her a temptation she had never expected to feel.

# CHAPTER 11

TEMPTATIONS
JANUARY 1914–FEBRUARY 1924

T emperamental, moody, contradictory, and unreliable"
was how Mary Berenson described Belle upon her return
from Chicago.

To hear Mary tell it, her poor Bernhard was enduring a living
hell.

Though Belle had seen B.B. every day, arranged meetings for
him with collectors, done everything in her power to serve him,
lunched and dined and slept with him, she was manifestly no
longer in love with him. She admitted as much without shame.
She continued to feel deep and lasting affection for him.
Tenderness, admiration, even veneration. He remained, she
said, the love of her life. But yes, she was sleeping with the publisher Mitchell Kennerley. So what? Yes, Kennerley had her
read all the manuscripts he was planning to publish. Yes, he purchased her preferred brand of face powder in Paris. Yes, he had
chosen her new perfume, Houbigant's Essence de Violette. Yes,
they spent much of their time together, both day and night. So
what?

When B.B. forbade her from seeing Kennerley again, she
merely shrugged her shoulders. "But, my dear, that's a terrible
idea. Because when I *don't* see M.K., it only makes me want to
see him even more!"

Mary, for her part, had withdrawn her support of B.B.'s liaison with Belle. While she didn't go so far as to call her a whore,
it was obvious that *the Greene woman* had fallen dramatically
out of favor.

Clearly, Mrs. Berenson said, J.P. Morgan's death had

removed the last of the impediments keeping his librarian on the straight and narrow. Belle drank more than ever, swore, smoked, flirted, and frequented the most outrageous denizens of the bohemian demimonde. Not content merely to keep up her old habits, she allowed herself to entertain countless other solicitations as well. B.B., in his jealousy, demanded to be informed of these.

"All right," Belle responded flippantly. "You want to know about every one of my temptations? That's fine."

Matter-of-factly, she began to reel them off.

Temptation number one: to see Harold Mestre again. Her former fiancé claimed not to be able to live without her and was begging her once more to marry him. What to do? Dine and dance with him? Newly returned from San Francisco, he simply would not leave her alone. "I've told him that all proposals of marriage will be considered in alphabetical order as soon as I turn fifty."

Temptation number two: to accept the job offer made by the French art dealer Seligman, who wanted her to manage the New York branch of his company at an annual salary of fifteen thousand dollars.

Temptation number three: to accept kickbacks from the Duveen family of art dealers, who were offering her a commission on every object she advised Jack Morgan to sell them. "They think I'm an idiot," she chuckled, recounting the anecdote to B.B. "Allowing myself to be bought off by the Duveens would make me as rotten as they are—and destroy my reputation, to boot!"

Was she not aware that Berenson himself worked for them, and received twenty-five percent of the profits on transactions encouraged by his certifications of authenticity, and on all the business he referred to them? Or *was* she aware of it, and simply making fun of him?

B.B.'s head swam with conjectures, but he did not confide in her about his secret arrangement with the Duveens. Nor did she tell him about the only true temptation in her life.

Since the encounter with her father, Belle had felt so troubled, so lost, that she suddenly felt as if Berenson, Kennerley, Thursty, and all her other close friends belonged to a completely different period of her life. She had tried hard to pick up the threads of her previous existence, and at times she had almost succeeded, only to drop them again. Not even Jack Morgan, not even her brother and sisters, not even her mother could really ground her in the present reality anymore.

Everyone put her absent quality down to exhaustion, and perhaps depression. To her grief at the Big Chief's death, and the heavy workload of drawing up an inventory of all his possessions. To the fear of seeing his most beautiful masterpieces scattered to the four winds and of failing to save the Morgan Library, and the need to build a new relationship with "Mr. Jack." Perhaps, they thought, it was all just too much.

How could any of them possibly guess the truth: that she was dwelling on an unfinished conversation? An endless internal monologue on the future, the very survival, of her own loved ones?

*Could it be that Father was right, after all? That none of us will ever find peace, unless we tell the truth?*

\*

"You're going to identify yourself as a colored woman? *You?*" Genevieve had screamed the words.

"I never said that!" protested Belle.

Locked into the bathroom so that no one would see them argue—or, more importantly, *hear* them—mother and daughter were embroiled in a conflict fiercer than any they had ever had. And of the two, it was Genevieve who was the more vehement.

"It would be suicide!" she raged. "You'll lose everything! And for what? Just to satisfy that silver-tongued huckster—just to please your *father!*"

Belle's confession of having gone to Chicago, and the belated account she had just given her mother of the trip, had unleashed a wave of absolute, uncontrollable terror in Genevieve. None of her children had ever seen her in such a state of panic, not even once.

"I never said that!" Belle repeated. "I've just been thinking about what might happen if Louise's husband or Ethel's fiancé found out that we aren't who we claim to be. Or if Russell's very chic and very racist girlfriend found out that he's deceiving her, that he isn't a van Vliet, or a da Costa, or a Greene. That he's not descended from an old Virginia family, much less the Dutch or Portuguese aristocracy, but from an African tribe. And, even worse, if their children should learn that they aren't who they thought they were—that they'd been lied to about their origins—that everything about their lives, absolutely *everything*, is a lie?"

Genevieve clutched Belle's arm and shook it furiously. For her, normally so placid, the gesture was startlingly violent.

"Why did you go to see your father behind my back?"

Backed up against the bathtub, Belle tried vainly to free herself, to explain.

It was no use.

Genevieve would not listen. "We've talked about this before, and I *forbade* you to do it!" She took a deep breath before pressing on. "Did he even ask about us? About his son and daughters? Or anyone? No, of course not. He doesn't give a damn! And you come back with your head and your heart in a complete mess! *Why* did you visit him, when you *knew* how I felt?"

"To resolve the stalemate."

"What stalemate?"

"The blackmail. The fighting. I don't know—to put an end to

the fear. Family secrets lead to so much disaster! And I was thinking of the consequences for Russell's children, too, and Louise's, and Ethel's. The consequences for future generations are so—"

Genevieve lost what little composure she'd had left.

"*Consequences!*" she shrieked. "You should have thought of that before, Belle! *Before!* Let me remind you—you're the one who wanted to pass for white! You're the one who imposed silence on all of us. *You're* the one who made us keep the secret! And that vow is just as binding for you—*more* so—than it is for any of us! And let me also remind you, in case you've forgotten, that you're not the only one involved here. Louise married a white man last year. Ethel and Russell are about to marry whites. The die is cast. There is no going back!"

Belle reached over to unlock the door and leave the bathroom. Genevieve seized her arm again.

"Just one more question, my girl, before I let you walk out of here: just how far has your father brainwashed you? I lived with his powers of persuasion for twenty years; I know how good he is at it. But are you really ready to give up your beloved books, in the name of 'truth'? To lose your incunabula, your codices, in order not to lie anymore? Your seventy-six Coptic manuscripts that are being restored at the Vatican Library as we speak?"

Belle looked away.

"Look at me!" ordered Genevieve.

Taking Belle's chin in her hand, just like her own mother, Hermione, had taken hers during their last discussion in Georgetown, fifteen years earlier, Genevieve put her face very close to her daughter's.

"Answer me this: can you give up the Morgan Library?"

Eyes downcast, Belle allowed herself to be examined, scrutinized, studied to the very core of her being.

She searched her own conscience at the same time.

Finally, she shook her head.

"I want to hear you say it," Genevieve commanded. "Can you give up the library?"

"No."

Belle's tone was flat. Final.

"Well then, muzzle that conscience of yours and shut up! Do you hear me? Keep your mouth shut. Remember your grandmother's words: *'If you renounce your true selves, may your secret stay safe.'* If none of us give the truth away, no one will ever know it."

"So be it," murmured Belle, ceding to her mother's will.

"Now. Come into the living room and help me oversew your sister's wedding veil."

The subject was closed. Forever, they thought.

*

The shock of the encounter with Greener had, nevertheless, opened up some new horizons for Belle. One of these was a renewed interest in Asia, and there were others, as fresh as they were exciting.

She began to study Chinese history, culture, and philosophy, tutored by the great sinologist Friedrich Hirth, professor at Columbia University.

There were meetings in Professor Hirth's home with a young and particularly charming Japanese scholar, a specialist in China, Taoism, and Lao-Tze.

There were travels with B.B. in the northern United States, to visit the country's most prominent Asian art collector, Charles Freer.

There were long weeks of work in Detroit, on Freer's collection of pottery, bronzes, sculptures, and paintings.

"I love the immensity, the mysticism, the self-forgetfulness of Chinese landscapes," she wrote to her admirer Sydney Cockerell, curator of the Fitzwilliam Museum in Cambridge, England.

"My time with Freer, under the guidance of our old friends Mary and Bernhard Berenson, has changed my artistic life yet again, and allowed me to look beyond certain strictures of European art. A revelation!"

What Belle did not tell Cockerell was that the exploration of these masterpieces in the company of "our old friends" had reignited a passion in her that refused to die.

To the very depths of her soul, she shared with B.B. the thirst for knowledge, the hunger to know as much as possible. He had already begun purchasing Chinese art in New York before the trip to Detroit and would continue to do so afterward, soon coming to dominate that segment of the market and becoming one of the foremost specialists in Asian *objets d'art*.

Looking, *seeing*, with Berenson remained a breathtaking experience, stronger, much stronger for Belle than any other. And if Mary had thought their love was on the wane, she was largely mistaken.

More smitten and more in harmony than ever, they had hardly come back from Detroit when they were off to Baltimore to visit another art collection.

"On one hand," she wrote to him upon returning from one of their jaunts, "I hate myself for not having understood immediately, when you came to New York, all that you would mean to me. On the other, I'm so glad to have realized it before it was too late. My joy at sharing these moments with you has been even greater, perhaps, than our happiness in Italy.

"It was wonderful to be crazy about you once, wonderful to be in love with you the way I was four years ago. But loving you the way I do now is unquestionably deeper, truer, more real. Don't you agree?"

No. Berenson did not agree. He would have greatly preferred her love for him to be less "deep," for her to be more "crazy about him," the way she had been four years ago.

But as they approached yet another separation, their renewed passion allowed him to believe that he hadn't lost her. That Belle Greene was his for life, come what may, and that he could return to the Villa I Tatti in peace, or nearly so.

And so they parted calmly, swearing to meet again soon.

Belle was in desperate need of that serenity. For the day after B.B.'s departure was the anniversary of the Big Chief's death.

March 31, 1914. One year without him.

She would close the bronze doors of the Morgan Library, draw the blinds in the windows of its three rooms, and celebrate in silence, alone with Mr. Jack in the West Room, the memory of the man they had both loved so much.

"It was one of the hardest days of my life," she wrote to B.B. on April 1, "and I am still in a stupor."

*

"You and Jack seem to be getting on well enough, I see," announced Junius grumpily, taking a seat in Belle's office.

Junius! *My mad, bad, beloved Junius!*

She was so happy to see him. How many years had it been without a word from him?

She gazed at him fondly.

He had hardly changed, even after all this time. As trim and fine-featured as ever, with his narrow shoulders and boyish physique. Hair a bit sparser, perhaps. The same sensual mouth with that slight disdainful twist to the lips. The intense blue eyes behind gold-rimmed spectacles—the same spectacles he'd worn during the Princeton years. And the same dislike of emotional display, the same use of sarcasm to distance himself from it.

That standoffishness, which had given him such an air of mystery in his youth, had become, at age forty-seven, a rather off-putting sort of detachment.

To this was added his sense of guilt regarding his wife and children, guilt that had stiffened his temperament and put him constantly on the defensive. In this endless dodging of both flattery and reproach, in this resistance to any kind of personal importunement, he had lost the lightness, the suppleness he'd once possessed.

But his caustic sense of humor remained, as well as his air of self-deprecation. And, when it came to Belle, a tenderness that he concealed behind his gentle mockery of her.

"Despite all of your complaints, Miss Belle da Costa Greene, your swearing, your huffing and puffing . . ." He cast an eye around the North Room with its sumptuously painted ceiling, its Renaissance chimney, the books lining its walls, "All around you is nothing but 'order and beauty; luxury, peace, and pleasure'. And at a time when Europe is falling apart, no less. England has declared war on Germany; the Kaiser's troops have entered Brussels; Lorraine is in flames; young Germain Seligman has been sent to the front; and your friend Berenson has changed his name from 'Bernhard' to 'Bernard,' to seem less German—that should tell you all you need to know about the current state of the world! But here, as far as I can tell, nothing ever changes. Miss Greene prospers, and the Morgan Library with her."

It was September 1914, and Junius had allowed himself to be talked into crossing the ocean to attend his daughter Sarah's wedding, which would be performed by three bishops with much pomp at St. George's Church, in the home parish of the late Morgan patriarch.

Junius adored his daughter. There could be no question of his failing to walk her down the aisle.

He was desperate to avoid the endless social niceties at Constitution Hill, however. The thought of receiving guests as master of the house alongside Josie Dear, the need to pretend nothing had changed, exasperated him. And he found his future son-in-law to be a bore, far below what he had aspired to on Sarah's behalf. On this point, as on so many others, he was in disagreement with Josie Dear, who was very much in favor of this socially acceptable young man.

All of these conflicts had plunged him into a state of anxiety he found himself unable to overcome. Despite having just arrived back home, he thought only of returning to France, where other matters awaited him, matters far more important than his family drama.

There was so much to do to care for the wounded who, since the terrible bloodbath of the Battle of the Frontiers on August 22, had been pouring into the American military hospital at Passy. Junius, who had never been a very practical man, had volunteered to serve as quartermaster, finding money for medical supplies and recruiting nurses. His sojourn in the United States was partly intended to raise funds for that purpose.

But his hopes were to be dashed. Woodrow Wilson's America did not wish to hear talk of the war, and clung to its neutrality. Only Junius's cousins Jack and Anne Morgan, ferociously anti-German themselves, were supporting his efforts. They both understood the necessity of aiding France and England, and Jack in particular was working tirelessly, loaning money to English banks and funneling it to them secretly by way of Canada.

For the rest, though, Junius was no longer part of their world—except when it came to the white marble palace whose design he had once overseen, his late uncle's magnificent library on 36th Street.

He made a great show of arranging his visits in advance, and of signing the guest book like any other foreign visitor admitted to the temple, but the truth was that he showed up every morning and spent entire days in the vast reading room—except for his frequent side-trips to the North Room, where his former protégée reigned. He would sit down across the desk from her and bend assiduously over the catalogues she handed him.

No indiscreet questions, Belle, please. Nothing too intimate. She had tried to broach any number of personal subjects, but he resolutely denied her access to all of his secrets.

And so their common ground remained the same as always: their mutual love of rare objects. On this subject, they could talk for hours, their voices low, like two conspirators hatching a plot.

What future did Jack envision for the engravings? The manuscripts? The *objets d'art*? What was happening with the plans to sell them?

". . . when he told me he wanted to get rid of the faïenceries from the Hoentschel collection, I thought I would faint," whispered Belle, exaggerating, as usual. "And when he talked about letting the Iranian antiquities go, I wanted to kill him."

"The Asian collections don't interest him," murmured Junius, leafing through the three hundred pages of Belle's *Inventory*.

It was a gargantuan, positively titanic piece of work.

Marked everywhere, unmistakably, by Belle's genius.

He could be proud of his old pupil. And even proud of himself, for having seen, in the young employee who had drawn up the first catalogue of his donations to Princeton, a librarian of this caliber.

Well aware of Belle's love of flirting, he didn't dare look her in the eye. He was too afraid she would take advantage of his admiration. Nonetheless, he hadn't failed to notice the ways in which she had changed. She was a mature, polished woman now, breathtakingly modern. He had never had much interest in hats and feminine furbelows, and he knew nothing about fashion. But, by God, Belle knew how to display her charms to advantage. No one else could have carried off that outlandish jewelry, the dozens of bracelets on her arms, the wraparound skirts so suggestive of trousers. On her, the couturiers' most daring creations looked not just natural, but elegant.

But enough about her appearance.

He preferred to listen to her accounts, heavily peppered with jokes, of her quarrels with his cousin. A complex relationship if ever there was one. But neither Jack nor Belle ever brought up the possibility of a separation anymore.

"He's gone and chosen that bastard Charles Fairfax Murray to negotiate with the art dealers behind my back. Some artistic adviser—the most ignorant art historian alive!"

Junius couldn't refrain from giving her a sardonic glance over his pince-nez.

"Fairfax Murray . . . the great Berenson's arch-enemy, if I'm not mistaken? Bernard *without* an 'h,' of course. You weren't hoping, by chance, that *he* would be recruited instead, were you?"

She glared at him witheringly.

Could he be sniping at B.B. out of jealousy? Was it possible? Junius refused to tell her anything about his own mistresses, never confessed anything about his dissolute life in Paris, and now he wanted her to confide in him about her affair with B.B.? Well, he could forget it! He already knew too much, anyway. She evaded the topic.

"Your cousin told me that Fairfax Murray might be an idiot, but at least he wasn't a Jew!" Belle rolled her eyes. "But he isn't a *complete* moron, for all that, your cousin; he's even rather intelligent sometimes. He gave permission for all of his father's collections to be put on display at the Metropolitan last year. An incredible event. Historic. Nothing like it had ever been seen in New York, or anywhere in America! He loaned every object we had in New York, and all the wonderful things from Prince's Gate, too. The curators went absolutely insane with desire; it was obvious that they considered all those masterpieces to be theirs from that moment on. Two hundred and sixty Renaissance bronzes, which the public loved; nine hundred miniatures; thirty-nine tapestries; more than fifty paintings by Old

Masters . . . The problems started when it was time to take it all back. Jack has generously donated some of the most precious paintings to the museum—even the Raphael, the *Madonna Colonna*, the painting Mr. Morgan paid the most for. He did it without hesitating. His father would have been proud. Like you, with your Virgils that you donated to the Chancellor Green. And Jack donated almost seven thousand other priceless objects to the Met, too."

"Good! Jack's seen the light, then!" said Junius approvingly. "That's seven thousand pieces that won't be scattered to the four winds. *They're* safe, at least."

Junius had always wanted people—as many people as possible—to be able to enjoy his family's treasures. And Belle's latest idea, her new obsession with opening the library to the public, had been seeded in her by Junius himself, back in their Princeton days. They shared the same dream: for the Morgan Library never to become an empty shell. For the rooms to remain *living* places. For researchers and scholars from all over the world to come and work there freely.

"Safe, I suppose," she grumbled. "The problem is that your cousin still needs money. A lot of money, to pay the inheritance taxes, and the debts, and the twenty million dollars bequeathed in the will. Always the same complaint. He has a fortune in companies, shares, buildings—God knows what else—but no cash. He had to sell his box at the opera for ready money, so goodbye to my lovely little evenings with Madame Butterfly! What's worse is that he's planning to sell Fragonard's *Progress of Love*, which was hanging on the walls at Prince's Gate. If the Duveens manage to get their hands on those four paintings—that Louis XV gave to Madame du Barry, for heaven's sake!—and then sell them to some barbarian, it'll be an irreparable loss for us. I think—I hope—that I've convinced him not to touch any of the library's manuscripts. The ones that were dear to his father's heart, especially."

"Or any of the ones that are dear to yours! Stop with the doom-and-gloom routine, Belle; my dear old cousin is wrapped around your little finger, the same way J.P. was."

She simpered. "You're exaggerating."

"Ha! You've got Jack eating out of your hand. And you know it."

"I hope that's true." She looked thoughtful. "I'll admit that he came back from his last trip to London a changed man. Much more agreeable than before. He even told me that speaking to Charles Read and all the art dealers and British Museum curators made him realize how much they respect me. Don't laugh, Junius, it's true! And I won't deny that I was very touched when Mr. Jack had himself driven straight here when he got back from Europe. He and his wife came to the library without even stopping at home first, and this was after being away for months! Incredible, isn't it? From the ocean liner right to the West Room. Just like *my* Mr. Morgan used to do!"

Junius shook his head. His teasing air had vanished. He knew how much patience it had taken on Belle's part, how much hard work and tact and determination and subtle maneuvering, for his cousin to seek—and find—pleasure in the Morgan Library. She had managed to make her library a refuge, a haven where Jack could relax and forget his anxiety over the war in Europe, his fears for his beloved England. And Junius could only admire her for it.

He could imagine Jack's feelings, as well. His attraction, not to Miss Greene's appearance, or even her intelligence—Junius knew Jack was far too devoted to his wife to be interested, sexually or emotionally, in anyone else—but to the values that Belle espoused.

It was a fascination that Junius himself shared entirely. Hadn't he left everything—financial security, the bank, his family—to follow the siren call of his quest for beauty and knowledge?

"Be careful," he said now, his tone light. "Be very careful, Belle. If you keep telling Jack the history of the Caxtons, and showing him the magnificence of the Gutenberg Bibles, and making him appreciate those illuminations you adore so much, he'll stop going home at all. The love of books is contagious, you know. And my cousin—like *your* Mr. Morgan—is a dyed-in-the-wool capitalist who needs to immerse himself in something other than finance. He dreams of beauty too, and peace, and understanding. He knows what the Morgan Library can be now. For himself, and for his descendants. For America. When he's tied up the loose ends of the succession, you won't be able to get rid of him. Keep sharing the magic of the incunabula with him, and soon you'll have created another omnipresent employer, whose passion for rare books will swallow you whole."

She shook her head, disbelieving. "Mr. Jack will never replace the real Mr. Morgan!"

"Not in your heart, perhaps. But . . . who knows, maybe you'll end up loving him as much as you loved his father. Jack is taking his place everywhere. He's a perfect double. He orders his suits at the same Savile Row tailor in London and smokes the same enormous cigars by the hundreds, which he has shipped from Cuba just like the old man did. He drinks the same Chinese tea, the same brandy, the same Musigny Grand Cru. He puts the same flowers in his buttonhole and has the same fob for his watch-chain. He donates the same sums of money to the same hospitals, makes the same gifts to the same charities. He's reproducing everything, continuing everything! And the same thing will be true with his love of this library. Soon enough he'll be constantly underfoot; mark my words!"

Belle laughed. "Perish the thought!"

Junius chuckled, too. "You'll see. He'll come every day to hear tales of all the wonders in the vault."

"Jack, a permanent resident? What a nightmare!" Belle paused for a moment, thinking. "Actually, you're not entirely wrong. He's taking more of an interest than I expected him to. He's even read a fair amount! I was wrong about him. He has no taste whatsoever, but he's not a boor. Not as much of one as I thought, anyway! And he's braver than I realized. His hatred of the Germans, his resistance to President Wilson's policy of neutrality, his disobeying that policy by sending munitions to France behind Wilson's back . . . I find it all quite impressive. Despite all my efforts to the contrary, I'm touched by some aspects of your cousin's personality. He's truly generous, and truly thoughtful. Unlike you, who never write to the people who care about you! Not even a couple of lines to your loved ones! Indifference personified!"

Junius flushed. *Indifference personified.* His wife and children said the same thing. That he was indifferent, cold, self-absorbed. Accusations, always accusations.

Stung, he rose. It was time to go and change his clothes, to put on a dinner suit for that evening's damnable social engagements.

She tried to keep him from leaving. "I've missed you so much, you know, Junius. I've wondered endlessly how you were. And I was worried about you—terribly worried!"

He waved the admission aside. "Worried? You? Nonsense! You've got no more heart than a goldfish!"

Seeing her expression, he tried to soften the sarcasm.

"I beg you to reassure me, Miss Greene," he said, smiling, "that you haven't suddenly started going in for mawkishness and sentimentality! Don't tell me you've become—horror of horrors—a *romantic*, in your old age?"

With a pang of melancholy, she watched as he left the room, closing the door behind him. She couldn't help feeling, deep down, as if they had never really known each other . . . with the exception, perhaps, of that night in the Roma camp at Princeton. Never truly understood one another. *My mad, bad, beloved Junius.* She had thought they shared so much. Junius, her master, the man to whom she owed *everything*, had no inkling of what she felt for him. Nor of who she truly was.

And vice versa.

Why had he cut ties with his past? Why was he living in Paris, so far from his family? She didn't know.

Two strangers.

\* \* \*

"Ethel, daaarling," she wrote to her sister on stationery still bordered in mourning black two years after the Big Chief's death.

"What is everyday life like as a married woman? Tell me everything! Are you happy? Yes? No? Tell me all of it, my Blonde, all of it! Give me an idea of the conjugal experience!

"You'll never believe what's going on here; it's a miracle: the Morgan Library and I are both doing splendidly—under the protection of six bodyguards, each more handsome than the last!

"Who would've believed it? But it's true; ever since the *Lusitania* was torpedoed by the Germans—more than a hundred Americans died—the war has become a very personal matter for my employer."

What Belle didn't need to spell out for her sister, for the news had made headlines in early July 1915, was that a pro-German activist had attempted to assassinate Jack Morgan. The man, determined to keep Jack from selling arms to France, had gone to the Morgans' country home, where the family was vacationing, and taken Jack's two daughters hostage at gunpoint. Jack and his wife had rushed the man, who had fired, hitting Jack twice in the stomach. The couple had managed to disarm the would-be assassin and tie him up, then handed him over immediately to the police. Jack's wounds had not been life-threatening, and he was recovering gradually.

His cool-headedness during the attack, and his wife's bravery, had won universal, if grudging, respect—even from Belle, who now whole-heartedly admired them both. The only fly in the ointment: Jack was now obsessed with ensuring the safety of his employees at the library. The police feared further assassination attempts because the failed shooter had apparently been acting on orders from Berlin, and his pockets had been stuffed with grenades. Nothing would be easier than blowing up Mr. Morgan in the West Room, where he had set up his permanent professional base—and the Misses Thurston and Greene along with him.

"So you see, he's afraid for my life," Belle wrote to Ethel.

"And now that he has sold the Fragonards and his beautiful collection of porcelains at high prices, thanks to me—I had to lock him in his office so I could negotiate with the Duveens without him, and keep him from allowing himself to be fleeced—he's letting me mistreat him as much as I like.

"I don't mean to say that he's suddenly become susceptible to my charms, though—he remains *scandalously* blind to them, in fact! No, he is utterly in love his wife, and he considers me a dear friend. He's begun asking me to receive his business associates at the Morgan Library, to arrange for his board meetings to be held here, and to help him protect his financial interests, here and in Europe.

"He has even given me permission to purchase any works I think necessary for our collections—and to bid high for important manuscripts. And you know what sort of figures I mean, when it comes to enriching the library.

"And here I thought that everything was frozen—fossilized—done. But I've never had so much freedom!

"Isn't life amazing?"

Bliss, across the board.

In 1915, Belle's relationship with Mr. Morgan the younger

was wonderfully close, almost as close as it had been with the Big Chief.

Without the magic, of course.

But also without the jealous scenes. Without the emotional undertones. And without the quarrels. A harmony all the more unexpected because Jack had always disapproved of his father's intimacy with his librarian.

And as if this minor miracle weren't enough, Belle had just pulled off another: the nomination of her lover, the publisher Mitchell Kennerley, as head of the Anderson Auction Company, the great auction house that had taken charge of the Hoe sale and broken every sale-price record in the international history of book collecting.

With Kennerley as president and chief executive of such an auction house, Belle would have up-to-the-minute knowledge of everything that was about to be put on the market, and would have preferential, even unlimited access to bargains.

Their affinity was not based on passion. They were not madly in love. Rather, theirs was a playful and easy companionship, in which they were equally emotionally invested. With time, their liaison—after beginning as a mere one-night indulgence, among others—had become a stable relationship, rooted in an intimacy far deeper than it appeared on the surface. They shared the same frenetic pace of living, the same tireless work ethic, the same taste for luxury and intense feeling. The same adventuresome nature when it came to pleasure in all its forms. For almost three years now, their affair had been not only physical, but intellectual and spiritual, as well.

In truth, dear B.B. had been wrong when he sneered disdainfully, at first, at the possibility of any competition from "a Kennerley." And right when he had come to fear it. The man was a worthy rival.

Kennerley was thirty-seven years old and charm personified, with energy and imagination to match Belle's own. He was what

Americans referred to, *à la française*, as an "entrepreneur." He had just moved his publishing house to new premises in a six-story building on 58th Street, which he had christened the Mitchell Kennerley Building. The penthouse served as both his private clubhouse and storage for his stock of unsold books. He specialized in publishing avant-garde writers and had no experience with auctions, but was proving to be a great connoisseur of rare books. A true bibliophile. "Without books," he would sigh, taking a leisurely sip of his whisky, "God would have no voice." He was passionate about ancient bindings, the beauty of old paper and elegant typeface, the provenance of the books. Another point in Kennerley's favor as far as Belle was concerned: he dared the impossible. Even when that meant standing up to the powerful Anthony Comstock, creator of the New York Society for the Suppression of Vice and king of censorship in the city.

Comstock fought unstintingly to uphold Puritan values; he opposed progress in all its forms and had made it his business to terrorize the intellectual community for nearly a quarter of a century. No cultural event of any importance could be held without his presence. People used flattery to get into his good graces curried favor with him, placated him. He was even reserved a choice seat at auctions. This was how he had come to attend the illustrious Hoe sale, had, in fact, been seated just a few chairs away from Belle in that little theater on the top floor of the Hyde Mansion. On a sunny winter morning in 1913, Comstock, accompanied by two police officers and a federal commissioner, had shown up at Kennerley's publishing house and clapped him in handcuffs. He had violated ethical standards, Comstock claimed, by publishing a novel called *Hagar Revelly*. And so he had come to have Kennerley arrested, his bail set at the outrageous sum of fifteen hundred dollars, and seize all copies of the offending book. Any other publisher in his place would have paid the fine and rapidly withdrawn the novel from the market.

Not Mitchell Kennerley.

From behind bars, he had called on his friends in the press, whom he regularly entertained in his office at soirées well supplied with liquor, and asked them to print his open letter in their papers. "*I published this novel in January 1913,*" he wrote, "*at a time when its subject was a great discussion point of the day, for it dealt with the ridiculously low salaries paid to shopgirls in large department stores, and their perverse effects on the morality of these young women. Such a book can only be shocking to those who have not ventured beyond the narrow boundaries of provincialism in politics, literature, the arts, and even the understanding of life.*" On February 5, 1914, the date of his trial, the courtroom was packed. The most famous personality in the literary world, Miss Belle da Costa Greene, was there to cheer the defendant on, as were hordes of writers, literary critics, and suffragettes, all of whom had eagerly devoured *Hagar Revelly*. The jury delivered its verdict four days later, an unalloyed victory: an acquittal for Kennerley.

As a result of this fracas, Kennerley was now viewed on the New York literary scene as the embodiment of a courageous publisher. Not necessarily a publisher of bestsellers, but one who tirelessly defended freedom of thought, a hero and a champion of scholars and intellectuals.

The reality, however, was somewhat different. The waiting room of his office was invariably teeming with novelists, poets, and essayists demanding their unpaid royalties. With suppliers whose bills he had not settled. With former mistresses he now employed as secretaries at sky-high salaries, as compensation for dropping them romantically. And with the pretty young women he invited for a drink in his sixth-floor penthouse—followed by an interlude in the bedroom there. The jealous tendencies of the Mitchell Kennerley Building's receptionist—one of his former flames—meant that his current favorite, Miss da Costa Greene, was forbidden entry, forcing her to wait for the boss outside in her car to avoid the scandal of a hysterical scene. But whenever Kennerley headed for the lobby calling out "I'll be in the Turkish baths at the Biltmore Hotel!", everyone on his staff knew that he was going to lunch with Miss Greene, and that he wouldn't be back in the office that afternoon—and probably not for several days.

This was the man whose candidature for head of the Anderson Auction Company Belle had supported. Their personal closeness now extended to the book market and the countless professional opportunities that opened up for both of them.

A master-stroke, on both sides . . .

. . . with one faint nuance. Kennerley, whose financial needs were bottomless, tended not to differentiate between his personal expenses and those of the auction house that employed him. He tended to help himself frequently, generously, and openly from the till, a practice that Belle castigated him for, not just privately, but everywhere.

While Belle might have been perfectly happy to spend much of her time in the company of a lover with dubious morals and a flexible conscience, her own integrity remained as strict as ever. She was scrupulously careful to avoid any blurring of her personal interests with those of Jack Morgan and his late father. Her tooth-and-nail fight to protect Mr. Jack's possessions from the covetous Duveens, her prudence in managing the immense sums of money with which he entrusted her, and her unshakeable loyalty to the library's cause had belatedly earned her the respect of the whole Morgan family. J.P.'s widow and daughters might well bemoan what they saw as her moral indecency and vulgar vocabulary—which Belle fought mightily to restrain in their presence—but they had finally come to trust her.

In the autumn of 1916, Jack gave Belle another raise, and the dazzling success of this "young person" in her work for two generations of bankers made newspaper headlines once again.

Oddly, the publicity made her less nervous this time than it had in the past. She agreed to give interviews and even posed for photos. To the reporters' questions about her future marriage plans, she replied with a laugh: "So far, I haven't found anything more exciting than my work at Mr. Morgan's library. But, I promise, as soon is there is any news on that score, you shall all be the first and only ones I tell!"

At thirty-seven, though officially twenty-seven, Belle seemed, as always, to be aging in reverse. What was more, she could feel the vice-like fear that had gripped her all her life loosening its hold at last.

In the summer of 1915, her father had finally been able to collect the inheritance from his Wears cousin. His own share *and* that of Russell, a son the Philadelphia courts had declared legally dead. She was betting on Professor Greener's silence from now on, since there was no longer any incentive for him to reappear.

"'Opportunity Will Come to the Prepared,'" the *Evening Sun* quoted her in its headline of October 19, 1916, "'and Success is a Matter of Undivided Loyalty.' So says Miss da Costa Greene, one of the most powerful career women in the world."

Belle now had the power to make and break careers.

Not only that, but she could spoil her little sister and marry her to the son of a prominent New York physician—a boy with whom Teddy was madly in love and whom, for once, had managed to win the approval of "one of the most powerful career women in the world."

There was one condition, of course. Teddy had to renew her vow never to have children. On this point, her older brother and sisters had all kept their word. Neither Louise, nor Ethel, nor even Russell had procreated, even though they had all been married for years now. How had they avoided it? That was a mystery. But the facts were the facts.

Marriage, fine. But no children.

Teddy swore up and down to keep the family promise.

Her true love's name was Robert Mackenzie Leveridge. An engineer, like Russell. Tall and blond, with a dazzling smile. The embodiment of joie de vivre. And of innocence, too, despite being twenty-six years old.

Significantly younger than his fiancée, nevertheless. Teddy, in keeping with Greene tradition, though she claimed to be freshly twenty-one, was really ten years older. A detail her future husband didn't suspect in the least.

The wedding, set for September 1, 1917, would be the last major social event before the dispatch of American troops to Europe. Congress had voted on April 6 to join the war, in alliance with France, England, and Russia, and since then, young soldiers had been training in droves. Robert Mackenzie Leveridge, mobilized as part of a machine-gun battalion in May 1917, was currently stationed at Camp Wadsworth in South Carolina. He had just been given leave to marry and would return to the training camp with his wife after the wedding, until his departure for the front.

Watching their little Teddy walk down the aisle on Russell's arm; Teddy, advancing toward the man she loved; Teddy, radiant in her sumptuous Worth wedding gown, Genevieve and Belle beamed with happiness even through their tears.

Standing together in the front row, mother and daughter exchanged a glance. They were both feeling the same sense of wonder. Who would have thought this scene possible? Their baby girl, pledging herself for life in front of three bishops at Saint Thomas Church on 5th Avenue, site of New York's grandest Episcopalian weddings?

\*

"I can't bear any more of these sanctimonious biddies endlessly knitting socks for the soldiers . . . ridiculous—so irritating . . ."

It was August 8, 1918. Belle had just returned from a benefit at the Metropolitan Opera, a frequent activity these days.

Like every other woman in the world, she fully supported the war effort. She even belonged to several committees, including the American Committee for Devastated France, of which she was among the most active members.

With her customary energy, she was also working to raise funds for the American Red Cross, recently reorganized by an associate of Jack's, supported by the Morgan Bank. Her efforts included putting on art exhibitions to benefit needy mothers and widows and donating a thousand dollars from her own pocket to the YMCA, for wounded soldiers.

The evening at the Metropolitan had ground on for so long that Genevieve had sent Belle's maid to bed and was waiting up in the living room herself to help Belle undress. The walls around them looked oddly bare. Bernardo Daddi's *Madonna and Child* and *Annunciation*, those marvelous Renaissance paintings B.B. had given Belle, along with the Persian miniatures and Chinese vases she had collected, were all on loan for exhibition.

Belle's brother and sisters had all flown the family nest. Uncertain of what financial disasters the war in Europe might bring, she had thought it best to be cautious and moved herself and her mother into a smaller apartment on 38th Street. Genevieve was still settling in. In addition to her room, the flat featured an office, which was also large enough to double as a bedroom for Teddy while her husband was away, and a small room for the maid. Belle had set up her own quarters behind a set of double doors that separated them from the common rooms; she was keener than ever to ensure her own privacy— and to share her bed with whomever she chose.

". . . they knit in restaurants," she complained now, throwing her gloves down on the sofa, "they knit at the museum—they even knit at the opera, between acts. When all they would really have to do is sell a few of their smallest diamonds, or order a cheaper bottle of champagne, to afford to ship *thousands* of ready-made socks straight to Europe!"

Genevieve had set about undoing the dozens of tiny buttons on the back of Belle's evening gown. "Thank God Russell is too old to fight," she commented abstractly, as if they were just finishing a long conversation on the subject. "And my sons-in-law, too. Well, two of them, at least. But our poor Teddy—"

"She'd do better to stop being so damned lazy and come help us on the committees."

Belle was undressing quickly and without inhibition, pulling out hairpins and removing her jewelry, stockings, and high-heeled slippers and tossing them indiscriminately in all directions. At this rate, she would be completely naked when she left the living room.

Her words came out a mile a minute, as she fidgeted beneath her mother's hands.

"Teddy needs to shake off her blasted lethargy! We need heads and hands everywhere. At the Red Cross, at the Women's City Club, and even at the library. She'd be kept plenty busy, filing receipts for the donations Mr. Jack is making to charitable associations—rather than lying in bed all day, worrying herself sick!"

"She misses Robert. She's afraid."

"She *knew* they were going to have a short honeymoon. She *knew* he was being sent to France when he finished his training. She knew all that when she married him, and she knew it when she was living with him at Camp Wadsworth. When he left—"

"When he left, poor Teddy hadn't even had three whole months with him."

Belle shrugged. "We're at war, Maman. Not exactly the best

timing, if she was hoping to settle down to peaceful married life."

At Christmas, the commanding officers of the 27th Infantry Division had sent all the wives of the 104th Machine Gun Battalion back home. And so Teddy had returned to her mother's house—or rather, her sister's, at the address Robert had provided on his enlistment papers under *Next of Kin:* 145 East 38th Street. He had joined his wife there a few days before shipping out, on a week's leave in New York.

Teddy hadn't yet recovered from those seven days of happiness. Robert had left her on the platform at Grand Central Station in the spring of 1918, sailing from Newport News, Virginia, on May 17. He had reached Calais on May 30 and had been fighting in Flanders ever since.

"They *were* sweet, both of them, when they were here," Belle conceded. "And it *was* awful to see them have to part. Teddy is truly a mess without him. But I'm not too worried; with our troops over in Europe now, the Allied victory can't be far away. Robert will be back here before too long, you'll see. And soon enough he'll irritate us just as much as Louise and Ethel's husbands!"

"Let's hope so. Because poor Teddy—"

"Stop calling her 'poor Teddy'!"

"—is going to have a baby."

Belle, who had been about to depart for her own rooms, froze.

"What did you say?"

Her voice was low, her face white. She advanced on her mother. Genevieve didn't blink.

"Teddy is pregnant."

Belle couldn't speak for a moment.

"That *idiot*," she gasped at last. "It isn't *that* hard to be careful!"

"Teddy is a married woman, my dear."

"So what? Louise and Ethel are married, too! And they've done what was necessary. One way or another, they've acted to make sure we're safe. I'd even say they've sacrificed themselves, to protect us all from disaster—and now, because of that irresponsible—that little wet rag who refuses to grow up and does whatever she wants . . . ! Of *course* it would've been Teddy," Belle raged. "A public nuisance. Can't keep her promises. She *swore*, though! How many months pregnant?"

"I don't know."

"She can't be very far along. Robert was here at the end of April. First week of May, at the latest." Belle counted on her fingers. "Four months. She can still have an abortion."

Now it was Genevieve's turn to explode.

"How can you suggest something so horrible?" she gasped.

"Teddy won't be the first, or the last. And she has no choice. She can't take a risk like this."

"I'll *never* do that!"

Teddy had flung open the door of the office that was serving as her bedroom. Petite and delicate, extremely slender like all the da Costa Greene women, she looked barely more than a teenager. In her long white nightgown, her dark curls tumbling around its lace collar, she was the heroine of a romantic novel come to life. Very unlike Louise and Ethel, with their pale complexions and flaxen hair. Nor did she much resemble Russell and Belle, though like them she could have passed for Mediterranean; in fact, they had always dressed her up as Bizet's Carmen for costume parties when she was a child. The role of the fiery Spanish Gypsy suited her physically, her siblings thought, but it did not match her passive nature.

They were wrong. Teddy's soul was far more passionate than her indolence suggested.

She had begged her mother to announce her pregnancy to her brother and sisters, knowing that the news wouldn't please them. After all, before she was married, hadn't they made her reaffirm their solemn vow never to have children? Dreading Belle's reaction especially, Teddy had waited up for her return home tonight, eavesdropping on her and Genevieve from behind the door. But the thought of an abortion, the moment Belle suggested it—the idea of that flooded her with horror beyond any family dust-up.

"Never!" she repeated now. "I'm going to have my husband's child."

Pitilessly, Belle turned on her. "Maybe. But what will your husband think, when he comes home from the war? Tell me— what will Robert think, when he finds his wife with a little Black baby in her arms?"

Teddy was silent. Belle supplied the answer herself.

"He'll think you slept with some Black man. Or that you're Black yourself. Either way: not good news for a white man. Not good news, period. He'll find out that you were lying to him, that I was lying to him, that Russell and Maman and our whole family were lying to him. And he'll be right! And how do you suppose *his* family will react? Knowing your father-in-law, the powerful Dr. Leveridge, he'll cry scandal from the rooftops. And then what will happen to you, a woman who got married lying about her name, her age, and her race? Robert will sue you for divorce on grounds of fraud. And what about your baby? If you think Robert will acknowledge it, you're fooling yourself. And you're fooling of yourself if you think we'll be able to keep living here, too! No more apartment on 38th Street, no more of the luxuries you're used to. You've never known any other kind of life, but *we* have! If your baby comes out Black . . . it's back to square one for all of us."

Teddy had dissolved into tears.

Genevieve, appalled by the brutality and bleakness of Belle's words, tried to separate them.

In the end, Belle left the two of them to retreat into the office together—but not before pulling Genevieve aside for a word.

"Teddy's playing her own game now, and you're protecting

her because you want grandchildren. You both want to have your cake and eat it, too. But you should have thought of the consequences before. Those are your own words—Lord knows you've said them to me often enough! We in this family are bound together by our secret—we're in this together. If none of us turns traitor, no one will know. Well, someone *has* turned traitor now. Someone is putting the rest of us in danger. And you're giving her your blessing?"

"You are," Teddy sobbed, "the most hideously racist person in the whole world!"

And Genevieve dealt the killing blow, a mere five words:

"As monstrous as your father."

*

There was nothing for Belle to do but accept the inevitable. To watch with exasperation as Teddy's belly grew rounder. And to beg God to spare them what she saw as certain catastrophe.

The tension at home was unbearable. Teddy would not speak to her, and Genevieve remained inscrutable. When they were alone, the two women talked of nothing but the baby, knitting booties feverishly.

By late September, Belle could stand it no longer. Abandoning what she now called "the 38th Street nursery," she decamped to one of Kennerley's Manhattan *pieds-à-terre*. And so she was not present when the letter addressed to Mrs. R.M. Leveridge arrived at their apartment that October.

Teddy's scream when she read the letter would be, for long weeks, the last sound that came from her mouth.

*Died, August 17, 1918, at the Esquelbecq Hospital, from wounds sustained in combat.*

Robert Mackenzie Leveridge had been killed trying to save two of his comrades on the front line at Poperinge, in Belgium. He was posthumously decorated for bravery. He was twenty-seven years old at the time of his death. He never knew he was going to be a father.

From that autumn day forward, Teddy did not speak or eat. She couldn't even get out of bed.

The jubilation of the armistice a few weeks after the fateful letter, the shouts of joy in the street, the brass bands and fireworks, plunged her ever deeper into depression.

She grew more grief-stricken by the day, and her condition more alarming. She had sunk into a bottomless abyss from which nothing, not even the baby kicking in her belly, could pull her. She had lost the will even to breathe and refused to acknowledge the life growing within her.

Genevieve, seeing Teddy so utterly bereft, feared that she might try to end her own life. It was a terror that Belle shared. They made sure never to leave her alone. They were so afraid of losing her that they poured all their hopes into the arrival of her baby.

It was Belle, now, who reminded Teddy that her beloved husband would live on in his child. But to no avail. Teddy was too far gone in her sorrow to register such a message of hope.

And when her labor pains began in January 1919, her body was so weakened by grief that the midwife thought herself duty-bound to inform the family: this would not be an easy birth.

\*

Just as Robert would surely have done during Teddy's labor if he had been there, Belle paced in front of the bedroom door, waiting anxiously for news. Genevieve, armed with basins and towels, had vanished inside and not reemerged. Belle could hear Teddy's gasps and the midwife's exhortations.

Unable to rein in her anxiety, Belle allowed a thousand

contradictory emotions to wash over her. *Please let Teddy hold on . . . please don't let the baby be stuck . . . please let her live . . . please don't let this baby destroy our lives!* She had given the doctor a single instruction when he arrived from the hospital: "Save the mother."

A sudden wail made her blood run cold. She dashed toward the bedroom. The midwife blocked her way and asked her to wait.

Who could have anticipated Belle's reaction at the first sight of her nephew?

When she breathed in his baby scent and felt the weight of the little body in her arms, when she cradled him against her breast and saw his tiny fist wrap around her finger, she was overwhelmed with a tenderness she'd never felt before, and that no one else had ever seen in her.

It didn't occur to her, not for an instant, to check beneath the blanket to make sure the baby had ten fingers and ten toes. Nor even, and more importantly, to rejoice at the sight of his creamy complexion and fluff of blond hair. She didn't mention any of that, didn't give the slightest sigh of relief. There was no outward sign of any anxiety whatsoever.

He was, she decided then and there, the very image of *her* Mr. Morgan. The resemblance was incredible! His eyes were the same shape. And the mouth was exactly the same.

It was a declaration that would have appalled many.

But not Teddy.

She couldn't bring herself to hold her son. She couldn't even look at him. When he was offered to her, to hold and coo over, she pushed him away.

Had she chosen a name for her little boy?

Teddy turned her face to the wall and did not answer.

How would she feel about giving him his father's first name? Wasn't that the tradition in Robert's family?

Belle, who had realized, rather belatedly, that her exclamations over the newborn's similarity to J.P. Morgan were rather tactless, now began to gush over the baby's resemblance to Robert Leveridge. Incredible! The very image of him!

Robert Mackenzie Leveridge, Junior.

While Belle marveled at the baby, stroking his little cheek and referring to him already, with infinite love, as "daaarling Bobbie," the young mother wept inconsolably.

*

It fell to Belle to choose a nurse for the baby, and then a governess. Bobbie's well-being, Bobbie's diet, Bobbie's clothing, Bobbie's education: she saw to everything, supervised everything. She was everything to him.

Teddy, sunk in depression, was unable to care for the boy, or even muster an interest in him.

And so, at eighteen months of age, Bobbie's first word was not Mommy, or even Grandma, though Genevieve was very much present. No—it was the name of the woman who played with him for hours, sitting with him in his large playpen or lying flat on her stomach on the living room floor. The woman whose return he awaited in the evenings, the woman toward whom he ran when he heard her key in the door. *Bull.* The same nickname Miss Thurston had once given to Miss Greene. A happy coincidence.

Later, Belle would become "Auntie Bull," and later still, in a play on words when the boy began to learn French as a young teenager and discovered that *belle* meant beautiful, "Beautybull."

But it was Belle's behavior that remained the most startling aspect of the whole situation. She spoiled Bobbie rotten. She remained a workhorse, certainly, taking an avid interest in every new rare book and manuscript that hit the market, going out on the town every night, and traveling. To the Vatican to monitor the restoration of the Coptic manuscripts, which had been interrupted by the war, and to London, for a sale she'd managed to have postponed from January to May 1919—an unheard-of compromise on the part of Sotheby's, due solely to the birth in New York of Miss da Costa Greene's nephew. She continued to dine at the castles of the English aristocracy and to entertain constantly in her own home. To indulge in romantic flings that lasted one night or ten. To carouse with Kennerley, as well as doing business with him for Mr. Morgan's library. To write to B.B.—interminable letters that he still complained were too short—and to meet him in hotels all over Europe.

But the center of her life had shifted. In the close confines of the North Room, poor Thursty was subjected to endless tales of the naughtiness and mischievous doings of one Robert M. Leveridge, Junior.

*

As luck would have it, Belle's investments, far from having declined, as she had feared in 1914, had tripled in value during the war.

Her personal fortune now enabled her to move her little tribe into an immense duplex very near the library. Bobbie, Teddy, Genevieve, the governess, the cook, and the maid would share the ground floor, while Belle took the floor above, which had its own bedroom suite and reception rooms. The two apartments were connected by an interior staircase not far from Bobbie's room, in case he had a nightmare and awoke crying and the governess didn't hear him.

After moving five times, Belle would live here, at 123 East 38th Street, for more than twenty years. Anything to provide a stable life for Bobbie.

The love between the boy and his "Beautybull," formed in the very first hour of his life, was mutual and total.

The perfect harmony of the situation, however, was rudely shattered when Teddy began to get back on her feet at last.

She was finally pulled from her depression by a former suitor, one Robert M. Harvey, who had courted her in their youth and now asked her again to marry him. Belle hadn't trusted him years ago, and she didn't trust him now.

The grandson of Irish immigrants, Harvey worked as a manager in a carpet factory and remained too poor to provide Teddy with any kind of financial stability. He only cared about his pipe, his beer, and his pals, Belle warned her sister. To hear Belle tell it, Harvey was not only poor, he was ignorant, too, living in a tiny backwater town and spending all his time with country bumpkins. And her disapproval deepened due to the fact that, if Teddy married Robert Harvey, she would take her son away to live somewhere else.

Panic. The thought of being separated from Bobbie had become unbearable. Belle began to lose sleep. Her customary flippancy, her seeming inability to be emotionally touched by anything deserted her completely; she did not even try to hide her terror. Whenever the subject came up, she fell apart. Would Teddy really deprive Robert Leveridge's son of an education worthy of him? Would she really spirit him off to be raised in Paxtang, Pennsylvania, denying him everything his aunt's position and his grandmother's love could do for him in New York?

Genevieve, for her part, no longer knew which camp she belonged to. It was true that Harvey wasn't the most exciting prospective husband for Teddy, but he had just returned from the war. He was a brave young man. And if he could restore her youngest daughter's will to live, she would welcome him with open arms.

Teddy was unsure. She wasn't deeply in love with Harvey, but she felt lucky to be offered his devotion and loyalty. It was like being thrown a life preserver in the midst of her overwhelming sorrow. He would rescue her from widowhood and provide a ticket out of the duplex on 38th Street that she hated. She was chafing under Genevieve's constant attentions and Belle's alternating generosity and despotism. She felt as if she were being crushed between her mother and sister, those two forces of nature. And she needed a man by her side.

The problem for Teddy, the main concern by far, was Bobbie. She knew herself to be lacking in maternal instinct and blamed herself bitterly for it. Fate had driven a wedge between her and her own son, and now the toddler saw her as a stranger. He rarely kissed her and never came looking for her. And she, despite her efforts, could not manage to overcome her discomfort and timidity in his presence. It was a truly awful situation. Unable to play with him, unable to cuddle him, she felt paralyzed around him and only ever wanted to get away.

Would she really deprive the little boy of his aunt's love for him, to inflict him on a stepfather who didn't care much one way or the other?

When Bobbie turned two in January 1921, the battle was still raging.

Belle continued to oppose Teddy's remarriage—or, more precisely, her imminent departure with the baby. She had openly declared war on her younger sister, and Teddy was not equal to it.

And so she ended by giving in. Or, rather, she bought her freedom by agreeing to leave her son behind.

It was agreed. Belle would provide financially for all of Bobbie's needs until he reached adulthood.

To avoid complications when it came to the administrative formalities that Bobbie's education would require, Belle would be granted legal guardianship of the boy. Teddy even gave her sister permission to adopt Bobbie, with all the necessary paperwork signed and notarized in good order. There were only two conditions. One, that Bobbie must always be aware that Teddy was his biological mother and, two, that he would spend all his school vacations with her in her new home.

The transaction was concluded in less than five minutes.

At forty-two, Belle da Costa Greene was luxuriating in the kind of happiness she thought she had sacrificed forever.

She was a mother.

A foster mother, an adoptive mother, a mother utterly smitten with the most adorable little boy ever to walk the earth.

\* \* \*

On the morning of February 17, 1924, a glacial wind blew through the streets of New York. The front steps of the palace on 36th Street were solid sheets of ice.

Bobbie, flush with the power of his five years, was determinedly trying to climb the icy stairs. He refused to let anyone hold his hand; he wanted to climb the stairs that Bull climbed every day, and he wanted to do it "all by myself!" He wanted, above all, to see where she went when she left the house every morning. Bull had promised, that day, to show him her domain.

She kept a careful eye on the boy, ready to catch him if he fell but, in keeping with her old motto "Live and let live," leaving him to battle the fierce wind and the height of the steps on his own.

Their long winter coats stood out darkly against the white marble as the woman and the small boy made their way slowly up the stairs. It didn't matter; Belle could take as long as she wanted to reach the top. She just had to be careful not to slip herself, should Bobbie need rescuing. Especially since she was carrying under one arm a pile of newspapers that she wanted to show Jack Morgan.

The press conference held at the library the previous day had been an ordeal for Belle, even though it had also marked a victory crowning years of hard work.

Jack had only agreed to receive the journalists if Belle made the speeches and acted as guide in his place. He hated the press as much as his father had, to the point that it was a true phobia. But Belle, convinced that it was absolutely necessary to put on a good show, and to cast the decision he'd made in the most glittering light, had begged him to personally entertain the thirty individuals she'd selected. Reporters and photographers able to grasp the importance of the event. She would remain by Jack's side, she promised, and feed him any necessary prompts. They would be a double act. But *he* should be the one to usher them around the West Room and the galleries of the East Room, and even the recesses of the vault; *he* should be the one to show off the Lindau Gospels and its gem-encrusted cover, the Cambridge Bible possibly kissed by King Charles I of England on the scaffold, and all the other treasures in the collections . . . that were no longer his private possessions.

And today, the *New York Times*, the *New York Tribune*, the *Boston Daily Globe*—all the major newspapers in the country, a stack of which she was clutching beneath one arm—had published Mr. Jack's photo, and all bore the same headline: SCHOLARS CALL GIFT MOST SPLENDID OF THE KIND EVER MADE: MORGAN GIVES LIBRARY TO THE PUBLIC.

It was Belle's moment of triumph. Her lifelong dream, realized at last.

"Yesterday, Mr. J.P. Morgan offered, in memory of his father, the first John Pierpont Morgan, the international banker and great collector, his private library—the famous Morgan Library, of an importance equal to that of the British Museum and with an estimated value of between eight and fourteen million dollars.

"Moreover, Mr. Morgan has made a donation of one and a half million dollars for the upkeep of the building, the conservation of the works it houses, and the enrichment of its collections.

"A board of directors composed of six people will henceforth be responsible for the management of the institution. Mr. Morgan will be the president of this board and Miss Belle da Costa Greene director of the library for life.

"Rumors of Mr. Morgan's intentions regarding the library have been rife in Europe, with requests for consultations already piling up on Miss Greene's desk and researchers prepared to line up in droves in front of the magnificent Renaissance palace on 36th Street. The success of the venture is ensured, and the John Pierpont Morgan Library will soon be invaded by students from all over the world.

"University scholars and amateur book-lovers alike consider this donation the most splendid gift of its kind ever made, in the whole history of Knowledge."

Belle Marion Greener had achieved her greatest goal, that dream Junius had instilled in her at Princeton twenty years earlier.

The treasures possessed by the Morgans were no longer destined to be seen only by friends of the family. No longer reserved solely for the powerful and privileged of the world. The manuscripts, the incunabula, the engravings, all the wonders Belle continued to acquire, could now be accessed freely by anyone who wished it.

It was true that, since the war, the guest book had become a sort of showpiece of famous names from around the world. There were the signatures of Édouard Herriot, mayor of Lyon; of the writers Arthur Conan Doyle and Agatha Christie; of the poet Robert de Montesquiou. The signature of Marie Curie would soon be added to the list. Visiting Mr. Morgan's library had become a must for prominent figures passing through the city. Belle, overjoyed, welcomed them all eagerly. But her interest was not limited to those happy few. Quite the contrary.

"To offer to the largest possible number of people, as Junius always said, all that may contribute to the education of students, the culture of America, and the posterity of humanity."

Mission accomplished.

And yet, for Belle, the adventure had only just begun. Her position at the head of the institution—the unassailable Queen of Books, Belle da Costa Greene, Lady Directress of the John Pierpont Morgan Library—meant that she could continue to pursue her dreams, to do her work the way she wanted to, for the rest of her life.

She was already working to organize several exhibitions at the New York Public Library on 42nd Street and was in the process of selecting the pieces to be loaned for a show she was calling *The Arts of the Book* at the Metropolitan Museum. This event would display to the public the rarest and most magnificent specimens of the Morgan collections. Rows of glass display cases would be set up in the rooms of the museum as the six members of the Morgan Library's board of directors finished overseeing the construction of a long-awaited annex to the white marble palace, fitted out with acoustic provisions for the lectures Belle intended to host, and lighting and ventilation of breathtaking modernity.

There was no end in sight to Belle's eternal quest to preserve beauty and transmit knowledge.

On the loggia, Bobbie hesitated. Intimidated by the statues rising in the niches, by the tall bronze doors that blocked his way, he was too afraid to continue.

Reaching for Bull's hand, he clung to it tightly.

She bent tenderly over him.

"When you're all grown up, my daaarling," she murmured in his ear, "you'll be able to come here without me. You won't need anyone's protection to go inside. And all the beautiful books I'm going to show you? You'll be free to read them and study them whenever you want."

The boy nodded.

Hand in hand, their two small figures vanished through the heavy bronze doors.

*

Maternity. Posterity. Belle had conquered it all.

At least it seemed so, in 1924.

# Epilogue

## Morgan's Nigger Whore

**Eighteen years later, May 1942. 535 East Park Avenue, New York**

B ull, I'm going out!"
A tall young man, strikingly handsome but still with a slight boyish roundness to his face, seemingly just out of adolescence, had appeared in the doorway. Less blond than he had been in babyhood, but far more attractive even than he appeared in the countless photos in Belle's office at the library.

A real dreamboat, as Belle might have said once.

Seated at her many-drawered desk in the living room, she turned around.

"Sexy!" she exclaimed, with an admiring whistle.

In the snug khaki uniform of the U.S. Army Air Forces, with his helmet and flight jacket, Bobbie cut a seductively dashing figure.

*A pearl before swine when it comes to his girlfriend and those jackass parents of hers. Cretins, the Taylor-Buchets, all of them.*

True to form, Belle never approved of her loved ones' amours.

She would have adored to spend this evening with him. The countdown had begun; he was returning to his base in Maine tomorrow, and from there he would fly to Europe with the B17s of the 327th Bomb Squadron.

Her memories of the massacres perpetrated during the Great War left Belle in no doubt of the butcheries to come. How could the world bear the horrors of another global conflict? She shivered.

It was Bobbie's last night in New York, before hell. His final furlough.

*Stay calm*, she told herself sternly.

"You're going out?" she exclaimed, keeping her tone light. "At this hour? Where?"

He laughed. "Are you planning to keep asking me these sorts of questions much longer? You're forgetting yourself in your old age, Bullie! May I remind you that I'm twenty-two years old, and it's only six o'clock. But I do love you like crazy, my Lili."

"Where are you going?" she repeated.

"To the Taylors', to pick up Nina and take her to dinner. Is that a satisfactory answer?"

"It is. And as far as Nina goes, I'm glad that's all you're planning!"

"What?"

"Dinner."

"Actually . . . no. I was thinking of asking her to marry me." Belle frowned.

"What nonsense are you talking now?"

"Like my father did with my mother. Before he went to the front."

"Don't joke about that!"

"I'm not joking. Now—*ciao, daaarling . . .*"

The front door of the opulent apartment on Park Avenue, into which Belle had just recently moved, closed behind him.

She sighed. Any one of Bobbie's previous flirtations—and Lord knew, there had been a lot of them—would have been better than Nina Taylor-Buchet. The girl was vapid and affected. Like thousands of other young society women. She wasn't even very pretty. Cute, at best. But she saw herself as having sprung from the thigh of Zeus, just because "Daddy" sat on the board of directors of some club or other, and "Mommy" bought her clothes at Bergdorf Goodman. They made a big production of being a "good family" and gave themselves grand airs, but really they were just uncultured rubes. As pretentious as they were fabulously rich.

And Bobbie had allowed himself to be impressed by them! He was too naïve. Sweet, beneath his roguish airs. A truly *nice* boy.

Don Juan, but with a heart as soft as a marshmallow. The worst of seducers.

Belle sighed again. Luckily, Bobbie's liaisons were usually short-lived. Though . . . he seemed quite smitten with this one. He must have it *very* bad, to be talking about marriage . . .

Well, the distance would take care of that. It was the only positive thing about these dreadful circumstances.

Still, the mediocrity of this girl, in such difficult times, felt vaguely threatening.

Bad vibrations.

Shoving her dark thoughts aside, Belle returned to her papers. She was looking for the copy of the will she had filed with her lawyer six years earlier. She wanted to rewrite it. But first, she had to inventory her current assets. Stocks, jewelry, works of art, apartments, cash. Her fortune had become truly substantial. The Taylor-Buchets must be rubbing their hands together with glee; their daughter had landed quite a catch. Her sweetheart's aunt was planning to leave him a substantial inheritance.

*Please God, don't let Bobbie marry that little ninny!*

It was true, though, that she was leaving a tidy sum to both of her sister's children.

*Both* of them.

Teddy, the ink hardly dry on the certificate of her marriage to Robert Harvey, had violated the siblings' oath again by giving birth to a second child, a girl she had named Belle Greene Harvey, in tribute to the star of the family. Another miracle: little Belle was a beauty who bore a striking resemblance to the original. The same gleaming gray eyes, sharp as a fragment of ceramic. The same sensuous mouth and slender body. And on top of it all, a porcelain-pale complexion and strawberry-blonde hair.

*Me, but blonde*. Beautybull's ultimate fantasy.

In her letters to B.B., which were rare these days, she dwelt often on the subject of "blondes," her rivals in this world. And on the elegance of her namesake, who was not so tiny anymore: Belle Green Junior was turning eighteen today, and, to mark the occasion, her aunt wanted to arrange a nest-egg for her future. This was why she was looking for her old will now and calculating new amounts to bequeath.

Still, Belle Greene the younger was a niece. Well-loved, certainly. But a niece.

Bobbie, though—Bobbie was her beloved boy, the one she had raised and educated, enrolled in the best schools, dragged along to museums and the opera, and to the homes of her friends, New York's great art historians and collectors, and to London and Paris and Venice, too. How many times had they crossed the ocean to Europe together? They had always been excellent traveling companions. She never grew bored by him, and he never had more fun than when he was with her. At every age. Even when they squabbled, even when he gave her a hard time.

She had taught him to look, to listen, to feel.

To live.

The result: despite his boyish transgressions, Bobbie had been admitted to Harvard University with honors. Top honors, even. Harvard, the alma mater of Bull's friend, the famous Bernard Berenson. And of Bull's father, Richard Greener, of whom Bobbie knew nothing at all.

By mutual agreement, Bobbie's aunt, mother, and grandmother had chosen to conceal his family history from him. To keep quiet about the origins of the da Costa Greenes. All of them, even Russell, had steadfastly adhered to the vow of silence that guaranteed their survival. For Bobbie and for Belle Junior: silence.

The elder generation had suffered enough from carrying such a weighty secret for so long. Why burden the younger ones with it? If they didn't know, they wouldn't have to be afraid of discovery. If they didn't know, they would be free to carve out their own destinies. If they didn't know the secret, they couldn't betray it.

In any case, nothing about Bobbie or Belle Junior, absolutely nothing, suggested the slightest hint of their African roots. The drop of Black blood that would have made them unacceptable in the eyes of the white world probably went too far back now for them or their own children to run the risk of being unmasked.

Was there any real reason, anymore, for the da Costa Greenes' terror of cutting their own throats by giving birth to Black babies? The latest genetic research seemed to conclude that the danger of that was virtually non-existent.

In any case, Bobbie had grown up wholly ignorant of the significance of the word *Negro* for his loved ones. Completely unaware of what the concept of segregation could have meant in the apartment at 535 Park Avenue. He knew the meaning of the word, certainly, and deplored it, just as he deplored discrimination. But he had no idea of what these things involved, socially, for those closest to him. The truth was that, like all white children, he never thought about Black people. He did not know any personally, other than the housemaids who made his bed when he spent weekends at his friends' homes.

Bobbie had been educated at a private school where the word "slavery" was rarely pronounced and the history of the Civil War taught in such a condensed version that the students learned very little about it.

English-style cap, cream trousers, navy-blue blazer embroidered with the school's crest. Theater, music. Tennis, football, hockey—all the sports. Six pupils per class, the sons of powerful industrialists and the nephews of tycoons named Rockefeller, Vanderbilt, and Astor. The very best teachers. Then Harvard, at age eighteen . . .

. . . until he abandoned it all to become an actor, reporter, and aviator in Los Angeles.

He had left Harvard after his third year, without bothering to complete his degree, without even having begun the medical studies he'd planned. Didn't he want to become a physician, like his paternal grandfather, the renowned Dr. Leveridge? Farewell to those vague ambitions. *Vive l'indépendance!*

He might have been the best-educated, the most civilized young man on earth—the most affectionate, without a doubt—but Bobbie was also a hotshot flyboy who loved nothing in the world so much as freedom. Adventure. Risk. Speed. To pursue adrenaline rushes and sow his wild oats with a group of friends very different from the ones whose company had been imposed on him.

He wasn't the son of Belle Greene for nothing! The words she had written to B.B. nearly forty years earlier could just as easily have applied to Bobbie now: "I think that, in most of us, lies the desire to break the rules. I know that the need to go beyond all I have experienced before never leaves me. That's just how it is, *fiamma mia*; the taste for excess runs in my blood, and my love for you won't change that one bit."

When it came to alcohol, flirting, and fast cars, Bobbie was a carbon copy of his Bull—with one exception. Where *he* was the heir to a fortune, Belle had had to prove herself in every way, to build everything from scratch. And since her earliest youth, the credo of Belle Marion Greener had not changed: without education, without knowledge, nothing else mattered—there could be no salvation.

And so Bobbie's decision to leave university without taking his degree had caused an uproar at 535 Park Avenue. It was viewed as a tragedy, even. By Belle and also by Teddy Harvey in Pennsylvania. And even by Bobbie's gentle grandmother, who had been furiously opposed to his change of course.

Darling Genevieve had passed away last year, at the venerable age—the true age—of ninety-five. A record, in the 1940s.

Belle's close friends, those who had had the privilege of meeting *Madame mère*, talked endlessly of their fond memories of the charming old lady, so elegant, so genteel—and so well preserved for her "eighty" years!

Of course, Genevieve's obituary in the newspapers had been, like so much else, a lie. The *New York Times* had written that she was born in Richmond, Virginia, to a father named Robert van Vliet and a mother called Genevieve da Costa. Her death certificate listed her as white, and all the information Belle had supplied and sworn to was false.

Lies to the very end, of course. Of course.

The only true thing was the affection that had bound Genevieve and Belle. Theirs had been an unconditional love, a rare closeness. Mother and daughter had lived together for more than half a century. They had shared everything.

Genevieve had been the cornerstone of the family. The author and the custodian of their smooth passage from one world to another. After having worked tirelessly so that her children could pursue their chosen careers, she had trained the most brilliant of her daughters—effortlessly, as it seemed—to carry on her own work. To help. To support. To protect others. And then, her role now definitively embodied by another, she had allowed herself to relax and enjoy life's pleasures, before withdrawing peacefully from this life.

Genevieve had left an immense void behind her, and Belle would never fully recover from her loss.

That had been in March 1941, a month before Bobbie joined the Army Air Forces. He had enlisted in California, impulsively, without asking anyone's advice. And without necessity—the Japanese had not yet bombed Pearl Harbor, and the United States wasn't at war.

Now he found himself in the eye of the hurricane. Having entered the 92nd Bomb Group as a mere cadet, he would depart for combat with the rank of first lieutenant. A brilliant promotion. And it promised adventure enough to satisfy even him.

He would be among the first groups of American soldiers to

be flown across the ocean, inaugurating the North Atlantic Air Ferry Route between Newfoundland and Scotland. From there he would be stationed at Bovingdon, a Royal Air Force base in Hertfordshire, to carry out missions against the Nazis in concert with the English. What would Bobbie's role be during these cross-Channel raids? Pilot? Navigator? Bombardier? Spotter? Belle couldn't keep all the crew positions straight. On the other hand, she was perfectly clear about the fact that a damaged aircraft was a deathtrap, and that it was exceedingly rare for aviators whose plane was hit to return home alive.

She didn't want to think about it.

They still had one day to spend together in New York. They should enjoy it.

They should enjoy every moment.

She wasn't young any more herself, and there was no time to waste on regrets and ratiocinations. Though she still had the same girlish figure as always, the same sense of humor and impudence, the same ability to make idiots cower with a single withering stare, the same tendency to swear loudly at anyone who contradicted her—in short, though she carried her fifty years lightly in the eyes of the world, nothing could change the fact that she was actually about to turn sixty-three.

Late to live alone for the first time. And late to live in fear.

Belle had thought she knew every facet of fear. And yet, this evening, she realized that she had forgotten them all a while ago.

Had she felt safe for too long?

The admiration she enjoyed in Europe in the highly prestigious world of books, the respect accorded to her by university chancellors in every large American city, her power over the art market and in the museum sphere had long placed her far above the fray. And the esteem of a man as solid, as important as Mr. Morgan continued to protect her from gossip.

Simply put, Belle da Costa Greene had become an institution in herself. She had reigned over her venerable kingdom for so many years that no one even thought to wonder about her age anymore, or where she had been born. The vague rumors that had once swirled about her mysterious past had dissipated like fog.

Safe at last.

Her friendship with Jack had been a real surprise. He had proven to be a bibliophile almost more interesting than the Big Chief. Certainly his taste was more sophisticated. The death of his adored wife in 1925 had devastated him to the point that he could find comfort only at the Morgan Library. While it was true that the library was no longer his property, he was still its president, and his two sons sat on the board of directors. The Morgan Library remained his refuge. A haven both sentimental and intellectual. And so harmony had reigned for nearly twenty years in the white marble palace that rose, majestic and unchanging, at the corner of Madison and 36th Street. Unchanging, had it not been for the war.

Since March 1942, Belle had been working to ensure the safety of the library's treasures. A bombing of New York seemed very unlikely, but how could anyone be sure, especially after the surprise attack on Pearl Harbor? And in light of the destruction visited on London's monuments by the Blitz, better safe than sorry. Using the evacuation of the British Museum as her model, Belle had had crates of books, manuscripts, and *objets d'art* transported to several underground shelters located in different areas of New York. Another herculean endeavor.

But *protect, preserve, and transmit* remained her keywords of the moment, and now a fourth directive had joined the others: *conceal from the Germans*. This had been the advice of her colleague Daniel V. Thompson, "Dan" to his friends, head of the laboratory at the Courtauld Institute of Art in London.

Though he was twenty-three years younger than Belle and thirty-seven years younger than Berenson, Dan was a correspondent of choice for both of the former lovers. An American based in the United Kingdom, he had replaced the faithful Charles Hercules Read, now deceased. B.B. used his communications with Dan to catch up on news of their "B.G.," their "Tartar Queen," their "Queen of Sheba," his former flame who never wrote to him anymore, he said, unless he wrote to her first.

Bobbie, for his part, preferred Dan to any of Bull's other friends. He had even chosen Dan to be his godfather when he was a child.

Belle found it immensely comforting to think that Dan would be in London at the same time Bobbie was based at Bovingdon, that the young man would stay with Dan and his wife and their little girl when on leave, that he would be able to visit Dan in his laboratory at the Courtald institute.

She didn't hear him come home, despite the fact that she'd been listening from her bed for the sound of his key in the door, and her hearing was as sharp as ever.

She couldn't sleep. She'd told herself over and over that many thousands of other wives and mothers endured the same terrors on the night before their husbands and sons departed for the battlefield, but it was cold comfort.

And she never had managed to unearth her will. Her anxiety in that regard was becoming obsessive. Yet it was accomplishing nothing. She should have done the same as Bobbie. Gone out. Gotten drunk. Flirted. Toyed with the idea of accepting a marriage proposal—why not? Her former fiancé Harold Mestre had passed away years ago, and Mitchell Kennerley was sunk deep into alcoholism. But there were still others knocking at the door.

She had no heart for gallivanting tonight, though.

She just wanted to wait up for Bobbie. So she wouldn't miss the chance to say goodnight to him. And maybe have a last glass of bourbon together in the kitchen. Or a little conversation like they used to have when he was small, Belle perched on the edge of his bed while he slowly grew sleepy.

What the hell was he doing out there at this hour, with that Nina?

Was he spending the night with her?

Of course he was! The last night with his lover. Of *course* he

wouldn't be home tonight. Just as long as he didn't get her pregnant, like his father had done with Teddy!

Shortly before sunrise, Belle got out of bed, just to make sure
Bobbie wasn't there.

But the light was on in his bedroom. So he *was* home, and he
wasn't sleeping, either. She knocked. No answer. Then she
thought she heard movement in the living room. She found
Bobbie there, sitting—huddled, really—on the floor next to her
desk, which was in wild disarray. All the drawers had been emptied, their contents dumped everywhere. The family papers she
kept in the desk—official documents, deeds of sale, photos, even
old albums were scattered on the floor all around him.

The room looked like an archaeological excavation.

"What are you doing?"

The fear and confusion on his face when he looked up at her
struck cold terror into her heart.

His face was white. Distraught. Devastated. He seemed to
have aged by ten years. Her first thought was that Nina must
have broken things off with him. Or maybe they'd had an accident, and she was dead.

"What's happened?" she asked, her voice quivering.

He looked down again, avoiding her eyes, and didn't answer.
She knelt next to him. Seizing a few sheets of paper from the floor
at random, she cast an eye over them. Genevieve's death certificate.

"Were you looking for my will?"

He shook his head.

"Then what are you doing with this old stuff?"

She picked up two of the albums, yellowing photos askew in
their cardboard slots. He must have been leafing through the
albums feverishly, to leave them in such a state.

She paged quickly through the photos from the early part of
the century, official portraits taken by professional photographers
at Saint Thomas Church: the family and all the notable figures

who had been invited to the wedding of Russell da Costa Greene and Miss Josephine Wells. There, elegant on the arm of Josephine's father, was Genevieve—Mamie-Genevieve, as Bobbie called her—in her long striped gown, her wide-brimmed hat tilted rakishly over one eye, and Aunt Louise, with her speech-therapist husband in a top hat . . .

Belle repeated the question a third time:

"Why are you looking at these papers and old pictures? What are you looking for?"

"My grandfather," he said abruptly.

She raised an uncomprehending eyebrow.

"Dr. Leveridge wasn't at Uncle Russell's wedding, silly. This was in 1914. Your parents hadn't met yet."

He laughed tonelessly.

"But you knew your father, didn't you?"

"My father?"

Belle's blood turned to ice. Where was Bobbie going with this? Sensing the danger, she tried to stall for time.

"No . . . I never knew my father. He died before I was born. Just like yours."

"Really? Even though Aunt Ethel and my mother were born after you?" He wrenched the album from Belle's hands and tossed it across the room. Why was he acting so bizarrely?

"I just meant that I don't have any memories of my father; by the time I was old enough to remember anything, he was already dead."

"And you don't have any photos?"

"It wasn't so common back then."

"Are you joking?" Bobbie paused for a moment, reflecting. "There isn't a single trace of him, of any kind, anywhere. You never talk about him in your letters. He's not in the photos, even the oldest ones. Mamie-Genevieve must not have loved him very much, not to have kept a single memento of him! Not even a portrait miniature. Not even a few strands of hair in a locket. But if her husband was a Negro, like Nina's father says . . ."

The shock was so great that Belle couldn't speak. She felt as if she'd been punched in the throat.

"What are you saying?"

She had turned as white as Bobbie.

"I'm saying," he replied, his voice low as he fought to keep it steady, "that according to what Mr. Taylor said when I asked him for his daughter's hand in marriage this evening, my grandfather's last name wasn't Greene, but Greener. Richard Greener, to be precise. According to Mr. Taylor, he was a Black activist who used to run amok around Washington D.C. According to Mr. Taylor, Mamie was Black, too. Not born in Richmond, as she claimed, but in the Black ghetto of Georgetown. I'm not allowed within a hundred yards of his daughter, he said, because my ancestors came from coconut trees in Africa. He says I'm a lying nigger, just like them, pretending to be white."

Belle was paralyzed, unable to speak, unable even to think. It didn't occur to her for a second to tell Bobbie the truth. Her only instinct was to deny it. The old reflex.

". . . just where did your Mr. Taylor dig up all this rubbish?" she managed at last.

"A private detective agency. Nina told him we were in love and wanted to get married. So he hired them to investigate. To investigate *you*."

Belle, reeling, tried to deflect the issue.

"It's a tired old story, my dear. There was no need for detectives to unearth it. Those rumors have been going around for decades. I suppose your Mr. Taylor also told you that I owe my brilliant career to the fact that I'm old J.P. Morgan's illegitimate daughter? Of course! Or did he give you the other version—that I slept with not one, but two Morgans, father and son, to get where I am? Or was it the third version, perhaps? That I'm daughter, sister, and mistress to both of the J.P. Morgans? Queen of incest in New York?"

He hesitated. Should he repeat the abominable things Taylor had really said?

"Something like that," he hedged.

"And you believed him?"

"I'm asking *you* the question, Bull. Is it true?"

"True that I'm Jack Morgan's mistress?" She gazed at him severely. "What do you think, Bobbie?"

"*Is it true*," he repeated, his voice full of quiet desperation, "that my grandfather was a Black activist named Richard Greener? Is it true that my ancestors—that I—"

She cut him off.

"I have no idea who Richard Greener was. But I can tell you one thing: he wasn't your grandfather. And as for the rest—as for Mamie being, as your informer says, a Black woman from Georgetown?" Her voice was rising. "Just look at her! *Look* at your grandmother, since you've got her photo right there in your hands! And while you're at it, look at all of them, *all* the women in your family!"

She flipped angrily through the pages of the album, jabbing a finger at the figures. "Look at your aunt, Louise *la blonde*; look at Ethel-of-the-flaxen-hair! Look at your mother. Do they look like what you're describing? Not to mention your sister—and look at *yourself*, child!"

Seizing Bobbie's elbow, she pulled him to his feet and steered him to the mirror.

How many times, since the beginning of this terrible night, had he scrutinized himself in the glass, staring at his nose, his mouth, his hair, carefully searching his own face, terrified, for proof of what he had just heard? It had been the first thing he'd done when he returned home after the horrifying revelation at Nina's.

"Take a good look at yourself, Bobbie. At that tall, blond-haired young man in an officer's uniform. Do you see him? First Lieutenant Robert Mackenzie Leveridge. Do you think he looks Black? Really?" She shook him. "You have to stop with this ridiculousness. Stop it immediately! I realize that the foul things

Nina's father said have shaken you up, but there are limits to how far you should trust malicious gossip."

They stood side by side in front of the mirror, Bobbie's face a good foot higher than Belle's. But it wasn't his own face that he stared at with a kind of appalled fascination now. He was examining hers. And he saw her now as he had never seen her before. He saw the golden tint of her skin, the limpid pupils of her gray-green eyes, her overly prominent nose, the fullness of her lips. And her rebellious hair, which she hadn't taken the time to twist in a chignon.

In this light, beneath Bobbie's gaze, the rapt and wild look in his eyes, she felt herself transforming. Turning into what he was seeing.

In her dressing gown, without makeup, without the rice powder that lightened her skin, without the pomade that smoothed her hair, she was no longer simply the exotic beauty that he had always admired, but also—more importantly—she was "Morgan's nigger whore," as these bastards had dubbed her.

It was undeniable. The revelation was as excruciating for her as it was for him.

Morgan's nigger whore.

They stood, paralyzed by the same horror.

An infinite loneliness now descended on them both, crushing their bodies, flooding their souls, invading every part of them.

Bobbie sat unmoving on the couch, head down, as if struck by vertigo. An abyss seemed to have opened at his feet. Belle stood at the bay window, looking out at the city. The sun had risen, the tall silhouettes of the skyscrapers black against the rosy gleam of the dawn sky.

The thing she'd dreaded for so many years had finally happened. She stopped arguing with Bobbie, stopped trying to deny anything. She was quiet now, trying to assess what the consequences of the truth would be for him.

Thinking of the future, and thinking fast.

He mustn't see the Taylor-Buchets again, mustn't get within a hundred yards of them. He would have to cut ties with them immediately, without a letter of explanation, without a word. Silence. He would end up with a broken heart, which was never good for a soldier on the eve of combat. But who hadn't had their heart broken at his age? And everyone recovered from it eventually. Marriage to that girl would have been a disaster, anyway. In any case, there could be no possibility of his marrying her now.

More worrying, and far more dangerous in Belle's view, was the question of Bobbie's position in the army. He was so proud of his squadron, so proud of his training comrades, so proud of their friendship. The boys of the 92nd Bomb Group, 327th Bomb Squadron. But if those white men discovered his secret, if they learned of Lieutenant Leveridge's African roots, their attitude would change.

Belle remembered all too well what had happened to one of her father's protégés, the West Point cadet whose classmates had slit his ears after giving him a merciless beating, shouting that he was Black and that they would not live and die alongside a colored man.

Rejected, humiliated, and shamed, Bobbie would be court-martialed for having lied about his race. He would be transferred to a Black infantry regiment as a low-ranking soldier. How would he survive it? Physically as well as in terms of education, tastes, and temperament, Bobbie was a white officer.

The truth was that he didn't belong anywhere anymore.

Her spirit rebelled against the thought. The Greeners had escaped poverty, humiliation, injustice—all the atrocities to which whites subjected Blacks. They had pulled themselves up out of the squalor and ignorance in which the whites had deliberately confined them. They had gotten out of the ghetto. And her child was not going to go back there now!

There could be no doubt that Bobbie knew where he came from now. His expression in the mirror just a short while ago, the

way he had looked at his Beautybull's face, her lips, her
hair . . . he knew.

But neither of them had *said* anything conclusive. The
Greenes' secret had not been spoken aloud. The mystery had
not been revealed.

Yet without words to lift the veil, without words to make
things definitive, the shadows and the silence would linger.

Forehead pressed to the window, Belle murmured:

"Forget what you think you found out tonight. Forget what
those bastards said to you. Even if you should have doubts one
day, even if you should wonder about what you heard in their
house, keep it to yourself, and keep your damned mouth shut.
Never admit—to *anyone*—what you think you know because
you're wrong, and you don't really know anything about it!"

"Why are you still trying to pull the wool over my eyes?" He
shot a despairing look at the back of her head, which she didn't
see. "What's the use of lying?"

His voice took on an infinite sadness.

"Why are you lying to me, Bull?"

"When have I ever lied?" she snapped.

She turned away from the window and came to sit down
beside him. She was fighting to keep calm, to reason with him.

"What really happened tonight? Nothing. Except maybe a fit
of madness in a family of racist trash. A fit of madness, Bobbie.
No more, no less. You shouldn't see that girl again, or even write
to her. Those people are nothing. My advice is to forget the
whole thing, not to mention it, and to keep on living your life
just like before. That's all."

He laughed bitterly.

"Just like before?' Do you actually think that's possible?"

"To keep on living, anyway—yes. That's really the only thing
I believe in, anyway. Living. And, at the moment, *surviving*."

She took his hand. He didn't pull away, but allowed her to
raise it gently to her lips.

He smiled faintly.

"Message received, Bull. I'll do my best."

*

Bobbie left later that same day.

He refused to let her accompany him to the train station, but he couldn't keep her from walking him out to the street. They hugged for a long time in silence.

Eyes closed, she relished being his arms, breathing in his scent, soaking in his warmth and life.

Finally he pulled away. She followed him to the corner of 60th Street, where he stopped her.

They stood there on the sidewalk together one last time, gazing at each other, trying to smile.

"Be good, Bullie. No hijinks while I'm gone!"

She couldn't think of a witty reply. Her mind was otherwise occupied. What could she say—what could she *do*, to protect him? She had never believed in fate. "Opportunity will come to the prepared," she had said once. Who could she call, who could she write to so that nothing would happen to her beloved boy?

Even in the most difficult circumstances, she had always found a solution. Always overcome adversity.

He touched her cheek gently. Tucked in a wayward strand of hair that had escaped from her chignon.

She had never felt so utterly powerless. So helpless.

Without speaking again, he walked away in the direction of Grand Central Station.

Eyes full of tears, throat tight, she watched his tall figure recede down the broadest and most fashionable street in New York, the symbol of her many triumphs.

How do you change the course of destiny?

Bobbie

Lieutenant Robert Mackenzie Leveridge, Junior, one of the most daring and popular aviators in his squadron, returned safely from multiple air raids in France.

Through his acts of valor, he made it possible for the crews of other planes hit by enemy fire to return home, escorting damaged planes and keeping them covered until they reached the safety of the RAF Alconbury base.

Several months later, on August 3, 1943, he shot himself in the head after receiving a letter from his fiancée.

This letter, which bemoaned his Blackness and asked him to have himself castrated, had been opened by English censors and its content communicated to the high command of the United States Army Air Forces based in Cambridgeshire.

The American military authorities refused to give his family any information at all concerning the circumstances and reasons for his suicide.

Adding to the weight of their grief, the mystery of Bobbie's death left his loved ones in an agony of confusion.

Dan Thompson of the Courtauld Institute of Art, the man who knew his secret, also chose to remain silent.

Still in possession of the letter from Nina Taylor-Buchet that Bobbie had entrusted to him, but wishing to spare his friend

Belle Greene any unnecessary suffering, he requested that his heirs not turn the letter over to her until his own death.

But Belle, who was older than Dan, died first.

She never received the key to the mystery of her adopted son's death.

The letter, once placed in a sealed envelope, can still be found today among the personal papers of Dan Thompson, donated by his descendants to the American Art Association.

Bobbie was laid to rest in England alongside his brothers-in-arms, at the American military cemetery in Cambridge, Section B, Row 1, Grave 36.

BERNARD AND MARY BERENSON

Bernard Berenson had not seen Belle since the summer of 1936, in Salzburg. In the letter he wrote to her on the day after their reunion in Austria, he complained about not having met her nephew, of whom she had spoken so much.

By that summer of 1943, the summer of Bobbie's death, life had become extremely difficult for Berenson. The Germans had occupied Florence. Jewish by birth, he ran the risk of being arrested and deported. Thought to have fled to the United States, he had actually gone into hiding at the villa of a friend, just three miles from I Tatti. He would remain there for thirteen months with a charming female companion named Nicky Mariano, initially hired by his wife Mary as . . . a librarian. Twenty-two years B.B.'s junior and completely in his thrall, Nicky had been seeing to the well-being of both Berensons since 1920, and she knew Belle, with whom B.B. had arranged for her to travel on occasion.

Mary, who was not Jewish and did not run the same risks as

B.B., continued to live at I Tatti, having removed and hidden away its collection of treasures. She remained there despite having been physically and mentally ill for years.

Mary's lover Geoffrey Scott had left her in 1917 to marry an English lady of aristocratic birth, who had been B.B.'s mistress for a time and remained their neighbor in the hills of Fiesole. Mary's despair at this abandonment, further aggravated by her husband's constant recriminations on the subject, led her to throw herself out of a window, a suicide attempt from which she never fully recovered. She died in 1945, aged eighty-one, with B.B. and Nicky at her side.

After the war, the famous Bernard Berenson, surrounded by adoring, beautiful women and idolized by young art historians who sought his company, spent many happy years with Nicky at the Villa I Tatti, finally realizing with her the dream he had tried to impose on Belle: "She works with me, thinks with me, feels what I feel. She is the ideal companion."

Their relationship would last until his death in October 1959, aged ninety-four. He bequeathed his opulent villa, his library, and his collections to Harvard University.

## JUNIUS SPENCER MORGAN II

Belle's dear friend continued to live in Paris, never resuming marital life with his wife Josephine—though he did not divorce her, thus sparing her a scandal that would have damaged her social standing. In 1924, his son Alexander joined him in France to study Beaux-Arts architecture.

A leading collector of engravings and *objets d'art* and a prominent book collector and patron of the arts, Junius donated many of the most precious objects in his collections to the

Firestone Library and the Museum of Beaux-Arts at Princeton University, the New York Public Library, and the Metropolitan Museum. He offered these four institutions a number of absolute masterpieces over the years, including the entire corpus of his *Virgiliana;* his Dürer engravings; paintings by Van Dyck, Claude Lorrain, and Van Ruysdael; and other treasures.

His dedication to assisting wounded soldiers during the First World War led to his being awarded the Légion d'honneur by the French and receiving the Order of the Crown of Italy in 1932, for having protected the culture of the Old World and developed it in the New.

Ill with heart disease, he died of a coronary infarction on August 18, 1932, while traveling with his sister in Switzerland. He was sixty-five years old. His funeral was held at the American Cathedral in Paris. He is buried in the Morgan family plot in Hartford, Connecticut.

Belle made sure that Princeton University paid him the homage that was his due and personally edited the obituary written by a former classmate for the university newspaper, adding many details and clarifications for which Junius's friend thanked her warmly in their letters.

She always considered Junius her greatest mentor and cherished her memories of him for the rest of her life.

## JACK MORGAN (JOHN PIERPONT MORGAN II)

Struck by "collecting fever," a malady he described—not without humor—as incurable, Jack himself became an avid bibliophile, doubling in ten years the number of volumes his father had left to the Morgan Library.

Following the first attempt to assassinate him in 1915, Jack would survive two further attempts that left him deeply shaken. On an April Sunday in 1920 at St. George's Church, an insane gunman killed Dr. James Markoe, who had been J.P. Morgan's personal physician and close friend, by shooting him in the face at close range. The killer was obsessed with the rumor that the Morgans were responsible for the sinking of the *Titanic* and determined to avenge the victims. Mistaking Dr. Markoe for Jack Morgan, he had shot the wrong target. Six months later, on September 16, a horse-drawn wagon loaded with dynamite exploded in front of the headquarters of the J.P. Morgan & Co. bank at 23 Wall Street, killing 38 people and wounding 300 others, including Jack's oldest son. Morgan himself, the great capitalist, targeted this time by anarchists, was not in the building.

These violent occurrences had a lasting detrimental effect on Jack, and he began to suffer from a form of paranoia. He never recovered from the deaths of his mother in 1924 and his wife the following year. He was severely impacted by the economic crisis of 1929, and the Morgan Bank was significantly weakened. Still, he remained one of the most important financial figures of the interwar years.

Jack Morgan died of a stroke, aged seventy-five, on March 13, 1943, thirty years almost to the day after his father's death. His funeral, which he wished to be exactly like that of John Pierpont, Senior, was celebrated at St. George's, with the same texts read and the same hymns sung. And in his will, Jack left Belle the same amount of money his father had: fifty thousand dollars.

His death after so many years of friendship devastated Belle. To lift her spirits, Ada Thurston—"Thursty"—who had retired in 1934 after twenty-eight years of loyal and dedicated service to the library, wrote to her, "Thanks to you, he was able to evolve from the closed-off individual we first met to someone capable of appreciating all sorts of people and having a wide variety of interests. He may not have fully realized it, and his family may not have, either, but he owed that new openness of mind and curiosity about the world to you. You can be proud of yourself for that."

Thursty's words were no consolation. Belle felt as if she were reliving the Big Chief's death.

It came only four months before that of Bobbie.

## BELLE AND HER FAMILY

Belle never recovered from the loss of her nephew.

She concealed from the world the fact that it had been a suicide, and convinced Harvard University to include Robert Mackenzie Leveridge, Junior on its list of students killed while serving their country. Bobbie's name figures today on the wall of Harvard Memorial Church, alongside those of the other heroes of the class of 1940.

Belle refused to answer any letters from Nina Taylor-Buchet, who seemed unaware that Bobbie had killed himself and wanted details of her fiancé's death. Nina did not press further for answers and did not even show up for a meeting she had requested with Dan Thompson, who had agreed to provide her with some explanation but warned her that it might upset her.

Belle herself was never certain of Bobbie's motives, but how could she not have guessed?

The shock of his death affected her so deeply that she suffered several attacks of powerful grief over the years, so debilitating that they weakened her physically, to the point that she became unable to use her legs.

Fate continued to deal her a series of painful blows, including the deaths of Thursty in 1944 and then her favorite sister

Ethel, who passed away in 1945 aged sixty-five. She had already lost her older sister Louise to a poorly treated case of influenza in 1933. And, of course, both of her parents.

Richard Theodore Greener had died on May 2, 1922, aged seventy-eight. He had never stopped denouncing the injustices to which his Black brothers and sisters were subjected, continuing the fight by means of articles and speeches. Succumbing to a cerebral hemorrhage after many relatively peaceful years living with his Platt cousins, he was buried in the Platt family plot at Graceland Cemetery in Chicago. There was no mention of his illustrious career in any white newspaper; however, Black newspapers all over the country paid tribute to the greatness of his struggles, describing him as "one of the most highly educated, intellectual, and important colored men in the United States." The headline of the *Cincinnati Union* read: THE LAST OF THE OLD GUARD HAS DEPARTED.

None of his children attended his funeral.

On his death certificate, under the category of "race," the medical examiner, going on his physical appearance and residential address, had listed him as white. A final, tragic irony.

\*

After World War Two, rumors began again to swirl about the shadowy past of the Morgan Library's "Lady Directress." How old was she really? Where was she born? Where did she get her olive skin and fiery temperament?

Belle had plenty admirers at the library who dreamed of lifting the veil concealing the mysteries of her life, but neither did she lack detractors who coveted her professional position. She was—perhaps—a colored woman, people said. It was now, for the first time, that the possibility of her "passing" was mentioned.

She refused, then and always, to answer questions about her life, or to cooperate in any way whatsoever with friends who tried to pin down her memories. To all of them, she gave the same refusal, claiming a general dislike of attempts to tell a personal story—hers or anyone's. Her answer to anyone who tried to change her mind was always the same: "Not interested!"

In reality, the thought of her past being turned inside-out after her death horrified her.

Belle Greene, Junior, her niece, never learned of her African roots. She married a white man and had two children; why burden them with their heritage? Why make their future needlessly difficult? Nothing had changed in America, and racial segregation was at its peak. Though the "one-drop rule" had not been voted into law in the North—not officially, at least—racism was everywhere, and discrimination and inequality had never been more acute. Inequality of education, health, justice—and civil rights.

Enough of these injustices! There was only one way for Belle Marion Greener to break the chain weighing her family down: to erase every trace of it. Not to leave behind the slightest thread for the curious to pull on.

She would destroy everything. Burn it all. Photos, letters. All of them. Without sorting, without choosing.

And so Belle spent the late winter of 1948 hard at work in her apartment at 535 Park Avenue. Burning hundreds of thousands of papers in her state—as an invalid who could barely carry the boxes to the fireplace—was a herculean task, of the type that had marked her whole career.

Night after night during the months of January, February, and March 1949, she consigned the relics of her life to the flames. By the advent of spring, all of it had been consumed. The many volumes of her private diaries had gone up in smoke, as had the countless letters from Bernard Berenson—even the ones in which he declared his love for her, and the ones in which he wrote about his research as a historian, his discoveries. More than two thousand pages of them.

When Berenson himself learned of this auto-da-fé, he wrote with horrified rage, "She has destroyed forty years of my life story!"

Belle demanded that B.B. do the same with her letters. He couldn't bring himself to do it.

B.B. had reason to be angry.

Belle, who knew better than anyone the value of archives and the importance of manuscripts, and who still fought to protect, preserve, and transmit the annals of history, had just deliberately and systematically reduced her own recollections, and those of her loved ones, to a heap of ashes.

The only personal document to survive the massacre was Belle's last will and testament. Filed away with her notary in July 1936, she didn't try to recover it. In this document, she left her fortune to Bobbie; her furs, diamonds, and Cartier watches to her mother, sisters, and niece; and her works of art to the Morgan Library. What did it matter to her now? Her dearest ones were dead. The two surviving women of the family, Teddy and Belle Junior, would share the spoils, and Russell would serve as executor. The rest—the collections of Chinese vases and Persian miniatures, the paintings received as gifts from B.B., the antique jewelry, and all the valuable books went to the white marble temple on 36th Street. As planned. There were no other names to add, no names to remove. Although Belle had been all over the world and had friends numbering in the hundreds, her will mentioned no heir.

In this sense, her old will had remained wholly current, focusing, to the last, on the two centers of her life: her family and the library.

In April 1949, the twenty-fifth anniversary of the opening of its collections to the public, the Morgan Library put on an enormous exhibition in tribute to the woman who had breathed life into it and embodied the genius of the place. Miss Belle da Costa Greene. Displayed in her North Room office, and in the two other rooms where so many dramas had played out, were the most priceless trophies of her career: *Le Morte d'Arthur*, of course, and Lord Amherst's Caxtons, as well as the ninth-century Gospel Book from Reims Cathedral and the Lindau Gospels, which she kissed reverently each time she held it in her hands before replacing it in storage in the vault. Two hundred and fifty wonders that she had sought out, tracked down, rescued, and offered to scholars.

This event would be Belle's crowning moment. Her friends and colleagues concocted another surprise for her, as well: an extraordinary volume of written tributes to her. Everyone contributed, even Berenson.

Belle never read it.

Stricken with cancer, she died at St. Luke's Hospital in New York on May 10, 1950. She was seventy-one years old.

The minister who eulogized her at St. Thomas's Episcopal Church subtracted fifteen years from her age and lamented the fact that Miss Greene had been taken from her friends in the prime of her life. So young. So eternally young.

But Belle was wrong when she thought she'd left nothing for posterity.

### The Saga of Miss Greene's "Secret"

At the time of Belle's death, Nina Taylor-Buchet's parents were anxious to avoid damaging their daughter's reputation by divulging the story of Nina's affair with the nephew of the woman they had the abject gall to call "Morgan's nigger whore." The conclusions of their investigation into the African-American origins of the Greene family did not, therefore, go beyond the limits of their own inner circle. A few newspapers hinted at the question in their articles noting Belle's death, but in the 1950s no one dared raise the subject aloud.

Nevertheless, one of Belle's admirers, the great book collector Anne Haight, was determined to gather information about her past.

Thirteen years after Belle's death, Anne asked their mutual friend Dan Thompson if a certain "Richard" was listed in the Harvard alumni directory, Dan having studied there himself. Belle would have been the third child of this Richard, Anne said, born in 1883 in Alexandria, Virginia.

In her letter to Dan Thompson, dated 1963, Anne specified that she had received this information from the wife of Russell Greene.

Dan probably did not reply to the letter, since, in the 1971 edited volume *Notable American Women*, to which Anne Haight contributed an article on Belle, there was no mention of any "Richard." In addition, the date and place of Miss da Costa Greene's birth in the article were incorrect.

Illness prevented Anne Haight from continuing her pursuit of the truth about Belle. She died in 1977.

It was not until 1999 that the historian Jean Strouse discovered Belle's actual birthplace and date of birth, during her research into the life of J.P. Morgan: November 26, 1879, in Washington D.C. Strouse also revealed Belle's relationship to Richard T. Greener for the first time in her biography of the great financier.

It would be a further three years before an exhaustive thesis on Richard Theodore Greener was written by Michael Mounter, a PhD student at the University of South Carolina, in 2002. Unfortunately, this thesis remains unpublished.

The denouement of the story came in 2007, when the first biography of Belle da Costa Greene appeared, written by Heidi Ardizzone, the fruit of a deep archival dive that revealed Belle's secret at last.

In total, more than half a century would go by before rumor became certainty, and the truth came to light

But what truth? The mysteries of Belle Greene's life are far from fully solved. And the saga continues.

## POSTSCRIPT: THE STEAMER TRUNK OF ONE RICHARD GREENER
## CHICAGO 2009–NEW YORK 2024

In the early hours of an icy morning in 2009, a demolition company is tearing down the slums of one of the poorest areas on the south side of Chicago. The foreman of the small team, an African American man named Rufus McDonald, enters one house to take a final look around before moving in with his bulldozer. The place is a shambles, its windowpanes broken, doors torn off their hinges, wooden beams termite-ridden. Everything of any value has been looted by squatters. There is nothing left to save. All the same, McDonald goes upstairs. And there, in plain sight, he finds a steamer trunk covered with labels. "There's something here!" he bellows. From outside, his colleagues shout that they've already seen it. He opens it anyway. A mass of old papers written in several languages, documents printed on the letterhead of government agencies, membership cards for various organizations, a few books . . .

Almost instinctively, he collects everything he can carry, returns to his truck, and stuffs it all into the plastic sacks he uses when running errands. Then he climbs back into his bulldozer and shifts into gear.

When his wife asks him to get the two stinking sacks out of the kitchen, he tells her he's taking them to a second-hand bookstore.

The bookseller there identifies a Harvard diploma dating from the 1870s, and another from the University of South Carolina, dated 1876. He is even able to make out the name of the recipient: one Richard Theodore Greener. The name rings a faint bell in his mind . . .

Three years later, in March 2012, the *Chicago Sun-Times* publishes an article by a famous journalist, with the headline: "It Gives Me Goosebumps: Remarkable Find in South Side Attic."

By now, the bookseller to whom Rufus McDonald brought his find has done some research on Richard Greener: the first Black student to graduate from Harvard, the first Black professor at the University of South Carolina, the first Black attorney to have his diploma ratified by the Supreme Court of a Southern state. The first Black American consul posted to Vladivostok. And, on top of all of that, the father of the famous "Lady Directress" of the Morgan Library. As for the steamer trunk, it is probably the one brought back by Greener from Russia, which he believed lost in the Great San Francisco Fire of 1906. How did it end up in this house, which does not correspond to any address where Greener is known to have lived? It's a mystery. And what other treasures did the trunk hold? What other relics were crushed to dust by the bulldozer?

McDonald decides to sell the papers, the value of which has

been estimated at more than one hundred and twenty thousand dollars—a sum that would enable him to put all of his children through college. But to whom will he sell them, and how? He has no experience in the world of bibliophilia.

In 2013, the University of South Carolina buys all of the documents relating to itself for fifty-two thousand dollars. Harvard's negotiations for the rest of the papers, including the diploma of the first Black student in its history, prove trickier.

Offended by the disdain the Harvard representatives display toward him, and by their ridiculous offers—seven thousand five hundred dollars for the whole lot—Rufus McDonald announces his intention to burn everything. Farewell to the memory of Professor Greener!

His remarks are picked up by the press, which protests the scandal of this planned destruction. McDonald defends himself by saying that he has no other way to arouse the interest of collectors.

Finally, McDonald decides to turn his treasure over to a Chicago auction house. Despite the publicity resulting from his earlier remarks, Greener's diploma is bought by an anonymous bidder, with no counteroffers in the room, for only twelve thousand five hundred dollars.

McDonald's disappointment is only exacerbated by the fact that the diploma ends up in Harvard's archives, anyway. It is unclear if the anonymous buyer has donated it, or if they were in cahoots with the university the whole time.

One thing is certain: Richard Greener has become one of Harvard's most vaunted sons, and his portrait by the artist Stephen Coit will soon be hung in Annenberg Hall, among its great alumni.

Not to be outdone, in February 2018 the University of South Carolina erects a splendid statue of Greener, standing nearly nine feet tall.

And still the saga is not over, as Rufus McDonald continues to sell off his trophies through 2018.

The auctions have now become heated battles fought in the country's most prestigious auction houses. And the spirit of a certain Belle da Costa Greene, with her passion for winning the manuscripts on which she set her heart, seems to be present in the collectors bidding for her father's possessions. The press associates the names of Belle and Greener at every opportunity now, shining the spotlight on the dual destinies of father and daughter.

Both of them, each in his or her own fashion, have come to embody the struggles of Black intellectuals to have equal access to knowledge, justice, and freedom.

The torch is now passed back to the Morgan Library, which has never stopped adding to its collections and putting on superb public exhibitions and now plans a major retrospective dedicated to Belle da Costa Greene. The façade of the white marble palace, built between 1903 and 1905 by Charles F. McKim, with its lionesses, its statues, and its tall bronze doors, has been fully restored, and its gardens will soon follow suit. The Annex, built in 1928 on the site of the private mansion belonging to Jack Morgan's late mother, contains new exhibition spaces. There is also a third building, designed by the great architect Renzo Piano, which includes a new reading room and considerable storage space.

All of these expansions and refurbishments perpetuate the spirit of the woman who inspired the Morgan Library's modernity, and her memory is deeply cherished. The photograph taken of her by Baron Meyer graces postcards on sale in the museum bookstore; her portrait by Helleu is featured on tote bags. And a terra cotta bust of her by the sculptor Jo Davidson is proudly displayed in a room still known to the library's curators as "Belle's office."

In 2024, to mark the one hundredth anniversary of the Morgan Library's opening to the public, Belle's professional correspondence with the great scholars and book dealers of the time—the contents of the library's archives, which she did not think to burn—will be put on display. The history of her acquisitions during the golden age of American collecting will be explained. The many prizes that marked her life and career will be exhibited. And her six hundred and eleven letters to Bernard Berenson will be scanned and put online.

It seems, then, that the rebellious *grande dame* who attempted to deny posterity any trace of herself did not succeed. Her genius and her work are stronger than oblivion. They live on.

The life of Belle da Costa Greene seemed to me to be so exceptional, so novelistic, that I felt I had to stick to the facts as I knew them without altering anything, even in the case of peripheral episodes involving secondary characters that may seem minor.

For example, the incident in which Junius Morgan, pistol in his pocket, goes to visit the Roma at night is an authentic detail, related by one of his friends in the *Princeton Journal*, in his vivid tribute to Junius written the day after his death in 1932. Likewise, during the banking panic of 1907, the sequestration of the country's leading financiers in J.P. Morgan's library really happened. Belle's reading of Morgan's will in his private train car, and the Big Chief's unexpected visit to the Greene family at their rented country house in Tuckahoe are factual, as well—as are the scenes of Bernard Berenson with his wife at the Villa I Tatti and his tantrum on the balcony of the Hotel Europa in Venice in front of Belle and Geoffrey Scott.

All of Belle's professional achievements at Princeton and in London and New York are, of course, established fact.

With the same desire to adhere to what is known, I chose not to interpret events I couldn't learn a great deal about, but to leave them unexplained. These include the reasons for Junius Morgan's permanent move to Paris in August 1909, his absence from his uncle's funeral in 1913, and the omission of his name from J.P. Morgan's will, in which absolutely everyone else is mentioned. What really happened? Despite exhaustive research on Junius, I could find no answer besides the failure of his marriage, which didn't seem to me like enough to justify J.P. Morgan's drastic break with his favorite nephew. So I have left Junius's actions a mystery, since I cannot shed any further light on them. However, his wide-ranging tastes and the quality of his collections should arouse the interest of art historians who may, I hope, pursue further research into this fascinating character.

Neither did I want to invent any of the countless letters Bernard Berenson sent to Belle over the nearly forty years of their relationship, as she herself chose to burn them.

Fortunately, we have her answers to B.B., carefully preserved at the Villa I Tatti, which run to thousands of pages. And we have the correspondence between Berenson and his wife, including the many letters in which they discuss Belle Greene's personality with their mutual friends.

It was the vast corpus of letters from Belle to B.B., as well as all the other correspondence I was able to consult in various archives, that provided food for my imagination, allowing me to describe her affection for and relationship with J.P. Morgan, the confidences she shared with her sister Ethel, and the gossip passed on by Ethel Grant (taken from Grant's letters to Berenson, which are also preserved at the Villa I Tatti). Belle, complaining about this friend who betrayed her in every possible way, was right to write to B.B. on September 2, 1911, that Ethel would do better to "pour her ink straight into the sewer."

Most of the dialogue in this book is taken from letters exchanged between the various protagonists.

Conspiracy theories concerning J.P. Morgan's role in the sinking of the *Titanic* continue to play a role in the mythos of the tragedy. In 2014, a documentary entitled *Was the* Titanic *Deliberately Sunk by J.P. Morgan?* claimed yet again, despite all logic and evidence to the contrary, that Morgan was behind a plot to sink the ocean liner.

Finally, and obviously, that terrible letter from Robert Leveridge's fiancée, the letter Belle's nephew received in England in 1943 and that he entrusted to the director of the Courtald Institute before his suicide, really existed. The original document can be found today in the Archives of American Art, among the papers of Daniel Varney Thompson.

Readers will find a list of my other sources, published and unpublished, in the general bibliography that follows. But first and foremost, I want to give credit to the four biographers whose books have never been off my desk in all these years. First, Heidi Ardizzone's *An Illuminated Life*, a herculean work that gives new insight into every area of Belle's life and the traces she left behind, and Jean Strouse's masterful biography *Morgan*. Next, Michael Mounter's exhaustive PhD thesis on Richard Theodore Greener. And, of course, *Being Bernard Berenson* by Meryle Secrest, which provides some keys to the complex personality of that great art historian.

BIBLIOGRAPHY

Published sources

AMHERST, William Amhurst Tyssen-, *Catalogue of the Magnificent Library of Choice and Valuable Books & Manuscripts, the Property of the Rt. Hon. Lord Amherst of Hackney.* London: Dryden Press, 1908.

ARDIZZONE, Heidi, *An Illuminated Life: Belle da Costa Greene's Journey from Prejudice to Privilege.* New York and London: W.W. Norton & Company, 2007.

ARDIZZONE, Heidi, and LEWIS, *Earl, Love on Trial: An American Scandal in Black and White.* New York: W.W. Norton & Company, 2002.

AUCHINCLOSS, Louis, *J.P. Morgan: The Financier as Collector.* New York: Harry N. Abrams, 1990.

BARNET, Andrea, *All-Night Party: The Women of Bohemian Greenwich Village and Harlem, 1913–1930.* Chapel Hill: Algonquin Books of Chapel Hill, 2004.

BASBANES, Nicholas A., *A Gentle Madness: Bibliophiles, Bibliomanes, and the Eternal Passion for Books.* New York: Henry Holt, 1995.

—"Henry E. Huntington's 'Little Game'," *Gazette of the Grolier Club*, New Series, 44 (1992): 5–17.

BERENSON, Bernard, *Aesthetics and History.* New York: Pantheon Books, 1948.

—*The Bernard Berenson Treasury*, edited by Hanna Kiel, with an introduction by John Walker and a preface by Nicky Mariano. New York: Simon & Schuster, 1962.

—*The Central Italian Painters of the Renaissance.* New York: G.P. Putnam's Sons, 1897.

—"Contemporary Jewish Fiction," *Andover Review: A Religious and Theological Monthly* 10 (December 1888): 587–593.

—"The Death and Burial of Israel Koppel," *Harvard Monthly* 6 (July 1888): 177–194.

—*The Drawings of the Florentine Painters*. Chicago: University of Chicago Press, 1938.

—*Essays in Appreciation*. New York: Macmillan, 1958.

—*The Florentine Painters of the Renaissance: With an Index to Their Works*. London: G.P. Putnam's Sons, 1896.

—"How Matthew Arnold Impressed Me," *Harvard Monthly* 5 (November 1887): 53–56.

—*Italian Painters of the Renaissance*, vol. 1: *Venetian and North Italian Schools*, and vol. 2: *Florentine and Central Italian Schools*. London: Phaidon, 1968.

—*Looking at Pictures with Bernard Berenson*, with an introduction by Hanna Kiel, and a personal reminiscence by J. Carter Brown. New York: Harry N. Abrams, 1974.

—*Lorenzo Lotto: An Essay in Constructive Art Criticism*. London: G.P. Putnam's Sons, 1895.

—*North Italian Painters of the Renaissance*. London: G.P. Putnam's Sons, 1907.

—*One Year's Reading for Fun (1942)*, introduction by John Walker. New York: Alfred A. Knopf, 1960.

—*The Passionate Sightseer: From the Diaries, 1947–1956*. London: Thames and Hudson, 1960.

—*Rumor and Reflection*. New York: Simon & Schuster, 1962.

—*The Selected Letters of Bernard Berenson*, edited by A.K. McComb with an afterword by Nicky Mariano. Boston: Houghton Mifflin, 1963.

—*Sketch for a Self-Portrait*. New York: Pantheon, 1949.

—*The Study and Criticism of Italian Art*, Third Series. London: George Bell & Sons, 1916.

—*Sunset and Twilight: From the Diaries of 1947–1958*. New York: Harcourt, Brace & World, 1963.

—"The Third Category," *Harvard Monthly* 3 (November 1886): 66–83.

—*Three Essays on Method*, Oxford: Clarendon Press, 1927.

—*The Venetian Painters of the Renaissance: With an Index to Their Works*. London: G.P. Putnam's Sons, 1894.

—"Was Mohammed at All an Impostor?," *Harvard Monthly* 4 (April 1887): 48–63.

BERENSON, Bernard, and COSTER, Charles Henry, *The Letters between Bernard Berenson and Charles Henry Coster*, edited by Giles Constable in collaboration with Elizabeth H. Beatson and Luca Dainelli. Florence: Leo S. Olschki, 1993.

BERENSON, Bernard, and STEWART GARDNER, Isabella, *The Letters of Bernard Berenson and Isabella Stewart Gardner, 1887–1924*, edited by Rollin Van N. Hadley. Boston: Northeastern University Press, 1987.

BERENSON, Bernard, and MARGHIERI, Clotilde, *A Matter of Passion: Letters of Bernard Berenson and Clotilde Marghieri*, edited by Dario Biocca. Berkeley: University of California Press, 1989.

BERENSON, Mary, *A Modern Pilgrimage*. New York: D. Appleton, 1933.

—*A Self-Portrait from Her Diaries and Letters*, edited by Barbara Strachey and Jayne Samuels. New York: W.W. Norton, 1983.

BLAKELY, Allison, "Richard T. Greener and the 'Talented Tenth's' Dilemma," *The Journal of Negro History*, no. 59 (October 1974): 305–321.

BOND DAY, Caroline, *A Study of Some Negro-White Families in the United States*. Cambridge: Peabody Museum, Harvard University, 1932.

BRUCCOLI, Matthew J., *The Fortunes of Mitchell Kennerley, Bookman*. New York: Harcourt Brace Jovanovich, 1986.

BURMA, John H., "The Measurement of Negro 'Passing'," *American Journal of Sociology*, no. 52 (July 1946): 18–22.

CANFIELD, Cass, *The Incredible Pierpont Morgan: Financier and Art Collector*. New York: Harper & Row, 1974.

CHADDOCK, Katherine R., *Uncompromising Activist, Richard Greener, First Black Graduate of Harvard College*. Baltimore: Johns Hopkins University Press, 2017.

CHERNOW, Ron, *The House of Morgan: An American Banking Dynasty and the Rise of Modern Finance*. New York: The Atlantic Monthly Press, 1990.

COHEN, Rachel, *Bernard Berenson: A Life in the Picture Trade*, New Haven and London: Yale University Press, 2013.

CONNORS, Joseph, and WALDMAN, Louis, A. (eds.), *Bernard Berenson: Formation and Heritage*. Massachusetts: Harvard University Press, Cambridge, 2014.

COSTAMAGNA, Philippe, *Histoires d'œils*. Paris: Grasset, 2016.

DAVIS, Angela, *Women, Race & Class*. New York: Vintage, 1983.

DOWLING TAYLOR, Elizabeth, *The Original Black Elite: Daniel Murray and the Story of a Forgotten Era*. New York: HarperCollins, 2017.

DUGGAN, Brian Patrick, *Saluki. The Desert Hound and the English Travelers Who Brought It to the West*. London: McFarland & Company, 2009.

DUPONT, Inge, and HOPE, Mayo (eds.), *Morgan Library Ghost Story*. New York: Fordham University Press, 1990.

DURLACHER, George, *Eighty-five Years of Art Dealing: A Short Record of the House of the Durlacher Brothers*, London: 1928.

ELLIOTT, David B., *Charles Fairfax Murray: The Unknown Pre-Raphaelite*. Leicester: Book Guild, 2000.

FABRE, Michel, *Harlem 1900–1935: De la métropole noire au ghetto, de la Renaissance culturelle à l'exclusion*. Paris: Autrement, 1993.

FAULKNER, William, *Light in August*. New York: Random House, 1932.

FAUSET, Jessie Redmon, *Plum Bun, A Novel without a Moral*, Frederick A. Stokes, 1929.

FORSTER, E.M., *Howards End*. London: Penguin Classics, 2012.

GATEWOOD, Willard B., *Aristocrats of Color, The Black Elite: 1880–1920*. Arkansas: University of Arkansas Press, 2000.

GENNARI SANTORI, Flaminia, "European 'Masterpieces' for America. Roger Fry and the Metropolitan Museum of Art," in *Art Made Modern. Roger Fry's Vision of Art*, edited by C. Green. London: Merell Publishers Ltd, 1999: 107–118.

—*James Jackson Jarves and the Diffusion of Tuscan Painting in the United States*, in *Gli anglo-americani a Firenze: idea e costruzione del Rinascimento*, conference proceedings, Fiesole, 19–20 June 1997, edited by M. Fantoni, D. Lamberini and J. Pfordresher. Rome: Bulzoni, 2000: 177–206.

—"The Taste of Business. Defining the American Art Collector 1900–1914," in *Across the Atlantic. Cultural Exchanges between Europe and the United States*, edited by L. Passerini. Brussels: Peter Lang, 2000: 73–92.

—"Holmes, Fry, Jaccaci and the 'Art in America' Section of *The Burlington Magazine*, 1905–10," in *The Burlington Magazine*, no. 145 (2003): 153–163.

—*The Melancholy of Masterpieces. Old Master Paintings in America 1900–1914*. Milan: 5 Continents Editions, 2003.

—"I musei e il mercato dell'arte," in *Il Rinascimento Italian e l'Europa, vol. 1: Storia e storiografia*, edited by M. Fantoni, Treviso, Angelo Colla Editore, 2005: 489–510.

—"Renaissance *fin de siècle:* Models of Patronage and Patterns of Taste in American Press and Fiction (1880–1914)," in *Victorian and Edwardian Responses to the Italian Renaissance*, edited by John E. Law and Lene Østermark-Johansen. Routledge, Ashgate, 2005: 105–120.

—"Medieval Art for America: The Arrival of the J. Pierpont Morgan Collection to the Metropolitan Museum of Art," *Journal of the History of Collections*, 22 (2010): 81–98.

—"'I Was to Have All the Finest': Renaissance Bronzes from John Pierpont Morgan to Henry Clay-Frick," *Journal of the History of Collections*, 22 (2010): 307–324.

—"An Art Collector and His Friends: John Pierpont Morgan and the Globalization of Medieval Art," *Journal of the History of Collections*, 27 (2015): 401–411.

—"'This Feminine Scholar': Belle da Costa Greene and the Shaping of J.P. Morgan's Legacy," *Visual Resources*, vol. 33, nos. 1–2 (March–July 2017).

GENNARI SANTORI, Flaminia, and VIGNON, Charlotte, "From Private Homes to Museum Galleries. Medieval Art in America from 1890 to 1940," in *Gothic Art in the Gilded Age*, edited by V. Brilliant. Paris: Periscope, 2009: 53–64.

—"J. Pierpont Morgan, Joseph Duveen e le collezioni americane di maiolica italiana," in *1909 Tra collezionismo e tutela*. Florence: Giunti, 2010: 281–291.

GREENE, Belle, *The Pierpont Morgan Library: A Review of the Growth, Development and Activities of the Library during the Period between its Establishment as an Educational Institution in February 1924 and the Close of the Year 1929*. New York: Pierpont Morgan Library, 1930.

—*The Pierpont Morgan Library: Review of the Activities and Acquisitions of the Library from 1930 through 1935: A Summary of the Annual Report of the Director to the Board of Trustees*. New York: Pierpont Morgan Library, 1937.

—*The Pierpont Morgan Library: Review of the Activities and Acquisitions of the Library from 1936 through 1940: A Summary of the Annual Report of the Director to the Board of Trustees*. New York: Pierpont Morgan Library, 1941.

—*The Pierpont Morgan Library: Review of the Activities and Acquisitions of the Library from 1941 through 1948: A Summary of the Annual Report of the Director to the Board of Trustees*. New York: Pierpont Morgan Library, 1949.

GREENER, Richard T., "Professor Greener and the Colored

Race, Letter to the Editor of *The New York Times*," *The New York Times*, 21 January 1881.

HADLEY, Rollin Van N., *The Letters of Bernard Berenson and Isabella Stewart Gardner 1887–1924*. Boston: Northeastern University Press, 1987.

HERRMANN, Frank, *Sotheby's. Portrait of an Auction House*. London: Chatto & Windus, 1980.

HOBBS, Allyson, *A Chosen Exile: A History of Racial Passing in American Life*. Cambridge, Massachusetts and London: Harvard University Press, 2014.

HOCHMANN, Michel, *Colorito, la technique des peintres vénitiens à la Renaissance*. Turnhout: Brepols, 2015.

HOMBERGER, Eric, *Mrs. Astor's New York: Money and Social Power in a Gilded Age*. New Haven: Yale University Press, 2002.

HUGHES, Langston, *The Ways of White Folk*. New York: Alfred Knopf, 1934.

—*The Big Sea*. New York: Hill & Wang, 1940.

—*The Short Stories of Langston Hughes*. New York: Hill & Wang, 1997.

HURST, Fannie, *Imitation of Life*, New York: Perennial Library, 1990.

HUTCHINSON, George, *In Search of Nella Larsen: A Biography of the Color Line*. Cambridge: Harvard University Press, 2006.

JAMES, Henry, *The Outcry*. Cambridge: Cambridge University Press, 2016.

JOHNSON, James Weldon, *The Autobiography of an Ex-Colored Man*. Boston: Sherman, French & Company, 1912.

KOPPELMAN, Constance, "Belle da Costa Greene," in *American National Biography*, edited by John A. Garraty and Mark C. Carnes. New York: Oxford University Press, 1999: 518–519.

KROEGER, Brooke, *Passing: When People Can't Be Who They Are*. New York: PublicAffairs, 2003.

LARSEN, Nella, *Quicksand*. New York: Alfred Knopf, 1928.

—*Passing*. New York: Alfred Knopf, 1929.

LEFÈBRE, Raoul, *Recuyell of the Historyes of Troye*. Ghent: William Caxton, 1473–1474.

LEHR, Elizabeth D., *"King Lehr" and the Gilded Age*. New York: J.B. Lippincott Company, 1935.

LOUCHHEIM, Aline B., "The Morgan Library and Miss Greene," *The New York Times*, 17 April 1949.

MALORY, Sir Thomas, *Thus Endeth Thys Noble and Joyous Book Entytled Le Morte d'Arthur*. Westminster: William Caxton, 1480.

MARIANO, Nicky, *Forty Years with Berenson*. New York: Alfred Knopf, 1966.

—*The Berenson Archive: An Inventory of Correspondence Compiled on the Centenary of the Birth of Bernard Berenson*. Florence, Villa I Tatti: The Harvard University Center for Italian Renaissance Studies, 1965.

McCANN, Carole R., *Birth Control Politics in the United States, 1916–1945*. Ithaca: Cornell University Press, 1994.

MINER, Dorothy, *Studies in Art and Literature for Belle da Costa Greene*. New Jersey: Princeton University Press, 1954.

MINER, Dorothy and LYON HAIGHT, Anne, "Belle da Costa Greene," in *Notable American Women, 1607–1950: A Biographical Dictionary*, edited by Edward T. James, and Janet Wilson James, Harvard University Press, Belknap Press, 1971: 83–85.

MOORE, Jacqueline M., *Leading the Race: The Transformation of the Black Elite in the Nation's Capital, 1880–1920*. Charlottesville: University Press of Virginia, 1999.

MORGAN, Junius Spencer, "The History of the Text of Virgil," in *The Tradition of Virgil*. Princeton: Princeton University Press, 1930.

NICHOLSON, Virginia, *Among the Bohemians: Experiments in Living, 1900–1939*. New York: William Morrow, 2002.

OSBORNE, J. W., "A Liaison to Remember: the Friendship of

Belle da Costa Greene and Bernard Berenson," *Biblio*, vol. 2, no. 11 (November 1997): 38–41.

PATTERSON, Jerry E., *The First Four Hundred: Mrs. Astor's New York in the Gilded Age*. New York: Rizzoli, 2000.

PFEIFFER, Kathleen, *Race Passing and American Individualism*. Amherst: University of Massachusetts Press, 2003.

RICCETTI, Lucio, *Alexandre Imbert, J. Pierpont Morgan, e il collezionismo della maiolica italiana, fino al 1914*. Florence: Edizioni Polistampa, 2018.

ROSENBACH, A. S. W., *A Book Hunter's Holyday: Adventures with Books and Manuscripts*. New York: Books for Libraries Press, 1968.

—*The Unpublishable Memoirs*. Sydney: Leopold Classic Library, 2015.

ROTH, Philip, *The Human Stain*. London: Jonathan Cape, 2000.

SAARINEN, Aline B., *The Proud Possessors: The Lives, Times, and Tastes of Some Adventurous American Art Collectors*. New York: Random House, 1958.

SAMUELS, Ernest, *Bernard Berenson: The Making of a Connoisseur*. Cambridge: Harvard University Press, Belknap Press, 1979.

—*Bernard Berenson: The Making of a Legend*. Cambridge: Harvard University Press, Belknap Press, 1987.

SANDWEISS, Martha, *Passing Strange: A Gilded Age Tale of Love and Deception across the Color Line*. New York: Penguin Books, 2009.

SECREST, Meryle, *Being Bernard Berenson: A Biography*. New York: Holt, Rinehart and Winston, 1979.

—*Duveen: A Life in Art*. Chicago: Chicago University Press, 2004.

SELIGMAN, Germain, *Merchants of Art, 1880–1960: Eighty Years of Professional Collecting*. London: Forgotten Books, 2015.

SHARFSTEIN, Daniel J., *The Invisible Line: Three American Families and the Secret Journey from Black to White*. New York: Penguin Books, 2011.

SHAW, Stephanie, *What a Woman Ought to Be and to Do: Black Professional Women Workers during the Jim Crow Era*. Chicago: University of Chicago Press, 1996.

SIMPSON, Colin, *Artful Partners: Bernard Berenson and Joseph Duveen*. New York: Macmillan, 1986.

SINCLAIR, Andrew, *Corsair: The Life of J. Pierpont Morgan*. Boston: Little, Brown, 1981.

SMITH, Jane S., *Elsie de Wolfe: A Life in the High Style*. New York: Atheneum, 1982.

SMITH-PRYOR, Elizabeth M., *Property Rites: The Rhinelander Trial, Passing, and the Protection of Whiteness*. Chapel Hill: University of North Carolina Press, 2009.

SOLLORS, Werner, *Neither Black nor White Yet Both: Thematic Explorations of Interracial Literature*. Cambridge: Harvard University Press, 1997.

SOLLORS, Werner, TITCOMB, Caldwell, and UNDERWOOD, Thomas A., *Blacks at Harvard: A Documentary History of African-American Experience at Harvard and Radcliffe*. New York: New York University Press, 1993.

STERLING, Dorothy, *We Are Your Sisters: Black Women in the Nineteenth Century*. New York: W.W. Norton, 1984.

STILLWELL BINGHAM, Margaret, *Librarians Are Human: Memories in and out of the Rare-Book World, 1907–1970*. Boston: University Press of New England, 1973.

STOCKETT, Kathryn, *The Help*, Penguin Books, 2009.

STRACHEY, Barbara and SAMUELS, Jayne, *Mary Berenson: A Self-Portrait from Her Diaries and Letters*. New York: W.W. Norton, 1983.

STREHKLE, Carl Brandon and MACHTELT, Brüggen Israëls, *The Bernard and Mary Collection of European Paintings at I Tatti*. Milan: Officina Libraria, 2015.

STROUSE, Jean, *Morgan, American Financier*. New York: Random House, 1999.

SYNNOTT, Marcia G., *The Half-Opened Door: Discrimination and Admissions at Harvard, Yale, and Princeton, 1900–1970*. Westport: Greenwood Press, 1979.

TALTY, Stephan, *Mulatto America: At the Crossroads of Black and White Culture: A Social History*. New York: HarperCollins, 2003.

TANABE, Karin, *The Gilded Years: A Novel*. New York: Simon & Schuster, 2016.

TONE, Andrea, *Devices and Desires: A History of Contraceptives in America*. New York: Hill & Wang, 2001.

TOWNER, Wesley, *The Elegant Auctioneers*. New York: Farrar, Straus and Giroux, 1970.

UPSON, Arthur, *The Collected Poems of Arthur Upson*, vol. I and vol. II. Minneapolis: Edmund D. Brooks, 1909.

VOELKLE, William M., and L'ENGLE, Susan, *Illuminated Manuscripts: Treasures of the Pierpont Morgan Library, New York*. New York: Abbeville Press, 1998.

WALD, Gayle, *Crossing the Line: Racial Passing in Twentieth Century U.S. Literature and Culture*. Durham: Duke University Press, 2000.

WETZSTEON, Ross, *Republic of Dreams: Greenwich Village: The American Bohemia, 1910–1960*. New York: Simon & Schuster, 2002.

WHITE, Walter Francis, *Flight*. Baton Rouge: Louisiana State University Press, 1998.

WILSON TOLFORD, Mary, "Belle da Costa Greene," in *Dictionary of American Biography, Supplement Four, 1946–1950*, edited by Edward T. James, and John A. Garraty. New York: Scribner, 1974: 344–346.

WOOLF, Virginia, *Roger Fry*. London: Penguin Books, 2003.

WROTH, Lawrence C., *The First Quarter Century of the Pierpont Morgan Library: A Retrospective Exhibition in Honor of Belle da Costa Greene.* New York: Pierpont Morgan Library, 1949.

## Press articles about major sales and about Belle Greene

"Hoe's Gutenberg Bible Is Sold for 50 000 dollars," *New York Tribune*, 25 April 1911.

"J.P. Morgan's Librarian Says High Book Prices Are Harmful," *The Sunday Magazine of The New York Times*, 30 April 1911.

"Morgan pays 42 800 dollars for a Book at Hoe Sale," *The New York Times*, 2 May 1911.

"Fifty Thousand Dollars for That Book!," *The World Magazine*, 21 May 1911.

"In the Public Eye, More or Less, at the Present Moment," *New York Daily Tribune*, 28 May 1911.

"Spending J.P. Morgan's Money for Rare Books," *The Sunday Magazine of The New York Times*, 7 April 1912.

"'The Cleverest Girl I Know' Says J. Pierpont Morgan," *The Chicago Tribune*, 11 August 1912.

"Women Who Are Paid Princely Salaries for Their Ability to Keep Secrets," *The Washington Post*, 16 February 1913.

"Beautiful Women of Society in Artistic Poses before the Camera," *The San Francisco Sunday Call*, 16 February 1913.

"Helleu Talks of Pictures He Did for The Times," *The New York Times*, 16 March 1913.

"Miss Greene Misquoted," *The New York Times*, 7 December 1913.

"In the Limelight," *Chicago Tribune Pictorial Weekly*, 2 May 1915.

"Opportunity Will Come to the Prepared and Success Is a Matter of Undivided Loyalty," *The Evening Sun*, 19 October 1916.

"Miss Belle Greene," *The Kenna Record*, 24 June 1921.

"Morgan Librarian," *The Times Literary Supplement*, 13 November 1948.

"Belle of the Books," *The Time Magazine*, 11 April 1949.

## Unpublished sources

MEMOIRS, THESES, AND DISSERTATIONS

ARDIZZONE, Heidi, *Red-Blooded Americans: Mulattoes and the Melting Pot in American Racialist and Nationalist Discourse, 1890–1930*, University of Michigan, 1997.

GREENE, Russell da Costa, *An Investigation into Methods of Dressing Land Pebble Phosphate Rock with a View to Effecting a Greater Saving*, University of Tennessee, 1913.

GREENER, Richard T., *The Tenure of Land in Ireland*, Harvard College, 1870.

JOHNSTON, Tiffany L., *Mary Berenson and the Conception of Connoisseurship*, Indiana University, 2001.

MOUNTER, Michael Robert, *Richard Theodore Greener: The Idealist, Statesman, Scholar and South Carolinian*, University of South Carolina, 2002.

ROPER, John Herbert, *The Radical Mission: The University of South Carolina in Reconstruction*, University of North Carolina, 1973.

SMITH, Stephanie D., *Passing Shadows: Illuminating the Veiled Legacy of Belle da Costa Greene*, Dominican University, 2015.

SWAN, Robert Joseph, *Thomas McCants Stewart and the Failure of the Mission of the Talented Tenth in Black America, 1880–1923*, New York University, 1990.

WHITE, Pamela Mercedes, *"Free and Open": The Radical University of South Carolina, 1873–1877*, University of South Carolina, 1975.

# Archival holdings

ARCHIVES OF AMERICAN ART, Smithsonian Institution, Washington D.C.
—William Mills Ivins Papers 1878–1974, Correspondence, 1908–1961, boxes 1 and 2.
—Mary Fanton Roberts Papers, Art Correspondence, series 4, box 1, folder 53.
—Jacques Seligman Papers, Correspondence, box 6, folder 6; box 42, folder 16.
—Daniel Varney Thompson Papers 1848–1979, Personal and Professional 1923–1979, box 3, folders 11 and 23.

ARCHIVES OF THE PIERPONT MORGAN LIBRARY, New York
—Morgan Collections Correspondence, 1906–1920 (Léon and Paul Gruel; Bernard Quaritch; Charles Hercules Read).
—Records of the Director's Office (Belle Greene), 1920–1940.
—John Pierpont Morgan Jr., Papers, 1910–1943.
—Records of the Director's Office (Greene-Adams), 1940–1950.
—J.P. Morgan and Amicorum: Manuscript Guest Books of Visitors to Pierpont Morgan's Library, 1908–1996.
—Last Will and Testament of J. Pierpont Morgan, 1913.
—"Junius Spencer Morgan, Class of 88," typescript tribute by Philipp Ashton Rollins, September 1932.
—Last Will and Testament of Belle da Costa Greene, 1936–1951.

NEW YORK PUBLIC LIBRARY ARCHIVES, Manuscripts and Archives Division
—Mitchell Kennerley Papers, MssCol 1634, boxes 1–10.

VILLA I TATTI ARCHIVES, Harvard Center for Italian Renaissance Studies, Villa I Tatti, Florence

—Letters by Belle da Costa Greene to Bernard and Mary Berenson 1909–1925, boxes 60–64 (Ber 8).

—Letters by William Mills Ivins (Billee Ivins) to Bernard Berenson 1924–1925, folder 71.1 (Ber 8).

—Letters by Ethel Grant to Bernard Berenson 1910–1912, folder 58.33 (Ber 8).

—Letters by Ethel Grant to Belle da Costa Greene 1912, folder 58.34 (Ber 8).

—Letters by Senda Berenson, married name Abbott, to Bernard Berenson 1910–1911, folder 23.2 (Ber 8).

ARCHIVES OF PRINCETON UNIVERSITY LIBRARY, Manuscripts Division, Department of Special Collections, Morgan Family Papers, C0553

—Letters by Junius Spencer Morgan II to his wife Josephine Perry Morgan. 1905–1913, box 16.

ICONOGRAPHY
SOME PORTRAITS OF BELLE DA COSTA GREENE

## Photographs

Ernest Walter HISTED, portrait series, 1910 (Berenson Archives, Villa I Tatti, Florence).

Theodore C. MARCEAU, portrait series, 1911 (Archives of the Pierpont Morgan Library, New York).

Baron Adolph de MEYER, portrait series, 1911 (Archives of the Pierpont Morgan Library, New York).

Clarence H. WHITE, portrait series, 1911 (Berenson Archives, Villa I Tatti, Florence).

## Sketches, watercolors, and terra cotta

Laura COOMBS HILLS, *Belle da Costa Greene*, 1910 (The Pierpont Morgan Library, New York).

Jo DAVIDSON, *Belle da Costa Greene*, 1925 (The Pierpont Morgan Library, New York).

Paul HELLEU, *Portrait of Belle da Costa Greene*, 1912 (The Pierpont Morgan Library, New York).

Henri MATISSE, *Female Nude before a Figured Curtain*, before 1912 (The Pierpont Morgan Library, New York).

René PIOT, *Belle da Costa Greene*, 1910 (Berenson Archives, Villa I Tatti, Florence).

William ROTHENSTEIN, *Head of Belle da Costa Greene*, 1912 (The Pierpont Morgan Library, New York).

# Filmography

ASANTE, Amma, *Belle*, 2013.
—*A United Kingdom*, 2016.
FARRELLY, Peter, *Green Book*, 2018.
KAZAN, Elia, *Pinky*, 1949.
—*Gentlemen's Agreement*, 1947.
KRAMER, Stanley, *Guess Who's Coming to Dinner*, 1967.
LEE, Spike, *BlacKkKlansman*, 2018.
PECK, Raoul, *I Am Not Your Negro*, 2016.
TAYLOR, Tate, *The Help*, 2011.
WERKER, Alfred L., *Lost Boundaries*, 1949.

# A Brief Glossary of Book Terms

**Autograph:** A document written by the hand of its author. There can be autograph letters (handwritten by the author), signed autograph letters (handwritten and signed by the author), and signed autograph manuscripts (handwritten and signed by the author).

**Bibliophilia:** The love of books. Bibliophiles are individuals passionately fond of books.

**Binding:** The act or art of binding the leaves of a book

**Blind-stamped percaline:** Cloth binding decorated with illustrations in relief

**Breviary:** Catholic religious book containing all of the prayers of the Divine Office except the mass

**Broadside:** A book in which the printed page is not folded

**Codex:** The gathering of leaves of paper, parchment, or other similar material; or a book by another name. Usually refers to an ancient manuscript.

**Cover:** The part of a book that protects its pages and usually includes the title, author's name, and the name of the publisher. A cover is called "blank" when there are no credits, or "dummy" when it is has temporary paper covers before being bound. A paperback book has a paper cover, while a bound book has a stiff cardboard cover covered with leather, cloth, or paper.

**Crest/Coat of arms:** Heraldic symbols dating back to the Middle Ages and symbolizing a family, a city, or a people. Usually stamped on the front board of a binding.

**Deluxe edition:** Also called "luxury editions," these are copies of a book printed on high-quality paper and often with illustrations or ornate bindings that are not available in the standard edition. Rare and numbered, they are highly prized by collectors.

**Duodecimo:** Book produced from full sheets printed with twenty-four pages of text, twelve to a side, then folded twice to produce twelve leaves. The leaves are then trimmed along the folds to produce twenty-four book pages.

**Edge:** A book has three edges; these are the three sides other than the spine. They are the fore edge (opposite the spine), the top edge (head), and the bottom edge (foot).

**Edge-gilding:** The application of a fine layer of gilt or gold to the edges of a book

**Edition:** All the copies of a book printed from the same plates or typesetting

**Ex-libris:** Inscription indicating the owner of a book. This inscription can take the form of handwriting or a printed or engraved label or square of paper bearing initials, a symbol, a crest or arms, or a name. It is usually pasted to the inner board of a volume. Ex-libris is a collecting theme for many bibliophiles.

**First edition:** An original, or *princeps* edition (from the Latin for "first") is the first appearance of a book in its first printing. Subsequent editions are called revised editions. Some of these editions are limited to a small number of copies and numbered, which makes them valuable items sought after by collectors.

**Flyleaf:** Blank sheets of paper placed at the beginning and end of a book to create a barrier between the binding and the main body of the book

**Folio:** Large-format book in which the sheet of paper is folded once, thus giving two leaves, or four pages

**Frontispiece:** Illustrated page that precedes and usually faces the title page of a book

**Gilding:** A thin layer of gilt or gold applied to a book. Gilding may be applied to the spine, the boards, and even the edges of the pages.

**Half leather binding:** A style of bookbinding in which spine and the corners of both the front and back boards of a book are covered with leather, while the remaining portions of the front and back boards are covered with a different material

**Illumination:** Small decorations (often ornate letters) illustrating the pages of a book or a manuscript. Illuminations were very common in medieval manuscripts, books of hours, and religious texts.

**Incunabulum:** From the Latin *cunabulum*, meaning "cradle" or "beginning." A book printed during the years between the invention of printing by Gutenberg (1450) and 1501. True collector's items, these books date from the transition period between the era of the codex and the printed books of the sixteenth century.

**Inside cover:** The inner surface of the cover of a bound book

**Laid paper:** A type of paper made on wire molds (called laid lines and chain lines) that give a characteristic watermark of close thin lines

**Limited edition:** Edition of a book deliberately limited to a relatively small number of copies. Usually numbered and often signed by the author, these copies are highly prized by collectors.

**Manuscript:** The original form of a book when it is first written by the author

**Morocco:** Thick leather with a visible grain, usually made from Moroccan goatskin. Often used in bookbinding due to its beauty and strength.

**Nerves:** Raised bands on the spine of a book formed by the sewing threads used to stitch the quires together

**Octavo:** Book produced from full sheets printed with sixteen pages of text, eight to a side, then folded three times to produce eight leaves. The leaves are then trimmed along the folds to produce sixteen book pages.

**Paperback:** A book bound in blank or printed paper that is glued to the spine and constitutes the book's cover

**Plates:** Full-page illustrations printed separately from the text of a book

**Printer's mark:** In the earliest days of printing, these marks, also called colophons, were inserted by printers at the end of a book to verify that they had produced it. Located on the title page from the sixteenth century onward, the marks can be very simple or take the form of a monogram or a logo.

**Provenance:** The history of the ownership of a book

**Publication date:** The date on which a book is officially put on sale

**Quarto:** Book produced from full sheets printed with eight pages of text, four to a side, then folded twice to produce four leaves. The leaves are then trimmed along the folds to produce eight book pages.

**Quire:** A set of pages created by the folding and cutting of a large sheet of paper. Medieval manuscripts are usually composed of multiple quires stacked and sewn together with linen thread.

**Roan leather:** Sheepskin tanned with plant extracts, used for ordinary bindings. The lifespan of these bindings is shorter than that of Morocco, calfskin, or shagreen.

**Scritta paper:** Extremely thin, fine, tissue-like yet strong paper, used to reduce the thickness of a book

**Shagreen:** Rough rawhide leather usually made from the skins of goats, donkeys, or mules, and used in binding to cover part or all of a book

**Spine:** The part of the book that is visible when it is stored on a bookshelf

**Tissue guard:** A thin sheet of tissue paper placed protectively over an illustration

**Vellum (binding):** Ivory-colored calfskin specially prepared for use in binding, finer than ordinary parchments.

**Vellum (paper):** Very white, ungrained paper that evokes the smoothness of binding vellum

**Watermark:** A faint imprint made in paper that becomes visible only when the sheet is held up to the light. The watermark typically includes the brand and maker of the paper, and sometimes the date of manufacture.

**Yellowing:** The darkening of paper when it has been exposed to light

## Acknowledgments

I began following Belle's trail quite by chance, four years before the coronavirus pandemic began. It was in Italy, during a working lunch with two prominent scholars, Vincent Jolivet and Luca Pesante, that the achievements of the great art historian Bernard Berenson came up. In that little restaurant just a few steps from the library of the École Française de Rome, we discussed the richness and beauty of the library in the hills of Florence that Berenson had bequeathed to Harvard University, and the extraordinary collections of that other American library where some of us had conducted research, the Morgan Library in New York. It was then that Luca Pesante mentioned the name of Belle da Costa Greene, which rang a faint bell for me, as I had heard her spoken of in the Morgan Library when I was researching Robert Louis Stevenson almost thirty years earlier. Back then, Belle's personality had intrigued me enough that I had asked a few questions about her career . . . before allowing myself to be swallowed up entirely by the whirlwind adventures of Fanny Stevenson.

By that evening on the very same day of our lunch, I was looking through my old notes again.

As luck would have it, just a few days later I made the acquaintance, at the home of mutual friends, of Flaminia Gennari Santori, director of the Barberini Museum and the Corsini Museum in Rome. Nothing at all to do with Belle, at first glance.

But, seated together at the end of the table, we tried amidst the hubbub to have a conversation. Leaning close so that I could hear her, she talked about her years of study in the United States and the articles she had written on . . . Belle da Costa Greene. You could have knocked me over with a feather. We were probably the only two people in the room who were familiar with that name. We fell into each other's arms.

How can I possibly thank her here?

The die was cast. I couldn't get Belle's face out of my mind.

How, too, can I adequately thank Ilaria Della Monica, curator of the Berenson Library Archives at the Villa I Tatti, who allowed me not only to consult the hundreds of letters from Belle to B.B., but also all of the letters from Berenson's other correspondents, in which they discussed the enigma that was "Miss Greene"?

And the director of the Morgan Library, Colin C. Bailey, who gave me such a warm reception in New York? And Christine Nelson, the Drue Heinz curator of literary and historical manuscripts at the Morgan Library; Daria Rose Foner, research associate to the director; and Maria Isabel Molestina, head of reader services, whose help was so invaluable in the archives of that magnificent library?

Thanks also to Jean Bonna, the great collector who took the time to initiate me into the secrets of his passion for bibliophilia, warmly welcoming me into his home in Geneva and allowing me to accompany him to major auctions in New York.

I would also like to express my gratitude to Brigitte Benoist, who explained the mysteries of bookbinding to me and showed me its splendors.

I owe the writing of this book, more than ever before, to the help and support of wonderful friends.

I would especially like to thank Danielle Guigonis, whose skill, work ethic, and generosity I have admired since I was a teenager.

My lifelong friends, my first readers, whom I have never ceased tormenting for years by sending them chapters fresh from my pen, demanding their reactions at all hours of the day and night—Delphine Borione and Vincent Jolivet in Italy; Frédérique Brizzi and Jean Yves Barillec, Carole Hardoüin, and Michel and Frédérique Hochmann in France; and Renée Cho and Joanne Yeck in the United States—know how grateful I am for their infinite patience, advice, and honesty.

My deepest thanks also to Alessandra Ginobbi and Andrea Fortina, Isaure Angleys, Odile Bréaud, Aurélie Le Roy, Marie de Geloes, Cécile Pozzo di Borgo, Francine van Hertsen, and Rosie Yangson for their constant help in every possible way.

As I neared the end of my research, the closure of archives and the inability to travel due to COVID-19 forced me to call on the assistance of bibliophiles, curators, and librarians with whom, in this period of confinement, I could not meet in person. It would be impossible, unfortunately, to list here everyone all over the world who took time out from their work to answer my questions. But I hope all of those new friends, who had the immense generosity to dig through their personal libraries for documents I needed, and to scan for me the hundreds and hundreds of pages I asked them for, know how grateful I am to them. Without that incredible chain of mutual aid, this book would not have been written.

I would also like to say to Garance, Leonardo, and Lavinia Ferrario how precious their affection is to me. And to Frank Auboyneau how deeply thankful I am for his love.

Finally, I would like to express my particular thanks to my French publisher Flammarion, especially to Anavril Wollman, who has done so much for this book. I hope my editor Teresa Cremisi, whose unfailing warmth, support, and faith during these last five years, knows how much of this adventure is thanks to her.

I would like also to say a huge thank you to Edizioni e/o and to my publishers in Italy, Sandro Ferri, Sandra Ozzola, Leonella Basiglini; to Michael Reynolds in New York, and to the wonderful staff of Europa Editions worldwide, who brought me back to my beloved America with this book, and for having entrusted its translation to Tina Kover, to whom I am deeply grateful for the elegance and the outstanding quality of her work.

Belle da Costa Greene
by Laura Coombs Hills, circa 1910

Belle da Costa Greene
by Theodore C. Marceau, 1911

BELLE
de COSTA
GREENE

Belle da Costa Greene
by Clarence H. White, 1911

Belle's father, Richard T. Greener,
circa 1885

·BELLE da COSTA GREENE· ·1911·

Belle da Costa Greene
by Clarence H. White, 1911

The Morgan Library,
circa 1905

The West Room:
J.P. Morgan's office

Belle da Costa Greene
by Theodore C. Marceau, 1911

The entrance to the North Room: Belle's office

The vault with its treasures

The mentor to whom Belle owed her career: Junius Spencer Morgan, circa 1889

The Lindau Gospels, one of Belle's first acquisitions

John Pierpont Morgan by Edward Steichen, 1903

Bernard Berenson at the
Villa I Tatti, circa 1903

Belle da Costa Greene by Clarence H. White, circa 1911, in an outfit
drawn from a collection by Paul Poiret

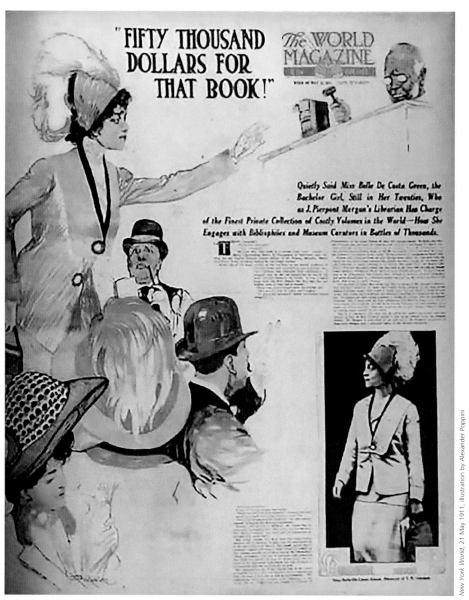

"Fifty thousand dollars for that book!"
*The World Magazine*, May 21, 1911

Photo inscribed by Belle to her friend, the book collector
Rosenbach, whom she referred to affectionately as "Rosie"

The prototype of the car Belle drove in 1912: her Pierce-Arrow Roadster

The publisher Mitchell Kennerley in his office at the Anderson Galleries, with the photo of his muse, *Belle in Profile* by Clarence H. White, prominently displayed on his bookshelves, circa 1920

J.P. Morgan shouting
at the reporters mobbing him,
1910

J.P. Morgan magnetically
"attracting" European works
of art with his dollars

*Belle da Costa Greene*,
by Paul-César Helleu,
with her cigarette

*Belle da Costa Greene*,
by Paul-César Helleu . . .
*without* her cigarette

Richard T. Greener as he looked during his last meeting with Belle

"Just because I'm a librarian doesn't mean I have to dress like one!"

Belle da Costa Greene playing up her exotic looks with her "Egyptian jewels," miniature on ivory by Laura Coombs Hills